Healing Love

Cottonwood Series
Book 1

Sophie Dawson

All the quotations of Scripture used are from the World English Bible. I chose this version for two reasons. The first is that it is public domain in the entire world. The version which would have been used in 1875 is the King James Version. This is not public domain in the United Kingdom. The second reason is for readability and ease of understanding.

™ - World English Bible

This is a work of fiction. Names, characters, places and events are products of the author's imagination or are used fictitiously. Any resemblance to actual persons, living or dead, locales or events is entirely coincidental.

Copyright © 2012 Susan D Ewing
All rights reserved.
ISBN-13: 978-1469911472

Dedication

To my husband Ivan, who has supported me in his own way for all the years of our marriage. I've been interested and tried many things. When I told him I was writing a novel his comment was, "That's something you've never tried before."

Thank you for allowing me to express myself in all those ways over the years. I love you.

Acknowledgements

This book and the rest of the series would not have been possible without the advice and help of a number of fellow authors who took me under their collective wings. They provided much needed counsel and shared their knowledge of writing, point of view, and the occasional: "That's just stupid."

These friends are from around the US whom I met on Christianwriters.com and ciaindie.freeforums.org. They encouraged me, edited drafts, fixed awkward sentences, and just chatted. I've learned so much about writing from them. I cannot lift one above the others as all have become very dear to me.

There's one other whom I must acknowledge as the one who has taught me the most about our Lord. For years I'd prayed for a pastor who would teach down deep and dirty in the Scripture. My prayer was answered in Pastor Cajun Pauley. I've been privileged to be shepherded by him since Dec. 2000. Thank you my friend and brother for the support, stricture and love you and Lynn have given me all these years.

Chapter 1

Lydia Walcott walked quickly down the path along the brook, trying not to glance back. She knew her brother Cyrus would be out in the field all day and wouldn't be expecting her until supper, but fear caused her to keep looking back. She carried the faded floral carpetbag in her right hand, wishing she could change it to her left but the pain in her wrist and arm kept her from doing so.

Just another mile, she thought, as she reached the footbridge crossing the brook that separated the Walcott and Cuttler farms. Often Lydia would stop in the middle of the bridge and look for glimpses of fish swimming below, but not today. Another mile and Aggie could look at her arm and tend it. Please, Lord, help me get away. I can't do what Cyrus wants, I just can't.

She hurried along the path between two fields separated by a row of hedge trees. None of the buds were swelling on the black branches yet, but birds were evident by their songs. Finally Aggie Cuttler's house came into view. Lydia increased her speed, entering the yard to the barking of Aggie's dogs.

"Hi, Buster. Hi, Angus," she said to the large, unkempt mongrel dogs as Aggie came out of the small clapboard house and down the steps.

"What are you doing here this early, child?" Aggie asked, her voice betraying her Kentucky hills background. Aggie and her husband had moved to Iowa thirty-five years ago with their young family.

"Oh, Aggie," Lydia cried, falling on her knees before the old woman. She clung to Aggie's legs like a brokenhearted child clings to a parent, even though she was twenty years old, finally releasing the pent-up emotions of the past few days.

Aggie gathered the child of her heart into her arms as Lydia gave way to the tears she had held in for so long. Tears for her unending grief at the deaths of her parents seven years ago. Tears of fear born at that time as her brother dominated and abused her more and more. Tears of betrayal at this last straw of her brother selling her.

Aggie laid her grey-haired head softly on the auburn one of the young woman. When the tears eased, she pulled back and gently wiped Lydia's tears away with her handkerchief.

"Oh, Aggie. He ... he wants me to marry Gus Botwright. I can't do it. I just can't. Two days ago Cyrus told me I had to marry Gus. When I told him I wouldn't he beat me worse than he ever has before."

Aggie looked at Lydia's black right eye and cheek, her face grim.

"Gus is just as bad as Cyrus and isn't a believer," Lydia said. "I can't and won't marry him."

"Are you hurt anywhere else?"

"I think he might have broken my wrist or arm. It hurts so much. I can't use it. He also hit me on the back and it hurts very badly. I've had a terrible time doing my chores and his, and dressing myself."

"Come in and we'll tend to it." Aggie's face and voice were steel.

They walked into the house, Aggie going to the cupboard and retrieving the satchel in which she kept her medical equipment. Lydia set her tattered carpetbag on the floor and sank into one of the two ladder-backed chairs by the table. She laid her head on the table, waiting for Aggie to gather her supplies.

"Now let me see your arm. This'll hurt as I try to see if it's broke."

Lydia extended her left arm to Aggie who, as gently as she could, probed Lydia's severely swollen hand and forearm. The bruising circled her wrist, extended up her arm and down onto her hand. Lydia brought her right hand up to her mouth and bit her index finger knuckle to keep from crying out.

"Look's like he broke the bone on the outside near your wrist," Aggie said as she set the arm on the table with great care. "I think it's a clean break. At least I hope it is. I'll have to pull on it to set the bone. It'll hurt like the very dickens."

She went out to the shed and brought back some straight sticks that had been split so that one side of each was flat and sanded smooth. Pulling the cotton bandaging from the leather satchel, she wrapped each of the three sticks. She also pulled out an old piece of leather.

"Here, you'll need to bite on this 'stead of your finger if you want to still have it after I'm done settin' your arm."

Lydia looked at the old leather, wondering how many of the people Aggie had tended had bitten on it before, and who they were.

As she reached for it, Aggie said with a chuckle, "I wash it after each time it's used. Sometimes I have to soak it in whiskey if someone real grimy's used it."

Lydia put the leather between her teeth and bit down. Aggie looked her in the eyes and, turning her attention to the arm, grasped it above the break with one hand and took Lydia's wrist in the other. She gripped tightly and then pulled with strong, even pressure.

Lydia sucked in air as she bit down harder. Stars flashed on and off before her eyes. She thought she'd pass out, but just then the bone slid into place and Aggie let go.

"You still with me, girl?"

"Y-y-yes," Lydia stuttered, spitting out the leather, taking deep breaths to help clear her head.

Aggie picked up one stick, and laying it on the back of Lydia's arm began wrapping the arm with bandages. After she had wrapped the first one enough to keep it from falling off, she took another, laid it on the outside of the arm and continued wrapping. After she placed the third one along the bottom of the arm extending up onto the palm of Lydia's hand, she tied off the bandage and sat back.

"Now," she said, "what about the rest of your bruises? I can see your face and eye, but I know he didn't stop there. He never has before and I imagine he was plenty mad."

"I'm sure my back is well bruised, and it hurts, but I'm managing the pain."

Aggie looked sternly at Lydia, who stood and turned her back toward the older woman. Aggie pressed and prodded as gently as she could. "I can't find anything that causes me alarm. You just be very careful."

Lydia and Aggie sat in the quiet of the house for a while. Lydia, feeling safe for the time being, reveled in the love she knew Aggie felt for her. With her husband gone and her children all moved further west, Lydia knew that Aggie was sometimes very lonely. The many hours she'd spent in this kitchen had not only given Lydia a sense of being loved but must also have helped assuage Aggie's loneliness.

Aggie got up, filled the kettle and began the makings of the chamomile and herb tea she knew would ease the pain. Lydia saw the glances sent her way and knew her dear old friend worried about what was ahead. When the tea was ready, Aggie poured them each a cup and sat down at the table.

"Aggie," Lydia started hesitantly, "I need your help. Would you help me to get away from here? I can't marry Gus, and Cyrus will only keep beating me until I finally either die or give up and marry him."

"Of course I'll help you. Have you a plan?"

"Lord forgive me, but I told Cyrus a lie yesterday when I agreed to marry Gus. I told him I couldn't take the beatings and would go along with his plan. I don't intend to do that. I want to leave Ringle and go somewhere away from here. I hope to be able to get work washing or sewing or cooking in a boardinghouse. Anything to make a living. You know I don't need much. I've never had much so I wouldn't know what to do with it if I had it," she finished with a small, twisted smile.

"I thought I'd take the train and go as far as the money I have will take me. I took some of Cyrus's money, but since we own the farm together I figured some of it would be mine. I didn't take much for fear he would notice and be even madder."

Lydia was silent for a few moments, thinking about how Cyrus, eight years older, controlled her life, allowing her little or nothing. She had had to use her mother's dresses to remake clothing for herself as her body grew and changed from age thirteen to twenty. Although they had inherited the farm jointly, Cyrus would let Lydia have only absolute necessities. These he purchased when he was in Ringle, the nearest town to the farm. He did not allow her to go to town, except occasionally to church.

"Sounds like a good plan to me," Aggie said. "What can I do to help?"

"I brought some food with me, bread, apples, cheese. I left fresh bread, biscuits and stew for Cyrus's supper. Also, a note saying I was coming to see you and might not be home tonight, that you were making soap. He knows I often stay when we do that so he won't miss me until tomorrow night."

"That was smart of you."

"Would you be willing to take me to Ringle so I can catch the train there?"

"Of course. We'll need to put that arm in a sling. And we need to do somethin' about the bruisin' on your face. When we get to Ringle I'll go into the mercantile and get some of that cosmetic stuff the doxies use and cover up the bruises. If someone sees you they'll be sure to remember you, and we don't want that when Cyrus starts lookin' for you and askin' questions."

"That's a good idea. Would you also buy the train ticket? That way the agent won't be able to say I bought a ticket."

"Sure, honey."

Aggie took an old dishtowel and folded it into a sling, tying it together at the back of Lydia's neck. Then she went to her trunk, opened it and rummaged around until she found a length of heavy tan canvas. Cutting off a wide strip, she tied each end to the handles of Lydia's carpetbag.

"What is that for?" Lydia asked.

"Since you can't carry anythin' in that hand, you can put the canvas over your head to the left side of your neck and across your body. It'll help you carry the bag without so much strain on your arm. I carried my babies that way when I needed to work, both in the house and in the field. Lets you use your hand without settin' the bag down. Less chance of someone stealin' it."

"What a good idea. It was so heavy, but I didn't want to set it down and rest on the way here."

Aggie made sandwiches for Lydia to eat on the way to Ringle. They headed out to the barn and Lydia put her bag in the wagon while Aggie harnessed up the horses. Tying their wide-brimmed bonnets on their heads, they headed away from the pain of Lydia's past.

"We clean forgot one thing," Aggie said.

"What?"

"To pray. You'll need the Lord's help and blessin' and we need to go to him." Aggie looked sideways at Lydia as she drove the wagon toward Ringle, Iowa.

"Oh, how could I have forgotten? I was so intent on getting to you, and getting away, that it just went out of my head."

"So we do it now." Aggie halted the horses, reached over, and clasped Lydia's good hand. They closed their eyes. "Dear Father," Aggie prayed, "you know all that's happened in Lydia's life, her folks dyin' of the fever, Cyrus being so mean an' ornery to her and beatin' her an' all that. She's handled that as brave as can be. But now, Lord, Cyrus is wantin' her to marry an unbeliever. Your word says that we shouldn't be unequally yoked and so her refusal to marry Gus is within your will. Besides that, Gus is just as lowdown a snake as that no-count brother of hers."

Aggie paused. She was getting worked up; her emotions were causing her hand to tighten on the reins, making the horses shy. "So, Lord, we come to you askin' for your blessin' and protection on this journey that Lydia's goin' on. You told Abram to set out for a land you'd show him. Our Lydia's steppin' out in faith that you have a place all picked out for her, just like you did Abram. Help her, protect her. Help her find that new place to live with people who're believers in you and your Son, Jesus. Keep her safe from evil men on the train and in the town you already have planned for her. We know you have plans for her. Plans for her good and not for evil. She's had enough of that the last few years. And so, sweet Jesus, we come in your name praisin' you. Amen."

"Thank you so much for your prayer and everything else you've done for me." Lydia squeezed the hand she held. "You've been such a blessing in my life, especially since my folks died. Without you, I don't know how I could've stood it."

"Well, I love you like one of my own. Let me know you lit somewhere and are makin' your way."

"Of course I will. It may be some time before I can, but I will as soon as I'm settled. Oh Aggie, I'm going to miss you so very much." Lydia leaned over and kissed Aggie on her weathered cheek.

"I'm going to miss you too, honey, but I know you're doin' the right thing. God wouldn't want one of his marryin' a nonbeliever, specially one who's the way Gus is."

Aggie had known something like this would happen one day. She'd watched as Cyrus became more and more abusive to Lydia, and had feared that her young friend would stay with her brother until he beat her to death.

Chapter 2

When they came into town Aggie pulled the wagon into the alley behind the livery, away from the busy street. She didn't want prying eyes to see Lydia in the condition she was in.

"You stay here," she said, "and I'll run those errands. I hope we're close to the train arrivin'. What way d'you want to be goin'?"

"I don't know. I haven't thought that far. I only wanted to get to you."

"Well, we'll see which way the next train's headed. Give me some of your money and I'll get you that ticket."

Lydia handed Aggie a small drawstring bag and Aggie headed off to the mercantile and the train station. Lydia sat quietly in the wagon. The trials of the last few days had brought a fatigue that weighed heavily as she waited for Aggie to return. She closed her eyes, thinking she would pray, but shortly she started to doze. She started awake when the wagon lurched as Aggie climbed up.

"Well, the next train's headed to Burlington, and soon. I got to thinkin' that it might be good to head there, then you can go most any way. Might throw Cyrus off when he starts lookin' for you. What d'you think?"

Lydia, still foggy from her nap, thought about it. "Might be a good idea. With all the junctions there, he'll have to figure out which way I went."

"That's what I thought. You just get off there and buy a ticket for as far as you want and have money for. An' here's that jar of paint to cover up that bruise." Aggie handed Lydia the drawstring bag without telling her that she had used her own money.

"Thank you so much, Aggie."

Just then they heard a train whistle in the far distance. Aggie handed the ticket and small jar to Lydia, who smiled and handed the jar back to Aggie.

"With no mirror and only one hand, I can't do this. Would you please make me like a painted woman?"

"Sure enough." Aggie chuckled, taking the jar and gently smearing the color over the bruises that covered most of Lydia's cheek, eyelid and forehead. Handing back the jar, she said, "You're presentable now. Let's get to the station and get you on board."

They climbed down and Lydia retrieved her bag from the wagon, pulling the canvas strap over her head. She was pleased with the way it crossed over her chest and held the bag on her right side. Her shoulder supported most of its weight. She adjusted her bonnet so that her face was shielded from view.

As they walked the distance to the station, the train was pulling to a stop. The conductor swung down and placed the step, allowing the passengers to step off.

Lydia looked at Aggie. Tears were in both sets of eyes, the hazel ones below the gray hair and the green ones below the auburn.

"You go on now and get aboard that train. I'm a gonna head back to my place to start makin' some soap. When Cyrus comes around there'll be new soap a sittin' there for him to see."

The two ladies hugged each other, Aggie being mindful of Lydia's injured back, and then slowly separated. Lydia walked to the train and the conductor handed her up the steps. She disappeared from view as she entered the car, then reappeared and took a seat by the window. She waved to Aggie as the conductor shouted, "All aboard."

The train began pulling away from the station, with both women praying for the many uncertainties of Lydia's journey.

"Ticket, miss?" asked the conductor.

Lydia, seated by herself as the car was not crowded, handed him her ticket.

"Going to Burlington, I see. We'll be arriving at eleven forty-five. Sure is a fine day for early March. Warm, but not too much wind."

She saw his eyes flick to her sling.

"Hurt yourself, did you?"

"Yes. Nothing time won't take care of."

"Well, if you need anything you just let me know. I must get on to punching the tickets. Have a pleasant trip."

"Thank you." Lydia returned her eyes to her lap.

As the conductor moved on, she took off her coat. It had been her father's and was too large and long, but Cyrus would have noticed if hers was missing. It was unseasonably warm for early March, but Lydia knew the weather was fickle in Iowa. The sleeves were rolled back, and she hadn't had time to shorten the hem; it reached clear to the floor. She had to walk with care so as not to trip. She stared out the window, not seeing the fertile land passing. Feeling lost and alone, her thoughts went back to the day before, and her lie to Cyrus.

"I've decided to marry Gus," she had told him. She laid her spoon down, finally gathering the courage to begin her planned escape. She kept her eyes focused on the uneaten food before her, hands in her lap. "I can't take any more. I only hope Gus won't be like you."

The pain in her body had kept her awake the previous night, during which she'd thought and planned. She knew she couldn't stay to marry Gus Botwright, and her brother would beat her to death if she didn't. She fought hard to keep her voice neutral and not say too much. She knew she was lying, and wanted to keep her words as few as possible. The simple breakfast of oatmeal, leftover biscuits and bacon had been the easiest meal she could think to prepare. She knew cleaning up would be a problem, but she didn't ask for help, knowing it wouldn't be forthcoming.

"Good. You've come to your senses." Cyrus shoveled food into his mouth. He hadn't shaved or combed his hair, which was similar to the auburn color of Lydia's. "You aren't as dumb as I thought. Know a good man when you see him."

Lydia kept her eyes down and said nothing.

"Well, I'll just go to town and let him know," Cyrus said. "Need some parts to fix the seeder wagon, too. Can get those at the same time."

"Please," Lydia said, "c-c-can we wait until after planting to do it?" She hated that her nervousness caused her to stutter.

"Why?" Cyrus looked at her, his anger flaring.

Lydia didn't raise her eyes for fear he'd think she was challenging him. "I was thinking you'd be wanting a wedding to show that you're a prosperous farmer and could afford to send your sister off with several new dresses and linens. Mine are patched and have been adjusted and lengthened with fabric from Mama's things. Do you want the people of Ringle to see me married like that?"

"You want me to buy you a trousseau? Well, I ain't gonna," Cyrus snapped.

"No, Cyrus, just some fabric so I can make two new dresses. One to be married in and another to show what a good provider you are. You might attract some lady to be your wife. You'll want a housekeeper after I'm gone. You wouldn't want her to think you can't provide for her, would you?"

"Well, I guess not." Cyrus's voice was petulant. "Okay, fabric for two dresses and some gewgaws to make them pretty. I'll choose the fabric, though. You'd probably buy the most expensive there was in some dumb color."

"Thank you," Lydia said quietly. "Maybe you could get it today so I can start on them. That way you won't have to stop the seeding or planting when you get busy."

"Um, I was thinkin' the same thing. Headin' to town anyway, like I said. I bet Gus and I'll be doin' some celebratin', so don't expect me home for dinner or supper. You'll have to milk and do the other chores tonight."

"Yes, Cyrus, I will."

Cyrus left shortly after, taking money with him that Lydia knew would not only buy the supplies but would also be spent at the tavern for the celebrating. She was glad, for it gave her more time to make her preparations.

She had done the housekeeping chores as quickly as she could without using her broken arm, or her stiff back from the pounding of the night before. Going to the trunk that held her parents' things, she extracted her father's coat and a white wool shawl that had been her mother's, which Cyrus never let her use. With great care, she climbed to the loft and pulled down the tattered carpetbag, bringing dust along with it. Taking it outside, she shook it and beat the dust out with the rugbeater. It still looked like what it was: a sagging, floral carpetbag faded to a dirty brown.

Back inside Lydia gathered her meager belongings together on her bed: her high-button shoes, which were tight but could still be worn, her threadbare undergarments, two pairs of black wool stockings, and her two other dresses. All had been lengthened at the waist, cuffs and hem with fabric taken from her mother's dresses. She had let out the bodice seams and inserted gussets beneath the arms to allow for the changes in her body over the last seven years.

She went back to the trunk and pulled out the last two of her mother's dresses. Those she hung on the hooks in her room to disguise the fact that hers were gone. Before she closed the trunk for the last time, she took out her mother's locket, a gift from her father. It was actually a watch. The front opened to reveal the watch and the back to reveal the engraving. Lydia opened the front, wound the watch, and set it to the same time as the mantle clock. Then she opened the back and read: To my lovely bride, Hannah. With love, Thaddeus. May 26, 1846.

Lydia wrapped the watch in a pair of her stockings and stuffed it into a shoe. She packed everything into the carpetbag and slid it under her bed, all the way back into the farthest corner. Her Bible, toothbrush and toothpowder, nightgown, brush and comb would go in tomorrow just before she left.

Lydia spent the rest of the day doing Cyrus's chores and preparing food to give herself as much time as possible before he missed her. Everything took so much more time because of the pain in her back and face, and her broken arm, but she managed to do everything she wanted. Then she fell into bed, exhausted, not even taking time to read her Bible.

The next morning at breakfast Cyrus gloated that he and Gus had had a great time celebrating her upcoming nuptials. After Cyrus fixed the seeder, he left to prepare the farthest field for sowing the oats. Lydia hastened to pack the last of her items, put on her father's coat and her old wide-brimmed bonnet, and then opened the drawer that held the cash. Counting out the amount she hoped Cyrus wouldn't notice, she left as quickly as she could for Aggie's.

"Burlington. Next stop Burlington, Iowa," the conductor called as he walked through the railroad car.

Lydia, who'd been praying, started at the sound.

The conductor paused as he walked past. "Miss, if you'd wait until the others have passed by, I'll help you get your bag off."

"Thank you. That would be quite kind of you," replied Lydia. She looked over the other occupants in the car. All seemed to be men in black suits. "How long until we arrive in Burlington?"

"About ten minutes. Do you have someone meeting you at the station?"

"No, I'll be switching to a different train."

"The C.B. & Q. is headed west around one-thirty. Is that the one you're catching?"

"Uh, yes. The C.B. & Q. I'm heading to visit out west."

"Nice trains they have. Comfortable, not the bench seats we have but padded ones. You'll have a comfortable trip."

"Thank you, I'm looking forward to it."

The conductor moved on, leaving Lydia to review the conversation and make sure she'd been truthful in her vague replies. She pulled her coat carefully over her left arm first, and then put her right into the sleeve. Pulling the sling over her head, she inserted her arm into the support. Grabbing the handles of the carpetbag, she placed it on the seat beside her.

Well, Lord, please guide me as I head to wherever you've chosen for me to go. Keep me safe and use me to glorify you in all that I do.

The whistle blew as the train slowed down and pulled into the station at Burlington. Men got up and hurried down the aisle, trying to be among the first to get off. Lydia stifled a small gasp as she rose and her back protested the movement. Bag in hand, she followed the men to the end of the car.

The conductor took her bag and stepped to the platform. He set the bag down then reached up to take Lydia's hand and help her down the steps.

"Now, you take care, miss. Be sure to sit in the last seat in the car. The conductor will keep an eye on you there so none of the others passengers bothers you."

"Thank you so much. God bless you for your help and guidance. You've helped me with the jitters I had riding the train alone. You've been very kind."

"Well, I have a daughter just about your age and I sure would hate to see her have problems riding a train alone, so I tend to watch out for the ladies. Sort of my little mission work, you might say. You have a good visit out west."

"Thank you."

Lydia picked up her bag and turned to go into the train station. Others streamed past her to board the train she'd just left. She looked at the large gray stone station, so much larger than the one in Ringle. Taking a deep breath and squaring her shoulders, she entered the building.

A sign hanging from the ceiling indicated the direction of the ladies' retiring room and the ticket counter, along with other services available in the station. She headed to the ladies' room.

After seeing to her personal needs, she looked critically at her face in the mirror. She could tell where the makeup was on her face but thought it wouldn't be noticed by the casual observer. Deciding she didn't need to touch it up, she left the room.

Walking toward the ticket counter, she saw a man reading a printed schedule and went to the display. The schedule for the C.B. & Q. train the conductor had spoken about would be arriving at one-thirty and leaving at one thirty-five. Above the ticket counter was a chalkboard with the list of stations at which the train would stop, and fares to each town. Looking down the list Lydia saw she could go to Cottonwood, Iowa and still have some money left. She'd need some to get her through the next few days, before she could find work and a place to live.

After purchasing her ticket, Lydia went back outside to wait on a bench positioned under an awning against the building. Settling on the bench, she looked across the tracks toward the Mississippi River. Shining in the midday sun, the water stretched over a mile wide. The leafless trees on the other side, the bluffs in the distance and the plowed fields all attested to the might of the river, and the determination of those who worked the fertile soil. Looking to her left, she saw a ferry landing, docks and several boats. Downriver she saw the railroad bridge spanning the great waters. Watching the activity on the busy river was a new experience and one she relished.

Shortly after one o'clock she reentered the station, used the ladies room and got a drink at the water fountain. She marveled at the fresh water bubbling up with no one pumping a handle. She went back outside to wait for the train. It arrived on time. Climbing aboard, Lydia took the last seat in the car. Shortly, she heard a shout of "All aboard" and the train began to move.

The conductor from her previous train had been correct about the cushioned seats. Lydia gave thanks for the comfort, as the wooden bench seats of the other train had been hard for her bruised back to bear. She took out her Bible, and turning to the Psalms began to read.

Chapter 3

"Doc! Doc!"

Through the open window of the exam room, Sterling Graham heard the man whose horse was skidding to a stop outside. He finished wrapping the cut on the small boy's foot and picked up the shoe, which would not fit over the bandage, and handed it to the boy's mother.

"Guess Millie's time's come," he said.

"Yes, I guess so. Sounds like he's pretty worked up," said Mrs. Betsy Phelps, the mother of the recently bandaged five year old.

"Now Billy," Sterling said, "you need to keep that foot clean for at least five days. You wouldn't want it to get all infected, so stay inside. Better to be in for five days now than a whole lot more later when the weather's nicer." He smiled, ruffling the boy's brown hair.

Just then a panicked Vince Stanton burst into the room. "Doc, you gotta come quick. Millie's time has come. She's birthing the baby."

"Okay, Vince, I'm coming. How far apart are her pains?" Sterling watched the expression of the father-to-be as it ran the gamut from anxiety to confusion, concentration and, finally, relief.

"About an hour."

"Will you go to the livery and have them hitch up my buggy? That'll save us some time. Bring it back and we can head out to your place. Is anyone with her?"

"Yeah, her ma is. She came a couple of days ago so she'd be here when it was time." Vince dashed back out the door heading to the livery.

"First baby always makes the father crazy," Betsy said with a chuckle. "He truly believes the baby will be born before you get there. We'll just be getting out of your way. Let Ben know what the bill is, and we'll get you paid."

Betsy and Billy left the room and Sterling picked up the supplies he'd used on the small foot, putting them in the used equipment pan to be washed.

Ben, Betsy and Billy, Sterling thought, smiling to himself as he wiped off the large exam table that dominated the room. It always tickled him that all three names in the Phelps family started with B. Putting the thought aside, he went into the waiting room to see who else was there.

Mrs. Henderson had come for the monthly check of her heart. That could wait until tomorrow. Jackson Mueller was here to get medicine for his cough. Horace McHenry had to have the stitches in his hand removed. Sterling ticked off the list of patients in his head, doing a quick triage.

"Horace, head into the exam room and I'll get those stitches out. Jackson, I'll go get your medicine now. Mrs. H., can you please come back tomorrow for your check?"

"Sure I can," Mrs. Henderson said, smiling. "Nothing like a new baby coming into the world. More urgent than an old lady like me. You tell them I'll be praying for an easy birth and a healthy young 'un."

Sterling retrieved the medicine and handed it to Jackson. "Just lay the money on the counter, Jack. I need to get these stitches out before Vince comes back and hauls me out the door."

"Okay, Doc. You have a good baby now, you hear me." Jack grinned at Sterling and dug into his pocket.

Sterling went back into the exam room and started removing Horace's stitches. He'd cut the hand badly repairing some machinery on his farm. Sterling thought the machines might be more dangerous than they were worth, but more and more farmers were purchasing them. Just as he cut the last stitch and pulled it out, the men could hear the buggy coming up the street. Sterling reached out, closing the window.

"Just like a bat outta you know where," laughed Horace. "You better get a move on. He might just leave without you."

Sterling grinned. "He might at that," he said as they walked to the entry.

Sterling drew on his coat, turned the 'Open' sign to 'Closed', picked up his black leather medical bag and grabbed his gray Stetson.

"Come on, Doc. Millie needs ya. Let's go," Vince yelled.

Horace and Sterling exchanged twinkle-eyed glances as they walked to the buggy.

"I'm sure we'll get there in time, Vince. How about you ride on out on your horse and get back to Millie, letting her know I'm coming? Might ease her mind a bit." Sterling stashed his bag under the seat.

"Good idea, Doc."

Vince leaped down from the buggy and Horace grabbed the bridle as Baxter, Sterling's horse, shied at the sudden jostling of the buggy. Vince ran to untie his own horse, jumped into the saddle and took off at a gallop down the street.

"Now I can travel at a safe speed out to the farm," Sterling said to Horace. "I learned a long time ago it isn't safe to ride with an expectant father."

"I'll bet it was your pa who told you that." Horace held Baxter's dark brown head while Sterling climbed into the buggy.

"You're probably right, Horace. Pa told me so much, and so often, that sometimes I think I thought of it. See you later. Take care of that hand."

Horace let go of the horse's head and Sterling followed Vince Stanton at a much calmer speed.

Lydia looked up from her Bible, glancing out the window. She'd spent the afternoon reading many of the Psalms. Now she wondered how much time had passed and how far it was to Cottonwood. The landscape passing by the window was variations of black, tan and brown. The rich black soil of the Iowa plains that had been turned over in the fall contrasted with the tan stalks of the fields that still needed plowing. Hedgerows, maple, oak and willows along the creeks all stood bare, without a touch of the green that would start appearing in a few weeks. Here and there, the tall forms of the cottonwood trees towered above.

The sky, which had been clear and blue when Lydia's journey began, now had the gray overcast of clouds.

Lydia touched the windowpane. The temperature had dropped.

Typical March, she thought, hot and windy one moment and cold and windy the next. She hoped it wouldn't rain. She didn't relish walking through an unfamiliar town in the rain, or after it for that matter. The streets would be muddy and slippery.

The conductor came along just then, and Lydia raised a hand to get his attention.

"Excuse me, sir. Do you have the time, and can you tell me when we'll arrive in Cottonwood?"

"It's three forty-seven and we'll be in Cottonwood at five thirty-three if we don't get delayed anywhere along the line." He moved on down the aisle, stopping and speaking with another passenger.

Now she knew why her stomach was calling. The last time she'd eaten anything was that morning in the buckboard with Aggie. Lydia opened her carpetbag, taking out the cloth-wrapped bundle with the bread, apples and cheese. Making a sandwich, she said a quiet prayer of thanks and bit into the bread. The apples were somewhat wrinkly, since they were about the last of the past year's crop. She had canned applesauce and sliced apples in the fall, but left the bounty in the cellar.

After finishing her meal, she resumed looking out the window. The sky, she noted, had turned darker than it should be for this time of the evening, and she wondered if the weather would turn ugly. Just then, drops of rain started spotting the window. With a sinking feeling, she watched the rain increase as the train headed into the storm. Soon the rain began to stick and slide down the window as it turned into sleet, and then into ice.

Oh Lord, Lydia prayed, *I know we should be thankful for all things but I'm finding it difficult to thank you for this weather. So far you've protected me and made my way easy. I thank you for that. Now I ask that you continue your protection and help me find a place to stay for the night. You know I have little in the way of money so I would appreciate it if you find me a place that's clean, safe, and cheap.*

The train car darkened as the evening progressed. Lydia looked out the window, becoming more and more dejected as time wore on. It seemed to her that the train had slowed some since the ice began falling. They wouldn't make it to Cottonwood on time. Each time they stopped at a station she could see more and more ice building up on the buildings and trees. She wondered if the ice could cause the train to slip off the tracks. She prayed it would keep on the rails.

At last she heard the conductor calling, "Next stop, Cottonwood. Cottonwood coming in five minutes." He paused in his passage through the car and gave Lydia a look of concern. "Miss, do you have someone meeting you at Cottonwood?"

"They might not have made it to the station with all the ice. I'll see, and if not I'll stay in town. I can wait until the ice is gone."

"Okay. I'll help you down the steps. No one else is getting off in Cottonwood."

"Thank you. That will be a help. Will you please tell me what time it is?"

He pulled out his pocketwatch. "It's ten-twelve. We've been delayed over two hours because of the ice storm."

The train whistle blew, announcing its arrival in Cottonwood. When the train came to a stop, the conductor placed the step on the station platform, helping Lydia to the slippery surface and over to the white clapboard station under the wide overhang. He looked around the side of the station, trying to see if anyone was coming for her.

"I don't see anybody. You sure you're going to be all right?"

"Yes. I'll wait here a little while to see if they come, then go over to the pastor's. I know I can stay there with his family." She silently asked forgiveness for the lies.

"Okay. All aboard!" he yelled, moving back to the train. He threw the step back onto the platform and leapt up. He waved goodbye, looking a little uncertain at leaving her there, alone.

Lydia looked around. The station was closed. The evening was getting darker and the ice kept falling, coating everything with a glistening blanket. She walked around to the front of the building, staying under the overhang. There was no need for her to venture out until she had some idea where she was going.

She scanned the streets in front of her. One stretched east and west, parallel to the tracks, and one intersected it in front of the station. Looking east along the street she thought she saw stockyards: nothing that way. Looking north, she saw several unlit storefronts but none that looked like a hotel or boardinghouse. In the dim light, she wasn't able to locate the church either. She knew she needed to find shelter before the last of what little light there was died with the fast approaching night.

A dim light shining over a block away caught her eye. Maybe she could get help there. She surveyed the ice-slicked street. Adjusting the strap crossing her chest, she stepped carefully into the street. She did not want to fall; she was afraid that if she did she'd be unable to get back on her feet. The ice coating looked to be about half an inch thick. Crossing the street, Lydia was thankful to be a decent skater. Slipping and sliding, she managed to get onto the boardwalk in front of the buildings. Hugging close to the wall, she was able to avoid the ice, which was shielded from a narrow strip of the walkway by the overhang of the roof.

Reaching the other end of the block, she saw a lantern hanging from the eve of the livery stable across the street and wondered if someone who usually stabled there was out. Was the livery owner coming back tonight? Why else would he leave the lantern lit? Would the stable be unlocked? Could she find shelter there for the night?

She stepped out into the street. Another coating of ice layered itself onto her coat and bonnet. Placing each foot judiciously, she crossed the ice. Slipping, she almost fell, but was near enough to the building to grab onto the corner. Pausing to catch her breath, she moved along the front of the livery to the doublewide doors. Looking around, and feeling extremely guilty for trespassing, she lifted the bar, opening the door just wide enough to slip through. Once inside, she pulled the door shut with the inner bar, dropping it back in place and sighing in relief.

The interior was dark. She could hear the snuffling and movement of horses both to her right and left. It seemed more noises were coming from the right, so she felt her way down the left wall until she came to the row of stalls. She edged her way along the side of the nearest stall, rounding the front corner.

Snorff.

Lydia jumped as if she'd been shot. "Oh my word, you scared me," she said to the horse.

He put his head over the rail, snuffling and sniffing, seeming to look for a treat.

"I have nothing for you. No, wait." Digging in her pocket, she found an apple and held it out to him. The horse took it from her hand, bobbing his head up and down as if to say thank you. She could barely see him, but thought he was tan in color.

Continuing along the stalls, Lydia finally came to one that was empty, with the stall door open. A small amount of light filtered in the window above the stall from the lantern that hung outside. There was no evidence of occupancy on the floor, and the straw in the corner had not been scattered. Deciding not to look further she closed the stall gate.

She removed her wet, icy bonnet, shook off the ice and laid it over the feed trough, hoping it might dry by morning. Then she took off her coat. The outside was covered with ice but the inside had stayed relatively dry inside the thick wool. Shaking the ice from the coat was a difficult job one handed, but she finally managed to shed most of it. Moving to the corner with the bedding, she spread the coat open on the straw, lay down and pulled it close around her head, body and feet.

Forgive me, Lord. I doubted your provision. I didn't fall; I found a dry place to stay. It surely is cheap, and the horses give a little warmth to the place. Thank you, also, for making my pa so tall. With his coat I can wrap myself all the way up so nothing sticks out but my nose. Please don't let whoever might come in tonight notice me. I am so tired, and I ache all over. Please let me sleep. I know tomorrow is in your mighty hand. With that she snuggled into her warm cocoon and drifted into an exhausted sleep.

"It's a perfect little boy, Vince," Sterling said as he came out of the bedroom. Vince looked as white as the proverbial sheet and Sterling smiled. New fathers, he thought. They all looked the same after the first baby was born: scared to death. They liked the making part but now was when reality set in.

"Vince. Vince."

"Huh? What'd you say?"

"It's a boy. Millie is fine, too. You go right in and see them. Patty has her all spiffed up pretty for you. I'm going to head back to town. I'll come back and see her tomorrow."

"Okay, Doc. Wait! It's icy out. Want to stay here tonight? Could be dangerous getting back to town."

"No, thank you. Baxter and I have been out in ice storms before. We'll take it easy. We usually travel through the grass or fields--they're bumpier but less slick. You get on in there and meet your new son. Congratulations, by the way. See you tomorrow."

Vince waved back at Sterling before heading into the bedroom.

Sterling pulled on his coat and hat, grabbed his medical bag and headed out the door, nearly ending up on his backside as he slipped but managed to grab the doorframe for support.

The ice storm had stopped, the sky had cleared, and the nearly full moon created a shimmering fairyland. Trees, totally encased in ice, twinkled; grass sparkled like diamonds, and the paths and road looked like highways in heaven. Sterling surveyed the vision around him, marveling at the dichotomy of the beauty and danger of the sight.

Wow, Lord, what a sight. It's beautiful, but I need your protection to get back to town safely.

He stood in the moonlight, tall, well proportioned, his features as if carved by a master sculptor. With cautious steps he walked to the barn where Baxter and the buggy waited for him. *Thank you, Lord, for a safe delivery, and for the life you brought into the world tonight. Keep the family safe, healthy, and with a heart that longs for you.*

Harnessing the horse and leading him out of the barn, Sterling closed the barn door. Climbing into the buggy, he called for the horse to begin the trek back to town. Doing as he had told Vince, he guided the horse into an unplowed field, making the trip in decent time. Still, it was almost one in the morning when he arrived back at the livery and he was dog-tired. He unhitched the buggy in front of the carriage shed, deciding he was too tired to wrestle it in. That job could wait until it was light. The weather had warmed and the fairyland was melting, promising a muddy landscape in the morning. Pulling open the stable door, he allowed Baxter to walk towards his stall, the second on the right, while Sterling closed the doors.

"Well, old boy, we did well tonight. How about a scoop of oats?" Sterling said quietly.

He scooped the feed into the trough and rubbed Baxter down. When he was finished he closed the stall gate and went to the cot the livery owner allowed him to use when he got in late. He took off his coat and threw it and his Stetson onto the floor, kicked off his boots and fell onto the cot. Pulling a blanket over himself, he closed his eyes and went to sleep.

Chapter 4

Hearing the unfamiliar sound of men's voices, Lydia was drawn from the depths of a deep sleep. Her mind still foggy, she uncovered her head and looked up at the gate of the stall. Silhouetted there was a tall man in a cowboy hat. She couldn't see his features and her heart began to pound, fearing that Cyrus had found her.

Jumping up, she grabbed and donned her still damp bonnet, thankful that the right side of the brim had lost its starch and flopped down, covering that side of her face. She wondered if the makeup was still covering the bruises. She didn't want the man to see her until she was sure they were concealed. Her back screamed in pain at her sudden movement, causing her to take a sharp breath.

She heard scurrying steps and hushed voices retreating. She looked toward the stall gate again and saw a second, shorter silhouette, join the first.

"Looks as though you have a problem, Doc," the shorter man said, betraying an English origin. Both men were staring at her.

"Me? Seems as if she stayed in your livery last night, so the problem is yours, Theo."

"Don't think Clem and Eustace think that way. They saw the girl and just hightailed it out. You know what gossips they are. They know you stayed here last night and so did the young lady. It'll be all over town by eight o'clock."

"So? I didn't even know she was here and I figure she didn't know I was either."

"Doesn't make any difference. You know how gossip is. A gossip goes around telling secrets. Proverbs, I think it's eleven-thirteen, but I'll check on that."

"No need, I get the picture," Sterling said grimly.

"Hey Luke, go and get the sheriff, will you," Theo Ralston said to a young man standing in the doorway. "I'm thinking we should run this by him." He turned to Lydia. "Not that you're in any trouble with the law, young lady. Hey! Where you getting off to?"

Lydia had pulled her coat on, crept out into the alleyway and slowly edged behind the men before they noticed. She kept her face half covered with the fallen side of the hat brim, intently watching them.

"I just got up from sleeping all night long. Just where do you think I might be going?" Lydia surprised herself with the sassy reply. Quickly, she lowered her eyes to the floor. She had forgotten to put on the sling so she held her broken arm up against her chest. She was glad the sleeve of the coat was long enough to cover the wrapping and splints.

"Oh, sorry, ma'am. It's right out back through that door." Theo pointed the way, his cheeks turning a bright shade of red. "You don't think she'll take off do you?" he asked Sterling.

"No. She left her bag. She'll be back in when she gets done."

When Lydia reentered through the open back door she saw a man she realized must be the sheriff come in through the front and join the two men by the stall. Sliding to the side of the door she had come through and moving into the shadow, she listened without being observed.

"What's this I hear of a girl sleeping here last night?" asked the sheriff. "Luke didn't seem to know much other than that."

Sterling and Theo looked at each other to see who would answer first. Finally Sterling spoke up.

"Well, Drew, I'd been out to the Stanton place delivering their baby. It's a boy, by the way. Nice and healthy. Millie's fine, too. Anyway, I rode back after midnight, tired from the day and driving over the ice. I decided to sleep here, and basically fell onto the cot and didn't wake up until a while ago. I noticed that the gate to the last stall was closed and looked in. Saw the coat on the floor wrapped up around someone. About that time Theo and the rest came in, talking, and she woke up, popped out of the coat, grabbed her bonnet and stuck it on her head."

"Where is she?" The sheriff was a tall, lean man with gray eyes and a ready smile under his mustache, the color matching the sandy brown of his hair. He carried his hat in his hand, having removed it when he came in.

"She went to the necessary," mumbled Theo.

"I'm here," Lydia said softly. The men turned to her and she stepped out of the shadow. "I didn't mean to cause any trouble. I came in on the train last night. It was icing something fierce. I saw the lantern hanging out front and came to see whether someone could help me find a place to stay. I didn't think anyone would mind me sleeping in here. I'll pay you whatever you want, sir," she said to Theo. "I'm sorry if it was a bother to you." She kept her face turned down the entire time she spoke.

"No bother, miss. Could be a great deal of trouble for the doc, though," Theo said.

Drew and Sterling exchanged glances. "Eustace Taylor and Clem Baumgarden were with Theo when he and Luke came in this morning."

"Lovely, just lovely. Just what we need is those two spreading this around town." The sheriff rubbed his hand down his face. "I think we'd better head over to Pastor's place. We'll need his thoughts on this. Come on, missy. Let's go. You got a bag or anything?"

"Right here," Sterling said, picking up the worn carpetbag and handing it to Drew.

"Okay. Let's go."

Lydia moved forward, meeting up with Drew and Sterling and walking out of the livery between them. Neither man noticed how she was practically trotting to keep up with them. The two tall men ignored the boardwalk and strode up the street.

Sterling was at a loss as to how to deal with this problem. He'd lived in Cottonwood all his life, and it was home. That the gossip could hurt his medical practice concerned him. He knew there were people who lived for learning of and commenting on the lives of others. He'd never been the subject of the intense gossip. He didn't like it. He was also concerned about the young woman. Who was she? How had she ended up alone in Cottonwood during an ice storm without friends or family to meet her at the station? How could he help her?

As they continued along Main Street, past the shops, stores and other businesses, Sterling hoped that between the three of them--Drew, Pastor Peter and himself--they could figure out what to do. They'd been friends since childhood and shared a deep love for the Lord. Sterling knew that whatever counsel his friends gave would be based on the Word.

Neither man so much as looked back to see if she was following as Lydia desperately tried to keep up with them. She was worried. Was sleeping in the livery such a big problem that not only did the sheriff have to get involved but now the pastor, too? What would the men do if she couldn't keep up? Her stomach clinched in a knot of fear.

The ice had melted, the sun was shining and the morning was chilly. Here and there puddles gathered as rivulets of dirty water traced paths through the muddy street. In an effort to keep her long coat from tripping her on the slippery surfaces, and fighting the pain in her back, Lydia didn't look at the buildings or people around her as she moved faster and faster. She struggled to maintain her footing but lost the battle. Splat! Her foot caught in the hem of the coat, sending her facedown in the mud.

The men turned at the sound and looked back, stunned at the sight of her lying flat in the street. She lifted her face from the mud.

They looked at each other. Drew held up the carpetbag he carried, shrugging his shoulders. With a grimace, Sterling walked back and, grabbing Lydia under the arms, pulled her to her feet. She stifled a painful gasp. Sterling reached into a pocket and withdrew a semi-clean handkerchief, holding it out to her.

"Thank you," Lydia said, spitting mud out of her mouth. With her right hand, she began wiping her face. She stopped, suddenly remembering the bruise on her right cheek. She wiped around her eyes, taking care to leave most of the mud covering her bruised cheek and eye. Wiping around her mouth, she hoped to stop the grime flowing over her lips. She gritted her teeth at the pain in her broken arm, which she had fallen on, and at the pain shooting through her back.

Sterling picked up the bonnet that had come off in her fall. "What made you trip?" He looked from her face all the way down to her boots. She was dripping with mud and held her arms in front of her chest, the right hand holding the left.

"You two were walking so fast. I tried to keep up," Lydia replied in a pleading voice, looking down at her mud-covered coat. "Your legs are so much longer than mine. I'm sorry I couldn't keep up. I'll do better." Taking the hat, she shook it out and placed it gingerly back on her head, making sure the brim still hid the bruised side of her face.

"I'm sorry," Sterling said. "You should've said something. I think we were both going over the situation in our minds, and just walked without paying any attention to you. We should have been more thoughtful."

Lydia could feel his gaze, but she kept her head lowered so all he saw was the top of her muddy bonnet.

"Let's get going," Drew said. "Folks are starting to stare. No sense in giving them any kind of show."

Sterling turned back toward the pastor's house, but then stopped, swung around and scooped Lydia into his arms. She gasped, both with the shock of being picked up and carried, and at the pain in her back where Sterling's arm held her. She laid her left arm across her body, cradling it in her right arm. It still throbbed from her fall.

"Hi, Drew. You're here early. Do you need something?" Ella Lendrey said as she opened the front door.

"Yes. We have a problem that we need Peter for and ..." Drew's nervous glance back drew Ella's attention to the young woman being carried by Sterling and to the seriousness of the unexpected visit of her husband's best friends. "We're going to need your help too," Drew said. "She fell in the mud and, well, she's in need of a bath."

Ella saw Drew blush, realizing he was embarrassed at the thought of the girl and what she needed.

"I can see that. You go start drawing water and I'll get the pot onto the stove. Sterling, you go around to the back entry. We'll use the kitchen door. You men can wait in Peter's office while I help her bathe. I'll get the stove heating and bring Peter to the kitchen."

When the men had turned to do her bidding Ella closed the door and went to get her husband.

Sterling set Lydia down on the back steps. "You might want to take off your shoes before you go in. No sense messing up Ella's floor more than you have to."

Lydia sat down and began untying her work boots. Her fingers were trembling, not only from the cold but also from nervousness. She didn't understand the problem about the night in the livery, but was glad to have found the pastor's house. She felt she'd be in safe hands here. The pastor's wife seemed to be a kind woman.

Sterling pushed her hand away from the slimy strings. She'd not made much headway in untying them with her cold, muddy fingers. He worked out the knot and loosened the laces, beginning on the second shoe after finishing the first. Lydia watched his hands. They were nice hands: long fingers, beautifully tapered, with well-trimmed nails. At the moment they were covered with mud but she could tell they weren't the hands of a farmer or laborer. The liveryman had called him Doc. He was either a medical doctor or a horse doctor. Then she remembered him telling the sheriff he had delivered a baby last night.

"'Scuse me," Drew said as he came back carrying a bucket of water. Lydia jumped up, nearly tripping in her hurry to get out of his way. Sterling steadied her with a hand to her elbow. After Drew passed, Lydia slipped out of her boots and took off her coat.

"I don't want to get mud from the coat in the house," Lydia said, hiding her broken arm behind her back and handing the coat to Sterling.

She walked up the steps and entered the kitchen just as Ella and a man Lydia assumed was her husband came in from the hallway. They were a nice-looking couple. Ella's blond hair and warm round face seemed to welcome everyone with her smile. Her husband was somewhat taller than his wife, with ash-blond hair and eyes of blue.

"Oh, my, you are a mess, aren't you? I'm Peter Lendrey, pastor of Cottonwood church, and this is my wife, Ella." Peter grinned. His smile, like Ella's, welcomed Lydia into the house and she felt as if she belonged there.

"I fell. The street was slippery." Lydia was cold and wet. She crossed her arms, glad the position hid the splints.

"It must have been. Where's your coat?"

"The doctor has it, and my boots. I'm enough of a mess without bringing them into your clean kitchen."

Just then two children squeezed in from behind their parents. The girl had strawberry-blond curls all over her head. She looked to be about four and was wearing a navy, flowered dress and white pinafore. The boy, around seven, was a miniature of his father, without the blue eyes; he had the brown eyes of his mother.

"These two scamps are Rye and Janie," Ella said. "Now you two go upstairs and play. We have much to do down here. So scoot."

"Man, is she a mess," Rye said.

"Yeah. We'd get into a lot of trouble if we came home looking like that." Janie's eyes were as big as dinner plates.

"Your mother told you to scoot," Peter said.

"Going," both children said simultaneously. With one last look at Lydia they rounded their parents, and the sound of them running down the hall and up the stairs echoed through the kitchen.

During this exchange, Drew and Sterling had been filling the large pot on the stove.

Peter reached into the pantry and grabbed another pail, joining the bucket brigade. "No school today," he explained. "Rye's teacher had to go to Ottumwa for a family wedding this weekend."

"Come sit down," Ella said gently, leading Lydia to a chair.

"I don't want to get it muddy."

"A little dirt won't hurt it. I have two children who, despite their comment about trouble if they come home muddy, have tramped through the front hall in muddy boots more times than I want to remember." Ella chuckled, then frowned a little. "Once they made a muddy mess in the front hall just before the deacons arrived for a meeting."

Lydia gave a small smile then sat down.

Ella went into the pantry and brought out a tin hipbath and a bar of soap. "I'll go and get some towels. Do you have any other clothes with you? I can get some of mine if you don't."

"My bag's on the back porch. I'll get it." Lydia went to retrieve it as Ella gathered the towels.

The men brought in three buckets of water and set them on the floor. They'd be used to cool the hot water from the pot when it was put into the bath. They stood looking uncomfortable, waiting for Ella to tell them what to do.

"Looks like the water's ready," Ella said when she came back with the towels.

All three men turned to look, saw the steam rising from the large pot and moved to reach for it. They bumped into each other in their haste, jumped back and looked at Ella sheepishly. They seemed nervous at the thought of helping prepare a bath for an unfamiliar woman.

"Peter, you take the pot and fill the tub. Sterling, take off your muddy coat. And Drew, take off your shoes. All of you head on into Peter's study, I'll let you know when we're ready to join you."

The men did as they were told, breathing a sigh of relief that they could leave the kitchen to the women.

"Men." Ella shook her head.

Chapter 5

Ella looked at the filthy young woman, seeing her splinted arm for the first time. She thought Lydia must have been keeping it out of view. Now Lydia's hand rested in her lap.

"I see you've hurt your arm," Ella said. "Did you injure it again when you fell?"

"I don't think so. My friend Aggie set it and splinted it."

"May I help you get out of these muddy clothes?"

Lydia stood and allowed Ella to undo the buttons running down the front of the dress. Ella then eased it off Lydia's shoulders and down her arms. Lydia turned to aid in the removal of the dress and Ella gasped.

"Oh, my word. Dear Lord, child. You have bruises all over your back." She lifted Lydia's chin and looked into her face. "Oh, no. Oh, no," Ella said, looking Lydia straight in the eyes.

Ella watched as tears streamed down Lydia's face, the trails of which revealed deep bruising on her face. She drew the crying young woman into her arms, stroking the back of her head, murmuring prayers for this unknown waif who had landed on her doorstep.

The two women sat down, facing each other next to the kitchen table.

"Lydia, I'm going to have to get Sterling to look at these bruises and your arm," Ella said when Lydia's tears were spent.

"Must you?"

"Sterling will be able to tell if any bones were broken in your face. Also, the men need to know the whole of why you were in the livery stable last night. I don't think you would have told them about this, would you?"

"No." Lydia bent her neck, turning her face to the floor.

"I'm going to go get Sterling now, if that's all right with you. He's a doctor and will know how to treat your injuries. Here's a wet washcloth. Would you wipe the rest of the mud off your face so Sterling can examine it?"

"Okay."

Ella heard a shuddery breath left over from Lydia's crying. Leaving her alone, she knocked on the office door and went in without waiting. Ella looked first at her husband, communicating to him without words that a new factor had come to light.

"Sterling, come with me. The young lady needs you to look at something."

Realizing his medical skills were needed, Sterling followed her to the kitchen. Lydia was sitting with her head bowed, her back to the door as they came through. Her threadbare camisole did little to hide the black and blue marks covering her back from her shoulders to below the top of the chair. Slowly, as if he were coming upon a timid deer, Sterling approached Lydia, making just enough noise to let her know he was there.

"You know I'm a doctor, don't you?"

"Yes. You delivered a baby boy last night."

"Will you please stand so I can look at your back?"

Lydia stood and stepped away from the chair. The sleeves of her dress hung from her arms and her head was bowed.

"Are you willing to tell me how this happened?" He knew, from dealing with other abused women, that some would not.

"Cyrus, my brother, did it." Lydia looked at the floor as she spoke.

"You'll need to see her face and look at her arm," Ella said. "I think he caused both. Am I right?"

"Yes," Lydia said.

Sterling looked carefully at the bruises on her back. They were rectangular with darker bruising in a regular pattern within each bruise. Why would anyone do this? he thought. And what did he use?

"I'd been pounding meat with a wooden tenderizing mallet. He used that. It was after he hit me, making me fall. That's when my arm bone broke."

"Why?" Sterling saw that Ella was nearly in tears from hearing Lydia's story.

"He wanted me to marry Gus Botwright. I'd told him I wouldn't. Gus is as mean as Cyrus. Gus had agreed to let Cyrus keep my half of the farm if I married him."

Sterling decided not to ask her to elaborate and instead examined Lydia's back as gently as he could. She said nothing, but several times she inhaled sharply as he moved his fingers over her bruises.

"I think there might be some cracked ribs. You must not have spine damage or there'd be numbness or paralysis. Now turn, and let me see your face."

Lydia did as she was bid, pulling up and holding the front of her dress together. Sterling had to lift her chin to look at her face. Her right eye and cheek were shades of blue and purple, but at least her eye was open. He gently touched and examined her eye socket and cheekbones.

"No bones broken. Your face and eye will be bruised for a while but that will fade with time. No lasting physical scars." Sterling said nothing about the emotional ones, knowing they would be longer in healing. He turned his attention to her arm, looking with interest at the splints Aggie had put on, now filthy from the mud.

"Do you know which bone in the arm is broken? I don't want to remove these splints until I can put a cast on it."

"Aggie said it was the one on the outside, near the wrist."

"The radius. Okay. Ella, you help her clean up now, but leave the splints on. I'll cast the wrist later." Sterling looked again at Lydia, who still stood with her head bowed as if in defeat. He was frowning as he left the kitchen.

"Come," Peter said at the sound of knocking on the office door. He saw from the grave expression on Sterling's face that he wouldn't like what Sterling was going to tell them.

"I filled Peter in on what I knew of events of the night and the morning, including what Clem and Eustace did," Drew told Sterling.

"Thanks." Sterling sat down in the chair next to Drew. "She's been beaten. First, with her brother's fist to her face, causing a fall which broke her arm, and then he took a meat mallet to her back. I think there may be cracked ribs. Judging from the severity of the injuries, she probably passed out and he kept hitting her."

"Why?" Both men asked at once, clearly shocked by what Sterling had told them.

"Because she didn't want to marry a man who, from the sounds of it, would be capable of the same sort of treatment. He'd bargained with her brother, Cyrus, letting him keep her part of the farm they own together. Probably inherited from their folks but I don't know that for sure. I think she ran away and ended up here."

"The evil of the heart of man," said Peter.

"You've got that right, Preach," said Drew.

Peter shot him a sour look at the use of the disliked nickname. Drew just grinned. The three men had grown up together in Cottonwood, and though four years separated the oldest, Peter, from the youngest, Sterling, they were fast friends.

"Now, tell me what you know about her," Peter said. "What's her name?"

Sterling looked at Drew, who looked back.

"Don't tell me you two didn't even have the decency to ask for her name," Peter exclaimed, shocked at their insensitivity. "I've been preaching here for, what, six years, emphasizing caring more about others and less about self, but no doubt you two dragged her here because you were concerned with what Clem and Eustace were going to be saying around town. Letting her fall in the mud and humiliating her, again, on top of the humiliation she's endured from her brother ..."

Peter eyed both men, severely disappointed in them, and himself, for not getting across his message of true, selfless compassion.

The other men looked sheepish and it was evident they were feeling worse than they looked.

"Unfortunately, you're right," Sterling said. "We hardly even let her go use the necessary when she woke up before we left the livery."

Peter looked at them silently with his piercing blue eyes, communicating his disappointment in his two friends who should have known and done better. Silence reigned for several minutes, as each of the men was lost in thought over his own failings.

There was a soft knock on the door. Peter got up from his desk, rounded it and walked to the door. Opening it to Lydia and Ella, he stepped aside to let them in. He saw a young lady with wet, chestnut-colored hair pulled back in a braid. She was wearing a calico dress that might once have been green but was faded to gray with so many washings. Oddly placed seams and different shades of gray showed that the dress had been altered several times. The right side of her face was badly bruised, and she held herself stiffly. The green of her eyes was emphasized by the discoloration. He could tell by her stance that her back hurt. Her left arm was held bent at the elbow, with the hand resting on her upper chest.

"Lydia's ready to meet with you now," Ella said, leading Lydia to a small settee positioned to the side of the desk under a window.

At Ella's mention of Lydia's name, Peter shot a disgusted look at Sterling and Drew, who wouldn't meet his eyes. He pulled a straight chair up next to the settee, sitting down before Lydia and his wife. Ella gently held Lydia's hand. Peter could see her fighting within herself to keep from trembling, but not being totally successful.

"You know who I am, Lydia. I'm Peter Lendrey, pastor of Cottonwood church. These two, who you've already met, are Doctor Sterling Graham and Sheriff Drew Richards." Peter's voice had begun gently but took on a stiffer tone as he introduced the other men. "Can you tell me a little about yourself and how you came to Cottonwood? I want to help you in whatever way I can."

Lydia glanced at Ella, who nodded and gave her hand a small squeeze.

"My name is Lydia Walcott. I lived on a farm with my brother Cyrus. He's older than I and after our parents died, when I was thirteen, he farmed and I did the housework and went to school. Cyrus had always been demanding, but after our folks died he got worse. He got mean. If something didn't suit him, he'd get mad. Then he started hitting. I got used to it some, and I could go to Aggie when I needed to get away. She lives on a farm about two miles from our place. She'd help me with things I couldn't do myself. Teach me. She loves me and helped me out yesterday. A few days ago Cyrus came home telling me that he had set me up to marry Gus Botwright. He's a blacksmith in town. Cyrus said that Gus would let him keep the half of the farm that was mine if I'd marry him."

Lydia shuddered, then continued. "I told Cyrus I wouldn't. Gus is as mean as Cyrus. I think that's why he couldn't find a girl in town to marry him. Everyone knows he's mean. Oh, I'm sorry. That's gossip. Please forgive me."

"Forgiven, Lydia," Peter said softly. "Please, continue."

"When I told Cyrus no, we argued. I told him I wouldn't marry Gus because he was mean and not a believer. Cyrus got so mad. Then he hit me in the face with his fist. I fell against the doorframe of my room and then onto the floor. My arm broke then, I think. Gus grabbed the meat tenderizer I'd been pounding meat with. He started hitting my back. After that, I don't know."

Lydia was shaking, so Ella put her arm gently around her shoulders.

Peter reached out and took her hand in a gentle grip. "You just take your time. You're safe here. Sterling, go get Lydia some water, will you please?"

Sterling looked at Peter, then rose from his chair. "Of course."

Sterling left thinking he should have thought of this himself.

The room was silent, as each thought about what the girl had gone through.

When Sterling returned Lydia lifted her head and looked at him briefly. He realized that it was the first time, since the moment she jumped up so startled in the livery from the depths of her over-large coat that she had looked straight at him. He had even had to lift her face while he examined her bruises.

"Thank you." Lydia sipped the water, took a deep breath, and continued. "I knew I wouldn't marry Gus, and I couldn't stay at home, so I took a day to pack and cook enough food for Cyrus so he wouldn't come looking for me too soon. When he left the next morning I went to my friend Aggie's house and asked her to help me run away."

Sterling, who'd known only love and support from his family, found it hard to think of what Lydia had endured at the hands of her brother.

"Aggie set my arm and took me into town. I took the train not knowing where I would stop. This town is the farthest I could go and still have a little money left for food and a place to stay until I could find some work. When I got off the train last night, everything was dark and the ice and all. I made it to the livery because of the lantern hanging outside. I found the empty stall and slept there."

Peter got up and went back to the chair behind his desk. He steepled his hands with his elbows on the desktop and closed his eyes. Sterling recognized that Peter was praying. Sterling and Drew bowed their heads and asked for the Lord's forgiveness for the way they had handled Lydia this morning.

Ella pulled Lydia's head to her, stroking her hair. "You poor child."

A knock sounded at the front door. Ella rose and left the room to answer it.

"Lydia," Sterling said, trying to look into her face. It bothered him that she wouldn't look at him. "Please forgive my and Drew's actions and inconsideration this morning. We handled everything poorly, and I'm sorry."

"Yes," Drew said, "please forgive me."

"You're forgiven," Lydia said softly, not looking at them.

Ella showed Luke Johnson, the boy from the livery, into the room. "I'm going up to see to the children," she said. "I'll also fix something to eat."

"Thank you, dear," Peter said. After Ella had gone from the room he looked at the young man. "Luke, what brings you here?"

"Thought I should let you know what's going around town. It isn't good. Mr. Taylor and Mr. Baumgarden went straight to Langston's Cafe and starting spreading that Doc had been found with a woman this morning in the livery. Said they'd spent the night together there. That stirred up some talk, let me tell you. They didn't say anything else, but you know how it goes in a small town. There's all sorts of speculating. Anyway, then someone sees Doc carrying a woman down the street with the sheriff and things just start up even stronger. People started pouring out of the cafe. I followed a couple of people into Pa's store, and they were filling Pa and Ma with the story, already making up stuff. I know my folks wouldn't like it much. The gossiping, that is. I figured that it was going on everywhere in town so I came here to let you know."

Peter rubbed his hands down his face and then looked at Lydia. She had her hand clenched so tightly in her lap that the knuckles were white. Her body trembled so hard Peter could see it from where he sat. He also saw that Sterling was watching her too, the look on his face evidence of how her story and Luke's news had affected him.

The sounds of running children were heard on the stairs, then Ella's voice and slower steps down the hall to the kitchen. A few moments later the kitchen door slammed. Ella opened the door.

"I've sent the children over to the Smiths' with a note asking to watch them until later," she said. "I know it won't be a problem. Tilly understands and has watched them before. I'm fixing sandwiches. If you've finished with your message, Luke, will you please come and help me?"

"Sure." The boy was fifteen, always hungry, and would be hoping to get a few early samples.

"So, Peter, what do you think we need to do to fix this?" Sterling said. "You know nothing happened. I didn't even know anyone else was in the stable."

"I know you're both innocent of any wrongdoing, Sterling. I know you'd never take advantage of a woman, it just isn't in you."

Peter sat at his desk, his hands steepled before him, praying. The others in the room sat in silence.

"If someone would lend me some money, I could get back on the train and go farther west. Wouldn't that fix it? I would pay you back, I promise. I'd be gone so the talk would die down," Lydia offered with a quiet, somewhat pleading tone.

"Yes, Lydia, that would work for you, but that would leave Sterling to face this down alone. It would give the people more reason to suspect something had gone on," Peter said.

"So what do you suggest we do?" Sterling's voice betrayed his irritation.

Peter glanced at Lydia, seeing her pull her shoulders in as if she were trying to disappear.

"I suggest that Lydia stay with us for a few days. You go along as you normally do. You have a good reputation in town. First Peter 2:12 says that when evildoers speak against you, by living a godly life he will be glorified. Titus 2:7–8 says: 'In all things showing yourself an example of good works; in your teaching showing integrity, seriousness, incorruptibility, and soundness of speech that can't be condemned; that he who opposes you may be ashamed, having no evil thing to say about us.' "

Peter turned to Sterling. "Sterling, you can live showing that you have nothing to be ashamed of. Don't defend yourself against the talk. Live and work with integrity, compassion and honor as you've always done. The talk will die down."

"Just like that. The talk and embellished tale will just fade away." The sarcasm in Sterling's voice was thick. "You're a diehard optimist or totally naive."

"I didn't say it would be easy, or of short duration, but it will resolve itself. Think of Rahab. She had a past of massive sin. It couldn't have been easy to live in the midst of Israel knowing that everyone knew her sinful life. They no doubt gossiped about her continuing the lifestyle. Yet she must have lived a righteous life to the point that Salmon took her as his wife and made her part of the direct line to Jesus."

Sterling rose and walked to the window behind Peter's desk. He stood silently, looking out.

"Pastor," Lydia's voice was timid, "I appreciate your offer to let me stay here but ... I would really rather go on west. I need to be able to get a job, and I think that might be hard here in town. I promise I would pay back the loan as soon as I was able. I don't need much. Just some train fare and maybe a little bit of food."

"I know that sounds easy, but could you leave knowing how difficult it will be for Sterling and not helping him in any way?"

Lydia was silent for a moment. "I suppose it would be very selfish of me."

A knock sounded at the door. "Come," Peter called.

Luke poked his head around the door with what looked like chocolate cookie crumbs around his mouth. "Ella said the food's ready, and you should all come and eat."

"Looks like you started without us," Drew said, smiling at the boy as he got up from his chair.

Sterling shot a glance at Peter that seemed to say, Give us a minute. Peter nodded and left, followed by Drew and Luke. Once the door had closed, leaving the two of them alone, Sterling went and knelt before Lydia. The lashes of her eyes created damp amber crescents on her cheeks.

"I'm sorry all this happened," he said. "I don't know what the answer is. I'm sure Peter and Ella would let you stay for a few days until we get it all figured out. I'm going to put a cast on that arm this afternoon."

"I don't want to be a bother. I'm cleaned up now. I could just--"

Sterling lifted a hand, cutting her off. "Let's not talk about that. I don't know what will fix this, but I do know that neither you nor I have eaten today, and I expect you didn't have much yesterday. Let's go eat and think on this. Okay?"

Lydia looked at the man before her, the stranger named Sterling, examining his face for the first time. It was a nicely shaped oval with clean lines, a shallow cleft in the chin, brown eyes, dark brown, slightly wavy hair, and his lips, though very serious now, looked as if they would smile easily. She already knew he was tall and lean. She held her hand out to him and he helped her rise from her seat.

Chapter 6

The meal was eaten in near silence, after which Drew and Luke left. Peter, Sterling and Lydia continued sitting at the table while Ella started doing the dishes.

"I'm going to go and get the things I need to cast your arm, Lydia. I'll be back soon." Sterling rose and left by the back door, picking up his boots and coat to put on outside. He really needed to get away from the Lendreys' house so he could think.

How and why had this happened? Sterling had been raised in a devout home with loving parents who had instilled in him the values and responsibilities of being a believer in Christ Jesus. He lived trying to be holy, righteous and blameless in the sight of God and man. He had followed in his father's footsteps to become a doctor, coming home and taking over the practice when his parents died. He treated everyone, whether they could pay him or not. He was well respected, and he liked it that way. He had earned it.

Now this.

He walked to the corner across from the block set aside by the town for a park. The day was sunny, so different from the night before. Looking over at the bench surrounding the huge cottonwood in the center of the block, he saw a gathering of the townsfolk. He waved as he crossed the street to walk along the north side of the park. One man gave a tentative wave in response. Another simply looked at him. A woman lifted her parasol, concealing her face.

He knew each one, had known them since he was a small child. They'd been friends of his parents and patients of his. These weren't even people he'd been concerned would believe the gossip. Didn't they trust him, respect him; know that he would never do what was being spread around town?

What if I haven't been respected all this time? The thought struck him like a mallet. What if people just playacted that they respected him? What if they had just been waiting for him to slip up? How would he convince them, without defending himself as Peter had suggested, that everything was innocent?

Sterling had turned north and was walking past the Taylor house. Eustace Taylor had been one of the men at the livery this morning. He was also the owner of the bank and mayor of Cottonwood. It just had to be Eustace with his love of finding a person's vulnerability and exploiting it. Sterling thought he also had the most stuck-up and snobby, gossipy wife, Beulah, who was always pushing their daughter, Magdelina, at him. Sterling knew that Eustace thought he would be a good catch, with the right professional and social standing in the town.

Sterling glanced up at the house, catching sight of the curtains being hastily pulled together. He quickened his pace, deciding he'd thought enough about the problem.

He turned his focus to the supplies he needed to take to the Lendreys', then realized, with a sickening feeling, that he'd left his medical bag at the livery. Now, instead of going straight back to the Lendreys' from his house he would have to go downtown to get his bag. How would people react as he walked past the stores? Would he be pointed at? Whispered about? The reactions of the people he'd seen in the park gave him a clue. He wasn't looking forward to the trip.

At home he washed, shaved and changed clothes; no sense in presenting a disheveled appearance to further fuel the gossips. Gathering the materials for the cast into a bag, he straightened his shoulders and with grim determination to ignore the situation left the house to head downtown and retrieve his medical bag.

"Here's your room. It has a pleasant view in the summer of the Ralstons' back garden. She lets me gather flowers for the church all summer. You've already met Theo Ralston--he owns the livery."

Lydia knew that Ella was chattering to try and get comfortable. Lydia placed her carpetbag on the floor by the bed and looked around the room. It was a pretty room painted light green, with a green, white and yellow quilt on the bed. There was a mirrored dresser with a white bowl and pitcher sitting on the top. The hardwood floor had braided rugs scattered about.

"This is beautiful. Thank you."

"It is a pretty room, isn't it? The church folks decorated the house before we arrived, after Peter finished seminary. Most of it I really like, but there's one room I don't, and unfortunately it's the parlor. I really can't change it yet. We've only been here since Rye was a baby." Ella's eyes took on a mischievous air. "I keep hoping the children will spill something on the furniture or damage a wall, and then I can change it."

Lydia laughed, and Ella joined in. "I'll get some water for you and then go rescue the Smiths from my children. They can be a handful."

Ella left the room and Lydia sat down on the bed. The emotions of the days leading up to her flight, the train trip, and now today's events had left her exhausted. She looked around the cheery bedroom, unable to dredge up any feeling of comfort. Defeated, she turned to prayer.

Heavenly Father, I'm so confused. You provided for me so well yesterday. Now, I don't know. I feel abandoned. I know you've said you will never do that but ... I'm so lost and afraid. I didn't mean to cause any problem. I just needed a place to stay. Now I've caused so much trouble for that man. Please, Father, let it be that his reputation and career don't suffer.

Ella knocked on the door just then and Lydia called for her to come in.

Setting the pitcher of warm water on the washstand, Ella turned to look at Lydia. "Are you all right? You look a little pale."

"I'm fine. Weary mostly." Lydia looked up at Ella. "I didn't mean to cause so much trouble. I only wanted to get away from Cyrus and Gus. I hope the doctor isn't angry with me. I didn't mean to harm him."

"No one thinks you're at fault. Those who left without knowing what was going on and then spreading rumors throughout town are. Sterling isn't the type to blame you."

"I hope not." Lydia looked back at the lands in her lap.

"Why don't you lie down for a while? Sterling won't be back until later and you could rest until then."

"Okay, I'll try."

Ella helped Lydia draw back the blankets and tucked her in as she would her own children. She closed the door softly as she went.

Lydia curled up on her side, drawing the cover over her shoulder. She felt so alone. Aggie was so far away. She didn't have enough money to go anywhere. She had no friends, no job, nowhere to live. Why, Lord? What am I supposed to do? I didn't mean to hurt anyone. A tear slipped from her closed eye as she tried to shut the problem out of her mind.

Sterling felt as if every person in Cottonwood were staring at him, judging him for something he hadn't even done. As he passed, conversations on the street stilled. A few people acknowledged him, but not as many as usual and not in as friendly a manner. It seemed as if even the store windows were condemning him. He finally arrived at the All-Purpose Store and went in.

Hal Johnson, the owner, looked up and came out from behind the counter. "Hi, Doc, glad you came in. I was wondering how things were with you. The people in this morning, they had some wild ideas about what happened last night."

"I'll just bet, and none of them really know or care about the truth."

"No, they don't. All they care about is finding something they can talk about, and if it hurts someone else so much the better. Would you like a cup of coffee?"

"Well, I should be getting back to the Lendreys' but maybe a quick one. I could really use a break from the stares I received on the way here. Also, did the plaster of Paris I ordered come in?"

"It did. It's in the storeroom along with the coffee. Come on back."

The men walked to a curtained doorway leading into the storeroom. A potbellied stove sat in the corner warming the room, with a coffee pot sitting on top. Hal took two mugs off a shelf, filled them with coffee and handed one to Sterling. Carrying his own mug, Hal crossed to a shelf on the other side of the room and picked up a package.

"Thanks," Sterling said as Hal handed it to him.

"So," Hal said, "what are you going to do about the gossip?"

"I don't know yet. Pastor says to just wait it out. That the whole thing will pass. I'm not sure, though. I'm afraid it might hurt my practice. What if people stop trusting me as their doctor?"

"Surely it wouldn't go that far." Hal's voice held disbelief mixed with concern.

"I hope not."

Just then the bell above the door to the store rang, indicating customers. Hal set down his cup, looked at Sterling and went back into the store. Sterling sat sipping his coffee, and the voices from the front filtered back to where he was sitting.

"So, Mr. Johnson, it was just as I suspected."

Sterling recognized the speaker as Harriet Baumgarden. He flinched at the sound of her voice. It grated on every nerve in his ear. He wasn't overly fond of the wife of Clem Baumgarden, who, along with Eustace Taylor, had run out of the stable before bothering to find out why he and Lydia had both spent the night in the livery.

"That doctor has a roving eye and now it comes out. Imagine, spending the night with a floozy in the livery stable. Clem said she was hardly wearing any clothes when he and Eustace found her. He only had on--"

"Now wait a minute, Mrs. Baumgarden. You know I don't like gossip and won't tolerate it." Hal's voice sounded forceful and strict. "Furthermore, I've known Sterling Graham all his life, and so have you. A more respectable man you won't find. He's a good doctor, and a giving, compassionate person, so you have no cause to think let alone talk about him like that."

"Well, I don't know. I'm not so sure anymore. Caught in the livery with a woman. What sort of man does that? I'm going to think long and hard about whether my family is going to continue using him as our doctor. I know the Taylors will, too. Imagine him treating Magdelina or any other single young lady. Disgraceful."

Sterling heard her march down the aisle, and then the jingle as she opened the door and slammed it behind her, indicating her displeasure at the conversation with Hal.

Standing up and setting his mug in the pan for dishes, Sterling looked up as Hal entered. "Not so good, huh, Hal. Seems I'll lose patients if I just wait it out."

"It's a possibility, although losing the Baumgardens ..." Hal left the thought unspoken.

No need to state the obvious, thought Sterling. The Baumgardens were known to be meddling gossips who enjoyed another person's failings. They were also difficult patients.

"Well, thanks for the coffee. I need to get to the livery for my medical bag. Lydia, that's the girl's name, has a broken wrist that needs to be cast." Sterling's discouragement was evident in his voice. He grabbed his Stetson, placing it on his head.

They walked out of the storeroom and down the middle aisle to the front door.

"If I, or the missus, can do anything to help, let me know."

"Your prayers would be welcome."

"That goes without saying, Doc. We have, and we will."

Sterling opened the door and walked out into a street that had always welcomed him before but now seemed threatening.

Chapter 7

Lydia came down the steps and looked around the corner into the parlor. She had slept for several hours but wasn't feeling very refreshed. The late afternoon sun illuminated the room. Ella certainly was correct. The room was horrid. The walls had wallpaper with muddy yellow and lavender roses in large bunches on a background of what she thought was supposed to be light blue. The sofa was a gray-blue with yellow stripes. The other chairs in the room had green upholstery so dark it appeared nearly black. There were several occasional tables, none of which matched in wood or design. Blue and yellow striped draperies with a yellow ball fringe hung at the windows.

Lydia took a step backwards and closed her eyes at the awful sight, and with relief headed into the kitchen.

"Ella, you are surely right about the parlor," she said as she entered the kitchen and saw Ella coming in with the children. "Whatever possessed them to decorate it like that?"

"I'm not sure. I think a couple of the ladies decided they were going to outdo each other and that's the result. Horrid, isn't it?"

Lydia nodded.

With a loud bang, the back door slammed and the ladies' attention turned to the two children who stood stock-still.

"Sorry," they both said.

"Try better next time," their mother said. "This is Miss Walcott. She's new in town. These two are Zachariah and Janie. We call Zachariah Rye."

"Pleased to meet you," Janie said.

"Yeah, me too," said Rye, eyeing her bruised face.

"Rye," his mother said warningly.

"Pleased to meet you, Miss Walcott," Rye corrected.

"What happened to your face? Did you fall? Does it hurt?" Janie's questions came on the heels of each other.

"Janie." Her mother gave her a stern look.

"I'm pleased to meet you both, also." Lydia smiled at the precocious children.

"Now, do you want some cookies for a snack before you do your evening chores?"

"Yes, please." Both children replied politely, still under the influence of their mother's warnings.

"May I have some milk too?"

"Of course, darling. You want some too, Rye?"

"Yeap. Err, yes, ma'am."

Lydia watched the conversation that brought back memories of her mother and father. The memories were bittersweet. It seemed so long since they had died, so long since she'd felt the love of a family.

Ella had poured milk and set a plate of cookies on the table when there was a knock at the kitchen door. Sterling opened it, poking his head in.

"Hey guys, save some of those cookies for me."

"Uncle Doc!" and "Better hurry or I'll eat them all" came from mouths with milk mustaches and crumbs.

Sterling stepped into the kitchen and set his medical bag and satchel on the floor. He mussed Rye's hair and gave a quick kiss to Janie's forehead. Then, he popped a whole cookie into his mouth.

"Mama says it's not polite to eat a cookie in one bite," Janie scolded.

"Sorry, Mama," Sterling said.

Sterling didn't look too sorry and Ella shot him a mockingly stern look.

"Lydia, I'm ready to cast that arm for you. I also brought the wrapping."

"A cast?" Rye queried. "You got somethin' broke?"

"Do you have something broken?" corrected his mother.

"My arm. It's splinted now. Your Uncle Doc thinks it'll be better in a cast."

"How'd ya break it?"

Sterling and Ella exchanged glances, wondering how much detail Lydia would give.

"I fell. I don't recommend it to anyone. It hurt very badly and still does, even after several days."

Rye's eyes were bright with interest. Janie's were more serious.

"Okay. You two want to help with the cast?" Sterling asked.

"Yeah!" both children said. "How?"

"I'll need water. You go get a bucketful, Rye. Janie, you get a big bowl."

The children climbed from their chairs, running to do their tasks.

Sterling lifted the satchel onto the table and Ella removed the empty glasses and plate. Lydia, who was sitting at the table, laid her arm down, and Sterling began unwrapping the splints.

Janie brought a large mixing bowl from the pantry, and Rye came in with the bucket of water. "Here's the water. Where do you want it?"

"Give it to me. I'll put it up here on the table. I don't think you can reach it."

Sterling took the bucket from him and the children climbed onto their chairs, sitting on their knees. Sterling opened the satchel and took out the container of plaster of Paris. He poured a good amount into the bowl and added water.

"Ella, can they get a little messy?"

"Sure. It won't be the first time and I'll bet it's not the last." Ella smiled, turning back the sleeves of both children.

"Okay. Now, assistants, you need to mix up the plaster with the water. It needs to be all mixed up and smooth. I'll keep watch and add more plaster or water if it needs it."

The children's hands dived into the bowl and started mixing.

"Eeuuw. It's gooey."

"It squishes through my fingers."

"Just like mudpies."

The adults laughed, watching the children stir the wet white paste. Sterling went back to unwrapping Lydia's arm. When all the wraps were gone and the sticks were on the table, he examined it carefully. It was still bruised from the break and dirty from her fall in the mud. Ella brought over a bowl of warm water, soap and a towel.

"How's this, Uncle Doc?" Rye asked. Both children held up hands covered with plaster, fingers spread wide.

"Pretty good, but I think it needs a little more water. You mix it in good, now."

"Okay."

"Will do."

Sterling dried Lydia's hand and arm, and began to loosely wrap it in muslin strips. He looked at the bowl of plaster. "That's just perfect for making a cast. You two did great. Now push that bowl over here and go wash your hands before it hardens and your fingers are stuck like that."

The children laughed and did as they were told. Ella had a pan of water ready for the cleanup.

"Here we go, Lydia. It'll start off cold but get warm as it dries."

Sterling began to spread the plaster over her muslin-wrapped arm, casting it from below her fingers to just short of her elbow. When it was done he said, "Keep it still until it dries. It'll take a couple of hours to fully dry and will have to stay on about five weeks. It should start to feel better in a few days. Then it will start to itch." He used the pan of water to wash the plaster off his hands.

"Okay." Lydia wondered if she could hold the heavy cast off the table for two hours but she didn't ask. She would keep the arm still.

"Sterling," Ella said, "would you stay for supper? It's close to five and I've prepared enough."

"Thank you, I will. You're a mighty fine cook." Turning to Lydia he said, "I have the wrapping for your ribs. Let's go into the parlor and I'll tell you how to wrap yourself."

"The parlor?" Lydia asked. "I thought you wanted me to keep my arm still." She hadn't even set her elbow on the table, and the weight of the cast caused a trembling as she tried to do as Sterling had instructed and hold it still for two hours.

"You can let your arm hang down. It'll just get things plastery if you set it on anything."

Lydia set her elbow on the table with relief. "But, the parlor?"

60

Sterling chuckled. "So you've seen it. Well, it is the only other room on this floor except Peter's office. I figure he's in there praying, studying or writing his Sunday sermon. I don't want to bother him."

Lydia rose from the table and Sterling stepped back, allowing her to lead the way. She paused when they arrived at the doorway, then entered, crossing to the sofa and sitting on the edge with her arm propped on her knee.

Sterling joined her, holding out the bundle of muslin strips. He explained how to wrap her chest to support her back and ribs. "It might be best if Ella helps you to start with," he said when he was finished. "It's pretty straightforward, though it can be awkward trying to do it by yourself. Do you have any questions?"

"Yes, I do have a question. Why did you want to come in here? We could have discussed it in the kitchen, then Ella would have heard, too."

"I wanted to speak with you privately." His tone had changed from the friendly banter in the kitchen, becoming more serious.

Lydia looked down at her lap. She was being very careful not to let the cast touch anything and holding it up was difficult. "Have you thought of a way to fix this situation?"

"No. I wanted to know if you had. From your question I figure you haven't either."

"No."

"I had to go downtown to fetch my medical bag before I came back here. My reception was not what I was used to. Usually, people are friendly. Even if we don't speak, we'll wave or smile a greeting. Today, many acted as if they didn't see me. Others just, I don't know, weren't normal. If it's okay with you I'd like to speak with Peter about the situation after supper. I'm not sure his 'just wait it out' is a good idea. Are you willing to do that?"

Lydia nodded, but didn't say anything. What choice did she really have? She was stuck in Cottonwood with no way to move on or make a living. She had no friends and knew no one except the Lendreys, the doctor and the sheriff. She could not, would not, return home.

Silently, she prayed that God would let her know what she was supposed to do.

Peter came out of his office when a knock sounded on the front door, just as Sterling and Lydia were leaving the parlor. He opened the door to a grim-faced Sheriff Drew Richards and stepped back, allowing Drew entrance to the foyer.

"How is it, Drew," Ella smiled, coming down the hall from the kitchen, "that you always arrive just in time for a meal?" Sheriff Drew Richards removed his Stetson, giving Ella a sheepish grin. "Don't worry, I'll feed you."

"Thanks, Ella. Hello, Sterling, Miss Walcott." Drew turned his hat around in his hands nervously.

"So, Drew. What brings you here?" Peter asked. He was afraid he knew.

"I thought I'd come and fill you in on what's been going on this afternoon. None of you are going to like it." Drew looked first at Peter, then Sterling, then Ella and finally Lydia.

"I need to finish fixing supper," Ella said. "You all go talk in Peter's office. I'll let you know when it's time to eat." She gave them a small wave, turned and went back to the kitchen.

"Come on into the office." Peter waved them through ahead of him, closing the door as he entered. He rounded his desk and sat in his chair while the others took their seats. Lydia sat on a settee under the window to Peter's left. Sterling and Drew sat in chairs positioned directly across from him.

"So, Drew, would you like to start?" Peter went straight to the point, feeling any delay or small talk was worthless.

Drew looked at Sterling then glanced at Lydia. "Well, there's been a lot of talk going on all day. The story, and that's what it's become, has been told, and retold, growing past any foundation of truth. Theo's been really good at trying to quash the talk, but some just don't want to hear what really happened. The Johnsons have tried to stop it by reminding people about Sterling's character and such. Hal won't allow the gossip in his store or even on the boardwalk in front. The town seems pretty divided between believing that Sterling and Lydia didn't know the other was there and did nothing wrong, and those who want to think the worst. That group has taken the incident and built it up as something planned and very sordid."

Peter noticed that Lydia had gone pale. He hoped she wouldn't faint. He'd keep an eye on her.

"I'm not surprised to hear you say that," Sterling replied. "I had to go to Johnson's store to pick up the plaster of Paris, and Hal and I were having coffee when Mrs. Baumgarden came in. She ... well, let's just say that she's on the side of those who are embellishing the story."

Peter thought Sterling was holding back from telling what Mrs. Baumgarden had said. He eyed Lydia again. Her color was better, but she was looking down at her lap.

"I'm concerned," Sterling continued, "that people will stop allowing me to treat them. My reputation as a doctor is important. If people don't trust me, how can I make a living?"

Silence reigned for several moments. Peter took in the worried look on Sterling's face. Drew looked at him with an expression communicating how seriously he thought the matter was. Lydia was still looking down, her fingers nervously fiddling with her skirt.

Peter had spent much of the afternoon in prayer. He'd asked God to mitigate the effect of the gossips. Prayed those hearing it would reject the notion of Sterling doing anything improper. That Sterling's career would not be affected. He'd asked that Lydia be spared embarrassment and shame since she'd done nothing wrong. Now, he wondered if the advice he'd given that morning to act as if nothing had happened would be enough to still the rumors. Sterling was one of his best friends. Could he and Drew stop the gossip and the blow Sterling's reputation and career were taking?

Looking at Drew, who, Peter knew, had left out details of the expanded version of the incident, he asked, "Drew, exactly what is being told around town?"

Drew squirmed uneasily, glancing at Lydia and Sterling before answering. "It's not pretty. It's said that

Sterling planned the get-together with a doxy and that this wasn't their first tryst."

"What?" Both Sterling and Lydia exclaimed, Sterling nearly rising from his chair.

Sterling looked at Peter. "Mrs. Baumgarden said that she thought the woman was a floozy," he said, with disgust in his voice. "I thought Hal might've been able to convince her that I wouldn't do anything like that."

"I'm not a ... one of those types of women." Lydia's voice was small, with a slight tremor.

Sterling quickly turned to look at her, his tone gentle as he spoke. "We know you're not. You're as innocent as I am in this."

Peter sat at his desk in his usual position: hands steepled, eyes closed. He prayed for guidance, for an answer to how to go forward. His time in seminary hadn't taught him much about dealing with a situation like this. Finally he opened his eyes, noting that both Drew and Sterling looked to also be in prayer. Lydia, he couldn't tell. Her neck was bent, her face hidden from his view.

He looked at the vulnerable young woman. Beaten and abused by her only relative until she had no choice but to flee. Arriving in Cottonwood at night during an ice storm. Taking refuge in a stable. Hoping to start a new life in a friendly town. What a welcome, Peter thought with disgust. *How, Lord, do we protect this innocent girl and give her a new, safe life?*

He switched his gaze to Sterling. Peter knew life wasn't fair, but why did this have to happen to a blameless, Godfearing man like Sterling? All Sterling had ever done was serve the people of Cottonwood and the surrounding farms with compassionate care. Now his career could be lost because of rumor and gossip. *Lord, help me help him.*

A word quietly slipped into his head. Peter blinked. The word seemed to be spoken in his mind again. *Really, Lord? That's your answer? Isn't that a little drastic?* The word sounded louder this time. *All right, Lord, I'll suggest it but you have to be the one to convince them.*

Looking at Drew, Peter was surprised to see the man looking intently back at him. Drew nodded once. Peter had the feeling that Drew had exactly the same word in his mind too.

Chapter 8

"Excuse me." Peter didn't want to interrupt their prayers, but felt the need to press on with the discussion. "I hope you've been praying for guidance. I know I have."

Lydia raised her head, looking at him. Sterling nodded.

"Have either of you received any answers?"

"No," said Lydia.

"I haven't heard any response. I know sometimes the answer is wait, but then I have a peace about the problem. I don't now."

Sterling looked first at Drew, then at Peter, who could tell he was frustrated with God's silence.

"Are you two open to ideas which may seem farfetched and drastic?"

"What do you mean?" Sterling's voice was filled with suspicion.

"Let's review," Peter said. He looked at Lydia. "You left home seeking refuge and safety, with a goal of working to support yourself. You ended up in the livery because of the storm."

She nodded.

"Sterling, you sleep at the livery at times when you get back late from a call. That's known some around town. You stayed there last night after delivering the Stantons' baby." He paused for a moment. "Now, because you two were found to have both spent the night in the livery stable, the rumors and gossip surrounding this threaten you both. Your reputation and career are both in danger of destruction, Sterling. Lydia, you're no closer to safety and finding the work you need. I know you said you would borrow money to move farther west but that still leaves you both with the same problems."

Lydia looked a little confused.

Gently, Peter said, "You would still be going to an unknown place trying to find shelter and a job with no one to help you."

Lydia's expression changed from confusion to despair.

"I've been asking God for some way to restore Sterling's reputation, and to fill your need for safety and support as well. The answer I've received will seem astounding, I'm sure. Please don't reject it without thinking it through and discussing it. I feel very strongly that this has come from God. If I'm not mistaken, Drew has received the same answer." Peter looked at Drew.

"Just what is this answer you two have received from God about my situation that he chose not to reveal to me?" Irritation colored Sterling's voice. He looked from Peter to Drew and back, all but ignoring Lydia in his frustration.

"You two could get married," Peter said.

Lydia gasped.

"Married!" Sterling fairly shouted the word. He tried to calm his racing pulse, which had taken off like a galloping horse.

"I know it's a shock, but unless you want to give up your practice here in Cottonwood and set up again a long way away, it's the only solution I see." Peter was looking straight at Sterling.

Drew stared at his hands, looking uncomfortable. "Several people said you'd do the honorable thing, if the girl was respectable, and marry her."

Sterling got up and started pacing the room. Move away from Cottonwood. Start a practice somewhere else. Leave all my friends, my home. Or get married. Get married to a perfect stranger. One who's been bruised in body and soul. Help her heal from all her brother's abuse. Spend the rest of my life in the same house. Have children with her ... The thoughts flew swiftly through his head until the last. At that one, both his thoughts and his pacing came to an abrupt halt. He dragged a hand through his hair.

A knock sounded at the door. "Come," Peter called.

Rye poked his head around the door. "Mama says supper's ready."

"Thank you. Tell her we'll be right there."

Rye pulled his head out and closed the door. They heard the sound of running feet, then the sound of slower steps replacing them.

"Father in heaven, we thank you for our food and ask for blessings on the hands that prepared it," Peter prayed. "We ask for you to give us wisdom this day so that we are within your will. Give us peace, and thank you that we are safe in your hands. In the name of our precious Jesus, amen."

After the prayer, the food was passed and coffee poured. Lydia, who was not a coffee drinker, asked for water. Peter decided that they wouldn't go back to the office right after supper; the more relaxed atmosphere of the kitchen might help with the discussion. The adults were silent as they ate, keeping their thoughts to themselves.

Rye and Janie seemed to realize that something serious was going on and also ate quietly, but Peter could see that Rye was twitchy with excitement.

Finally Rye burst out, "Seth and me climbed that big oak tree in their yard today. Real high, too."

"No broken bones, I see." Sterling grinned at the boy.

"We were really careful. We're really good at climbing trees."

"One thing Uncle Doc isn't," Drew contributed with a twinkle in his eye, "is a good tree climber."

"Oh, don't bring that up, Drew," Sterling said with a groan, a flush creeping up his neck.

Peter laughed.

Drew continued. "The easiest tree in the whole county to climb and Sterling here manages to fall out of it. Not only fall out, but break his arm in the process."

"Don't you pay any attention to them," Ella injected. "Sterling was only six at the time, with Drew being eight and Peter, the old man of the group, ten. I believe you two got into big trouble for letting Sterling climb that high, am I not right?"

"Yes, my love, you are correct. I got into big trouble, and I had to go apologize not only to Sterling but also to his parents for putting their precious son in danger. I'd always been a little scared of your father, Sterling, but that day I was terrified."

Everyone was glad Drew had lightened the mood with his tale, and talk became easier during the rest of the meal. Lydia ate silently. When the meal was finished and the cookie plate empty, Peter sent the children upstairs leaving the adults in the kitchen. Ella put the dishes into the sink and began washing them.

Deciding he better let his wife in on the suggested solution, Peter said, "Ella, I think that about the only way to fix this and keep it from destroying Sterling's career is for them to get married."

"What!" Ella turned from the sink so quickly that soapy water flew off the dishrag in her hand and onto the people sitting at the table. Chuckling, Sterling and Drew wiped water from their faces. Peter took it as a sign from God that the choice of the kitchen for the discussion was a good one.

"Good aim, my dear," Peter said, smiling.

Lydia's eyes, peeking up, sparkled with humor, which encouraged him.

"It seems that the gossip has taken on a life of its own. It could easily damage or destroy Sterling's career and Lydia's chance to find employment and a place to live. Do you have any other suggestions? I'm sure Lydia and Sterling would gladly entertain any you may have."

"Unfortunately, although I've been rolling it around in my head all day, I didn't even come up with that one," Ella said.

Lydia cleared her throat. "Pastor, is the doctor a believer?"

Peter looked at Sterling, then back at Lydia. "Why do you ask me?"

"Because you seem to know him well and would know where his heart lies. If I asked him, he could say he was even if he wasn't, just to fix his reputation. I wouldn't know the truth. You do know, I think. I will not even consider marrying anyone, for any reason, who is not a believer. I will not be unequally yoked."

"Very good reasoning. Yes, Sterling is a very devout believer. That's one reason I know he wouldn't have done anything in the night even if he had known you were there."

"Peter, I think Lydia and I need to discuss this between ourselves," Sterling said. "Could we use your office?"

"Sure, go ahead. We'll wait out here and eat more of my wife's great cookies." Peter grinned at his wife with big sheepdog begging eyes.

Sterling stood facing the office door he'd just closed after following Lydia into the room. He didn't know what to think, do or say. He was at a complete loss. *Why, Lord, why did this have to happen? All I want to do is live a quiet life serving you and others. Now this. Why didn't you stop the gossip and make people who know me believe that I wouldn't do what they accuse me of?*

He knew he wouldn't receive an answer. Sterling looked at Lydia sitting on the settee, eyes closed, her head leaning back against the top, slowly rocking it back and forth. Running a hand through his hair, he grabbed a chair, set it before Lydia and sat down.

"I didn't mean to hurt anyone. I only wanted to get away from Cyrus and Gus. I'm so sorry. If it would do any good I'd go back, but that wouldn't help you, would it?" Lydia had stopped rolling her head and sat looking at the ceiling. A tear slipped down her temple, getting lost in her hair.

Sterling's heart clenched. To think that her brother was so mean and greedy that he would beat her into submission turned his stomach. That she had no one who could have taken her in and protected her. She was taking all the blame for the gossip on those slight shoulders. It brought out an urge to protect her. The thought surprised him. Shocked him really.

Lydia's hair had dried, and a wispy halo surrounded her face. He saw that it had lightened as it dried, revealing auburn highlights in the chestnut. The column of her throat--the white skin disappearing behind the modest collar of her gown--appeared soft to the touch. She lifted her head to look at him.

Pulling himself back to the issue at hand, Sterling cleared his throat of its sudden tightness. "We need to decide how we're going to proceed. Let's start this with prayer, shall we?"

"Yes, let's. Will you please pray?"

They bowed their heads. Lydia started slightly when Sterling took her hand.

"Dear heavenly Father, we humbly come to you thanking you that you know the dilemma and how we should resolve it. We ask now for your guidance that what decisions we make are your will for our lives. Help us as we talk about it. Give us peace with whatever the decision we make is. Bless us with your will, not our own."

Sterling paused, and Lydia thought he must be finishing the prayer silently when he spoke again. "Lord, please forgive me, but I want to do violence against both Cyrus and Gus. They need you and are dead in their sin, but I want to beat them for what they've done to Lydia. So forgive me and give me peace with the fact that vengeance is yours. Help Lydia to forgive also. The sins were against her and I don't want her life tarnished with bitterness and hate. Please, Lord, answer this prayer in the name of Jesus, our Savior. Amen."

"Amen," echoed Lydia.

"Oh, I never gave you a chance to pray. Do you want to?"

"No, yours was very good. I hadn't thought that I might hold onto the hurt and turn bitter. I'll have to think and pray about that, but not right now."

They sat silently, Lydia with her head bowed, eyes on her folded hands.

Finally Sterling said, "Well, I guess we should discuss this. I know it doesn't seem fair to either of us, but we need to decide what we're going to do. Shall we go over the salient points? Sorry, that sounds so cold and sterile."

"That's okay." Lydia looked up at him. "I think it's best we go over whatever we think is important, although we covered the most important part in the kitchen. We're both believers and followers of Jesus Christ. If we keep him and his way in front of us, we can't go wrong."

"That's what I think. I also wouldn't have considered this if you weren't a believer," Sterling said. "My folks would probably come screaming from their graves and hit me upside the head if I married an unbeliever."

They both laughed, which broke the tension, and spent just a moment looking into each other's eyes.

"Since we know what's gotten us into this, why don't we get to the crux of the matter?" Sterling said. "Even though we're both innocent, it seems to me that almost everything would be set to rights if we did get married. My reputation would be repaired from whatever damage those gossips are doing out there, and you would be safe from your brother, as well as having a home and security."

Lydia began slowly. "I know you're right but, it just seems wrong to be giving in to those stupid gossips. 'One who brings gossip betrays a confidence, but one who is of a trustworthy spirit is one who keeps a secret.' "

"Ah, Proverbs 11:13. How about the verse right before: 'One who despises his neighbor is void of wisdom, but a man of understanding holds his peace.' That one seems to apply also."

"They've taken the gossip and turned it into slander of you. Leviticus 19:16 says, 'You shall not go up and down as a slanderer among your people; neither shall you stand against the life of your neighbor. I am Yahweh.' Now to appease them, you're supposed to marry me. It isn't fair to you."

Lydia looked so sad and concerned that Sterling almost reached for her hand to comfort her. "If we do decide to marry," he said, "I want you to know that no matter whatever happens, I promise you that I would never, ever strike you. Not only was I raised without that kind of treatment, I also took a vow to do no harm. I would never harm you. You could feel safe with me."

"Thank you. I could tell that you would never do that, but I thank you for the assurance."

"What are your thoughts? You haven't really expressed your opinion."

"I've been so lost the last few days it's hard for me to even think. I know that getting married is an answer but what if ... what if, later, you meet someone you fall in love with and want to marry? I would hate to stand in your way of happiness."

"I could say the same for you. All I know is that if we take vows, I will be making a covenant between you, me and God. Nothing will make me break it, no matter what."

"I would keep them also." Lydia let out a soft sigh, as if something heavy had been lifted from her shoulders.

"Oh, I'm twenty-seven, by the way," Sterling said. "How old are you?"

A little nervously, Lydia replied, "Twenty."

Sterling nodded, then thought for a moment. "We seemed to have decided to get married, haven't we?" Sterling was a little astonished that they had come to such a decision.

"Yes, I think we have. God doesn't tell us whom to marry so long as we're not unequally yoked. We won't be. Maybe God had his hand in this."

"Most likely," Sterling said. "I can support you, I don't want you to worry about that. I'm not rich by any means, but I've had a good practice. Let's hope that I'll have one after we get married. I also have the house that I grew up in. My folks left it to me when they died. It has my office and a couple of patient rooms connected. Makes it convenient to treat people, especially at night."

"I don't need much, and I have homemaking skills and will help you all I can."

"I might call on you some when I need a hand in the treatment. Nothing too much, mainly handing me things when I ask for them. Only if you want to, though. I don't need my wife fainting at the sight of blood." He grinned.

"Sterling," Lydia began, a little nervously, her voice shaky, "this is Friday. Would you mind if we didn't get married until Sunday? I'm exhausted from all the emotion and turmoil of the last few days. I could use tomorrow to rest and be ready on Sunday, if that's all right with you."

Sterling looked at her, saw the exhaustion in her face and even in the way she held her bruised body. "I think that would be a good idea. Besides, it would do those in church who've been spreading lies good to have to see what their gossip has wrought. Our getting married during service would surely do that. One last thing. Eventually I would like us to have a family. I hope you would too, but for the present I'd say that we should put that part of our relationship on hold until we know each other better."

Lydia's face blushed bright red again, but Sterling could only see her forehead and nose as she had dropped her face to look at the hands in her lap again. He realized she had been looking directly at him nearly the entire time they had been talking.

"I think that's wise for now. You can take the lead in that area if you want," Lydia said to her lap. "I don't think I could ever, well, you know ..."

"Yes, I know," Sterling said softly. "I'll take on that responsibility. But you be sure to let me know if you think you're, um, ready. Now let's go out and let the rest of them know."

All eyes turned to look at them as they entered the kitchen.

Sterling felt as if he were on display. "We've decided to marry on Sunday," he said, "during or after the service."

Sterling's voice didn't hold the joy that most grooms' would.

Lydia's face was serious, not delighted either.

"I won't say congratulations under the circumstances," Peter said, and Sterling could hear the relief in his voice, "but rather, I hope and pray this is the right decision and that you'll have a successful marriage. One that glorifies our Lord."

Drew simply nodded.

Ella looked as if she were going to cry. "I wish we could all be happier about this."

The group was silent for a while.

"Is it all right if I go upstairs now?" Lydia asked softly. "I'm very tired."

"Of course," Ella said. "I'll go with you. Let's take up pitchers up as we go. They're right here."

Lydia stood and poured warm water from the kettle on the stove into two ceramic pitchers, then she and Lydia headed to the stairs.

Drew left by the back door.

"I'll stand as your best man, Sterling," Drew said.

Sterling looked at his long-time friend. "I'd appreciate that."

"You all right with this, Sterling?" Peter asked.

"Guess I have to be, don't I? Seems sort of wrong and somehow right at the same time. We prayed for guidance before we started talking. Even so, I'm scared that we won't be able to make a marriage of strangers work. It's sort of funny, but I feel good that I can help her out of her difficulty. There's a sort of beginning of peace creeping in."

"If I know you, you'll do what you can to make this marriage work. Something tells me she will too. Just to warn you, though. She's been hurt deeply. She lost her parents at a critical time in her life and her brother, her only family member and someone she should have been able to rely on, betrayed her in a number of ways. She's been hurt both physically and emotionally. She'll have a hard time trusting you. That'll take time, and sometimes you just don't have the time with your medical practice." Peter was looking straight at Sterling, hoping he would get the true import of the words.

"All I can do is my best, and pray that the Lord will help me give her time to get to know me and to learn that she can trust me."

"How about we pray for God's help and protection for you both?"

"Yeah. I think that's a good idea." With that they bowed their heads and Peter began to pray.

Chapter 9

Peter stood at the pulpit looking at his congregation. They were sitting down after finishing a hymn. He took a minute to make eye contact with many of those sitting in the pews. A goodly number looked uncomfortable as his gaze focused on them.

"Our text for today is Exodus 23:1–2. 'You shall not spread a false report. Don't join your hand with the wicked to be a malicious witness. You shall not follow a crowd to do evil; neither shall you testify in court to side with a multitude to pervert justice.' "

As Peter's eyes swept the congregation, many people shifted nervously in their seats. Sterling and Lydia sat in the first row with Drew and Ella, along with her children. Lydia looked nervous, as if she felt every eye was looking at the back of her head. Peter watched as Lydia lowered her gaze to her lap and Sterling reached over to take her hand in his and give it a small squeeze. Peter knew this was difficult for both of them.

"This week I've been very disappointed by the amount of false witness that has swept through this town," Peter began. "I'd hoped that my preaching the way in which God wants us to live had been effective. I thought that those who come to church and listen to me week after week had taken it to heart. I am so sorry that I have failed you.

"My words have not passed the test of leading you to change your lives, to change how you act and react to unusual happenings in our town. My ineffectiveness eats at my soul. My failure as your pastor to affect your consciences so that you would choose to stop doing what is wrong and start living and acting as Christ would want you to brings my failure for God to the forefront. Please forgive that failure.

"The ninth commandment is: 'You shall not give false testimony against your neighbor.' In the past few days many have not only given false testimony, but have also passed it along, adding to it as it moves from person to person."

Peter's eyes--eyes that seemed to see into the hidden thoughts of a person--speared certain individuals he knew had spread the gossip. When he looked at them, they squirmed and looked away from his steely gaze.

"Psalm 101:5: 'I will silence whoever secretly slanders his neighbor. I won't tolerate one who is haughty and conceited.' Proverbs 10:18: 'He that hides hatred with lying lips, and he that utters a slander, is a fool.' Proverbs 6:16–19: 'There are six things which Yahweh hates; Yes, seven which are an abomination to him: Haughty eyes, a lying tongue, hands that shed innocent blood; a heart that devises wicked schemes, feet that are swift in running to mischief; a false witness who utters lies, and he who sows discord among brothers.' "

Peter paused, hoping his words had had some effect. "As you can see, God has a lot to say about slandering others. Slander has a companion: gossip. It does nothing but hurt and destroy. It harms the one spreading it. God says he will destroy the slanderer, the gossiper. These past few days have been difficult ones for a well-respected member of our community and a stranger seeking a safe harbor. Two innocent people have been slandered and gossiped about. Lies have been fabricated, inflated and believed. These two people, not guilty of any wrongdoing whatsoever, have been greatly ill-used. Harm has been done in ways many of you cannot imagine. When the young woman came seeking refuge in our welcoming town she was met with lies and gossip." Peter's voice was thick with sarcasm.

"Although no one knows her, she has been accused of appalling actions. A man in our congregation whom many of you have known all your lives as a God-fearing, compassionate man is the subject of gossip and rumor. This kind man has helped most of you in times of crisis and times of joy. Why didn't you believe in the character of this man that you know so well? Some of you decided to leave God's command and believe the slander of those with lesser character who spread the lies. The damage has been done. Dr. Sterling Graham's reputation and career have been jeopardized because of these lies. These lies have taken on a life of their own. Falsehoods as to the character of this unknown woman have been made up and believed by those who have never met her.

"Now, to show how honorable they are, these two people, who have been slandered by these lies, will live the rest of their lives bearing the consequence of that gossip spread by others. Although they are innocent of any wrongdoing, they have decided that they will do what they can to be honorable people. They have decided to wed each other."

There was a gasp from many in the pews. Lydia gripped Sterling's hand tightly. He turned slightly so he could see her face. It was tight with tension under the cosmetic covering her bruise, but he was relieved to see that her eyes, though bright with anxiety, held no tears.

"Sterling, Lydia, please come forward."

Lydia stood, Sterling beside her, and walked forward to a place in front of the pulpit. Out of the corner of her eye she saw that Drew and Ella had risen and were standing behind them.

"Dearly beloved," Peter began, "today we come together to join in holy matrimony this man and this woman ..."

Lydia heard the familiar words but could hardly believe this was actually happening. She looked at Sterling during the vows and saw that he was taking this in full seriousness, but she felt that the whole event painfully lacked the joy that was usually evident during a wedding.

Peter noticed, as he performed the ceremony, that many in the congregation realized they had played a part in bringing about the ritual before them and were deeply affected by the consequences of their sin. Two innocent people were now going to spend the rest of their lives together whether they wanted to or not, and all because those in a small town had nothing better to do than to delight in spreading gossip.

Finally the ceremony was over.

"I now pronounce you man and wife."

Peter didn't tell the groom to kiss his bride. Sterling and he had decided Lydia would be embarrassed enough without that sham show of affection.

Sterling and Lydia, followed by Drew and Ella, who signaled for the children to come along, walked down the aisle of the church and out the door. Other than the Lendreys, Drew and two others, this was the first time Lydia's face had been seen by the people of Cottonwood.

Sterling and Drew, both in dark suits, white shirts, black vests and ties, escorted the ladies and children across the street to the parsonage. After previous discussion the five adults had decided it would be best for them to leave straight after the ceremony and let the service continue without them. They also planned to eat dinner at Langston's Cafe, thinking it would be best to present themselves in public as soon as possible.

"You look nice," Sterling said to Lydia when they entered the house and moved into the parlor.

The couple had been given a few moments of privacy. Drew had gone to the kitchen, and Rye and Janie had gone upstairs to change out of their Sunday clothes with the help of their mother.

Lydia was wearing a deep-blue dress of polished cotton with pale-blue piping. Pale-blue collar and cuffs finished the contrast, giving the dress, though simple in design, an elegant look. Her mother's soft white wool shawl covered her shoulders. Rather than her work boots, Lydia had on her tight high-button shoes. The cloth used for her sling was a crisp white. Ella had dressed Lydia's dark auburn hair in a soft chiffon, with curls at the sides of her face and spilling out the back.

Lydia blushed, fingering her mother's locket. "It's a dress of Ella's. She insisted. She said none of my dresses were fit for a wedding. It was very kind of her. We shortened it a little for me yesterday. She wants me to keep it. Is that all right with you?"

"I guess so. It wouldn't fit her any more, would it?"

"No. We had to make other alterations also. I think she would be hurt if I didn't keep it."

"I wouldn't want to hurt either Ella or Peter. Not only have they done so much for you, but they're also very good friends of mine."

Lydia looked around. "Sterling," she said, "none of the rooms in your house look like this, do they?"

Sterling burst out laughing, breaking the tension. "I'm very glad to say no. Not that they don't need some sprucing up, but none are as bad as this."

Drew came in then and asked what was so funny. Sterling and Lydia looked at each other and smiled.

"Just look around you, Drew," said Sterling. "I think you'll be able to figure it out. Lydia was asking if there were similar rooms in my house."

Drew grinned and sat down in one of the chairs. "Not only are these ugly, but this chair isn't comfortable either."

They all chuckled.

Ella entered then, saying, "Service should almost be finished. Rye and Janie will be down shortly. We can walk over to the church and meet up with Peter, if you want."

"It might start to show people that we won't hide," Sterling said. "Do you want to do that, Lydia? I don't want you to if it'll make you uncomfortable."

"I'm sure I'll be nervous, but we might as well start the way we want to go on. Besides, it'll only be a short time before we go to the cafe." Lydia looked pensively out the window as she spoke.

The children came thudding down the stairs.

"Softly, softly," their mother said as the adults entered the foyer from the parlor.

Janie took Drew's hand, leading him to the front door. "We get to eat with Seth and Becky, Uncle Drew."

"We're taking a tin of cookies, sugar cookies," Rye added. "I'll go get it." He dashed down the hall to the kitchen.

"What have I said about running in the house?" Ella's voice was stern.

"Sorry, Mama," came Rye's voice from the kitchen.

"Let's go," said Drew when Rye came back carrying the cookie tin.

With the children leading the way, they trooped down the porch steps and across the street to the church.

Service had finished and people were milling around chatting. When Rye and Janie saw the Smith family, the Lendreys' neighbors, they looked up at their mother with questioning eyes. She nodded, and they ran off to join Seth and Becky.

Drew watched Rye run and jump with the metal container and smiled. "I wonder if those cookies will be anything other than crumbs when the tin's opened."

People were approaching them and Sterling knew Lydia was nervous. Her hand on his arm tightened slightly. He looked down at her, seeing the tension in her face. Lord, he prayed, please make this easy for her.

Mrs. Leila Henderson appeared in front of them as they neared the crowd, the sunshine bright on her snow-white hair. "Well, Doc, since you put me off last week because you had to go birth a baby and you weren't to be found yesterday, I'll be by tomorrow for sure. Now introduce me to your lady." She smiled at them all.

"Mrs. Henderson, this is Lydia Wal-- Lydia Graham. Lydia, this is Mrs. Henderson, a dear friend and patient, as you can tell." Sterling smiled at Mrs. Henderson in thanks for her support and friendliness.

"Pleasant to meet you, Mrs. Henderson."

"Now, you just call me Mrs. H. like everybody else does. Well, almost everyone." She looked at some of the others who were watching the group.

"Thank you, Mrs. H," Lydia said.

"Well, now. How about I stop in for a get-acquainted visit tomorrow after my monthly heart check? I'd like to welcome you to Cottonwood in my own way." Then she added in a soft voice, "Out of prying eyes and ears."

Just then an older couple with sour looks on their faces passed by without so much as looking at them. They weren't talking, and strode past with purpose to their steps. A young blond woman followed several paces behind, looking at the ground in front of her feet.

Sterling cleared his throat and said softly, "That's Eustace Taylor and his wife, Beulah. Eustace was one of the men at the livery on Friday morning who left just after you stood up."

Lydia didn't so much as glance their way, keeping her gaze on Mrs. H. "I'll look forward to your visit," she said. "I thank you for your warm welcome."

Peter arrived just then and took his wife's arm. "Good timing. Shall we head off to the cafe? Care to join us, Mrs. H? It's always a pleasure to have your company."

Mrs. H. smiled and said, "You were always a charmer, Peter." She took the arm Sheriff Richards held out to her and the six of them started off up the street.

Sterling kept Lydia a little back from the rest and said, "Are you all right with this? I don't want you to feel uncomfortable. You've gone through a lot and if this is too much we can bow out."

"No, I'm fine. Better to let everyone have their look. I know they're curious. I'm glad for the face cosmetic though. It would be more difficult if everyone could see the bruise."

"It'll be gone in a week or two. It should fade a little every day."

"I know. I'll keep putting on the cosmetic until it does though."

In the cafe they found a table for six along a wall and sat down. A waitress approached with menus and handed them around. "Welcome to the Langston Cafe. Coffee all round?"

"Just five. Mrs. Graham doesn't drink it. Would you like some lemonade?" Peter asked Lydia. "It's pretty good here."

"Thank you. That would be nice." Lydia was surprised that Peter had remembered her dislike for coffee.

They perused the menu as the waitress got their drinks. The special was fried chicken, mashed potatoes, cream gravy and corn. Cherry cobbler was the dessert for the day. After they ordered, Sterling noticed that several people were trying to look at them without being noticed.

"Well," said Drew quietly to Lydia, "at least the town's getting a good look at you today, first at church, and now here. Anybody who isn't in town today will feel like they've missed a good show."

Sterling saw Lydia blush, seeming to concentrate on straightening her utensils. He gave Drew a hard stare.

"I know it seems harsh and uncomfortable," Ella said, "but in a week or two it will all be old news."

83

"Several people came to me after service and asked for forgiveness for their part in the gossip," Peter said. "I told them that I wasn't the one who'd been sinned against and they should apologize to you two. I think some will, but I know not all."

"It'd be nice if some came to us, but I really don't expect it." Sterling blew on his steaming cup of coffee. "It's hard enough to come to a preacher and do that. Most won't come to those they need to." He looked at Lydia, who was folding her napkin, not looking at anyone.

Just then their meals arrived, and conversation centered on how good the food was.

Over dessert, a couple with a young son came up to the table, the man signaling to the men to stay seated.

"Hello," he said. "We thought we'd come and say welcome to Cottonwood, Mrs. Graham. I'm Ben Phelps, this is my wife Betsy and our son Billy. We farm outside of town about a mile to the south. Doc here took real good care of Billy's foot the other day."

"Yeah, Doc. It don't hurt near as much as it did."

Five-year-old Billy lifted his foot and waved it around, nearly losing his balance in the process. The adults all grinned at his antics.

"Glad to hear it, Billy. I'd hate to have you hurting more." Sterling steadied the boy by taking hold of his hand.

"We'll be going now. We just wanted to greet you and welcome you to town." Betsy Phelps smiled a welcoming smile as she drew on her gloves.

"Thank you. Nice to meet you all." Lydia was grateful for the Phelps' friendliness.

The greeting from a local family seemed to break the ice and several more families came to express greetings. When the welcomes slowed, the group rose, paid their bills and left the cafe.

"What a fine place to have in town. The food is wonderful." Lydia pulled her shawl up around her shoulders as they reached the boardwalk. This time Ella linked her arm through Lydia's and they walked along together.

Drew said he would escort Mrs. H. home and they headed off in that direction. Sterling and Peter followed their wives.

"So this is how it is after you're married, huh, Peter?" Sterling pulled his pocketwatch out of his vest, checking the time. Peter gave him a quizzical look. "Not even married three hours and I have to follow my wife while she walks with her friend instead of me."

Everyone laughed, but the ladies didn't change their places to walk with their husbands.

Chapter 10

At dusk, after spending the afternoon at the Lendreys', Sterling and Lydia approached Sterling's house and clinic, going up the walk that Sterling told Lydia would be lined with lavender in the summer. The two-story house faced east, with a wide porch that went across the front and wrapped around the side. Yellow clapboard siding was accented with white and dark green. Shutters bordered the windows and gingerbread-trimmed columns supported the porch roof. Two large bare trees would shade the yard and front of the house when the leaves appeared.

The clinic opened with a separate doorway and ran the length of the house's south side to the rear.

"Oh, Sterling." Lydia, somewhat in awe, stopped and gazed at the house. "It's lovely. You never said anything about how big it is. Only that you grew up in it and the clinic was on the side."

"I guess I never thought about it. It's just the house I've always lived in. Come, I'll show it to you." They continued up the walk and climbed the steps to the porch.

"The porch runs all the way around the side and across the back of the house. My mother wanted to be able to wash or cook out there when it was hot or rainy. That way she'd still be protected from the weather. I played along the side of the house on the porch as a kid. Under the porch, too, hiding from my sister."

He pointed to a spot in the corner of the porch. "There's a swing that hangs there, and I put out a small table and chairs in the summer. It's a pleasant spot to sit in the evening. Drew and the Lendreys come by some. My mother used to have ladies over during the day. They'd sew or knit or do whatever ladies do."

Lydia laughed softly. "I'm sure I'll continue that tradition of 'doing whatever ladies do.'"

Sterling opened the door and looked at her. "Has it always been your dream to be carried over the threshold?"

Lydia blushed. "I don't know. I guess I never thought of it. After my parents passed I never had time to daydream."

"I will if you want."

"I think I'd rather walk in than take the chance that you'd drop me."

"You wound me." Sterling laid the back of his hand on his forehead melodramatically. "I carried you most of the way from the livery, and now you think I can't carry you four feet?" Sterling smiled and held out his hand. "Will you allow me to hold your hand as we enter together?"

He bowed and swept with his free hand, indicating that she precede him. Lydia took his hand and led the way in.

The door was centered on the house. The floors were of oak, as was the trim around the doors and windows, and the staircase that divided the house. Crown molding framed the walls at the ceiling.

To their left was a sitting room with wallpaper of rose-colored peonies on a green background, a green settee, two chairs upholstered in green and rose stripes, and a few side tables. A Franklin stove sat in a corner ready to heat the room. Various knickknacks were scattered around the room. Lydia thought the look was pleasing, the colors subdued. She was thankful it wasn't like the Lendreys' parlor.

An unusual feature was a door on the south wall where a window might have been. This, Lydia thought, probably led to the clinic.

She turned to her right and surveyed the parlor. It was larger than the sitting room and boasted a fireplace in the north wall. Windows, looking out onto the porch, framed the fireplace with green draperies that were the same as those in the sitting room. Here, the walls were a green and light-blue stripe. Two settees faced each other on either side of the fireplace. They had a floral pattern with rose, blue and green. The other furnishings were similar in style to those in the sitting room. There was also a small grand piano along the wall backing the stairs.

"Do you play?" inquired Lydia, looking up at Sterling.

"Badly. Do you?"

"No. We never had one."

"You can take lessons if you want."

"Not yet. Maybe sometime in the future. I'll think about it."

Moving to the left of the staircase, they went down the hall. There were doors on either side of the hallway. Lydia looked back at Sterling with questioning eyes. He nodded, and she opened a door under the staircase. A storage area was tucked there. The shelves that stepped up the wall backing the stairs held kitchen linens and various other items. Closing that door, Lydia opened the one opposite. It opened onto another closet with coats and boots along one wall and shelves along the other.

"What good planning. Who thought of that?"

"My mother. When they were planning the house, I was told, she didn't like coats and boots and such littering up her house. She tucked another closet upstairs between two of the bedrooms. It's used to keep linens and things like that in."

They moved on into the kitchen. The sink with a pump was centered on the back wall below a large window with white curtains. The walls were painted a pale green. To the left of the sink counter was a door to the backyard. A large, well-worn table with four chairs surrounding it sat in the middle of the room, testifying to many meals made and eaten. A large iron stove was against the wall at the right end of the room, and next to it was a doorway leading into a formal dining room.

To their left was a pie safe atop a counter that provided workspace and storage beneath. Lydia opened a door beside it and found a good-sized pantry with a large icebox.

"Look here," Sterling said, opening another door beside the hall door. Lydia looked and saw stairs leading down. "My mother didn't want to have to go outside to get to her cellar so she had steps built under the stairs. Comes in real handy on cold winter days." He opened a narrow door in the wall next to the cellar door and pulled down an ironing board that was built into the wall. "This wasn't my mother's idea. She found it in a catalog and had it built when I was a teenager."

"Sterling, I don't know how to live in a house this grand. Everything is so big and well thought out and convenient. Your mother must have been very intelligent."

"Yes, she was. Too bad her son didn't get any of that," he joked. "See the little hall here by the back door?" There were hooks and a box bench with a hinged lid. "More of my mother's places for that 'litter'. I had another door put in to go into the clinic area. That way I can get there from either end of the house."

"Maybe you did get some of your mother's smarts."

They both laughed.

Sterling opened the door to the clinic and said, "Let's look at this before we head upstairs."

The clinic consisted of two narrow sleeping rooms for patients, an office, an exam room and a waiting room. The patient rooms each had an iron bed under the window, a side table with a lamp, and a small dresser with a basin and pitcher.

In Sterling's office, the rolltop desk was almost as wide as the room. The narrow shelves on the walls were filled with bottles and boxes, each labeled and set in order.

The exam room had an exam table, cupboard, various other items of medical equipment and a couple of straight chairs. A small desk occupied the corner by the door. The waiting room had a small counter, and several chairs lined the walls. Each of the rooms in the clinic had one window on the south wall, with the waiting room having another on the east wall.

"Very nice. Efficient, I would think," Lydia commented.

"It seems to work pretty well. Not if we have an epidemic with many very sick patients who need to stay, but most of the time. Let's head upstairs."

At the top of the stairs there was a landing extending to the exterior wall, where a windowed door lighted the area. As they reached the top stair Sterling suddenly stopped.

"Uh-oh. I forgot. All but the room I use have been closed off since my parents passed. They aren't ready to be used. They haven't been cleaned."

"You aren't expecting me to sleep ..." Lydia looked at him nervously.

"No, no," Sterling said quickly. "Let me think." He looked around, thinking. "How about you taking my room and I'll sleep in one of the patient rooms?"

"I think it would be more convenient for me to sleep down there," replied Lydia. "That way you won't have to move your things. I can clean the rooms up here soon."

"Are you sure you won't mind? I'll gladly move and let you have mine."

"I would prefer that you not move out of yours. It's no trouble. Also, if I don't get to these for a while, as I settle in, you won't be inconvenienced for a long time."

"Okay, if you really don't mind."

Lydia shook her head.

"There are four rooms." Sterling opened the first door on the right. "This was the room my mother used as a sewing room." In it was a table, a bureau, a couple of sewing chairs and a spinning wheel.

"I'll use it the same way."

"This room was my folks', but I've moved into it now." The room was wallpapered in red with a cream oriental floral design. There was a tester bed with cream curtains, a tall chest of drawers, mirrored dresser, chair, heating stove, washstand with a cream-and-red floral pitcher and basin set, and a tall wardrobe. The hardwood floor had large red-and-cream braided rugs on both sides of the bed. The draperies at the windows were deep red, with cream lace curtains behind.

By now night had fallen and they headed downstairs without looking at the other two bedrooms. Sterling went back to the porch and brought in her carpetbag. Lydia lighted two lamps and carried them into the clinic. They decided that the back patient room would be where Lydia would sleep. Sterling put the carpetbag on the floor. Lydia put one lamp on the table and set the other on the washstand. They stood looking at each other uncomfortably.

Sterling looked around and grabbed up the pitcher. "I'll get you a pitcher of water." With that he fled into the kitchen. Lydia heard the sound of him pumping the water and his steps back into the room. He set the pitcher in the basin.

"Thank you."

They looked at each other.

After several seconds Lydia said, "Um. Is the necessary close by? Or, um, a chamber pot?" She was sure she blushed, but in the dim light hoped he couldn't see it.

"Oh. Yes. Well, the necessary is out back. I think it'd be best if you don't go there tonight in the dark, not knowing the path. Here's the chamber pot." Sterling opened the door in the washstand.

"Thank you."

They looked at each other.

"You're sure this is all right for you?"

"Yes, thank you. I'll be fine."

They looked at each other.

"Well, I guess I'll go lock up and head upstairs."

"Goodnight."

They looked at each other.

"Oh shoot," Sterling said with frustration. "This is our wedding night. Can I at least give you a kiss?"

Lydia looked at him and nodded slightly. Sterling came closer and, putting his hands on her upper arms, pulled her softly to him. Lowering his head, he placed a gentle kiss on her lips. They ended the kiss as gently as it had started and looked at each other. Sterling slid his hand down her good arm, lingering there slightly as his hand met hers. Then he turned and left her alone in the room.

Chapter 11

The enticing aroma of coffee, bacon and something baking woke Sterling in the morning. He rose and swiftly preformed his ablutions, dressed and went downstairs. He entered the kitchen expecting to find Lydia at the stove. The room was empty, but the table held a plate of coffee cake topped with sugar strudel. A pot of coffee and a plate of bacon sat on the back of the stove keeping warm.

He went into the clinic hallway. The door to the room Lydia had slept in was open, but the room was empty. There was nothing to indicate that the room had been occupied. The bed was made, and there was nothing on the furniture that was not normally there. He opened the washstand door, relieved to see her clothing neatly folded there. He realized that her offers to go on west had frightened him into thinking she had run away. Then he remembered the smells that had woken him.

Going back into the kitchen, Sterling called her name. No one answered. He called again, and still no one answered. Becoming concerned, he walked through the dining room next to the kitchen. He circled through the parlor, looked out the front window and scanned the front yard, looked into the sitting room, and headed down the hallway to the kitchen. Just then the back door opened and Lydia stepped in.

"Where have you been?" asked Sterling sharply.

Lydia started. The smile on her face quickly changed to a frightened question.

"Oh! I'm sorry," Sterling said. "It's just ... it's just that when I woke to the wonderful smells coming from the kitchen and you were nowhere in the house I became concerned. I don't really know why. I just expected to find you in here and didn't. I'm sorry I snapped."

"You certainly startled me." Lydia tried to hide a frown and stepped over to the stove. "I'm sorry I wasn't here when you came down, but I had to go ..." she paused, blushed, and continued, "out for a moment."

Sterling looked away, his chagrin evident on his face. "Again, I'm sorry. I just expected to find you here. How about we start the morning over?" he said, hoping she would take the olive branch.

"I think that's a good idea." Her tone still held the hurt.

Sterling backed into the hall, cleared his throat and came into the kitchen. "Good morning, lovely wife of mine. The glorious smells wafted up the stairs and into my room, calling me to arise and greet the day."

Lydia burst out laughing. "Well, if you greet me every day with dreadful prose like that I'll be sure not to be here."

"You wound me to the quick." Sterling put his hand to his chest in exaggerated melodrama, falling into a chair by the table.

"You poor thing, you. How about some coffee and coffee cake to make it all better?" She poured a cup of coffee, plated up some bacon with a piece of the cake and set both before him on the table.

Sterling said grace then picked up a fork and took a bite of the cake. "Very good."

"Thank you. I made it in case Mrs. Henderson wants to visit today."

"You mean I won't get this every day?" Sterling had a wounded look in his eyes but a grinning mouth as he took another bite of the cake.

"As my mother used to say, 'You'll be as big as a house if you eat like that all the time.' "

Lydia sat at the table with her own plate of coffee cake and bacon. Instead of coffee, she had a glass of water.

"I assume you found the eggs and milk Daniel Windsor left," Sterling said. "He comes twice a week. If we need more, just let him know. I only cooked as much as I needed. I really only ate breakfast here most days but I suspect we'll eat here more now."

"I do know how to cook. I would hope that if you're going to be gone for a meal you'll let me know so I won't fix as much." Her voice held a touch of nervousness in making such a bold request.

"Of course."

They chatted about how Sterling's schedule usually went and how Lydia would occupy her time. She had given the backyard a quick look over when she had been out and said, "The garden is rather overrun. You haven't had time to keep it up, have you?"

"No. It was my mother's and she's been gone five years. I don't go out back much."

"I'll look over the garden and yard. Is it okay for me to plant a garden? Fresh vegetables are good in the summer, and preserving them makes for a good winter."

"There are fruit trees, also. Let me think. There are a couple of apple trees, a pie and sweet cherry, a peach, and maybe a plum. That is, if they're still alive."

"We'll see whether they come out. Most likely they'll need to be pruned, but that's no problem."

"That would be a problem for me. I know nothing about pruning trees." Sterling finished the last bite of bacon. "Thank you. Breakfast was very good." He glanced at the clock on the shelf by the stove. "It's time I opened up the clinic. If Peter's sermon and our marriage solved the problem, hopefully I'll have more than Mrs. Henderson as a patient today." He wiped his mouth on the napkin, rose from the table and walked through the rear door to his clinic.

After cleaning up the kitchen, Lydia went upstairs to finish looking at the rooms. Turning to the left at the top of the stairs, she found the last two bedrooms. Between the rooms was a small closet. One side was lined with shelves on which linens were neatly folded. Larger items leaned against the other wall.

The first bedroom had wallpaper that was patterned in blue on a yellow background. White ruffled curtains and blue drapes decorated the windows, and a blue, white and yellow quilt adorned the bed. The other room was painted tan with green-and-brown curtains and quilt. She thought that this must have been Sterling's room as a boy. She wondered if there had been a girl who had occupied the yellow and blue bedroom, then remembered Sterling saying that he had hidden from his sister under the porch.

Next, she went into the room Sterling occupied. The bed had been made, but it was lumpy. Lydia smiled, straightened the covers and fluffed the pillows. Going to the washstand, she poured the dirty water back into the pitcher, gathered the used towels and headed back down the hall. She paused by the sewing room, setting down the pitcher and towels. Entering, she looked over the furniture and other items in the room. This was a room in which she would spend many hours, she hoped. The white walls would keep it light and help her see her stitches even as the daylight started to fail. The bureau, she knew, would hold thread, buttons, pins, scissors--all the things needed to create with fabrics. With a small smile of hope she gathered up the pitcher and towels and headed downstairs.

   She put the dirty linen in a basket in the pantry and went outside to empty the pitcher. She looked out over the yard, noticing that it was larger than she had first thought. To the left were clotheslines parallel to a tall fence that bordered the entire yard. The necessary came next. Lydia hoped the walk to the outhouse would be lined with flowers in the summer, hiding it from view. Past that were fruit trees marching in order along the back fence. A brick walk ran down the center of the yard, with an overgrown garden plot between the walk and the fence.

   Lydia set the pitcher on the porch and stepped down onto the brick walk. First, she went and inspected the fruit trees. They were alive, but badly in need of pruning. She thought it should be done soon. She paced back up the walk to estimate the length of the garden. Then she turned and paced to the fence. In her mind, she began plotting out the garden with the different vegetables she would plant. She would have to ask Sterling what vegetables he liked. Or maybe the ones he didn't would be more useful. No sense in planting what he doesn't like, she thought.

   She went back into the kitchen and set the pitcher by the sink. She went into the pantry, deciding that Sterling was correct in saying he hadn't eaten at home much. The shelves were not well stocked. The icebox was a larger one than she had had at home. She found a few jars of preserved vegetables and a can of tinned chicken. Taking these, she went back into the kitchen and began making a pot of soup. Opening the can was difficult but she found that she could use the cast to hold the can in place and work the opener around. She couldn't find any yeast so she decided that dumplings would be good in the soup. These she would add later.

Searching the kitchen and pantry for some paper and a pencil she came up empty-handed. The same happened when she searched the parlor and sitting room. Going upstairs and searching the bedrooms produced the same result. She didn't want to disturb Sterling but she wanted to make a list of supplies she needed from the general store.

She quietly opened the door into the waiting room. A man and a woman looked at her as she entered the clinic.

"Good morning, Mrs. Graham," greeted the man. "I'm Vince Stanton. Doc delivered my baby son on Thursday. Brought him and his ma in for a check this morning. Doc came out to check them on Saturday. Everything seems okay but the missus wanted another check. I'm glad we got the doc. I'd a passed out for sure if he'd a been out on some other call." He gave a sheepish grin.

"Nice to meet you."

"I'm Gladys Ralston. My husband runs the livery," the woman said. She, like her husband, had an accent indicating their British origins.

"Pleased to meet you." Lydia blushed, thinking of what the livery owner might have told his wife.

"I'm real glad things have worked out. I'm praying that you two have a good marriage." Gladys reached out and took Lydia's hand, giving it a slight squeeze.

"Thank you. I appreciate your prayers." Tears welled in Lydia's eyes at the kind words. She blinked several times.

The exam room door opened and Millie Stanton, carrying her son, emerged, followed by Sterling.

"Millie," said Vince, "this is Mrs. Graham, the doc's new wife."

"Nice to meet you, Mrs. Stanton. May I ask your son's name?" Lydia looked from the mother to the bundle she carried.

"Call me Millie. His name is John but we'll probably call him Johnny." She pulled back the blanket covering the baby so Lydia could see him.

"He's beautiful, Millie. And please, call me Lydia." Lydia smiled at the new mother, who beamed with pride.

Vince, who had been speaking with Sterling, reached into his pocket and handed Sterling some money. "Thanks, Doc. Sure am glad you're here. Thanks for bein' there on Thursday. Don't know what I would've done without ya." With that the Stanton family left the office.

Gladys waited for the door to close and then laughed. "He sure is a nervous father. Did he faint while the baby was being born?"

Sterling grinned. "No, but Millie's mother and I kept him out of the room or I'm sure he would have. Gladys, why don't you go on in and I'll be there shortly."

Gladys smiled at Sterling and Lydia then went into the exam room.

"What brings you here?" Sterling asked Lydia. "Not that I mind, but I think you have a purpose. Am I right?"

"Yes. I can't find any paper or a pencil and I need to make a list of things to stock the pantry. You'll be eating air if I don't get to the store soon."

"Not a very filling meal. I'll get some from my office." Sterling was back shortly with the items. "Do you want me to go with you? It'll need to be after lunch if you do. Mrs. H. is supposed to be here shortly."

Lydia looked at him, trying to figure out if he wanted her to go by herself or have him go with her. She couldn't tell and didn't want to make the wrong choice. "Let's talk about it over lunch, okay?"

"Sure. Make your list and we'll talk then." With that he headed into the exam room.

Lydia walked down the hall and entered the kitchen through the rear door. She couldn't stop the sudden trembling as she thought about him checking her list. What would he do if he thought it was too long? He's not like that, he's not like that, Lydia told herself over and over as she stood in the kitchen. He's just trying to be nice.

Oh Lord, I know that in my head but my heart is still scared. Help me trust him. She took a deep breath and, sitting down at the table, began her list.

Several times she got up and went into the pantry or looked through drawers to check on things that might already be in the house. The items she didn't need were things used to make simple breakfasts: eggs, milk, lard, flour. Also in abundance were things that could be used to clean: vinegar, soap and ammonia.

Her list was a long one and she would make sure that it passed her new husband's approval. She would be a good wife, a wife that he would be proud of. By the end of the month Sterling Graham would forget the dreadful occurrence that had brought them to be man and wife.

Lydia was making dumplings to add to the soup when she heard voices and steps coming down the corridor. She looked up as Mrs. H. and Sterling entered.

"Good morning, my dear." Mrs. H. smiled. "Sterling gave me another month to live and I told him I wanted to visit with you, so here we are."

"I'll be back after I see my next patient. Is that enough time to get lunch?" Sterling asked Lydia.

"Most likely. I'm making dumplings for the soup and it'll be ready when they're cooked."

"Okay, see you shortly." With that Sterling left the way he had come.

"Mrs. H., please sit down. Would you like some coffee? And you will stay for lunch, won't you?" Lydia asked.

"No and yes," Mrs. H. said, taking a seat. "You just keep on doing your preparing." She paused. "There's no way other than to just come right out and ask. How are you doing, my dear? Not the best way to start a marriage or come into a new town."

"I'm doing as well as I think I can. Sterling is very considerate. We haven't had much time to get to know each other, but we're committed to making the marriage work. We promised to before God and we both take it seriously."

"Glad to hear it." Mrs. H. noticed the list lying on the table and picked it up. "My, what a list."

"Sterling hasn't eaten here very much. Only for breakfast most of the time. What I've made the soup with is pretty much what was in the pantry. I'll be going to the general store after lunch or I won't be cooking tonight. Sterling may come with me."

"From this list I can see that you won't be cooking much until you shop."

Lydia spooned the dumplings into the soup to cook. They continued to discuss the list for a while and then Mrs. H. started reminiscing about the Graham family. Sterling's parents, Eli and Grace, had come to Cottonwood as a young married couple and Eli started his medical practice in a storefront, living in the apartment upstairs. They were living there when their first child, Margaret, was born.

"They built this house just before Sterling came. Sterling was Grace's family name," Mrs. H. said. "Margaret was the same age as my youngest, Betty. They were best friends. Both are married and live away now. I miss them and their families."

Mrs. H. paused and stared off into space for a moment. "Eli was so happy when Sterling was born. You'd have thought he'd done something original and unique, having a son. And what a pistol that boy was. He's the reason the fence is so tall you know," she said with a grin. "He kept wandering away whenever he was outside. When he was only three he walked clear over to where Drew lived, about five blocks. Grace was frantic. One moment he was playing while she hung laundry, then she couldn't find him. They built a fence then, but he climbed right over it. So they built this one. It was tall enough that he couldn't climb it. One time, when he was about five, he dug under it and went over to Drew's again."

"Are you telling tales about me, Mrs. H?" Sterling asked as he came into the kitchen. The two women turned to find that Sterling was standing in the doorway, grinning.

Mrs. H. laughed. "Not tales, only the truth, only the truth."

"Well, I only dug under the fence once. I couldn't sit for a week after my pa got home and heard I'd escaped again."

All three smiled.

"The soup's ready if you're here for lunch," Lydia said, getting up from the table to serve.

"It sure smells good. I'm hungry." Sterling sat down. As Lydia dished up the soup he said, "I'm hoping my practice hasn't suffered from the gossip. I've been busy all morning. On Saturday I wondered. I was gone in the morning and only had one patient come in the afternoon. That isn't all that unusual but it made me wonder."

"I'm so glad." Lydia placed a full bowl of soup in front of Sterling and lesser bowls before Mrs. H. and her own setting. She poured coffee and water, and placed a plate of coffee cake on the table. Sterling said grace when she was seated and they began eating.

"Here's the list I made," Lydia said, handing the list to Sterling. She quickly looked back at her soup and took another spoonful.

"That's some list. We need all of this?" Sterling inquired. His tone was normal, just a little confused.

"If you want Lydia to cook decent meals for you, all those things are needed," said Mrs. H. "You don't want her to have to go to the store every day, do you?"

"I just had no idea. I've never cooked much. I'll go with you to help carry the things you'll need right away. Luke can bring the rest in the wagon after school."

"Thank you," Lydia said, grateful for the support Mrs. H. had given in validating the list. "I don't even know where the general store is or what other stores are in town."

"It's an adventure," Sterling said with mock excitement. "You will explore the town and gather your supplies. I will discover all that it takes to keep me from having to eat air."

Lydia looked at Sterling and they both laughed. Mrs. H., watching the two, felt her heart ease, thinking that they just might make a good couple after all.

Chapter 12

Sterling flipped the 'Office Closed' sign in the window and they walked Mrs. H. to her home, leaving her to her afternoon nap, on the way into the business district. The day was sunny, with a March chill in the air that made them pick up the pace of their walk. Lydia looked avidly at the stores they passed.

On the side of the street they walked along were Langston's cafe, the barber, and Hopkins' dress shop in the first block, and then the large general store, which took up that entire block. In the next was the bank and city hall. At the end of the street was the train depot. Across the street was the feed store, then the livery. On the third block from the station was a bakery, butcher and tailor shop.

Several people walking on the boardwalk stopped and looked at the couple as they walked toward the general store. Taking Lydia's arm, Sterling pulled her a little closer. She turned her head slightly and looked up at him with gratitude in her eyes at his protection. She didn't feel threatened by anyone, just uncomfortable to be the center of attention.

"We'll be a seven-day wonder, I hope," Sterling said.

Lydia was looking at the large sign above the door. "Johnson's All-Purpose Store," she read. "Why did they call it that?"

"Mabel Johnson didn't want it to be just a general store but an all-purpose store."

"This is different from general?" Lydia asked with lifted eyebrows.

"I guess so." Sterling smiled and Lydia chuckled.

They entered the store and Sterling guided Lydia to the back where the counter was. A man and woman came forward, greeting Sterling.

"Hello, Doc," Hal said. "Glad you came in. We wanted to meet your wife and welcome her to Cottonwood."

"Good afternoon, Hal, Mabel. This is my wife, Lydia. Lydia, Hal and Mabel Johnson are owners of the store." Lydia noticed that he hadn't said the name of the store and remembered their discussion about it.

"Pleased to meet you," Lydia said with a charming smile.

"Luke, the young man who was at the livery Friday morning and came to the parsonage, is their son," Sterling said.

"He's a good boy," his mother said, somewhat nervous at the mention of what had occurred on Friday.

"You should be proud of him. He was concerned about the gossip, investigated and came to tell us about it. He showed great character." Lydia's gracious comment caused Mabel to smile with motherly pride.

"My wife here says that my pantry's just not up to her exacting standards. She's made a list of the things she needs." Sterling handed the list to Hal. "Some of the things we'll want to take with us but Luke could bring the rest in the wagon after school, if that's okay with you."

They began gathering the items to purchase. Mabel helped Lydia find the things she wanted to take with them, putting them in the basket Lydia had brought from home. When they had everything, Mabel went back to the counter and Lydia went to meet up with Sterling. He was standing near the counter looking over her list, making sure they had everything. The sunlight from the window on the wall beside him cast him in a warm glow.

My, he's handsome, Lydia thought. I hadn't noticed before. She paused in her approach taking in the tall, slim but strong build of her new husband. The high cheekbones in the long lean face framed his brown eyes that she knew could sparkle with humor, be grave with seriousness, and gentle with compassion. His hair was dark brown with a wave that tended to slip down onto his forehead. She had noticed Sterling's long hands before and felt their gentle touch. At the thought, Lydia pulled herself back to their purpose and continued toward him.

"Sterling, it's time to start preparing the garden."

"Do you want to plant flowers or vegetables?"

"Both, actually. I'll plant flowers in the border around it and vegetables in the center. I'll need to buy seeds and starts. I didn't put them on the list."

"The seeds you can get here. Hal, do you have potato and onion sets yet?"

"Yes, they're over by the seed packets."

As they went over to the display of seeds Lydia asked, "Will you help me pick the vegetables you like?"

"Good idea. I sure don't want to spend the winter eating turnips."

As they picked out the seeds and sets, the store door opened and the voices of two women could be heard.

"I think it's just a shame, the doc being forced into marriage to that strumpet. I'll just bet we see her waist increase much sooner than we should."

"Yes, my Magdelina is just heartbroken. She was sure he would propose to her this summer. She spent yesterday and this morning weeping her heart out. She hasn't come out of her room since church yesterday. Fair breaks a mother's heart, it does."

"I'm sure it does, I'm sure it does." The voice held a nasal whine reminiscent of chalk grating on a chalkboard.

Standing at the seed display, Sterling shuddered. Lydia, face pale, looked at him sharply. He looked at her and shook his head fiercely. Taking her hand, he went around the end of the row of shelves filled with merchandise and walked right up to Harriet Baumgarden and Beulah Taylor.

"Ladies, I'd like you meet my wife, Lydia. These two gracious ladies are Mrs. Harriet Baumgarden and Mrs. Beulah Taylor. The aforementioned daughter is Mrs. Taylor's. This is my wife, Mrs. Lydia Graham."

"Hello, Mrs. Baumgarden, Mrs. Taylor," Lydia said. She wouldn't lie and say that it was nice to meet them. The two ladies, whose faces were bright with embarrassment, stuttered their greetings.

"I'm sorry to hear of your daughter's distress," Lydia said. "If she takes ill from her emotions please be sure to bring her to my husband. I'm sure he can find some sort of remedy for her." Lydia said this while inside she prayed: Lord, you promised to heap burning coals on the heads of my enemies if I'm kind. That was kind of me, wasn't it?

"Of course," muttered Beulah Taylor. She was a tall, slim woman who managed to look at everyone as if they were worms to be crushed by her shoe.

The other woman, Harriet Baumgarden, was wide, and although of average height evidenced no neck and was extremely shortwaisted, with arms to match. She was the woman with the discordant voice.

"We must finish our order and go to the butcher's, Lydia." Sterling placed his hand on the small of her back, guiding her away from the women.

"Yes. Until next time." Lydia nodded to the women, who nodded back.

Moving to the counter, Sterling paid for the goods and arranged for Luke to deliver what they wouldn't be taking. Mabel reached out and squeezed Lydia's hand, letting her know that she could count on her support.

Hal waved, and with a big smile said, "You come in anytime. You and the missus can have some tea and chat."

"I will, thank you." Turning from the counter, Sterling took her hand and, carrying the basket in the other, chose to walk down an empty aisle rather than encounter the two women again.

When they had exited the store Lydia tried to pull her hand from his. "Sterling, you're hurting my hand."

He had been holding it tightly in his anger at the two women who had, purposely, he believed, said such cruel things about someone they didn't know. And as for thinking he would have ever married Magdelina Taylor, of all people...

"I'm sorry," he said, loosening his hold on her hand. He kept holding it, not wanting to let go. "Just to make it clear, I would never, ever," he said forcefully, "have asked Magdelina Taylor to marry me." He shuddered.

"Let's not let them ruin our afternoon," Lydia implored. "It's all so new to everyone. Some will be like the Johnsons and Mrs. H. Others will be, well, not as nice. Like you said before, it should be a seven-day wonder. Some other thing will happen and the gossips will turn their tongues from us to another unfortunate."

"You're more gracious than I. I'm thinking about how I can cause them pain when they come in for treatment."

"Now, now," Lydia said. "I don't remember a Bible verse that says vengeance is the doc's, says the Lord."

Sterling chuckled. "You're right. I need to forgive, but that was so uncalled for. You did nothing, but they make up lies."

"Maybe God will bring on a plague of boils that you'll have to lance. It would be the Lord giving you the opportunity to do just what you want to do," Lydia said with mirth.

Sterling laughed. "Maybe I'll just pray for him to do that."

"Don't you dare."

"Okay, anything to please my wife, but just know it's a great sacrifice, which I'll remind you of at a later date."

Lydia decided that she wouldn't start bread until the next morning, but would make biscuits to have with supper. There were still two pieces of coffee cake left, so dessert was supplied. She would fry up a couple of potatoes which Luke would bring along shortly. Canned peaches and the pork chops they'd purchased at the butcher would round out the meal.

Dinner planned, she went down to the cellar to get the garden tools. She was gratified to find shelves filled with canning jars in one of the rooms. There was a room of clotheslines for winter washing. She noted that the ropes would need to be replaced. This could be done later in the year. She could use the lines outside until the winter weather.

"Lydia," Sterling called.

"I'm down here getting the garden tools." Lydia was climbing the stairs trying to hold onto the tools with her right hand, unsuccessfully. Several dropped back down the steps with a clatter. Sterling reached for the ones she still had, Lydia retrieving the fallen ones.

"Luke's here with the wagon. Do you want him to come in the front or through the back?"

"Through the back? Where's the gate? I didn't see it."

She went out the back door and Sterling went out the front to guide Luke to the back gate. Lydia found the gate in the fence by the clothesline and opened it as Luke backed the wagon along the clinic wall. She noticed that the latch was set high on the fence and smiled, remembering the story Mrs. H. had told about Sterling.

"You, wife," Sterling wagged a playful finger at her, "will allow us to carry these things in for you. You'll be more help directing and putting away."

Lydia went back into the house, blocking open the door so that the men could easily get in and out. With her directing them, they soon had the wagon unloaded. Sterling and Luke chatted for a few minutes before Luke went on his way. Lydia was busy unpacking the boxes of groceries when Sterling came back in.

"Looks as if a tornado went through here."

"It's not that bad. It has an organization to it. See, staples are here, canned goods here, spices here, vegetables over there. Now I need to decide where they'll go in the pantry."

"You decide and I'll help bring it into the pantry. It'll go faster with three hands instead of one." Sterling grinned as if he had said something witty.

Lydia, who had just turned to enter the pantry, rolled her eyes. Then she grinned too. He really was sweet to help her with this. Especially with her arm in a cast and her back starting to hurt after being on her feet most of the day. Cyrus would never have helped.

"Thank you for the help, Sterling. I appreciate it."

"Don't get too used to it. The sooner we get this done the sooner I can eat," Sterling said with a smile.

"Now the truth comes out. You work for food. I'll need to remember that."

"You've found me out, wife, and in only one day. At least I married a smart one."

They set to work laughing.

Chapter 13

It rained the next two weeks off and on, keeping Lydia indoors. She set about cleaning the rooms and arranging the kitchen to her preference. The next Monday dawned bright and clear. After finishing the breakfast dishes, she decided she needed to start working up the garden, knowing it would take longer than usual with her arm and back injuries.

Wearing the worst of her dresses and her work boots, she went out to the garden with the spading fork. She'd planned out where she would plant the different vegetables and so would start where she'd put in the potatoes, peas, beets and other cold-weather crops. She stepped off the bottom step of the porch carrying the spading fork, deciding to work up a few rows and plant as she went. That would take her several days.

Going to the far end of the garden, she drove the fork into the soil, stepped on it and thought about how to turn the soil with only one hand. Pushing the handle down and grabbing it in the middle, her elbow fitting into the handgrip, she was able to lift the fork and turn the soil over. It turned less than half the soil she could have turned with both hands but at least she could do it.

As she worked she thought about how supportive Sterling had been. He'd helped her with the groceries, both by going with her to the market and helping put the food away. While they were shopping he had stood up to the women in a gentle way, yet letting them know he was serious and well aware of their contribution to the gossip. He also, Lydia realized, had a sense of humor. Throughout this whole time he had shown gentle wit she had responded to and she had also, she realized, instigated some herself. Humor was something Cyrus lacked. He took himself too seriously for that. The only person she'd laughed with, since her parents had died, was Aggie.

Aggie. Lydia looked up from her work. She was supposed to write and let Aggie know she was all right. She stuck the spade in the ground and headed to the kitchen. She'd turned two rows from the walk to the fence and her back and arm were beginning to hurt.

She'd put paper, pen and ink in a drawer in the kitchen and so, after washing up she sat at the table to write her letter. Chewing her lip, she thought how to explain the events of her trip and marriage. Finally she decided to just start with the train ride and tell it straight through. As she was writing, Sterling entered the kitchen.

"What're you doing?" He set his empty coffee cup in the sink then went to the cupboard to get a clean one.

"Writing to Aggie. I told you about her, didn't I?"

"Yes. Um ... do you think that's a good idea? What if Cyrus found out where you are?"

"Aggie would never tell him. She knows what happened and will keep it secret. I promised that I'd write and let her know when I got settled. I'd forgotten until today. She will definitely be surprised with how my situation turned out," she said with a smile, then turned back to her letter.

Sterling poured himself a cup of coffee and looked out the window above the sink. Leaning closer to the glass, he squinted at the garden. "Lydia, were you working out in the garden today?"

"Yes, I started turning the ground so I can plant the spring vegetables," she said, not looking up from her letter.

"How did you turn the soil?" Sterling slowly turned to look at her.

"I thought I'd have problems because I only had one arm, but I figured out how." She described her method without looking up from her letter, ending with, "It'll take me longer because of my arm and back, but I'll get it done slowly, planting as I get it turned."

"No, you won't," Sterling said sternly. Lydia looked up swiftly at his words and tone, her eyes uncertain. "I will not have you aggravating your back turning the soil. We'll hire some boys to turn it for you."

Lydia quickly looked down, laying her pen next to the letter and placing her hand in her lap.

Sterling suddenly realized how his tone had affected her. He came to the table and pulled a chair up close to hers and sat down. Taking her hand in one of his and lifting her chin with the other he looked into her eyes. The uncertainty he saw there caused his heart to clench.

"Lydia, I'm sorry. I didn't mean to distress you. My tone was too harsh. My concern is that you not hurt yourself doing heavy work while you're healing. Once you're healed, if you want to dig up the entire yard you may do it with my blessing. I caution you, though, that if you grow that much produce it won't all fit in this house," Sterling said with a wry smile.

"I wish you'd talked to me about working up the garden," he continued. "Then I could've let you know that we could hire some boys to turn it. Please, come to me in the future. I want you to heal, and I don't want you overdoing. Please."

"I never thought about it. I've always had to do for myself, doing my chores no matter what. I had to do Cyrus's chores after he beat me. He'd gone to town and I knew he'd hit me again if I didn't."

"That's all I ask. Again, please forgive me for my tone. I didn't mean to upset you." Sterling thought about a man who would beat a woman so hard that he broke bones and then make her do both her chores and his own. The more he learned about Lydia's brother the less he liked him.

"Lydia, I want to check your back and look at your face bruises to be sure they're healing well. Will you let me?"

"Yes." She rose and went to the sink and pumped some water to wash her face, removing the cosmetic. She turned back to face Sterling. He motioned her closer and looked intently at her face.

"Blue, purple, green and yellow. You are very colorful, to be sure, but it's healing nicely. Now give me your right hand." Lydia looked at him sheepishly, but lifted her hand. He took it, turned it over and frowned at the blisters on her palm, both swollen and broken.

"I left my gloves for gardening at home," Lydia said.

"I see." Sterling still frowned at her hand. "Let's go into the clinic and put some salve on this." Then he smiled. "Another reason to hire boys. I don't want you making your hands all rough. I plan to hold them often and want them without calluses and blisters."

Lydia blushed and pulled her hand from his.

As they walked down the hall to the exam room Lydia said with a wry smile, "Don't hire too many boys to work. There's a farmer back home who told me that if you hire one boy, you have one boy. If you hire two boys, you have half a boy, and if you hire three boys you have no boys."

"Ha, I think he's right. I remember when I was a youth, and my friends and I were hired to work haying or weeding or whatever. The more of us there were, the less we got done. I'll remember that when I hire the garden workers."

After he bandaged her hand, Sterling looked at her and asked her to unbutton her dress so he could check her back. Lydia blushed deep red, then turned her back to him and fumbled with the top button using her right hand. The bandaged palm made her clumsy.

Sterling looked at her back and her very red neck. "Lydia, I am a doctor. I've seen more than you will show me. I'm also your husband. It's all right for you to do this. I only want to see whether you're healing well."

"I know. It's just ... I've never ... undressed before a man before, doctor or not."

She was having trouble with the buttons running down the front of her dress and he waited patiently. He knew he could and probably should leave the room and let her prepare herself in private, but something held him there. He didn't want to think it was his desire to be closer to her in all ways, but he couldn't convince himself.

Lydia's hand wrapped in the bandage just wouldn't work the button through the hole. *Please*, she prayed silently, please let me get these undone. Her fingers still wouldn't cooperate. If anything, they seemed to get even clumsier. *All right, Lord, I understand. The answer is no. Just help me with my embarrassment.*

She turned toward him, tears of frustration in her eyes, before she dropped her gaze to the floor. "I can't seem to unbutton this. Will ... will you help me, please?" Her face flushed with a new wave of red.

Sterling blinked, and blinked again. *Lord*, he prayed, *oh my, what are you asking of me? Help me keep my hands steady and do this with the detached attitude of a doctor. Please.*

He approached her and reached to the top button of the bodice. Looking only at the button, he willed his fingers not to shake and to actually be able to work the buttons. With relief, the first button opened after only a little fumbling. After the first one they seemed to get easier and easier. His shaking stopped, both on the outside as well as the inside. He calmed and gradually knew he could examine her as a doctor and not as a husband--who had yet to become one.

Lydia watched as each button slipped from its hole. With each one, she asked for God to calm her fears. He answered her with peace that increased with each button. When all the buttons were undone Sterling helped her take her arms out of the sleeves, leaving only a camisole covering her. She turned so he could examine her back.

"Where's the wrapping for your ribs?"

"I haven't been wearing it. I can't get it wrapped by myself."

"Why haven't you asked for help? I would have helped you."

Lydia could feel his hands gently pressing along her ribs. When he finished he turned her around. She saw concern on his face. "I ... I was embarrassed. I just couldn't ask."

"I understand your feelings. I really do. But you have cracked ribs in your back. They need support for them to heal. You haven't been supporting them, and even more, your work in the garden may have set back your healing. You're hurting in your back, aren't you?"

"Yes," she said to the floor.

Sterling moved closer and gently wrapped his arms around her. "Are the wrappings in the washstand? I'll help you wrap your ribs. Then I'll give you something for the pain. I'll also help you wrap your ribs every time until I think they're healed. Okay?"

"Okay." The word was little more than a whisper.

Overcome with sympathy for this wounded soul, Sterling kissed the top of her head. He set her from him and turning her around examined the bruises on her back and felt the ribs he knew were cracked.

"I don't think you did any more damage, but I do think you've hindered your healing. Now let's get you wrapped and you will lie down. Doctor's orders."

Chapter 14

After supper Lydia and Sterling spent the evening in the parlor. Sterling read a medical journal and Lydia held her Bible in her lap, staring at it but not reading. Instead, she thought over what had happened that day.

She'd been surprised by Sterling's reaction to her work in the garden. No matter if she had been ill or injured, Cyrus had made it clear that she had to do her work. If he was busy or wanted to go to town, she had to do his chores as well. Sterling, however, didn't want her to do heavy work while her injuries healed. He'd said that he wanted her hands to be soft for him to hold. He'd held her in his arms. He'd kissed her head.

Lydia thought back, wondering how long it had been since anyone besides Aggie had hugged her, had shown her any kind of affection. It must have been at her parents' funeral, seven years ago. She thought about the feeling of safety and wellbeing that had flooded through her when Sterling held her. She remembered that his kiss brought forth wonderful feelings of affection. These were familiar, but had been foreign for so long that she'd forgotten them. She wanted to feel them again, and more often. For that she knew she would have to trust Sterling more.

"Sterling," Lydia said, "thank you for caring enough to scold me about working in the garden and not wearing the wraps. It's been a long time since anyone cared enough to be concerned whether I was injuring myself." She paused, trying to decide whether to continue or not. Finally she said, "I'll be careful."

Sterling set his journal aside, stood and came over to where she sat on the other side of the fireplace. He sat down next to her. "You don't need to do heavy work anymore. We can hire that done for you, even when you're healed. If you wonder whether a task is too demanding, please, ask me what I think. That way we can decide together. We're in this together, you know."

"I know. It's just hard to trust."

"I can understand that. You haven't been able to believe that someone cares what happens to you. I understand it'll take some time for you to trust me."

He rose and held out his hand. "So, how about some tea? And maybe another serving of dessert?" She took it and allowed him to help her to her feet.

Sterling's conscience had been pricked, thinking about Lydia's letter to Aggie. After Lydia retired he decided that he better write to his sister. It really wasn't fair to keep her in the dark about his marriage, no matter how uncomfortable the thought of writing to her made him.

Settling in his office chair, he drew stationery from the drawer and placed it neatly on the desktop. He opened the inkwell, straightening the desk set a smidgen. Careful examination of the pen nib showed it to be in good condition. Checking the inkwell showed that it was full. He rocked the rolling blotter back and forth. Adjusted the oil lamp a bit. Picked up the pile of paper, knocked it on the desk, straightening the already straight stack. He sighed.

Enough dawdling, he said to himself. Just start writing and tell her the truth of what happened.

Dear Margaret, I hope this finds you, Reese and the children well. I have some news which I'm sure will be startling to you. I am married.

Sterling went on to describe the events, and Lydia--not her physical features but her character. As he wrote he realized that although she exhibited strength and ability she had a low opinion of herself and was afraid, much of the time, of failing to do something correctly. She was terrified of making a mistake. He had never been afraid of doing something wrong. His parents had used each failure as a chance to learn, and he had picked up this philosophy without really thinking about it. To live in fear of every little mistake must have been awful for her, he realized. He knew that her brother had beaten this fear into her and he determined to work to ease that fear. It really wouldn't be so hard for him. He was a pretty easygoing person. At least, he thought so.

He went back to his writing.

Please, Margaret, don't come flying down here. We're doing well but need time to get to know each other. We're still trying to get comfortable together. I know you'll want to meet her. Just plan to come later, maybe in late May or June. I'll let you know closer to then when will be a good time. Please keep us in your prayers. We want to make this marriage work to be a glory to God.

Sterling added the salutation, blotted the letter and addressed the envelope as the ink dried. He would mail it in the morning along with Lydia's letter to Aggie.

Lydia was grateful that Sterling kept his promise to hire two boys to turn and work the garden soil. When they were done she had them prune the fruit trees and help her plant the garden.

Matias and Nils Jorgensen, brothers ages fifteen and thirteen, came after school and on Saturdays, working hard and steady. Lydia was impressed with their work ethic and when she commented on it they looked at each other.

"We're supposed to do everything we do as if the Lord himself had hired us," Matias said. "Guess we just want to please him, and Da too. Da would have our hide if we didn't. We learned that the hard way."

"I understand what you mean," Lydia's eyes didn't have the smiling light the boys' did. "I do appreciate your hard work."

They were sitting at the kitchen table after completing the garden work. Time was needed now for the seeds to sprout and trees to blossom. Lydia had made a custard pie and given the boys each a large slice and a glass of milk.

Sterling had spent the last few days seeing patients in his office or making house calls, and he now came into the kitchen after returning from a house call. "So," he said, "my wife gives away pie to any slacking boy who shows up here?" The smile on his face told them he had heard the comments by both Matias and Lydia.

"Maybe if you did as much work as they did you'd get a piece of pie too." Lydia smiled back at him.

Sterling put on a hangdog face and all three laughed at him.

"I'll take pity on you today but don't expect it everyday." Lydia rose from the table and got the piece of pie she had cut and put on a plate for him earlier.

As Sterling ate his pie, Matias and Nils rose, put their plates in the sink and started to leave. Lydia thanked them again, giving them each the wages they were owed from the money Sterling had left for that purpose.

"Tell your father hello for us. Thanks again for helping out." Sterling stood and reached out his hand to shake each of theirs. The boys, obviously impressed with the adult gesture, shook his hand, nodded politely to Lydia and left by the back door.

Lydia, watching from the kitchen window as she washed the dishes, saw them hit each other on the arm, grinning and chatting as they went. "You surely made their day, shaking hands with them just as you would their father," she said.

"I remember what it was like being a teenager and wanting so much to be a man. There was one old gentleman who always shook hands when he greeted me and the other boys he met. It meant a lot to me--a show of acceptance as a man, even though I was still a boy, really. I remember that feeling and just want to pass that on, I guess."

Lydia looked at him. "You really are a very nice man."

"That is why you married me, isn't it?"

"Of course. What other reason would there be?"

"Well, my good looks, pleasant demeanor, intelligence, sense of humor."

"Not to mention your humility."

"Of course."

They both laughed at the silliness of the conversation.

"It's good we can joke about how we got together," Sterling said. "Otherwise it would put a strain on us getting to know each other."

Lydia blushed and went back to washing. "You're right. It does make me more comfortable. I hadn't laughed much for a long time ..." She let the thought trail off. "I have baked chicken planned for supper with roasted potatoes and green beans. If you're really good the rest of the day I'll make oatmeal muffins to go with it."

"I'll be good, ma'am, I promise." Just then the bell on the clinic door rang. "Duty calls." Sterling rose and handed her the plate and fork. "Gotta go be doc now."

After finishing the dishes and setting them to dry in the rack, Lydia went upstairs to the sewing room. She hadn't had much time to spend in the room and thought she might check out the drawers in the tall chest and the shelves. Sterling's mother had filled the top drawers with spools of thread in many colors, laces, trims, tins of buttons, pins, and a card of needles of various sizes and types. In the bottom were skeins of yarn, also in different colors and weights.

I wish I could have known her, Lydia thought. We have the same interests. I think we would have been friends.

She picked up the sewing basket sitting on the shelf. Looking through Sterling's socks, she found several that needed darning. Finding the darning egg, needle and thread, she sat by the window in the rocking chair darning socks and spending the time conversing with God.

Lighting the lamp on the bedside table that evening, Lydia changed into her nightgown. Putting her clothing and shoes away, she washed her face. Then she turned down the light. The window caught her eye. Only the bottom half was covered by white muslin curtains, and looking out she saw the silhouette of a man in the window of the house next door. She gasped as she realized that he would have been able to see her silhouette as she changed her clothes. She sat down suddenly on the bed. Someone was purposely watching her dress. What should she do? She wanted to talk to Sterling but this man might be a friend of his, maybe a lifelong friend. Would he believe her or not?

She contemplated, as she sat in the dark, trying to figure out a way to handle the situation without telling Sterling. She just wasn't sure he would listen and not blame her. Cyrus would have called her a slut for enticing the man. He would most likely have hit her at least once. Sterling hadn't shown any of that kind of behavior, but they had only been married for a short time. He'd promised that he'd never strike her, but would he believe her now and do something about the man next door?

Sitting in the dark room, Lydia remembered her commitment to trust Sterling more. She decided to speak with him in the morning.

Lydia woke to the sound of furious knocking at the front door. The room was flush with the soft light of early morning. She rose and was putting on her ragged robe when she heard Sterling's footsteps coming swiftly down the stairs. Knowing the person knocking would want him and not her, she went straight to the kitchen to stir up the coals in the stove and start coffee.

Sterling came into the kitchen, pulling his suspenders up onto his shoulders. "That was Ethan Smith, Peter and Ella's next-door neighbor. Both the children are sick and have a rash of some sort. I'm going to go check it out."

"Do you have an idea what it might be?"

"Several things come to mind. Scarlet fever, measles, even poison ivy. I'll know when I see them."

"Do you want anything before you go? I have bread and could make you a jelly sandwich. Coffee isn't ready yet. Do you want to go right away?"

"I want to get over there as soon as possible. If it's something contagious I want to figure out what it is so I can plan how to treat it. I'll take that jelly sandwich and eat it on the way. Coffee I can get when I get back. Tilly will most likely have some. I can get a cup from her."

Lydia followed him down the hall to the front door. "Here you are," she said, handing him the folded-over sandwich after Sterling pulled on his coat.

He grabbed his hat off the peg by the door, put it on his head, picked up his medical bag and, as Lydia held open the door, leaned over and gave her a quick peck on the cheek.

"Thanks for the sandwich. It's not as sweet as the maker, though." He smiled at her, which caused her to blush even more than the kiss had.

"Tell Tilly that if she needs any help to let me know."

"Will do," Sterling called back as he turned at the end of the walk toward the Smiths' house.

Lydia stood in the doorway in wonder over the kiss he'd given her. Her heart was skipping beats and to still it she took a deep breath.

After finishing dressing, Lydia went back to the kitchen to do some baking. She mixed up dough for bread. Everything took longer and was more complicated with her cast. Kneading bread dough with one hand was especially difficult and took twice the time. She hoped it would be healed soon.

A noise sounded at the back door. Lydia opened it to see Daniel Windsor delivering the milk, butter and eggs. Lydia had increased the frequency of deliveries so she would have enough for her cooking.

"Good morning, Daniel. Thank you."

"Morning, Mrs. Doc." He smiled at her. He'd declined calling her by her name and had started calling her by this moniker. Others in town were beginning to use it also. She was embarrassed, but figured nothing she could say would change his mind or that of the others.

"I saw the Doc over on Hawthorn Street. He's out early today."

"Yes, Ethan Smith came and said his children were ill. Sterling went right over there. Daniel, do you have a few more eggs? I thought it might be nice to make some bread pudding but I don't want to be short of eggs before you deliver next."

"Sure do. I can give you half a dozen more."

Lydia went back to kneading her bread after Daniel left, making the bread pudding from leftover dried pieces. Just before it went into the oven she heard the front door open. Putting the pan in to bake, she gathered the items she needed to make breakfast.

"It's chickenpox," Sterling said as he came into the kitchen. "Both children have it. I expect more will come down with it soon. I'll need to order more calamine lotion. There'll be a lot of itchy children before too long."

"You think this will spread?"

"Yeap, always does," Sterling said as he sipped the coffee Lydia had poured for him.

She fried bacon and then scrambled eggs, putting some grated cheese on the eggs just before they were done cooking.

"Looks good," Sterling said. He bowed his head, and after saying grace he dug in. "It'll most likely be a busy day. I figure others might be showing up with sick kids. Would you mail an order for me? I'll write it up after I finish."

"Of course. I can pick up some things at Johnson's and the butcher's. Is there anything else you want me to get or do?"

"Don't think so. I'll think on it."

The day was overcast, with a definite chill from the wind blowing from the northwest. Lydia had cleaned and shortened her father's coat. Although it still wasn't a great fit, at least she could walk without tripping.

She left the house after punching the bread dough down, leaving it for a second rise. She had Sterling's order for calamine lotion and her list. Carrying a basket for her purchases, she walked to the business district, hurrying in the cold wind. Outside the All-Purpose Store she met Ella.

"Lydia, good morning," Ella said. "You of course know about Seth and Becky Smith. Poor little things are all covered with spots."

"Yes, Sterling told me," Lydia said, following Ella into the store. "I'm sending off a medicine order for him. He's sure more children will come down with it. How are Rye and Janie?"

"So far, fine. They've played with Seth and Becky so I'm going to watch them carefully."

"Let me know if I can help Tilly in any way. Also, if your children get sick."

"Well, well, well. The new Mrs. Graham offering her help to any and all." An overly sweet voice spoke from behind them.

"Good morning, Magdelina." Ella's voice held just a hint of a pleasant tone.

"Lydia, this is Magdelina Taylor. Magdelina, this is Mrs. Graham, Dr. Graham's wife."

"Oh, I know who she is," Magdelina said dismissively. Her lips were turned up in a snide smile. She was a beautiful young woman with golden blond hair piled on her head in an elaborate manner. Her blue eyes, Lydia thought, held a combination of distain, sadness, pride and loneliness.

"I've heard of you, also. My husband indicated he knows you."

"Yes, we were special friends at one time. That was before you came to town, of course."

"Of course. Well, I must get this letter sent and do my shopping. Have a pleasant day, Magdelina. Ella, will you help me with some choices?"

Lydia turned away from Magdelina and went over to the post office area by the store's counter, her face stoic. She was pasting the stamp she'd purchased onto the envelope when Ella touched her elbow.

"There was nothing between Sterling and Magdelina," Ella whispered.

"I know," Lydia whispered back. "He told me that Beulah Taylor's been pushing Magdelina at him for two or three years. That was after we met Mrs. Taylor and Mrs. Baumgarden the first time we came in here. It was funny actually. When we heard Mrs. Taylor say that Sterling planned to marry Magdelina, he shook his head so hard I thought it might snap off."

Ella stifled a giggle and glanced back to see if Magdelina was watching them, but she had gone around the end of a display and walked out of sight down the next aisle.

"Do you really need my help with your shopping?"

"You can help me pick out what kind of fruit I should get to make a pie and tell me how much flour I need."

Ella laughed out loud. "I'm sure you're in great need of my help with those. Yes, I'll help you, and then you can help me pick out some black thread and buttons."

Smiling at each other they went to gather their items. Magdelina, coming back up the aisle, brushed past them with several items in her arms and her nose tipped to the ceiling.

Sterling came into the kitchen and rubbed his hand down his face. "I've had to cancel school for the rest of the week, maybe next week also. About half of the students have the chickenpox, so they'd be out anyway. I think many of the rest might come down with it too. It's surprising that so many haven't had it before now."

Lydia could tell how weary he was as he sat down. He had come home later than usual. She placed the meatloaf, butter beans, mashed potatoes and apple muffins on the table then joined him for the meal.

"You look tired," Lydia said after grace.

"I am." Sterling sighed, saying nothing for a few bites. "This sure hits the spot. I haven't had anything since breakfast. I've been busy all day."

"Is there anything I can help with?" Lydia looked at his tired eyes and reached over to squeeze his hand.

"I don't think so. Wait, you could fill the bottles with calamine lotion. I need to have at least two dozen filled."

"I'll do it after I get the dishes done. I want you to go to bed early tonight. I can't be the doc if you get sick from fatigue." She wagged her finger at him playfully.

"Well ... only after dessert. You did make some, didn't you? You sure fix great desserts."

Lydia smiled. "I just might have made a lemon meringue pie. I suppose you don't like those."

"One of my favorites. How about a big piece now, one before I go up, and say ... one for breakfast? Wouldn't want it to spoil, would we?" Sterling asked with a mischievous smile.

"My mother didn't allow sweets for breakfast. Tell me why I should."

"Doctor's orders?"

Lydia chuckled. "Well, here's one for now. We'll see about the other two. Especially the one for breakfast." She placed a large piece in front of him and began clearing the table.

"Come, sit and have some pie with me. I've been so busy. What have you been up to the last few days?"

Lydia plated a smaller piece for herself and sat down. "I've just been busy with household chores really. Cleaning, laundry, baking, things like that. It all takes much longer to get done with this cast. I did do a little hoeing in the garden. Now don't get all stern-faced. It was just a little with the hand hoe. I could do that with one hand."

She thought about telling him of the man next door watching her change but decided it could wait. She'd solved the problem for now. She'd either change in the hallway, if Sterling was upstairs, or not light the lamp in her room if he wasn't. She'd wait to discuss it until the epidemic was over. She didn't want to burden him with this now.

While Lydia did the dishes, Sterling worked in the clinic, arranging and straightening. They came together later for their evening devotions. When they were finished Lydia went to the kitchen and brought back a piece of pie, smiling.

"Here you go. When this is finished you're to head upstairs and go to bed. Mrs. Doc's orders."

"Yes, ma'am. I always try to obey Mrs. Doc's orders."

"I'll remember that," she said with an impish grin.

"Oops. Should have thought before I spoke, shouldn't I?" His smile echoed hers.

"I think so. You know, 'Be slow to speak' and 'It's better to be thought a fool than to open your mouth and confirm it.' "

"Ouch, wife. That hurts," Sterling said, taking the last bite.

"Now off to bed with you."

Sterling saluted and headed up the stairs. Before retiring for the night, Lydia filled twenty-four bottles with calamine lotion.

Chapter 15

Lydia awoke, hearing the front door close. She hadn't heard a knock or Sterling coming down the stairs. She sat up feeling as if her arms were weighted down. She stood, her legs feeling like wobbly jelly. Oh no, I can't get sick now, she thought. She needed to be able to make good meals. Sterling was so busy. She dressed slowly, pulling her hair back with a piece of twine.

Her head was aching but she made biscuits and fried some strips of bacon for breakfast. Taking a bite of bacon, she winced as she swallowed. She took a bite of warm biscuit, which went down easier.

She spent the morning doing light housework. Sterling didn't come home for lunch so she ate a biscuit and drank a glass of milk. Her throat still hurt and she was so very tired. Aching all over, she decided to take a nap. She put on a pot of beans and ham soup, setting the coal in the stove to burn slow and long so it would be ready whenever Sterling came home.

"Lydia." Sterling's call woke her from a deep sleep. Trying to get up quickly, she fell back onto her pillow, feeling worse than she had that morning. Getting up slowly, she looked at herself in the mirror. Her face was pale and there were dark circles under her eyes. She tied back the hair that had escaped from the twine, covered the dark circles with cosmetic, pasted a calm smile on her face and left the room.

She bumped into Sterling in the clinic hallway.

"Oh! You startled me," she said.

"Sorry, where were you? I called but you didn't answer."

"I took a nap and just woke up when you called. What time is it?"

"Quarter to seven."

Lydia was shocked. She'd slept the entire afternoon but was just as tired as she was when she'd lain down. "Have you been out all day?"

"Yes. Ben Phelps came early this morning saying Billy was sick. I went out to the farm and he has the chickenpox. I left a bottle of calamine lotion. Thank you for filling those last night. After I checked all those sick in town, I went around to the farms."

"I'll help with whatever you think I could do. Come, let's go and I'll dish up some soup. I made beans and ham soup and biscuits. You didn't get that piece of pie for breakfast, did you?"

"No, maybe I'll have two for dessert to make up for the one I missed this morning."

Lydia smiled but didn't reply. Her throat burned, her head ached, and she wanted to keep the knowledge from Sterling.

They ate in near silence. Lydia felt terrible. She ate very little as each bite sent knives slicing down her throat. Sterling was so tired from his long day that he didn't notice.

"I'm going to work in my office all evening. I'm very far behind in my paperwork. Will you mind not having our Bible time?" Sterling asked.

"No, you go right ahead and get your work done. I can entertain myself this evening." Lydia was relieved. She wouldn't have to put up a front all evening hiding her illness. She had no clue what she'd come down with and said a small prayer that it would be gone in the morning. She hated being sick. She also didn't want to put more of a burden on Sterling.

Sterling went to his office after finishing his second piece of pie. Lydia smiled softly as she washed the dishes. *He surely likes his desserts*, she thought.

Finishing the dishes, Lydia looked at the clock on the shelf: half past eight. This evening it had taken her twice as long to wash the dishes. Sitting down, she took a deep breath and laid her head on the table. She felt simply awful. Her throat ached, her head ached, her legs were weak, and she thought she was beginning to become feverish. *Lord, please, please make me well by morning. Sterling is so busy and tired. He doesn't need me sick.* She got up slowly and went to her room.

Lydia closed the door but didn't light the lamp. Looking out the window, she saw the silhouette in the window next door. She shook her head and began unbuttoning her dress with trembling fingers. She turned and went to sit on the bed to remove her shoes. She went down with a thud. She was too far from the bed. Landing on the floor, she knocked into the bed and sent it crashing into the wall. She sat there, stunned from her fall, and moaned as her head throbbed harder than before.

Sterling came running down the hall, paused at the door then opened it without knocking.

"Lydia, are you in here?" He heard a weak moan. "What are you doing in the dark? Are you okay?" He grabbed the matches off the bedside table and started to light the lamp.

"No, Sterling, don't light it. There's a man next door who watches. If the room is dark he can't see me change," Lydia's voice was soft and forced. She just couldn't keep up the pretense of being well any longer.

"What?" Sterling's voice held shock and anger. He looked out the window and saw the silhouette, then blew out the match and knelt beside her.

He could see her somewhat with the light filtering in from the hall. Lydia was leaning against the bed with her head in her hands. Her hair had been jostled out of its twine and hung around her face. Sterling brushed it back, and when his hand touched her face he started.

"You're burning up with fever. Why didn't you tell me?"

"You've been so busy, I didn't want to be a bother."

"Well, that's just stupid."

Lydia started crying. "I know. I'm sorry. I'll try harder."

"Oh, honey, I didn't mean that. It's my worry and frustration coming out in the wrong way. I'm sorry. Come, I'll help you with changing and getting to bed." He glanced out the window at the silhouette. "But not in here. You should've been upstairs before now. You can have Margaret's old room. Here, let me help you up."

Lydia kept crying. "I can't. I can't make it up the stairs. I'm just too tired."

Sterling got her nightgown out of the washstand, stuffed it in her lap, bent, picked her up and carried her out of the room. "See, problem solved."

He carried her up the stairs and set her gently on the bed in Margaret's room. He lit the lamp and closed the heavy drapes.

"Here, let me help you." Kneeling down, he untied and removed her work boots, then her wool stockings. He didn't notice how thin the stockings were or that her toes were almost through them. Lydia had unbuttoned her dress but had not gone any further.

"Do you want my help in changing? Or I can wait outside."

"If you'll help with my dress I'll be able to do the rest."

Sterling helped her stand then pulled the dress over her head. He tossed it onto the floor. "You're sure you can manage? I'll go get my med bag while you finish." Seeing her weak nod, he left the room.

Lydia untied her petticoat, letting it drop to the floor. Taking a deep breath, she unwound the wrapping for her ribs and pulled her camisole off, adding them to the growing pile on the floor. She picked up the nightgown, fumbling to find the hem, and pulled it on. Turning the covers back, she climbed into bed.

Sterling didn't quite know what to think as he descended the stairs. He knew Lydia didn't have much confidence and yet he'd heard from Ella how she'd handled Magdelina Taylor at the store. He knew she didn't want to burden him with things she felt she could handle, but not coming to him when she was ill, and very ill it seemed at first glance, indicated to him that she was unsure of her place and importance in his life.

Oh, Father, help me to show her that she doesn't need to put herself behind everything else. I don't know how to encourage her. Please, Father, let this illness be one I can treat and you can make of short duration. He grabbed his bag and took the stairs two at a time.

"You're running a pretty good fever, young lady." Sterling smiled as he took his hand from her forehead. "Let's sit you up so I can do the rest of the exam." He used his stethoscope, listening to her heart and lungs.

He felt her neck and said, "Open wide, please." He placed a tongue depressor in her mouth, looked in. "Your throat is covered in pox. I need to look at your back and chest."

Lydia blushed but untied the string at her neck and showed Sterling her upper chest.

"You never had the chickenpox, did you?"

"I don't know."

"Well, you have a good case of it now. It's even in your throat. I imagine it's pretty sore, isn't it?"

"Yes."

"I'll go bring up a bottle of calamine lotion. I'll put it on the spots on your back, also your arms and legs if you'll let me. You can do your front."

When he returned, Lydia leaned forward so he could reach her back. Finishing with all he could do he handed her the bottle and some cottonwool. When she was finished with the lotion he tucked the blankets around her, blew out the lamp and left, hoping she'd be able to sleep.

Sterling looked in on her the next morning before he went downstairs. She was still sleeping. He thought about feeling for fever but decided it could wait.

In the kitchen he set a pot of water for tea on the stove, scrambled some eggs and buttered several slices of bread. The water boiled and he steeped chamomile, then added lemon and honey. He hoped it would sooth her throat. Digging around in the pantry, he found a tray and after loading it with the breakfast he headed upstairs.

"Lydia," Sterling said softly. He set the tray on the bureau and approached the bed. Lydia turned over and looked up at him. The chickenpox had spread to her face. She looked miserable. "I'd say you're not any better this morning than last night. Am I right?"

She just nodded.

"I've brought some breakfast up. I need to get going but wanted to check on you first."

"I'm not sure I can eat anything. My throat is so sore." Her voice was hardly more than a whisper.

"It's just scrambled eggs, some buttered bread and chamomile tea. The tea should sooth your throat. It has honey and lemon in it. I'd like you to try and eat something. Even just a little."

Lydia pushed herself up to sit against the pillow. "Um ... I need ..."

"I have a chamber pot right here. I won't make that mistake again."

She smiled at his quip about having to go the first thing in the morning.

Sterling handed her a plate with a small amount of eggs, bread with the crusts cut off and a cup of tea. His plate held considerably more. He gave thanks and they started to eat.

"I'll be busy most of the day, but I'll stop in when I can to see how you are. Don't worry about meals. I can get lunch at the cafe and bring supper home, too. You stay in bed. Doctor's orders."

"I will." Lydia had eaten a few bites of egg and part of the bread. She sipped the tea. "This is soothing. Oh, would you please wind the clock? It's harder being sick if you can't tell what time it is."

Sterling glanced over his shoulder and looked at the white-and-blue china clock on the shelf above the stove. "Sure. You aren't going to eat anymore, are you?" He looked at her and the plate. She shook her head. "I'll take these things down."

He gathered up the dishes and took them down to the kitchen. Returning, he tucked the blankets around her.

"You're going to be down for a few days, but if you stay in bed you'll get over it sooner. In adults, chickenpox is usually worse than in children. Don't be surprised if you feel quite sick and itchy. Keep putting the calamine lotion on where you can. You stay put in that bed. Doctor's orders."

She saluted weakly, gave him a little wave and turned on her side away from him. Taking the hint, Sterling left the room.

Lydia woke later in the morning. She pinched her eyebrows together, hearing footsteps climbing the stairs. She figured it must be Sterling, but it didn't sound like him. She was surprised when Mrs. H. put her head around the door.

"I hope I didn't wake you," she said as she entered the room. "I saw Doc this morning and he told me about your chickenpox. I said I'd come here and keep you company. He mentioned that I was welcome to fix dinner, too." She laughed. "That man is always hungry."

"I'm glad you're here. It's very kind of you." Lydia's voice was weak.

"We should all have someone to tend us when we're ill. Let's you know you're loved. So, how badly are you feeling?" Mrs. H. picked up the clothing from the floor and, folding them, put them in a drawer in the bureau.

"Not very well."

"That's what I thought. How does some chamomile tea sound?"

"Sterling made some this morning. I'd like some if you don't mind making it."

"Of course not. That's what I'm here for. I'll be back in a few minutes."

During the day Mrs. H. spent time reading to Lydia, making meals, putting calamine on the pox and reminiscing. Sterling checked in twice but was kept busy with the epidemic.

Sterling came into Lydia's room that evening with a smile of anticipation on his face. Lydia thought he looked like a little boy hoping for a cookie.

"I have a surprise for you. It'll help with your itching. Do you feel like you can walk downstairs?" She nodded.

She went slowly down the stairs and Sterling led her to the kitchen. There was a sizable pot steaming on the stove. In the corner by the stove was a large copper bathtub. Lydia looked at Sterling questioningly.

"I bought this today. It's much larger than the tin tub we have. You should be able to get most of you into the water. I have an oatmeal bath ready. The oatmeal will help with the itching. You can soak as long as you want. Then we'll put on more calamine lotion. What do you think? Want to try it?" Sterling looked like a boy proud of how big the fish he'd caught was.

"That sounds wonderful. It was very thoughtful. Don't you want supper first? You have to be hungry. Mrs. H.

said there was enough soup from yesterday for supper tonight. Is that all right for you? I can make--"

"The soup is fine. You don't need to make me anything. Why don't you bathe, then we can have supper? I can do office work until you're finished."

"That would be lovely."

"I'll just get the bath ready."

Lydia sat at the table, her throat sore and her body itchy. When he was finished he left her to her bath. She sank into the murky water. She was able, with some adjusting, to get her torso and right arm under the water leaving her casted arm on the side of the tub. Sterling was right. It was soothing to her itchy skin. She laid her head back on the edge of the tub, wishing the bath would sooth her throat as well as it did her body.

Sterling tried to do paperwork but the thought of Lydia in the bath kept invading. She was his wife, but he'd promised they'd take things slowly. Not that anything would change while she was ill, but Sterling wondered how long it would take before their marriage was not one in name only.

The next few days passed similarly. Sterling made breakfast and brought it to Lydia in bed. After he left, Mrs. H. would come some time in the morning and spend several hours, making both a noon and evening meal. During the afternoon, Lydia would bathe while Sterling was out on house calls or seeing patients in the office.

Finally, Lydia stopped sprouting spots and the ones she had began to heal. Her throat also felt less on fire each day. As the days progressed she began to feel better and started taking over her regular chores. She tried not to scratch the healing scabs and kept up with the application of calamine lotion.

"Miss Spotty. How are you doing this fine evening?" Sterling said as he entered the kitchen.

"That's Mrs. Spotty to you, sir," Lydia shot back with a chuckle. "I looked in the mirror and I definitely agree with you. Just when I don't have to use the cosmetic to cover the bruise, I get spots all over my face. I am feeling better. I sent Mrs. H. home. She's been wonderful, but I know she was fatigued at being here almost every day. I sent supper with her so she wouldn't have to cook tonight."

"It was a blessing that she could come and help. You were pretty sick. Probably the most sick of all those who had the chickenpox. You were also the only adult who got them."

Sterling sipped the coffee Lydia had poured for him as she put their supper on the table. "School will start on Monday," he said. "Most of the children will be well by then. It will be good to get back to normal. Whatever normal means."

Chapter 16

The days passed in the 'normal' fashion Sterling had spoken about. Easter came and went. The garden began sprouting and the weather warmed. Lydia began to wonder if Sterling would ever check to see whether her back and arm had healed. She was tired of only having one hand to work with.

She was out in the garden on a day the sun warmed the air to a pleasant temperature. She'd planted some more lettuce, radish, beet and pea seeds, and was weeding among the hollyhocks that lined the walk to, and surrounding, the outhouse. Leaning down to pull a weed along the walk, she didn't hear Sterling's approach.

"Hi."

Lydia straightened and swung around so fast she almost hit his chest with her cast.

"Whoa there, girl!" Sterling jumped back, catching her arm and keeping her from falling as she lost her balance.

"Oh, Sterling, you startled me so. I thought you were out on a call."

"I gathered that. You could do some damage with that thing." Sterling smiled as he said it. "Maybe we should take it off so I'll be safe."

"I'm sorry, I almost hit you," Lydia said with contrition. Then her eyes lit up. "You want to take it off? Now? Let's go. I've wanted this thing gone for so long." She kept up an excited string of words as she pulled him along to the house.

In the kitchen, Sterling pumped water into a black-and-white speckled enamel roasting pan. "Do you want it warm or cold?"

"What for?"

"To get the cast off we need to soak it in vinegar water. It takes a while, and is messy, but it does work. Or," he said with an evil grin, bouncing his eyebrows up and down, "I can take my saw and cut it off."

"I'll take warm, please." Lydia said primly then smiled. "You'd never make it as an evil doctor. You're just not made for it."

Sterling put the pan on the stove and added more coal to the firebox. Lydia got the jug of vinegar out of the pantry along with some cookies. Sterling definitely had a sweet tooth.

"How long will it take to dissolve the plaster?"

"Most of the rest of the afternoon. When it gets soft enough, I have heavy shears that I may decide to cut it off with, but I don't want to bruise your arm. We'll see."

When the water was warm enough, Sterling set the pan on the table and added a large amount of vinegar. "Lay your arm in here. If it's too hot let me know."

Lydia did as told, finding the temperature comfortable. They sat in the kitchen, Sterling eating cookies, Lydia soaking her arm, looking at each other in silence. A knock and the clinic bell ringing as the door opened caused Sterling to go see who needed him. Lydia could hear voices and then small feet running down the hall.

"Hi, Mrs. Doc. Rye fell off the shed roof and bumped his head," Janie Lendrey said excitedly as she ran into the kitchen. "Mama thinks he has a cushion."

"What was he doing on the shed roof?"

"Trying to get Oscar, our kitty, down, he'd been up there all day, Rye thought he couldn't get down, I told him he could, but Rye climbed up anyway, can I have a cookie, the kitty jumped down just fine, but Rye fell, I screamed and Mama came running out the door." Janie's excited rush of words ended and Lydia handed her a cookie.

"So Rye fell. Did he pass out?"

"Don't know what that is but his eyes were closed for a bunch of time," Janie said around the cookie. "That's why Mama thinks he has a cushion. Is that the same kind as we have on the sofa, Mrs. Doc?"

"No, sweetie. It's called a concussion. It's a bad bump to your head. I think your brain bangs up against the bone in your head and gets a bruise."

"Did you have a con-- cushion when you stayed at our house? You had a big bruise around your eye."

Ella came in just then, her face wreathed in worry. "I'm going to get Peter. Sterling thinks Rye will be okay, but Peter doesn't know yet. He's at the Jorgensens'. Johann is down with his leg again. I just grabbed Rye when he woke up and came here. Can you watch Janie?"

"Of course. You go on. Plan to have supper here, too."

"Thanks. We will." Ella headed to the front door.

Janie watched her mother leave, then turned back to Lydia. "Whatcha doing?"

"Doc said it's time to take my cast off. I have to soak it to soften the plaster. Do you remember helping to put it on?"

"Yeah. It was messy but really fun. Can I help take it off?" Janie stood on her chair and looked into the pan. "That smells like pickles." She wrinkled up her nose.

"That's because it has vinegar in the water." Lydia was smiling at the girl. Janie was a precocious four-year-old who loved to talk.

"Can I help?"

"Well, I'm not sure how it will help, but you can try mixing the water around. Here, let's roll up your sleeves."

Lydia had Janie climb onto the table and allowed her to put her hands in the water. Janie swished the water around then started poking at the cast.

"Look! The water's turning white. I'm helping. I'm helping get the cast off," Janie cried with delight.

Lydia laughed. "You most certainly are. You can help all you want. Anything to get it melted faster."

Janie played in the water, pushing and rubbing the cast and turning the water milkier. "Oops," she said when some water splashed out.

"No harm done, but do be careful. Your mama won't like it if you're all wet when she gets back."

Suddenly Janie stopped and looked straight at Lydia. "Mrs. Doc, is Rye gonna die?"

"I don't think so," Lydia said gently. " Doc'll take care of him, and he'll probably have to stay quiet for several days."

"Abel Smith fell off the roof of the boardinghouse, and he died."

"I don't know the particulars of that. I don't know what happened."

"Can we pray for Rye, Mrs. Doc?"

"Of course. Do you want to pray?"

"Uh-huh." Janie pulled her hands out of the water, folded them and bowed her head. "Dear Jesus. Rye fell off the shed and bruised up his brain on his head bone. I don't want him to die. I love Rye even though we fight sometimes. Please make Rye better. Papa says we always need to say thank you for whatever you are going to do, so thank you, Jesus. Please make Rye better. Amen."

"That was a fine prayer. I know Jesus heard you."

"Papa says Jesus always hears our prayers. He says the Holy Spirit groans to the Father and that makes it easier for God to understand 'em. I don't see how groans can help God understand, but since the Bible says it we gotta believe it."

"You're right. We need to believe what the Bible says."

"Oh! I poked my finger right through the cast. Did you feel it?"

"Yes, I did. You're doing a great job. I'll bet it's fun too, isn't it?"

"Yeap. It's just about as much fun as when we put it on." Janie paused. "I wish Rye hadn't fallen off the shed. He could've been helping, too."

They heard the clinic door open and Peter calling for Sterling. A few minutes later Sterling and Peter came into the kitchen.

"Papa!" The little girl scrambled up and flung herself into her father's arms. "Rye's got a con-- cushion, that's a bruised-up brain, he fell off the shed roof trying to get Oscar down but Oscar got down by his self."

Peter hugged the girl, not caring that her hands were wet. "Yes, Janie. Doc told me. He'll be fine, but he'll have to stay here tonight so Doc can check on him. Mama's with him now."

"We prayed. I remembered to thank Jesus for what he's gonna do."

"That's so good of you, Janie. I'm proud of you."

Janie, switching topics again, said, "I'm helping Mrs. Doc get out of her cast, I poked a hole clear through, it smells like pickles."

Peter, confused, looked to Lydia for explanation. "The water has vinegar in it to help dissolve the plaster.

Janie's been helping it dissolve faster and doing a fine job of it," Lydia said with a smile for the girl.

"Let's see how it's going." Sterling reached into the water and lifted her arm out. "My, my, my. You have done very well with this, Janie. Maybe when you grow up you can get a job as a cast remover."

"That's silly, Uncle Doc. I'm gonna be a cook at a restaurant. Then I can make cookies every day."

"Mighty lofty plans there, my girl," said her father, leaning with his hands on the back of a chair after setting Janie onto the seat.

Sterling got his shears and began to work on the plaster. Carefully slipping the shears between the cast and Lydia's skin, he cut the softened cast apart, freeing her arm from its confines.

"Yuck," exclaimed Janie. "Look at your hand and arm. They're nasty," she said, scrunching up her face.

"That's from not being able to wash it and from soaking in the water so long. It makes your skin all pruney. Here, Lydia, let me see it." Sterling took her arm and gently moved her wrist every which way, asking her how it felt. Finally, he pronounced it healed.

"Praise God," Lydia said with relief. "I was surely tired of that thing. Now I need to think about fixing supper for us. You want to help, Janie?"

"Sure do. Mama says I'm the best help she knows."

"I'll bet you are. Now, you two men get out of here. We women will fix you up a nice meal."

"Yeah, scoot now," Janie said with the shooing motions she'd seen her mother do many times.

The men quickly left the kitchen, trying to hold in the laughter which threatened to bubble out.

After supper Ella and Janie went home but Peter stayed, planning to sit up in the room Rye would occupy during the night. Rye was sleepy and had a bad headache. Sterling would check on him periodically during the night. Peter joined Sterling and Lydia in the parlor while they had their evening devotions.

After Lydia retired, the men continued drinking coffee and eating cookies.

"How are you and Lydia doing?" Peter asked.

"Fine, I suppose. She's really skittish. If I come on her unexpectedly, she startles badly." He chuckled. "She about got me with her cast today. She was out in the garden and didn't hear me come up on her from behind. When I spoke she just about clobbered me as she turned around. I'd already decided to remove the cast today but that took away any and all doubt."

Peter laughed. "Yeah, you could've ended up with a black eye yourself."

"Believe me, I thought of that at the time."

"At least you got a very good cook. Dinner was great. Even on such short notice. The cookies are good too."

"You should try her lemon meringue pie. All I can say is that it's good enough to take first place from Beulah Taylor at the county fair."

"Not the best way to get on her good side, I'd think, but it'd do her some good to be humbled a little."

"I doubt Lydia will ever be on Beulah Taylor's good side."

"Probably not." Peter paused before continuing. "Janie surely likes Lydia. I think she might have helped her feel more secure about Rye. I appreciate that."

"Lydia is secure in her faith and can be very patient. She's helped other people, both children and adults, when they've been scared in the clinic. Not often, but I'm impressed when she does. I just wish she would begin to trust me more."

Sterling told Peter about the man next door watching her at night. Peter was not only shocked about the man's behavior but also that Lydia felt insecure in telling Sterling about it. Amos Watts and his wife, an older couple, had moved into town shortly before Christmas. Sterling had met them at the time, but they hadn't been very friendly and had since kept to themselves. They didn't attend church either.

"What do you plan to do about this?" Peter asked. "You can't have the man looking into your patient rooms."

"I know. I'm going to ask Lydia about making some draperies for the windows. I plan to plant some bushes that will grow tall along the lot line. That should take care of it. I don't want to get into a fight but I want to protect Lydia, and my patients too."

"They say good fences make good neighbors. Sounds like a good idea."

Just then they heard Rye calling from the clinic and went to check on him.

Lydia changed into her nightgown, noticing again how thin the fabric had become. Her camisole, equally thin, was covered by the wrapping for her ribs. Whenever she'd bathed, Sterling had helped her wrap the binding around over her camisole. Each time she had blushed, but as she became more accustomed to his touch her trembling diminished a little. Wondering how soon Sterling would ask for his husband's rights made her tremble anew. She had learned he was gentle and caring, and not at all like Cyrus or Gus, but still she was afraid. She'd lived on a farm so she knew more than some women but that did nothing to calm her nervousness.

Please, Father, help me to be less afraid. I know I need to be willing, but let it be longer before we--

A knock sounded at her door. Lydia jumped up, her eyes wide, and took a deep breath.

"Yes?"

"Lydia," Sterling said through the door, "I thought I might check your ribs to see if you're healed enough to stop wearing the wrap. Is that all right with you?"

"Just a moment and I'll remove it. Okay?" Hearing him answer in the affirmative she lifted her gown and untied the knot below her breasts. When the muslin and her camisole were in a pile on the floor and her gown's hem brushed her feet, she opened the door.

She sat on the edge of the bed, with Sterling sitting behind her. Running his fingers over her ribs, Sterling fought to keep his physician's detachment. Her ribs were healed. He stilled his hands on her back for a moment. He took a deep breath then lifted his hands and laid them in his lap.

"Your ribs are healed well. You can stop wearing the wrap." Sterling was pleased that his voice didn't falter when he spoke.

"Wonderful. Thank you." Lydia turned so he could see her face, but not anything else her threadbare gown might reveal. "How's Rye doing?"

"We just checked on him. He'd called out for Peter. He's doing fine, but tonight will let us know if he has something more than a concussion. He was a little hungry so I gave him some bread and butter. I'll check on him several times tonight, and Peter will stay in the room with him. I moved that comfortable chair from the sitting room in for him."

"Is there something I can do to help?"

"Not tonight. If he's okay through the night you might make him a special breakfast."

"I can do that. I expect Ella and Janie will be here early."

"I imagine so."

Conversation died down at that point. They sat on the bed looking at each other. Neither one spoke, but neither wanted the moment to end. Sterling picked up her hand and held it. Both felt the tension in the air. Sterling knew how afraid Lydia was, and although he wanted to do more than just hold her hand he knew he couldn't push her. He squeezed her hand and rose.

"I'm glad you're healed now. However," he said with an impish smile, "I still want you to hire the hard garden work done."

She laughed. "You'll get no argument with me on that. I like only doing the light work. Now I have to try and get you to let me hire the laundry done."

"Give an inch and you take a mile." On impulse, Sterling leaned down and gave her a quick kiss on her cheek and left the room.

He smiled as he walked to his room. First her head and now her cheek. I'm getting closer, he thought.

Chapter 17

Rye went home the next day with Sterling's assurance that he would suffer no lasting harm. He would not, however, be trying to rescue the cat again. Peter explained to him that God had made cats able to rescue themselves much better than a little boy could.

Lydia was sewing in the sitting room when there was a knock on the clinic door. Answering it, she smiled a welcome to Mrs. H.

"Come in. Have you been for your heart check?" Lydia asked as she ushered the older woman to a seat.

"Yes, dearie. I'm as good as I can be. Like Paul, I'm torn between wanting to be home with my Lord and wanting to be here with you all."

"Well, I for one want you here. Would you like some tea?"

"No, thank you. I received a letter from my great-niece, Rachel. She's my sister's granddaughter. She teaches in Council Bluffs. She asked if she could come and visit for a few weeks in the summer. You'll like her. She's my favorite niece. She's a little older than you. She has a sweet spirit and loves to have fun. I hope you'll welcome her."

"Of course I will. I'd like to meet someone who knows you well. My, my, the stories she can probably tell. I can't wait." Lydia raised her eyebrows in a mischievous manner.

"Maybe I should tell her she can't come. I wouldn't want all my secrets to be let out."

They both laughed.

"Let me know when she's to arrive and I'll invite several of the younger women from church to a tea," Lydia said. "I know Ella will want to meet her, and Betsy Phelps. The Phelps were the first people to come and speak to us after the wedding. You were with us at the cafe, remember?"

"I do. They're very nice people who live up to their beliefs."

"And Millie Stanton could probably use a day out to show off her baby."

"It's nice of you to think of them. I knew I could count on your welcome."

With that settled, Lydia showed Mrs. H. the sewing she was doing.

Sterling paused at the kitchen door. He looked at the letters in his hand then came into the room. "Hello, wife. Here's a letter from your friend Aggie, I think. That is, unless you've told someone else that you're here."

"No, just her," Lydia took the letter he held out and slit the seal. She stood and moved over to the stove to read.

"I received one from my sister today too," Sterling said, sitting down at the table to read his own letter. Without looking up, he said, "She and her family are planning to come for Decoration Day and stay for a week. They'll come on Saturday and not leave until Friday. I wrote them about our marriage. I know they want to meet you." Sterling wasn't all that happy about his sister coming, but he didn't say anything.

He looked up. "What's wrong?"

Lydia's face had turned white and her eyes were glued to her letter. She sat down at the table slowly. She looked at Sterling, her face serious.

"Aggie says that Cyrus was really mad when I left. Tore up the house. He came to Aggie's and accused her of hiding me. She held her shotgun on him and told him that I wasn't there, that she hadn't seen me since she'd made soap, and to get off her land and not come back. He told her that if she'd helped me escape he'd make her real sorry."

Lydia paused. "Cyrus went into town and told the sheriff that he had to go, find me and bring me back. The sheriff told him that since I was of age I was free to go where I pleased. Then Cyrus got drunk and smashed up the saloon. He spent a night in jail. When he got out he swore he'd find me and make me marry Gus."

Lydia's eyes were filled with worry and fear. "He can't do that, can he?"

Sterling pulled her up from her chair and put his arms around her. He could feel her slight tremble of fear. "No, sweetheart, he can't. We're married before God and man, with many witnesses. He doesn't know where you are. I won't let him hurt you. You're safe here."

He searched her face, praying that she'd listen and know he meant every word. Finally, he could see her relax.

She smiled a weak smile. "Thank you. What were you saying about your sister?"

"I wrote to Margaret when you wrote to Aggie and told her about our marriage. I knew she'd want to come right then, but I told her not to until later. I suggested the end of May or beginning of June, but that I'd write to her when I thought it'd be a good time. I should've known she wouldn't wait until I wrote and invited her. Now she states that she's coming for Decoration Day, along with her family, and they're staying a week. From Saturday until the next Friday," he finished rather weakly, looking at Lydia's stricken face.

"Oh my ... a week." Lydia took a deep breath and let it out slowly. She got up and took a piece of paper and a pencil from the drawer.

"What're you doing?"

"I'm going to write a list of the things that need to get done before they get here so I'll be ready. I won't be doing things at the last minute or miss anything that can be done ahead." She bent her head to the paper and began making a list.

"That's all? You just start making a list? No discussion or yelling or fighting?"

"What?" Lydia looked up. "You want me to yell at you for something you had nothing to do with? Sometimes, Sterling, you are a little strange." She went back to her list.

"This is all fine with you?"

"No, not really, but it is what it is. You were right to let her know about our marriage. It isn't your fault that she's disregarding your wishes."

"I suppose not. But how can you be so calm about it? You've just found out that someone you don't know is coming for a week with her husband and children and all you can say is 'it is what it is'?"

She looked up at him, and he saw that she wasn't as calm as she had seemed. Her eyes had that hollow look that came on when she was unsure and afraid. His heart clinched in his chest. He sat down and took the pencil out of her hand.

"Talk to me. Tell me how you feel about this. No, let me tell you how I feel first. That may help. I'm pretty mad at my sister right now. I specifically wrote that I'd let her know when they could come. I did suggest late May or early June but said I'd write. I wanted to speak with you about their visiting first. I thought maybe a long weekend. Maybe come Friday and stay until Monday, or maybe Tuesday. She took that away and seems to think she has the right to just invite herself and her family for an extended stay."

Sterling looked down. "She did this sort of thing when I was a child, too. She'd just announce that I was going to do this or that with her. Nothing I was ever interested in, either. No matter what plans I had, she just announced that I was going to ..." He was getting more and more agitated, remembering.

"It's okay, Sterling. It caught me off guard. I was surprised, that's all. I'll be ready when they come. The list-making helps me see that it's manageable. That calms me." She reached over and took his hand, clenched in his anger at his sister.

"I know her name is Margaret, but I don't know about her family." Lydia was making an effort to stay calm.

Sterling ran a hand over his face, forcing himself to let go of his frustration. "Her husband's name is Reese. He's a lawyer in Des Moines. I think he has aspirations in politics. His last name is Rawlings. They have three children. Connor is eight, Stafford is five, and Abby is twenty-eight months."

"Oh," Lydia said softly, looked down at her hands and blushed.

Sterling was confused at her blush and then it hit him. They used two of the bedrooms upstairs, and Margaret's family would need two. There were only three bedrooms. He fought hard not to smile. He wouldn't even let his lips twitch. Lydia would have to spend the week in his bed. Maybe she could be persuaded to stay there after his sister and family left.

Lydia was very nervous about the intimacy of dressing, undressing and voluntarily joining Sterling in bed every day for over a week. She wondered if she'd be able to sleep for even one minute each night. She looked down at her list. She took a huge breath and let it out.

"I'd like to know what the family likes to eat. I can plan meals they'll enjoy. If you can think about that for a couple of days then let me know, I can choose the meals and get a list of groceries I'll need. Also, if you know what the boys like to do I can plan for that. We could have the Lendreys over at least one time. That would give the children someone to play with. Are any of your or Margaret's toys still here? We could bring those out for the children."

She continued writing and talking until Sterling laid his hand on hers, stopping her. She looked up at him.

"Stop. It's a while before they come. Don't try planning it all now. We'll get it all planned and be ready for their visit. I think your idea of inviting Peter and Ella is a good one. We can invite Drew, too. He knows Margaret and Reese, and I'm sure he'd like to see them while they're here. If you ask, maybe Ella would invite the boys over for an afternoon or a day of play. School will be over by then, so both children would be available to play."

Lydia laid her pencil on the table. "You're right. I don't have to do it all now. I think I'll go see Ella tomorrow. She'll help me with all the planning."

Getting up, she put the paper and pencil on the counter and turned toward the stove. "I have a pot roast in the oven. All I need to do is make the gravy, set the table and dish everything up. You go wash up, and then you can pour our drinks."

Rising, Sterling gave her a hug. She leaned slightly on his chest for a moment before drawing away.

Chapter 18

Lydia walked up to the Lendreys' porch carrying a basket filled with rolls. She knew Ella would help with the plans for the visit of Sterling's sister and family. Still, she was nervous about asking for such a major, in Lydia's view, commitment. Arriving at the front door, she twisted the knob of the doorbell.

Ella opened the door with a smile on her face. "Good morning. What brings you here?"

"Good morning, Ella. I have ... that is ... well ... I brought you some of Gramma Lee's rolls." Lydia finally managed to get a complete sentence out of her mouth.

"Thank you. Please, come in and have some tea with me. Peter took Janie with him to visit some of the older people who don't or can't get out much. They love seeing a child, and Janie loves being the center of attention."

Ella could tell that Lydia wanted to ask something of her but was afraid to. She hoped a friendly chat over a cup of tea would ease Lydia's nervousness.

"The rolls look wonderful," she said when the tea had been poured and both ladies were seated at the kitchen table, the basket sitting on a chair by them.

"The recipe is from my grandmother on my mother's side. I would've brought you vegetables but it's too early. You don't plant a garden, do you?"

"Just a few tomato plants. With the children and my duties as the pastor's wife I don't seem to find time to do much gardening. Vegetable gardening, that is. I do like the flowers more. Even there, I have mostly perennials. They're much less work." Ella smiled with twinkling eyes. "Now, Lydia, what is it that you're so nervous about asking me?" Ella said, getting right to the point.

"Well ..." Lydia paused. "It's just that Sterling's sister, Margaret, and her family are coming for Decoration Day and staying for a week. I've never hosted anything like that. Cyrus never had anybody stay over who wasn't drunk and sleeping in the barn. They'd drink out there until they passed out and then leave in the morning."

"So you're nervous about how to plan and entertain them for a week." Ella reached over and patted Lydia's hand. "I know how you feel, in a way, anyway. When Peter and I came here to take the church I hadn't ever been a hostess or in charge of anything other than getting my brothers and sister ready for school or church. Suddenly I was looked to for guidance on about every decision that had to be made. It seemed like no one could decide anything without my input. But enough about me. Of course I'll help you. They have a couple of children, don't they?"

"Yes, three. Connor is eight, Stafford is five and Abby is twenty-eight months. Keeping children occupied all day for a week is ... well, not something I've ever done."

"You did very well with Janie. She loved going to your house."

"That was just for part of a day, not an entire week. I don't know Margaret, or her husband, and Sterling will be working and I'll be alone with his relatives. Margaret will be comparing the way I do things with the way her mother did. At least she and I can chat about female things, but what about her husband? I don't know how to talk with a man I don't know. How will I entertain them the entire week? I'm not used to being with people all day every day."

Lydia's words were coming faster and faster as she outlined the things she thought were giant obstacles. "I'll have strangers living in my house day and night. I don't know how I'll do it. How will I get my chores done? The laundry, baking, cleaning ... I don't know how I'll spend every night sleeping with Sterling."

She stopped her tirade suddenly. Realizing what she had revealed, her hands came up and covered her reddening face.

Ella rose and moved to get more tea. Pouring them both another cup, she sat down. Lydia's head was in her hands, resting on the table.

"It'll be okay." Ella murmured words of comfort until Lydia raised her head.

"I don't know what to say. I knew I was upset about Sterling's relatives visiting but ..."

"You and Sterling haven't progressed that far in your relationship, yet. It's all right."

"No, we haven't. I knew I was nervous about it but didn't realize how much. I've never slept with anyone, so even that will be strange to me. Oh! What if I kick him or pull the covers away?"

Ella chuckled. "He'll either kick you back or steal the covers from you. That's one of the adjustments couples make sharing a bed. Now, let's start making plans on how to entertain this family while they're here. When Peter gets home we can enlist his help since he grew up with Margaret and so will know something about her."

Lydia and Ella spent the rest of the morning talking over ideas and making lists. Ella offered to be a sort of joint host to lighten the burden on Lydia. Peter and Janie arrived shortly before lunch. Janie grabbed hold of Lydia like a drowning sailor and talked excitedly about her visits with the parishioners in her run-on sentences until she ran out of breath.

"My, it sounds like you had very good visits. How about you two wash up and we'll eat lunch. Lydia's staying so you can let go of her now."

As they ate, Ella told Peter of the Rawlings family's planned visit. She didn't mention Lydia's concern over the sleeping arrangements. As she outlined their plans he made comments and suggestions, generally agreeing with what they'd planned.

"You grew up with Margaret," Ella said to Peter. "What's she like?"

"She's tall like Sterling," Peter began. "Dark hair, too, blue eyes--"

"Not her appearance, Peter," Ella said with a little impatience. "What kind of a person is she?"

Peter smiled, and Ella realized that he'd purposely teased her and she'd fallen for the bait.

Lydia was astounded at the interaction. She would never have shown any indication of irritation around her brother. Cyrus would have slapped her.

"Papa teases Mama like that a lot. She falls for it every time," Janie said around the food in her mouth.

"She's right. It's sort of a standing joke around here." Ella laughed at herself. "Even if Janie said it with food in her mouth." Ella gave her daughter a stern look.

"She is at that," Peter said. "Let's see. Margaret's a good person. She's a faithful believer, a generous person with her time and talents. I haven't seen her in several years."

"Sterling was pretty angry with her for declaring that they were coming. He'd written that he'd let them know when they could visit. He ranted a little bit about her," Lydia said a little nervously. She didn't like telling of Sterling's emotional outburst.

"I'll just bet he was angry," Peter said with a slight grin. "She can be rather domineering and definitely wants things her way. She used to make Sterling play dolls or house with her when they were kids. He hated it. Even when he was a little older and we guys had plans to go fishing or something, she'd make him play with her or make him late to join us. Sometimes she'd insist that she come along or make him come home early. He'd sneak out early, some mornings, just to get away before she could tell him what he was going to do with her that day." Peter was grinning at the memory.

"Didn't their parents make her stop?" Ella asked. "It seems very unfair."

"They were busy with the medical practice. Mrs. Graham worked alongside Doc Graham and so was gone a lot, leaving Margaret in charge of Sterling. She's five years older than he is. I think they stopped it some, but when they were busy they just forgot and Margaret was able to dominate him again. I'm not saying they were bad parents, just busy. Like I said, Margaret is a pretty good person. I hope she's grown out of her domineering ways, but with Sterling it seems she still wants to call the shots."

Lydia heard the front door close and wiped her hands on the dishtowel. She turned around just as Sterling entered the kitchen.

"Hi, did you go talk with Ella today?"

"Hi back. Yes, I spoke with both Ella and Peter. Janie added her two cents' worth also. Do you want some coffee? I don't have any made, but I can make it quickly."

"No, thank you. A glass of water would be welcome, though. It's getting dusty, and my throat is dry. We could use another rain. So, did you all make lots of plans?"

"Yes, we have a good outline of things to do anyway. Peter told me that with Decoration Day on Sunday this year the town's having a parade before worship service. We thought we'd have a picnic here after it. Do you think your sister would help with that?"

Sterling nodded.

"Along with the Lendreys we'll invite Drew, the Phelps, Mrs. H. and I thought maybe the Stantons for the afternoon. I don't think Millie gets out much with the baby and I thought they might like to come. Is that all right with you?"

"Sure, that's thoughtful of you. I'll bet they'll come. They're quite young, and there aren't many couples their age around so they don't have much chance to socialize."

Lydia wondered if Sterling realized that she, at twenty years old, was about the same age.

"That will take care of Sunday. Monday, Peter's going to take the boys and Reese fishing down at the river. The plan is to have what they catch for supper but we'll have backup food ready just in case. I can get the laundry done while they're gone."

"Margaret'll help you with that, I think. Well, she'll tell you what you're doing wrong and how to do it." Sterling's voice had a bitter bite to it.

"Please, Sterling, try to have a positive attitude about this visit. I know she didn't wait until you invited her but please try."

Sterling sighed. "Okay. It's just that this is typical Margaret. She gets my back up with her pushing me around."

"Peter told us about how she was when you were growing up. I know it can be, and was, annoying, but she didn't really abuse you. She just played her older sister position to her advantage."

Seeing Lydia look down as she said this, Sterling felt the prick of conscience. He was complaining of his sister's behavior, but it in no way compared to Lydia's treatment by her brother.

"You're right. I do know she loves me. Sometimes too much to stay away." He smiled at Lydia, conveying repentance of his poor attitude. "I promise to be a good boy and play nice with my sister."

Chapter 19

The week passed with Lydia and Sterling both going about their various tasks. Sterling kept his office hours and went on house calls. Lydia tended to her garden, which was sprouting lettuce, onions, potatoes, beets, peas, broccoli, cauliflower and cabbage. She also stitched together strips of the muslin that had wrapped her ribs so she could make a new camisole. She wore it when it was finished, noting that the fabric was so much thicker than in her old ones.

Monday, being washday, found Lydia out in the backyard hanging out the washed laundry. The day was warm and breezy. When she was done hanging it out, she hoed in the garden. As she worked she sang.

Praise him! Praise him! Jesus, our blessèd Redeemer!
Sing, O Earth, his wonderful love proclaim!
Hail him! Hail him! Highest archangels in glory;
Strength and honor give to his holy name!

Lydia hacked at the weed until she was able to get it out by its roots. "All right, you stubborn jimson weed, you're not going to get started in my garden."

Praise him! Praise him! Jesus, our blessèd Redeemer!
For our sins he suffered, and bled, and died.
He is our rock, our hope of eternal salvation,
Hail him! Hail him! Jesus the Crucified.

She looked down at the garden. "My, you peas are growing nicely. I can't wait to have you creamed with some new potatoes."

Sterling came out the back door just as she started the last verse.

Praise him! Praise him! Jesus, our blessèd Redeemer!
Heav'nly portals loud with hosannas ring!
Jesus, Savior, reigneth forever and ever.

With Lydia singing in the background Sterling looked at the laundry hanging on the line. One item caught his attention and he walked over to the clothesline. It was a camisole, and Sterling realized that Lydia must have pieced it together from the muslin wrap she'd used on her ribs.

He looked closer at Lydia's clothing hanging there. Her undergarments and nightgown were so thin he could see the shadows of what was behind them. Her work dress, the only one he'd seen other than the one she was wearing, was oddly pieced with extra fabric along the sides, at the waist and hem. The sleeves had long cuffs of frayed muslin. Only dimly aware of her continued singing, Sterling lifted one of her stockings, noting that there was only two pair. The one he held in his hand was worn, with evidence of being darned several times.

Sterling turned and looked at her working in the garden. Lydia had her back to him, and her song of praise continued as he walked toward her. He stopped at the edge of the walk. Knowing he would startle her, he cleared his throat.

She turned swiftly, as usual her eyes wide. "Hello, how does the garden look?"

Sterling looked it over carefully. "Any turnips?"

"No."

"Then it looks just fine."

Lydia smiled. "I can still put some in."

"Don't do it on my account, please," he said, stressing the last word. Lydia's smile spread wider.

Sterling looked carefully at her clothing, for the first time seeing it for what it was: fit for the ragbag. He was ashamed of himself. They had been married over a month. He'd seen her every day in the same garments and never once noticed how ragged they were. He realized that the only dress she had that was fit to wear was the one Ella had given her to wear at their wedding. She'd worn it every Sunday since.

"Are you about finished here?"

"I can be. Weeding is one of those things that never ends. Kind of like laundry. Each day brings more. Why?"

Sterling thought for a moment. He didn't want to embarrass her, but she really needed new clothes. "I thought we might go to the store and get fabric for the curtains for the clinic rooms, if you aren't too busy."

"Okay, but will you let me get the clothes off the line first?"

"Sure. I'll help." Sterling tried to think of a way to bring up her clothing needs as Lydia washed her hands at the pump. Going to the line and unpinning the dress, he asked, "This dress is seamed up oddly."

"Yes, I suppose so. I had to add the extra fabric when I ... developed." Lydia's face reddened.

"Why didn't you get a better-fitting dress instead?"

"Oh, Cyrus didn't want to spend the money when there was fabric at home. So I altered the dresses. There wasn't enough to make a new dress."

She spoke matter-of-factly while she unpinned and folded the items she took off the line. Sterling thought angry thoughts about the selfishness of a brother who wouldn't even buy fabric for a couple of dresses. Then he wondered if he were any better. He hadn't even noticed, for over a month, that his wife was dressed in rags.

Lydia picked up the basket of laundry and started to carry it to the house. Sterling took it from her. "I'll carry that. You go on and get cleaned up so we can get going. Let's have supper at the cafe, too. Give you a night off from cooking and dishes."

"You'll get no argument from me. I wouldn't want to tempt you to change your mind." She ran on ahead, stopped at the steps to remove her dirty work boots then went into the house.

Sterling followed more slowly, thinking. He looked carefully at her boots when he reached the porch. They, too, were well worn. The leather was cracked and the laces were knotted from fixing breaks in the strings. He wondered if they were her brother's hand-me-downs.

Sterling watched Lydia descend the stairs. He winced inwardly. She had a scarf over her hair. To him it looked like a dishtowel tied around her head. She didn't even have a decent hat; her bonnet had been ruined in the mud. He felt lower and lower, humiliated by his lack of care for her.

"Do you have a color in mind?" she asked as they walked outside.

"What?"

"For the curtains. Do you have an idea of what you want?"

"Um, not really. What do you think?"

"I'd say a dark color, green or maybe navy. What about a print or stripe?"

Sterling didn't answer, as he was lost in thought.

"Okay ... we'll just decide when we get there."

He heard her mutter but didn't reply.

As they walked, Lydia chattered, obviously enjoying the day. Sterling could hear her talking about seeing evidence of God's creation in the budding of the trees, bushes, spring flowers and birds singing. He made no comment and concentrated on his problem. He was not enjoying the walk. Instead he was trying to figure out how to ask Lydia's forgiveness for not being aware of her need for new clothes. He was not a person to miss details; doing so could cost a patient's life. How could he have missed the fact that his wife's clothes were little more than rags? For the entire time he'd known her he hadn't paid enough attention to notice.

Just before they reached the business district they came to a large cottonwood tree with a circular bench built around it. It was in a lot owned by the city in hopes of establishing a park, but so far the only thing was the bench around the tree.

"Come, let's sit there for a while. I want to talk with you about something."

Sterling took her hand and led her to the tree. Lydia frowned. Sterling, concentrating on his thoughts, didn't notice her worry. They sat, Lydia with her head down and her fingers fiddling with her skirt, and Sterling wanting to find the right words. Finally, he took a deep breath and started to speak.

"Lydia, I need to ask for your forgiveness."

Lydia looked up sharply.

Sterling continued without seeing her reaction. "I've failed you. I, who takes care of others so diligently, have failed to provide for you as you need and deserve. Please forgive me."

"I don't understand. You've provided for me so well. You took such good care of me while I was sick, having Mrs. H. come and tend me. The bathtub, which I love and still use, by the way. You moved me upstairs when you found out about that man. Having Matias and Nils do the heavy garden work. How can you say you've failed me?"

Sterling looked at her. She expected so little and was so appreciative. She didn't even realize he hadn't provided her with proper clothing. She was going with him today to pick out fabric for drapes in her ragged dress, worn-out undergarments and socks, and work boots with knotted laces. Yet she didn't ask for anything from him or even expect it. How long had it been since she'd had anything new, he wondered.

He took her hand. "All those things are true, but I failed you in a fundamental way. I've failed to provide you with a basic wardrobe. You come into this marriage with clothes so worn out and ragged, and I don't even notice. I only realized when I saw the new camisole you made from the discarded fabric used to wrap your ribs. I saw it on the line today and how much better it was than any of your other things. You shouldn't need to make clothing from discarded bandages. I should've bought you new clothing as soon as we were married."

Sterling looked at her in anguish. "We're going to get fabric for you to make new draperies for my patient rooms--you wear rags, and I ask you to make new drapes. You don't even ask for the basic things you need. That's how I've failed you."

Lydia stared at him, her mouth open. She was completely shocked that he thought he'd failed her. "You haven't failed me, but if you think you have I forgive you. Yes, I'd like new clothing, but it's not important. I have that nice dress Ella gave me for the wedding. I wear it on Sundays and the rest of the time it makes no difference. I'm so much better off with you than Cyrus, or Gus for that matter. Worn-out clothing is the least of my concerns."

She leaned over and kissed him softly on his cheek. "I'm so much happier here, with you, than I have been since my parents died. Clothes just aren't worth risking that happiness."

Though she had done her best to reassure him, he still felt sad that she thought asking for needed clothing would be a risk. Having one nice dress, even a secondhand, altered dress, was enough for her to not risk upsetting him with a request. He realized that she had never asked for anything but to postpone the wedding one day, and for seeds and starts for the garden. Those were not really for her; she would preserve the produce from them for winter. She had never asked for one material thing for herself. Right then, he decided that he'd make this a day to shower her with not only the things she needed but with things she didn't. Little luxuries she'd never had or thought to have.

"Come on," he said, jumping up, grabbing her hand and pulling her to her feet, "let's go do some shopping. I'll see that you have new clothes, unmentionables, shoes, all kinds of fripperies that you ladies like--a whole wardrobe. We'll buy the fabric for the drapes, too, but we'll concentrate on getting you outfitted from the skin out."

Lydia blushed red. "Really? You want to buy me clothes, lots of clothes?" She looked and sounded confused.

Sterling stopped in his headlong stride down the street. "How long has it been since you had something new?"

"Since before my parents died, I think."

"Then it's high time. Come on, don't drag your feet." He laughed and started off again, holding Lydia's hand so she had to rush to keep up.

"Let's get the drapery fabric picked out first and get that over with." Sterling said as they entered the store.

"Let me catch my breath first, Sterling. You have much longer legs than me. You do get excited over the strangest things."

"Oh, I'm sorry. Are you all right?"

"Yes," she said with a laugh.

They walked between the shelves filled with canned goods, all manner of kitchen equipment from spoons, to pots, to stoves. Around to the left at the end of the aisle they came to the fabric department.

"Okay now, what color and type of fabric do you want for the drapes?" Lydia glanced at Sterling, who looked a little lost as he scanned the bolts of fabric.

"Dark. Something dark."

Lydia chuckled. "Dark is not a color or type of fabric."

"Good afternoon, can I help you with some fabric?" Mabel approached with a smile.

"Hi, we're planning on putting some draperies in the patient rooms of the clinic. What do you think would work for that, Mrs. Johnson?" Lydia asked.

"Call me Mabel, dear. Here's some nice broadcloth which will wash up well. I don't think you'd want a velvet or brocade." She indicated the bolts of broadcloth.

"Yes, Mabel." Lydia smiled at the shopkeeper as she ran her hand over the fabric. "It will need to wash well as they'll be washed a lot. I think this will work. What do you think, Sterling?"

"Does it come in dark?"

Lydia and Mabel laughed.

"I told him dark was not a color," Lydia said. "Here's a nice navy, which would work for either a man or woman. I don't think brown would be very comforting, and red might be just too cheery. I don't see a green ... I think that would work."

"I sold the last of the right shade of green a couple of days ago," Mabel said, pulling the navy out from the stack.

"Is the navy okay with you, Sterling?" Lydia looked around and saw that he wasn't paying attention to them;

he was looking at a rack of ready-made dresses. "I guess this is okay. Don't you agree, Mabel?"

Mabel looked at Sterling and smiled. "Yes, I think you're right. It's just perfect."

Lydia and Mabel discussed the amount needed and Mabel went off to cut it. Lydia joined Sterling at the dress rack.

"This is pretty, don't you think?" Sterling asked, holding up a bright pink satin dress. The dress had puce ruffles starting at the shoulders and meeting at the waist, then spreading again into two columns as they went down the skirt and around the hem in deep flounces. The sleeves had multiple puffs from shoulder to wrist. A stiff puce ruffle collar and puce ruffle cuffs finished the garment.

"It is unique." Lydia's response was a trifle weak.

Sterling grinned at her. "So you want it?"

Lydia missed the mischief in his eyes as she continued to stare at the dress.

"Let's look at some others, shall we? There are a lot of other dresses."

Lydia looked at him when he burst out laughing. "My, you are diplomatic." Sterling's voice was low. "I think this is hideous, but don't tell Mabel. She picked it out for the store. You go right ahead and chose what you want. These are going to be your clothes so you should get what you like."

"You have to look at me wearing them. I'd like your opinion."

"How about I let you know if I really like something or really don't? Is that okay?"

Lydia smiled impishly. "Only if you'll be truthful and not tease about ugly dresses."

"You wound me, wife. Here I pick out a dress and then you accuse me of not being in earnest."

Lydia looked at him with an attempt at a stern expression, but her lips twitched. She started looking over the garments on the rack.

"Hello, I thought I heard voices I knew." Ella approached with a smile.

"Hi, Ella. Lydia's just picking out some new clothes," Sterling said.

"Hi, Ella, where are the children?" Lydia inquired, looking around for them.

"Rye is in school and I left Janie with Peter. I actually want to get some shopping done. When she's with me she tends to get the 'I wants', so coming without her makes it easier and more enjoyable."

"I could use your help in picking out a couple of formal outfits, Ella. We're replacing some of my things, and Sterling here," she said with a wicked grin, "is not being much help."

"You wound me again." Sterling put his hand to his chest and staggered around a bit.

"If you can't help," Ella said to Sterling, "go do something somewhere else. Go talk to Hal or something."

"Well, then, I can certainly see that I'm not needed or wanted here."

Lydia stifled a giggle as Sterling strutted away like a woman with wounded dignity.

Chapter 20

"Oh my, is that a sight," Ella said. "A good one, really. I haven't seen Sterling in such a teasing mood in a long time. So you're getting along well? We haven't had much of a chance to really talk privately. How are you two doing?" Ella asked softly.

They looked through the dresses on the rack as Lydia answered. "We're doing well. We have our rough spots but for the most part we're getting along. We really haven't had many issues come up. Today though ..." Lydia looked thoughtful.

"What?" Ella inquired softly.

"Sterling was upset that he hadn't noticed that my clothes were very worn. He realized today, and so here we are. He was very upset with himself about it. He wanted us to have a good time picking out new things for me. Now we chased him away."

"I'm sorry. I would never have sent him away if I'd known. Shall I go and bring him back?"

"Not yet, I think." Lydia smiled. "He really wasn't being much help. Look what he picked out." She held up the pink dress.

"I see what you mean," Ella said as she looked at the outfit. "Let's see, here's one in a nice soft green which would look great with your hair."

The ensemble was light-green wool trimmed in lace at the neckline and bell cuffs, as well as the scalloped hems of the jacket and overskirt. The white buttons and underskirt gathers completed the look. Lydia thought it was the most beautiful outfit she'd ever seen--until she saw the next one Ella held up.

"Oh ..." She reached out to touch the fabric, her hand shaking slightly. "Oh, I don't think so. It must be terribly expensive."

Ella found the price tag. "Not overly. I'm a little surprised."

In sapphire-blue taffeta with puff sleeves, long cuffs and a nipped-in waist, the jacket was buttoned with knots made from the fabric. The skirt was decorated with box pleats at the hem.

"It's so very beautiful." Tearing her eyes away from the garment, Lydia looked at Ella. "Do you think it's too much?"

Ella showed her the price tag. "See? Besides, both of these will work for most of the year. You'll have three outfits for church and other formal occasions, including your wedding dress."

"You're right. I'll get these and make most of my day dresses and other things. The money I save by sewing will make up for the expense of these."

They carried the outfits with them as they went to find Sterling, who was in the shoe area.

"Sterling, we found two outfits suitable for church," Lydia said. "I can get fabric for the others that I need for everyday wear. These are nicer but cost more." Lydia smiled a teasing smile, causing her eyes to twinkle. "We'll let you try and help us pick out the fabrics."

"All right, but first sit down here and try on these shoes." He barely looked at the outfits, so intent was he on his own task.

Lydia sat and Sterling turned to a pile of shoes he'd picked out. Untying her boots, he pulled them off and chucked them over his shoulder.

"You will not be wearing these home. They will not be coming home. Here, give me your foot." Lydia held out her right foot and Sterling put on a black high-button shoe, using a buttonhook to work the twelve buttons into the holes. Along the buttonholes the leather was scalloped, decorating the shoe in a pleasing way.

"Does it fit?" Sterling asked.

"Wonderfully, I've never had a shoe so nice" Lydia was a little in awe of the quality of the shoe. "It surely is too expensive."

"Don't worry about the cost today. In the future I'll nag you endlessly about how much everything costs, but today you get the best." The twinkle in Sterling's eyes belied his words, reassuring Lydia when she looked up at him with doubt.

Ella laughed. "We'll certainly take you up on getting the best for her."

Lydia was still a little concerned over the cost of the outfits she had picked out, and what the shoes must cost. "We'll be careful and not go overboard, Sterling," she said quickly, "I don't want to waste your money on extravagances."

"Lydia, don't worry. I know you're not a person who cares much for fancy things. It's part of why we're here doing this today. You didn't consider your worn clothing as something important enough to mention. I'm just sorry I didn't notice it before." Sterling spoke in a soft but serious tone. Then his smile came back. "And just to show you that I'm being practical, too ..." He held up a work boot in brown leather with sturdy laces.

Lydia and Ella laughed. Lydia held out her left foot, allowing Sterling to put the work boot on it. After he'd laced it up, she held up both feet. They all laughed at the sight of a dress shoe and a work boot worn together. Sterling had also picked out a pair of soft brown slip-ons so she wouldn't have to wear the work boots in the house and around town.

The shoes chosen, Sterling took them to the counter along with the outfits Lydia and Ella had picked out. Telling them he would look around for other gewgaws ladies seem to like and that they should do the more serious shopping, he disappeared around the end of the aisle. Lydia and Ella went to pick out fabrics for day dresses, skirts and shirtwaists. Lydia also picked out fabric for two aprons as well as muslin for undergarments and nightgowns. Mabel joined them in this and the three ladies spent the time in friendly camaraderie.

"Are you planning on making all the rest of your clothes?" Ella asked, seeing the amount of fabric choices Lydia had made.

"I will make most, since I like to sew, and it'll save money. Also, I don't have the chores I had at home so I have more time. Sewing will be productive use of that time until the canning and preserving start."

"We'll have to get together to sew. I make many of the children's clothes as well as my own and some of Peter's. I have patterns, which you might not, that I'll let you use."

Lydia, not mentioning that she didn't have any patterns, said, "I'd like to get together to sew, and I'd be pleased to use some of your patterns, but I'll also get some of my own today."

They went to pick out ready-made day dresses. Lydia chose one dress of a dark red calico, a brown skirt and white shirtwaist. A brown pelisse, which went well with both the dress and skirt, was added to the growing pile.

Next, they picked out ready-made undergarments, stockings, a nightgown and robe. A straw hat, which could be decorated with colored ribbons, was considered seriously by the women and chosen. Taking what they had picked out to the counter, they went looking for Sterling. They found him by the brushes and combs, and he smiled as they approached.

"Get all the dresses and fabrics you want?"

"Yes, I decided on a day dress, and one skirt and shirtwaist. I'll make the others I need so we picked fabrics for them. I also chose some undergarments, stockings, and a nightgown and robe. Thank you."

"You're more than welcome. We should have done this long ago. Here, would you like a new brush and comb set? They have nice ones to choose from."

"No thank you, I have those already and they're fine. I could use some hairpins, though." Lydia picked up a box, knowing she really did need them. She'd been very careful not to lose any since she barely had enough to hold her hair in place. "I think what we've chosen now is enough. Besides, I'm getting hungry, and you promised we could eat in the cafe tonight."

"Such a demanding wife, I have. Don't you agree, Ella?" Sterling teased.

Ella laughed. "Don't get me into the middle of this. You two fight it out yourselves. I need to get to my own shopping."

"I hope I didn't keep you too long, Ella," Lydia said.

"Of course not, I enjoyed every minute. Not often do I get to spend someone else's money. Now you come and help me pick out some fabric for new britches for Rye."

Lydia laughed. "Back to the fabric department we go."

"I'll go pay for the items you've chosen. Give me the hairpins," Sterling said.

Lydia and Ella headed back to the fabrics, not noticing the other items Sterling picked up.

Dressed in her new shirtwaist, skirt and hightop shoes, Lydia stepped out of the back room where she'd gone to change. Sterling thought her smile even prettier than her new clothes.

"You have a lovely wife, Sterling." Ella's comment echoed his own thoughts.

"You're right." Sterling watched Lydia turning slowly before them to show them the entire view.

"Come, Ella, walk us to the cafe," Lydia said, joining them, and giving Hal and Mabel a delighted wave.

They left the store with Sterling carrying their bundle of purchases.

"Tell Peter I'll stop by tomorrow, I'd like to catch up with him," Sterling said to Ella when they reached the cafe.

"I will. I think he'll be in his office all day. Unless something comes up, of course. You have that, too, don't you?"

"Comes with the territory for both of us. Tell him it'll most likely be in the afternoon since I have house calls in the morning."

"Will do. Have a nice supper. Thanks for letting me shop with you, it was fun." After giving Lydia a quick hug, Ella headed home.

They entered the cafe and chose a table, Sterling holding the chair for Lydia. He sat down across the table and watched her place the napkin on her lap. The sunshine coming through the window behind her turned her chestnut hair into a glowing halo around her face.

"Did you have a good time getting the new clothes and fabrics?"

"Oh, yes." Her face shone with delight. "It was something I'll always remember. I've never had so many clothes, especially ready-made ones, in my life. Thank you. I can't say how much I appreciate what you did for me today. It was too much, really. I'd have been pleased with just fabric for the things I needed."

"I know, which is what made it more fun, even for me. Your delight at even the everyday things like stockings and work boots ... you expect so little and you're grateful for even the least thing. It humbles me. Again, I'm sorry not to have noticed."

"Please don't mention it again. I've forgiven you. Now it's time to forget it."

"Okay. So what are you going to have for supper?"

During supper Lydia told him about the curtains she'd make for the patient rooms, then about the clothes she would make for herself. Sterling listened, appreciating how much she knew about sewing, and her willingness to save money by doing so. When he commented on it she looked at him quizzically.

"I wouldn't know how to live any other way. We always made almost all of our clothing. Didn't your mother?"

"I think so, especially when I was young. Maybe she stopped as I grew up but ... she made most of the cushions on the settees. Some sort of sewing, I don't know what it's called."

"Needlepoint," Lydia said with a smile.

"Well, look who we have here, the doctor and his new wife out on the town. And don't you just look real spiffy now, Mrs. Graham."

Sterling stood, looking at the face of Clem Baumgarden. Beside him, Harriet Baumgarden managed to look down her nose at Lydia.

"Good evening, Clem, Harriet," Sterling said graciously, ignoring the tone and intent of the words. "This evening finds you well, I see."

"Yes, Doc. We're both doing well, so we decided to enjoy a meal out tonight," Harriet said in her grating voice while she looked Lydia over.

Lydia kept her eyes on her plate, her fingers making circles on the red-and-white checkered tablecloth.

Sterling noticed, and he didn't like the effect the Baumgardens were having on his wife.

"Well, we won't keep you from it," he said, hoping to encourage them to leave. It didn't work.

"Lydia," Harriet said, "I see you have new clothes. I'd noticed your other ones were rather worn. I'm glad you finally decided some new ones were in order. It wouldn't do for the wife of one of the leading citizens of Cottonwood to be dressed like an orphan."

"Yeap, girly, you sure do look mighty good. Bet that's given you ideas, huh, Doc." Clem laughed, poking Sterling with his elbow.

Sterling was not impressed with the man's attempt at humor.

"Thank you," Lydia murmured, not looking up from her plate.

Sterling hated seeing her like that. She hadn't kept her face down for a long time. He felt as if all the progress he'd made in helping her relax and accept herself was being destroyed.

"I have a table for you now," Sally said loudly as she came up to the table. "Come on with me and I'll seat you. The specials for tonight ..." Sally kept talking as she led them away.

"Lydia, are you all right?" Sterling said.

"Yes," she replied softly, her eyes still on her plate, her hands in her lap.

He picked up one of her hands. "Please don't let a couple of old gossips ruin our day. We've had such a nice time this afternoon. I enjoyed it so much, and I know you did too."

"I won't." Lydia finally raised her eyes to his. "They just bring back some uncomfortable memories. I know I need to ignore them, but it's hard. They remind me of ..." Her voice trailed off and her eyes flooded. She blinked away the threatening tears. "You're right. They can't ruin the day unless I let them. So, do you want dessert here or at home?"

"I don't know yet. What do you have at home? They have apple pie and chocolate cake here." He smiled as he said it.

"I have oatmeal cake and sugar cookies." She smiled back.

Sally approached, saying, "I'm sorry about that. I didn't have a table when they came in, and they wouldn't wait at the entry when they saw you."

"It's okay, Sally." Lydia said softly. "I know what they're like, so don't give it another thought. Sterling's trying to decide between your dessert offerings and mine at home."

"Oh Lydia," Sterling moaned, "you put me in a terrible position. If I choose dessert here, I'm in the doghouse with you, and if I choose to have it at home I'm in trouble with Sally. Wait, I have the perfect solution." Sterling's face lit up like a boy lighting fireworks. "I'll have some here and some at home. The pie please, Sally. I'll have the cake at home."

"Oh you, that's not what I had in mind. I was thinking either here or at home."

"I know." Sterling grinned.

Sally shook her head as she went away smiling to get his pie.

"Only cookies for you, and only a couple at that." Lydia's voice held a teasing, scolding tone as she brought the cookie jar to the table. They'd arrived at home and were in the kitchen.

Sterling was digging in the parcel he'd unwrapped. "Ah ha, found it," he said as he pulled a small item wrapped in brown paper from the clothing and fabrics. He held it out to Lydia. "Here, for you."

"What's this?" She took it and looked questioningly at him.

"Just a special little something I got for you today. Open it."

Lydia's eyes lit up. "Oh Sterling," she said, "you didn't need to get me anything else. We bought way too much today as it is."

"This isn't something you need. It's just, well, something pretty I thought you'd like. Open it."

Lydia slowly untied the string and folded back the paper. "Oh Sterling," she said slowly as she picked up the ivory comb, "it's beautiful."

The comb was decorated with swirled carving. As she turned it over she saw that the carving continued onto the other side. The three tines, though not carved, were curved in soft 's' shapes. "I've never seen anything like it, let alone touched or owned one. Thank you."

Running her fingers over the comb, Lydia went to the back hallway to look into the small mirror, with Sterling following. "I know this isn't how my hair should be when I wear it, but I had to look."

"You look beautiful." Sterling wasn't looking at the comb, but at her profile as she looked at herself in the mirror. "But there's another gift in the package. Come open it."

Lydia went back to the table and lifted a soft wool shawl from the paper. Navy blue with ivy vines and small white flowers embroidered on it.

"Oh, Sterling," she said, and then laughed. "I keep saying that, don't I? But really, you shouldn't have. It's so very nice and so very generous."

"Just don't expect to get things like this every time you go shopping." Sterling laughed too, but stopped when he saw Lydia's distressed face. "No you don't, young lady. I'm teasing you so don't take my words to heart. I know you'll never be one who spends too much. You're much too sensible for that. Besides, it's clear you don't really care much about material things."

"You're right. I will just say, thank you." He was surprised when she lifted up on her tiptoes and gave him a kiss on the cheek. "I'm heading out back for a moment. Only a couple of cookies for you, hear me?"

With that she left Sterling a little stunned, with a certain spot on his cheek tingling.

Chapter 21

The next day Sterling, after making his house calls, walked slowly down the street thinking. He was still bothered by his lack of awareness of Lydia's wardrobe needs. He knew he was a caring person--at least he thought he was--but this had caused him to doubt. He walked up the sidewalk to Peter and Ella's house.

Rye and Janie burst out the front door.

"Hi, Uncle Doc," they shouted in unison.

"Mama just baked cookies, snuggledoos, want some, they're real good, me and Rye had some and it's before lunch too, Mama usually doesn't let us eat cookies before lunch but she did today," Janie said.

"Yeah. She wanted Janie to be quiet so she let us have some," Rye said with a sly look at his sister.

"She did not!"

"Did too."

"Did not."

"Did too."

"Did not."

"That's enough. No matter the reason, just be glad you got the cookies," Sterling said, putting the end to the bickering. "What kind of cookies were they?"

"Snuggledoos," Janie said.

"Snickerdoodles." Rye corrected.

"Oh yeah. I can't ever memember that."

"It's remember, not memember," Rye said in disgust.

"Well, I'll remember to ask for more snuggledoos after lunch," Janie said, putting her nose in the air.

Rye just looked at Sterling and shook his head slowly, as if to say it's no use.

Sterling grinned at the duo. "Is your father here?"

"Yeah, in his office," Rye said.

Janie had leapt off the steps and was looking at a tulip blooming by the porch.

Sterling, sure of his welcome, opened the front door and called, "Ella?"

A return call came from the direction of the kitchen and he walked down the hall toward the kitchen, meeting Ella on the way, as the office door opened and Peter stepped out.

"Hey, friend, what brings you here? I don't see you much other than at church." Peter gave Ella a hug as he spoke. "Your wife keeping you on a short rope?"

"Don't tease him, Peter, he's still a newlywed," Ella scolded.

Sterling, a little nervous from their comments, tried to grin but felt he failed in the try. "I came to catch up with my best friend. If he has time, that is."

"Sure, any time. Come on into the office. Ella, would you please bring in some of those cookies I smell?"

"Of course. Sterling, do you want coffee, too?"

"No coffee for me," Sterling said. "One question. Are they snuggledoos, snickerdoodles or snuggledoodles?"

"What?" Ella asked, looking confused.

"The children called them by all three names. I was just wondering which was right."

"Snickerdoodles," Ella said with a laugh. "Janie can never get it right. A plate of snickerdoodles coming right up."

When the men were settled in the chairs in front of the desk Peter looked at Sterling and said, "This isn't just you catching up with a friend, but you coming to your pastor, isn't it?"

"You're right. I've discovered something I don't like about myself and want some advice."

Peter leaned back in his chair, waiting for Sterling to continue.

Sterling sat silently looking out the window for a few moments. "Am I a caring person, Peter? Do I really care about others?"

Peter looked at him. "Why do you ask?"

"I've been married, what, about a month now? How could I possibly have missed that Lydia's clothes were worse than rags? I didn't notice she needed clothes until I saw that she'd made a new chemise out of the bandaging we'd used to wrap her ribs. I'm a doctor, for heaven's sake. If I don't notice symptoms, the little things that most people miss, people can die. Yet, for a month I never notice that my wife wears clothing I wouldn't even keep for rags to wipe the floors. I asked her to make drapes for my patient rooms and she agreed, never mentioning that she needed clothes. She'd have made new drapes, never saying anything, and continued wearing those worn-out clothes for who knows how long."

Sterling ran his fingers through his hair. "You've preached and preached on this very issue. I was so sure that I had this down pat. Now I see that I don't."

Peter sat quietly, thinking and letting Sterling calm himself. He also knew the silence would encourage Sterling to reveal whether he'd figured out the real issue.

"Oh," Sterling put his head in his hands, "it's pride. It's that old sin of pride. I was proud of my ability to notice the small details of illness and I let that pride spill out of my medical practice and into the rest of my life."

"How do you make sure you notice the details in your dealings with patients?" Peter asked.

"There's a sort of checklist I run through in my head: color, fever, breathing, pulse, and so on. It goes on from there. You get the picture, I'm sure."

"Yes, I do. How do you notice details in non-medical areas?"

"Notice details? Hmm. Well, since Lydia's been here I notice that I always have clean clothes in the drawer. The house is clean and neat. The food she makes is great, and she always has dessert and cookies." Sterling smiled. "My office never needs picked up. I guess she does that, too. The garden is well kept."

"Do you notice anything different about the things you mentioned? The focus of your work is on the patient. Where is the focus outside of the office?" Peter watched as Sterling thought for a moment.

"I'm not sure I know what the difference is. Do you?"

"You notice the services done for you--clean clothes, clean house, clean office, good food, desserts and cookies, the garden, which will supply you with food ... Is there anything you notice about Lydia? Her character, her interests, her likes and dislikes?"

Sterling looked dumbstruck. "What a horrid husband I am, so centered on my own comfort. What kind of a husband or friend can I be when I only care about my wants?"

"Now don't go overboard." Peter held up a hand. "Are you the worst, most selfish person ever? No. Do you have areas in your life that need to change? Yes, just like the rest of us. That you've noticed and feel remorse for it means you're listening to the Holy Spirit about what flaw in your character you're to be working on. Many people never even admit they've sinned, let alone be remorseful of it. Beating yourself up about what a horrible person you are ... God already knows that. Now, since you know better, do better."

Peter paused, then continued. "First, of course, is confession and asking for forgiveness. After that, let's figure out what you can do to change and notice the details of other people's lives, especially Lydia's."

They spent the next few minutes in prayer, with Sterling pouring his heart out to his God. When they finished, Peter helped determine how Sterling could notice details in the lives of others, starting with Lydia. They wrote down a list of things that Sterling should find out about Lydia.

At the top of the page Peter wrote out Philippians 2:3–4: Doing nothing through rivalry or through conceit, but in humility, each counting others better than himself; each of you not just looking to his own things, but each of you also to the things of others.

"Now, Sterling, I recommend that you go confess to Lydia, and ask her forgiveness. She's who you've sinned against."

"I know," Sterling said. "The difficulty is that she'll just say that I've been so nice to her since she came, and that she's so grateful to me. It's hard to make her see. I had trouble with that yesterday. She just doesn't expect anything; she only hopes she isn't scolded or beaten. That probably made it easier for me to just ignore her needs. Not that it's any excuse. I'll speak to her, but she'll probably brush it off."

"How she reacts isn't your concern. You need to do it because Jesus says to go and leave your offering at the altar, and make it right with your brother, or in this case, your wife."

"I know, and I will. Thanks, Peter. I appreciate your counsel and your friendship."

They stood, heading to the office door.

"Well, I've known you since you were about three. If I haven't given up on you before, I don't see any reason to give up on you now." Peter slapped Sterling on the back, a little harder than necessary, but with a wide smile.

Chapter 22

Lydia stood with Sterling in the churchyard after Sunday worship service. People milled around, greeting each other. Children yelled and chased one another, enjoying the freedom after sitting still and quiet for so long.

"Mighty hot for the first week in May," Ben Phelps said as he came up to speak with Sterling. "Hi, ma'am. You look mighty pretty today."

"Thank you, Ben." Lydia was wearing her green outfit and the straw hat dressed up with a matching ribbon.

"Hi, Ben," Sterling said. "Have you started planting yet?"

"Not yet. Plan to tomorrow, but may have to wait if this heat brings a storm."

Lydia, who had been watching the children run around, looked quickly at Ben. "So you think it might rain?"

"Lots of times, when it's this hot this early it brings on a storm. Might be raining tonight. If it doesn't, I'll start planting the corn tomorrow."

Ben and Sterling continued to discuss the weather and planting season but Lydia's thoughts stayed on the possibility of a storm. She stood not hearing the conversation going on between her husband and Ben, remembering the time Cyrus had made her stay outside during a storm. He'd tied her to a tree near the barn, but not close enough for her to take shelter inside. She'd crouched down as far from the trunk of the tree as the rope would let her, knowing that the tree could attract lightning. She was still able to feel the terror and the tears, as well as the rain, streaming down her face. Her hands clinched on her reticule and she tried, with little success, to soften her grip.

A small hand slid along her forearm to her hand and Lydia was finally able to loosen the grip on the bag. Looking down, she saw Janie holding her hand.

"Hi, sweetie. You're not playing with the other children?"

"No, I wanted to be with you. We haven't done anything together since Rye had his cushion. Can we do something sometime?"

"Of course. Let me think. How about you come over next Saturday and we'll bake cookies? I'll speak to your mother about it. How does that sound?"

"Wonderful. What kind will we make? I like most kinds except molasses cookies, yuck. I like sugar cookies best, and after that snuggledoos."

"Hey, peanut, that's snickerdoodles," Sterling interjected with a smile, touching his finger to her nose. Ben had gone off with his family.

"I'll ask your mother," Lydia said.

"Ask me what?" Ella asked as she approached them.

"About snickledoos," said Janie. "I'm going to go to Mrs. Doc's on Saturday and make cookies. Maybe sugar or snickledoos."

"I was going to ask you if it was okay," Lydia said quickly, slightly nervous that Ella would think she was pushy.

"I think that'll be fun for both of you. What time do you want her to come over?"

They made arrangements for the cookie-making event. Peter joined them when he was done greeting his parishioners. They decided they would pool their Sunday dinners, and invited Drew and Mrs. H. to join them at the Grahams'.

"That was a fun afternoon," Sterling said after everyone had left. He picked up a couple of glasses, following Lydia into the kitchen.

"It was. We should do this sort of thing more often. Shall we plan to do it again, maybe inviting other couples or families?"

"Sure, not every week though. We all need a day of rest. I don't want you to overextend yourself." He picked up a towel and began drying the dishes Lydia was washing.

"You don't need to do this. I can do it."

"I know you can, but can't I help sometimes?"

"Well, yes, I guess so. I just don't know why you'd want to."

"You've helped me sometimes, so I thought I'd return the favor."

"Okay, I guess." Lydia was obviously confused and unsure, but Sterling just smiled and reached for another plate.

Lydia woke suddenly. Thunder crashed. She listened for a few minutes. It was coming closer. The storm Ben had predicted was making itself known. Lightning lit the room for a split second. Her eyes widened, her face filled with fear and she clutched the blanket. She didn't see the bedroom she was in. In her mind she saw Cyrus, angry at a thirteen year old who had burned dinner.

You stupid clumsy girl, can't you do anything right? Frying potatoes are easy and yet you let them burn. I'll see that you remember not to burn them again.

Lydia relived the struggle with Cyrus at he pulled her outside and tied her to the tree.

A night out here should help you not burn anything again.

She closed her eyes, blocking out the vision. The thunder made her jump. She slid down further into the bed, pulling the covers over her head.

"Please, Lord, please. Make it stop," she murmured between sobs of fear.

Sterling stood at his window watching the storm's approach. He'd always enjoyed storms. The power, the force of the wind, the lightning streaking its way from the clouds to the ground. The lightning and thunder came closer together, indicating the approach of the storm. The wind began picking up. Then he heard running feet coming down the hall. He turned his head as his door opened and a figure clad in a white gown flew through the door. Lydia leaped onto the bed and under the covers, pulling them over her head.

"Lydia," Sterling said softly, "are you all right?"

"Uh-huh." The sound was muffled as it came from beneath the covers.

"Are you sure?" Sterling sat on the bed.

"I'm fine." Lightning flashed, with only a small pause before the thunder sounded. Lydia visibly started.

Sterling slowly lifted the covers, sliding gently into the bed. Lydia grabbed him and buried her head against his chest. With each flash and crash, she jerked, holding Sterling tighter. He put his arms around her and pulled her firmly against him.

"So you're scared of storms. It's fine. You just hold me as tightly as you want. It'll be over soon." He continued whispering comforting words as the storm arrived and until, finally, it faded into the distance.

Sterling enjoyed the feel of her in his arms, hoping she'd stay. He listened closely to her breathing, wanting to be aware if she spoke. He noticed when her breathing evened out and her body relaxed into sleep. He kissed the top of her head softly then lay looking up at the ceiling with a wide grin on his face.

When he awoke in the morning she was gone.

"Good morning," Sterling said as he came into the kitchen. He'd spent the time he was shaving thinking about how to greet her this morning. He knew she'd be nervous and embarrassed. He didn't want to upset her and make her uncomfortable about what had happened last night. He didn't want to make it harder for her to-- eventually--join him permanently in his bed.

"Good morning," Lydia didn't look up from her concentration on her cooking.

Sterling approached and assessed what was she was fixing and whether it would burn if he interrupted her for a moment. Deciding that the bacon could cook without her attention for a couple of minutes, he took the tongs from her hand, set them down and turned her to face him. He lifted her chin.

"It's okay. I'm sorry I didn't know you were afraid of storms, but I'm glad you felt comfortable enough to come to me. It made me feel very much a husband protecting and comforting my wife. Thank you." He looked directly into her eyes while he spoke and then smiled. She smiled back, looking into his eyes. He saw her embarrassment fade.

"You're welcome. Now get out of my way so I can finish your breakfast," she said, shooing him in a teasing way.

Sterling laughed and did as he was told.

Chapter 23

"Hey, Drew." Sterling waved his Stetson at the sheriff across the street.

"Hi, I'm just heading to the office for a cup of coffee. Want to join me?" Drew called back.

"Sure." Sterling cut diagonally across the street, dodging the evidence that horses had passed that way.

"Here you go." Drew handed Sterling a cup and sat down at his desk across from his friend. Putting his feet up on desk and leaning back in his chair, he blew on his coffee.

"Good coffee. I didn't think you had it in you," teased Sterling after sipping the hot brew. He'd laid his hat on the desk that was covered with paperwork. Loosening his tie, he leaned back in the chair and enjoyed the break in the day.

"I have talents you don't know about and wouldn't believe if you did. So how is married life treating you?"

"It's pretty good. We're getting to know one another and being more at ease. Lydia is still pretty insecure and can be afraid I'll get mad at little mistakes, or even things that aren't mistakes but she thinks are. The other day I came home a little earlier than usual and I could tell she was upset that she didn't have any coffee ready. To me it's no big deal but I could see she was afraid I'd be mad."

"It'll most likely take a long time for her to get over that."

"I know. Anyway, married life is pretty good. The meals are much better and the house is neater. It's nice to have someone there when you come home. Nice to have company in the evening. Having someone to discuss Scripture with makes devotions richer, too. You should try it sometime," Sterling ended with a grin.

"Haven't met the right girl yet. When I do it won't take me long to escort her to the preacher."

Both men laughed. Sterling told Drew about his sister and her family coming for the holiday, enlisting Drew's promise to join in the events planned for the week.

"Lydia must have a lot of work getting ready for them."

"She's pretty nervous about it. She hasn't ever hosted any kind of party, other than our Sunday gatherings, let alone had to deal with house guests. Preach and Ella are going to help. Ella will, especially, with the preparations, the cooking, cleaning and such. I hired the Jorgensen boys to do the yard work, clearing out the leaves from under the porch and such. Lydia doesn't need to be crawling around on the ground doing that sort of thing. She'd do it without complaint, but I don't want her to. Besides, they can use the money. I know it's hard for them with no mother and Johann with his bad leg."

"Yeah, I hire them to clean up here and do small repairs. They're good kids."

"You could help me with something, my good friend and lifelong buddy."

"Oh boy, now it comes, the real reason for your visit. Not just a friend wanting to catch up with me but wanting a favor. I see how I rate. So what do I have to do for you?"

"Nothing too tough. Help me clean up and repair my porch furniture and the lawn swing."

"You still have that old swing? I thought it must've bitten the dust years ago."

"It can use some repair and maybe ... probably ... definitely ... a coat of paint, but it should still useable."

"When do you want to do this repairing of ancient furniture?"

"How about tomorrow? I know Lydia's planning to have roast beef for supper because I bought the roast yesterday. You can have a good home-cooked meal as payment. I'll ask Lydia to make a lemon meringue pie. Hers are the best I've ever tasted. Makes my mouth water just thinking about it."

"Okay. What time do you want to start the work?"

"Oh, about two I think. I can be done with my house calls by then. We should be able to finish by supper."

"If not, I get another meal when we do finish."

"Deal. Well, I'd better go and let my wife know we're having company for supper tomorrow, don't you think?"

"Yeah." Drew pulled his feet off the desk, stood up and tossed Sterling's hat to him. "Get outta here. I've got work to do. See you tomorrow."

"You two are certainly doing a good job," Lydia said as she came onto the porch carrying a tray with a pitcher of lemonade, glasses and a plate of cookies. She was dressed in a light-blue, flowered day dress; her hair was down, pulled back with a white ribbon.

The men set aside their tools, abandoning the work for the refreshments. They were working in the yard beside the house, the sun shining on their work area. Green leaves covering the maple tree and peonies sprouting along the porch gave evidence of the warm spring weather.

"Ah, ma'am, it ain't too tough fixing up that there furniture. Nothing that we big, strong, tough menfolk cain't handle." Drew stuck his thumbs in the belt loops of his canvas work pants and swaggered up the steps of the porch.

"Well, sirrah, I can certainly see that ya'll are big, strong, and tough." Lydia went along with the fun, speaking in an exaggerated southern drawl. "But," she paused for emphasis, "are you smarter than the tools, nails, and paint?"

"Sterling, you have yourself a mighty witty wife. I just hope she cooks as well as she insults."

Laughing, Sterling, in paint-spattered overalls, carried a small table onto the porch and Lydia set down the tray.

"We'll have to sit on the steps. The chairs aren't dry yet," Sterling said. "Do you like the color?"

Lydia and Sterling sat beside each other on the porch steps, with Drew sprawled out on the grass in front of them.

"They're white. Just like they were before." Lydia looked a little confused.

"Yes, they are. I didn't say the color was different, just if you liked the color."

"Funny, Sterling, very funny. You know, Drew, it's hard having a husband who thinks he's funny."

Drew laughed, Sterling groaned and Lydia poured the lemonade into glasses.

"Sterling," Drew said after he'd taken a long drink and eaten an oatmeal raisin cookie, "I really don't think that swing is fixable."

Sterling looked at the crumpled structure sitting in the grass. It was missing several boards, with others cracked or broken. Part of the frame was splintered.

"You're right. I didn't realize it was in such rough shape. I think it might be kindling. Lydia, what do you say we see if we can get a new one by the end of the month?"

"It's up to you, but how do you get a new one? They don't have them at Johnson's."

"I'll see if Johann Jorgensen will build it for us. He's pretty good at doing odd jobs and small carpentry."

"Okay." Lydia said hesitantly. She didn't have a good idea what a lawn swing looked like.

A knock came on the front door two mornings later. Lydia descended the stairs wondering if someone needed Sterling, hating to have to say he was out. She opened the door to a man with a well-trimmed beard, bib overalls that had seen many washings, and a beat-up, short-brimmed hat.

"Gute morning, Mrs. Doc. I'm Johann Jorgensen. Your husband asked me to come and build a lawn swing for you." He spoke with a thick Norwegian accent. "He said you would let me know what you wanted."

"Good morning, it's nice to meet you. Come in and we can discuss it over coffee." Lydia wondered what Sterling thought she knew about lawn swings. She couldn't remember having ever seen one, and the one she'd seen the other day had been little more than a pile of wood. She noticed as he entered that Johann had a severe limp in his left leg.

"Tack," he said, thanking her in Norwegian.

They went to the kitchen where Lydia poured coffee and laid out a plate of nut bread and butter.

Johann buttered a piece liberally, took a bite and smiled. "Um, yust as good as my Helena's. It's gute to remember. She was my wife. Died nearly six years ago. I miss her every day. Tack for the good bread."

"You're welcome." Lydia was taken with this man who still cherished his wife even after such a long time.

"Now," Johann said after washing the bread down with a swig of coffee, "what sort of lawn swing are you looking for me to build?"

"I really don't know. How are they different?"

"Well, you can have a single swing, or a double swing with the seats facing each other. It can be wide enough for one or two. It can have a roof or not. Can have ropes or wood as the swingers."

"So many choices." Lydia was a little distressed at having so many things to decide and not knowing what Sterling wanted. "Did ... did Sterling say how he wanted it made?"

"Yust said to ask you, and to have it done by Decoration Day."

"Oh," Lydia was at a loss. "What types have you built before?"

"All of the ones I mentioned. I will tell you that wooden swingers last longer than rope ones. Other than that, the choice is yust your preference."

Lydia hesitated and then decided she'd simply choose what she wanted. It could always be changed if Sterling had a different preference. "We have a two-person hanging swing on the porch, so how about a double for the lawn?"

Johann grinned. "Good idea. Now, one or two people wide?"

"Two, I think. Two people can swing across from each other, or two couples or several children."

"Ya. What color do you want it painted?"

"How about yellow and dark green to match the house. The other furniture is white so that would be pretty, don't you think? Oh, do you have those colors of paint?" Lydia added as an afterthought.

"Not to worry. Doc said to make it as you want it. I'll get it if I need it, but I usually have those colors."

"Wonderful. I think it'll be nice to add the colors." Lydia was enjoying the sensation of planning the details of the swing. She'd never done anything like this before and marveled that Sterling trusted her so. She hoped the colors would be all right with him.

She held the bread plate out to Johann, who gladly took another piece. Thickly buttered, he was savoring each bite when she said, "Mr. Jorgensen, I want to tell you how much I like your boys. They're delightful to have around and very good workers."

"Please, call me Johann. Tack. They are good boys. Their mama did a good job raising them. It's been hard with her gone. I'll yust be going now and build that swing. I can build it today and paint it tomorrow."

"So fast?"

"Ya. I'll bring it by this afternoon so you can see it before I paint it."

Lydia was sitting in the porch swing sewing when Sterling came up the walk.

"Nice looking swing, even though it's not painted yet. Looks like Johann did a good job." He climbed the steps and leaned against the column facing Lydia.

"Is it okay with you?"

Sterling thought Lydia sounded a little nervous "Yes. It's much like the other one. This is two people wide where the other one was one."

"Oh, I didn't realize that. Do you want him to change it? He could probably sell this one. At least I think he could."

"It's fine, Lydia, just fine. I asked him to make it how you wanted it. Please, it's fine with me. Besides, I might want to sit next to my wife and swing." He thought this might ease her nervousness, but it didn't seem to. She was sitting looking at the sewing in her lap.

He came over and sat beside her. "Okay, wife," he said in a teasing tone, "have you starched all my shirts stiff as a board or burned holes in them when you ironed them?"

Horrified at the thought, Lydia looked up at him. "No, Sterling, I'm very careful."

"Well, that sure didn't work. I was teasing you trying to get you to relax. How about this? What is making you so nervous?"

"The colors."

"The colors?" He looked back to the swing.

"Yes, the colors I asked Johann to paint the swing."

"So, are they purple with pink spots? Orange and brown stripes?"

"Yellow frame with a green seat. Like the house. Is that okay with you? I thought with the other furniture being white and on the porch, the yellow and green would look nice in the yard." She had started off speaking slowly but spoke faster and faster in her nervousness.

Sterling sighed inwardly. How long before she'd be able to feel secure enough to make decisions without being so nervous of his reaction?

He took her hand. "I told Johann to make it however you wanted. Whatever you chose would've been fine with me. Even purple with pink spots. I think your idea is fine, much better than what I would've chosen. It probably would have been white. I don't have much idea what colors are good. Yours is a better choice."

Lydia let out her breath. "I'm glad you approve. I thought you might not like the colors and would want white."

Sterling leaned forward and set his forehead against hers. "Please don't be afraid of making decisions. If I don't like something I'll tell you. I can't promise that I'll never show irritation, but I want you to have what you like. Also, I gladly leave all decisions concerning decorating the house and yard in your hands."

Chapter 24

Lydia was dusting in the parlor when she heard the wagon coming up the street. The sound indicated that it was moving fast.

"Whoa, whoa." The driver's call came through the open window.

She dropped the dust rag onto the table and hurried to the door. Her stomach clenched. Sterling wasn't home, and she thought this could be an emergency. She pulled the front door open and saw Daniel Windsor running toward her, taking the porch steps in one leap.

"Mrs. Doc, where's the doc? Charlie O'Sullivan got gored by his bull, he's bleeding real bad."

"He's not here. He went to see Jackson Mueller at the blacksmith's. Let's get Charlie into the clinic, then you go and find Sterling."

Lydia went to prop open the clinic door and ran out to help Daniel bring the injured man in. She stifled a gasp when she saw the unconscious man. He was lying in a pool of blood, with his head on his wife's lap.

She looked at the woman's pale, tear-stained face and, taking a deep breath, said, "Come, let's get him inside."

In his hurry to get help Daniel had just let the reins drop, and now after securing the horses to the hitching post he came to the back of the wagon and climbed in the back.

"Patty," he said to Charlie's wife, "I'm gonna need your help again gettin' him down outta the wagon. Mrs. Doc will help us. Once we get the doc I'll go out to the Stantons' and get Millie and Vince. She's gonna want to be with you and her pa."

Patty looked up at Daniel, then at Lydia and nodded.

Daniel took hold of Charlie's shoulders and pulled him gently from his wife's lap. Lydia pulled his legs to the edge of the wagon. Patty, her dress covered in blood, climbed down and helped Lydia with her husband's legs. As gently as they could, the trio carried Charlie into the clinic and placed him carefully on the examination table.

"Patty," Daniel said, "I'm gonna go get the doc. He ain't here, he's at the blacksmith's. I'll get him back as soon as I can."

After Daniel left, Lydia said, "Patty, sit down for a minute and take some breaths. I'm going to start some water to boil, then I'll be right back." She pulled the chair from the corner and helped the shaking woman sit.

Dear Lord, Lydia prayed as she went to the kitchen to put the water heating, *help Charlie. It looked really bad to me, with all that blood. I'm going to do what I can while we wait for Sterling, but you know I don't know much. Please, help me do the right thing. Please let Daniel find Sterling fast and get him back here. Help Patty deal with whatever is to come. Please, Lord, we all need your help.*

Lydia entered the exam room and looked at the unconscious man on the table. His trousers were soaked in blood and mud. A long gash ran up the inside of his left thigh. A rope was tightly tied around his leg up near his groin. His shirt, also covered in blood, showed evidence of his shoulder hitting the muddy ground. The smell let her know that it wasn't mud but manure he had fallen into.

Not good, she thought, tying on a large apron to cover her dress. Picking up a pair of long scissors, she started to cut off Charlie's pants.

"What are you doing?" Patty cried, jumping up from the chair.

"I'm doing what I can to get Charlie ready before Sterling gets here. These pants are covered in blood and manure and need to be removed. Cutting them is the easiest way. I don't have to move Charlie to do it."

Lydia continued cutting up the pant leg and Patty grabbed another pair of scissors from a tray on the counter and started on the other leg.

Good, thought Lydia. She isn't panicked enough not to see what's right to do and to help.

When she reached to the tourniquet she asked, "How long has this been tied on?"

"Um. ... I don't know."

"Do you know about what time this happened?"

"Between one and one-thirty, I think. Daniel had come to talk about breeding some of his cows to our bull. He does that every year. I was in the kitchen and I heard Daniel yell and then Charlie's scream. Daniel was yelling and chasing the bull away. He was pulling Charlie out of the bull's lot when I reached them. Blood was shooting out of Charlie's leg." Patty shuttered. "Daniel cut the rope belt Charlie uses and tied it around his leg. The blood stopped shooting out then. We put him in the wagon and hightailed it into town."

Lydia glanced at the clock. Quarter after two. The tourniquet had been on about an hour. Should she loosen it or wait for Sterling? If you left a tourniquet on too long it could cause the leg to die. Aggie had told her that. She'd wait until they got the rest of the clothes cut off. She had cut around the pant leg down to the table and was headed up to the waistband.

"How high should we cut it?" Patty asked.

"All the way to the top. Cut off the shirt too."

Lydia could see that Patty was blushing at the thought of her husband nearly naked before another woman. Lydia started cutting along the side of the shirt. When she'd cut high enough she grabbed a towel from the pile on the shelf and laid it across Charlie's hips. She heard Patty's relieved breath and they continued to cut away Charlie's garments.

When Lydia could see the extent of the man's injuries she blanched. He had a long, wicked-looking gash from just above the knee nearly to the groin. His leg was covered in blood and the muscle was exposed. His shoulder looked nothing like a shoulder; it was misshapen with a good-sized roundish wound that was oozing blood around grass and something else more deadly than mud. His chest was bruised and bloody. His lower left arm was swelling, bruised and misshapen. Lydia hoped it all looked worse than it was.

"I'm going to get some of the water I have heating," she said.

"Okay," Patty said.

As Lydia left the room, she heard Patty take a ragged breath.

She returned with a pitcher of hot water and one of cold. Combining them in a smaller pitcher, she tested the temperature. Then she began to pour the water over Charlie's shoulder.

Patty was picking up the tattered remains of her husband's clothes.

"I hope this helps wash out some of the dirt. It can't be good to have it just sit in there spreading who knows what kind of germs."

Patty nodded, grabbing a pile of towels from a shelf and sopping up the spilling water. Charlie moaned slightly. Patty jumped at the sound, tears again streaming down her face.

Lydia, having finished flooding the wound, wondered what to do next. Should she loosen the tourniquet or not? She prayed that Sterling would get here soon. Deciding that it would be better to loosen it in case it was getting too long to wait, she cautiously untied the knotted rope, loosening it slightly. Blood oozed out, but she could tell that the color of the leg was looking better.

Patty watched, blanching at the sight of the blood coming from the wound.

"The leg needs some blood. I know he's bleeding some but see how the leg's color looks better?" Lydia said.

Patty nodded but didn't say anything.

After a couple of minutes Lydia tightened the knot again. The bleeding slowed then stopped.

"Where are they?" Patty asked, her voice revealing her distress.

"I wish they'd get here too."

Lydia looked at the leg wound. There really wasn't anything other than rinsing the wound that she could do for it, but she was unsure if it would wash away clotting, and cause it to bleed again. There was nothing she could do for the arm either. Focusing again on the shoulder wound, she picked up some long tweezers, cautiously picking out bits of grass and other debris.

Patty sat down on the chair, weeping.

Finally they heard the wagon barreling up the street. Patty jumped up and ran out to greet it. Lydia put the tweezers into the used instrument bin along with the scissors. She kicked the towels on the floor into a corner and checked to be sure the floor was not too slippery. She could hear Patty talking as she and Sterling entered the clinic and hurried down the hall.

"You stay out here, Patty," she heard Sterling say. "I know you want to be with him but it won't be easy to watch and it'll be better for you to not see. Daniel's going to get Pastor, so you wait for them out here."

A weak "okay" came from Patty and Sterling entered the exam room.

Casting a quick look at Lydia, Sterling focused on his patient. Lydia stood silently. Minutes passed as Sterling examined every part of the wounded man.

"Can you help me with this?"

"Yes."

"I'll need boiled water."

"It's already boiling."

"Good."

"First I need to deal with this leg. The artery is torn open. That's why it bleeds so much. Daniel was smart to put the tourniquet on."

"I loosened it for a few minutes a little while ago. The leg pinked up some, but it did bleed too."

"Good girl."

Sterling turned to the cabinet and began gathering instruments, needles, thread, gauze, and other items he would need. They heard the wagon come and stop by the house again, then the sound of it moving away. Sounds of Patty sobbing, and the calming voice of Pastor Peter comforting her, caught the couple's awareness for a moment before they again concentrated on the task at hand.

Sterling washed in the water Lydia had brought earlier and began his cleaning of the leg wound.

"Thread the needles with about eighteen inches of thread. Pour some of the carbolic acid in a bowl and put the needles and thread in it. Then go and get some more boiled water."

Lydia did what he had instructed.

When she returned Sterling said, "Let's get as much done of this while he's still out. I don't want to give him very much chloroform."

Sterling asked Lydia to hand him needles and cut the thread. Several times, when he loosened the tourniquet, blood still oozed, but finally he had enough stitches in to repair the artery completely.

"It'll take a long time to wash this wound out. Thread some more needles for me, will you please? I'll need them for stitching this closed and the arm."

When the leg wound was done. Sterling moved to the head of the table and began concentrating on Charlie's shoulder.

"It's dislocated. I'll need to put it back in. I don't think you have the strength to help me. Please, go get Peter, will you? I'll set the broken arm while he's in here too."

"Of course."

Lydia went outside to get Peter, then waited outside the room. When the shoulder had been put back in place and the arm set, Sterling called her back in.

"I moved Patty into the parlor," Lydia said. "It's more comfortable and private in case someone comes into the clinic. I also told her to make tea or coffee, and eat anything she liked from the kitchen. I made chamomile tea for her. There's enough for you, too."

"Can you bring me some of the boiled water?" Sterling asked Peter as he left the room.

"Of course."

"This shoulder wound isn't as bad as it could have been," Sterling told Lydia. "The shoulder could've been broken. You rinsed it some and picked out some grass and such, didn't you?"

"Yes, I didn't think it was a good idea to let the dirt just sit in the wound."

"Good idea, thank you. Now it needs to be well washed out." Without looking at her, Sterling continued treating his patient. Charlie moaned and began to flounder around. Sterling grabbed the bottle of chloroform and mask.

"I need you to hold this above his nose and pour a few drops of the anesthetic onto the mask. As soon as he settles, stop and lift the mask. If he starts waking again use a couple of more drops. Not too much. Can you do that? I need him to keep still while I clean out this wound and then cast the arm."

Lydia nodded and took the bottle and mask. Sterling waited until Charlie was still again and Lydia had removed the mask. He nodded to her and went back to cleaning the shoulder.

To Lydia, the time in the exam room seemed to go on forever. She watched Sterling's methodical yet quick and efficient movements, and his thoroughness in examining and treating each injury the man had sustained. She'd helped him before with stitches, a boil, a nervous child with a bad splinter, but nothing as serious as this. He'd always been efficient, gentle and compassionate. She was impressed with his skill, the confidence with which he approached the different injuries, his overall competence as a doctor. His hands were long, lean, and gentle. Watching them made her skin tingle, which made her squirm slightly and she was careful not to allow Sterling to notice.

Something else hovered just out of reach in her mind. She tried to bring it to the forefront, but it remained illusive. The only thing she knew was that something was there for her if she could grasp it.

Sterling threw the scissors and needle into the used instrument tray. "Okay. That's all I can do for now. Let's get him washed up then move him to a bed."

Sterling rose from the chair by the bed, leaving Vince to sit with Charlie for a while. He peeked into the first door to his right. Millie, Charlie's daughter, was sitting by her mother's side. Patty looked worn to a frazzle but seemed to be sleeping. He crept past the room, trying not to disturb them.

"Where's Lydia?" he asked, looking around as he entered the kitchen. He glanced over to the kitchen table where Peter, Rye and Janie were playing a game of pick-up sticks.

Ella Lendrey looked up from the pot of soup she was stirring on the stove. "I sent her upstairs to change out of the bloody dress. You might want to check on her. She looked a little, I don't know, fragile, I guess."

"I will. Thank you for coming, Ella. You fixing supper will be a big help. Lydia did so well in a very stressful situation. She's helped with small procedures before, but nothing like this, and with me not here when they brought him. She handled everything wonderfully. Probably kept Charlie from losing his leg. He's still not out of danger but if she hadn't loosened that tourniquet he would have lost it."

"You be sure to tell her all that, Ster," Peter said, using the childhood nickname.

"I will."

Rye asked his father, "Is Mr. O'Sullivan going to die? Or lose his leg, Papa?"

"We won't know for a while. He was very badly injured. How about we pray for him?"

"I'll start, okay?"

Sterling heard Janie's tiny voice as he walked down the hall and started up the steps.

"Dear God, Mr. O'Sullivan got kicked by a mean bull. He got lots of owies, bad ones. Papa said you're the one who can heal every owie. Please make Mr. O'Sullivan all better and not hurt anymore."

Lydia sat on the edge of her bed. She'd given up after struggling to unbutton only three of the buttons running down the front of her stained dress. She held out her hands and watched them shake. The trembling had echoed throughout her body causing her to sit down, feeling that her legs would no longer hold her. She looked up, setting her hands in her lap, when a soft knock sounded on the door.

"Come," she said softly.

Sterling opened the door and stepped in. He studied her with the same intensity he'd used on Charlie. Closing the door, he came to the bed, sitting down next to her.

"You've had a difficult day. Are you all right?"

"I'm fine." She was looking down at her hands, a sure sign to him that she wasn't.

He tipped her face up. "You did so very well today. I am so proud of you. You kept your head in a very difficult and unfamiliar situation. You didn't freeze or fall apart. You thought out what might be good to do until I arrived, and did it. It made a big difference in how things might turn out for Charlie. Thank you."

He watched as her eyes filled and then overflowed with tears. He pulled her into his embrace, her head against his chest and held her, firmly but comfortingly.

"I was so scared," Lydia sobbed out. "Charlie was so badly hurt. There was blood everywhere. And mud that I knew was mostly manure. I had to get as much of it out as soon as possible. I wanted to do what I could to get him ready for when you got here. I had to stay calm to help Patty, she was so scared." Lydia clung to Sterling.

"You were wonderful. Thank you so much. Without you here, he wouldn't have the chance he has now. They wouldn't have known where to find me."

They continued to sit together in each other's arms, Sterling lending Lydia his strength while she cried out her fear and stress. He stroked her hair softly, murmuring words of comfort. Lydia's trembling slowly began to abate and she finally relaxed against him.

"Are you feeling better?"

"I am. It was just so ... I don't know."

"I understand. My first major emergency in med school ... afterwards I threw up. At least I made it to the water closet so my indignity was in private."

They sat for a little while longer, enjoying the feel of the comforting arms wrapped around each other. A soft knock at the door interrupted.

"Yes," Sterling called.

"Supper's ready. We can go ahead if you need more time. The children are hungry," Peter said through the door.

Sterling looked at Lydia. She nodded. "We'll be there in a couple of minutes."

"Okay." They heard Peter's steps as he descended the stairs.

Lydia had risen from the bed and was trying to undo the buttons on the front of her dress. Her fingers were still not working well.

"Can you help me? I can't seem to get the buttons undone."

Sterling swallowed. She was looking down at her buttons, not at him. He stood up and reached for the buttons. While he undid them, she reached up and began pulling pins from her hair, tossing them into a bowl on the dresser.

"All unbuttoned." Now his hands were trembling. He was glad Lydia didn't notice.

"Thank you." Lydia turned away, pulling open a drawer and taking out a white shirtwaist and dark brown skirt. Setting them on the dresser, she pulled the dress off her shoulders.

Sterling watched her in the mirror. Glancing at his reflection, he saw the intensity of his expression. He struggled to contain his longing. He'd felt so protective holding her while she cried out her stress. He wondered if she realized he was still standing behind her. Then Lydia lifted her face, their eyes meeting. She paused for a moment then continued changing into the clean clothing.

"Why?" Sterling asked when she was finished dressing.

"I didn't think about it when I started changing. When I saw you in the mirror I almost asked you to leave. Then I remembered that we'd be sharing your room when your sister's family's here. It seemed a little foolish to have you leave when in a couple of weeks we'll be sleeping together. Also, you saw me in my nightgown while I was sick. I'm more clothed without my dress on now than I was then." She blushed a little as she spoke.

"Well." Sterling cleared his throat, trying to get rid of the lump. "Let's go down and eat. I'm hungry."

"Me too," Lydia said with a shy smile.

Chapter 25

The night was hard on all of them, with Sterling, Patty, and Lydia all taking turns sitting with Charlie. When the chloroform wore off and he woke up in pain, Sterling was careful with the use of morphine injections. He knew of the 'soldiers' disease' many wounded veterans of the Civil War returned home with.

When the sun rose Patty was sleeping in the other patient room and Sterling was sitting with Charlie, writing notes about the case.

Lord, Lydia prayed while she cooked bacon for breakfast, *thank you for getting him through the night. Thank you that Patty is able to sleep now. Help Charlie heal, Lord, please. Thank you for Daniel and his caring and help yesterday. Bless him, Lord.*

Just then a knock at the back door brought her out of her prayer.

Daniel poked his head in. "Morning, how's Charlie doing?" He came in carrying the milk, butter and eggs.

"He made it through the night. Sterling says the next few days will tell. It's the leg and the wound on his shoulder. If they get infected it could be bad. Patty's sleeping now, it's been so hard on her."

"Tell her I plan to tend their stock until Charlie can."

"I will. That's very kind of you. Thank you for all you did yesterday."

"Wasn't nothing." Daniel looked uneasy at the gratitude. "Tell her I may take the stock to my place. It'll be easier for me to tend them there."

"Will do. How about an applesauce muffin? Hot out of the oven."

"Thank you, I think I will." He reached into the basket she held toward him, pulling out one of the steaming muffins.

"Hey, are you giving away my breakfast again?" Sterling came into the kitchen behind Daniel, giving him a pat on the back.

"Sterling, you need to learn to share. It's one of the things all boys need to learn before they grow up," Lydia bantered back, holding the basket out so he could take one.

"What about the girls? Don't they need to learn?" he said with a grin.

"I," she said with exaggerated snobbery, "learned long ago, like you should have."

They all laughed. Patty came in then.

"What's so funny? Did I miss something?"

"Not really. Just making fun of Sterling," Lydia replied. "Would you like a muffin?"

"Thank you." She looked as if she hadn't slept all night; her face was etched with worry.

"Patty, I'll be taking care of your stock while Charlie's laid up. Don't you worry about them."

"Thank you, Daniel."

"Well, I gotta get on with the route. Thank you for the muffin, Mrs. Doc. Praying that Charlie gets better real soon, Patty. Bye, Doc, Mrs. Doc." Daniel went out the back door.

"Charlie's sleeping," Patty said. "I just looked in on him. He looks so pale." She sat down at the table looking rather lost and forlorn.

"He will for a while. He lost a lot of blood yesterday. We'll need to get some liquids in him. Lydia, will you make up some chicken and beef broth? That'll give him liquids and some nourishment."

"Of course. There's the soup Ella made yesterday. Will he be able to eat some of that?"

"The broth, yes. The solids, maybe, we'll see."

They continued planning Charlie's care as they ate breakfast. Patty helped with the dishes while Sterling went back to check on his patient. His clinic hours would be starting soon.

"Patty, would you like to change into one of my dresses? Yours is, um, rather stained."

Patty looked down at her blood-covered dress. Remembrances of the events of the day before flooded her. She shuddered. "Yes, thank you, I would."

After Patty had changed and the two women were sitting at the table cutting up meat to make the broth, there was a knock on the door into the clinic hallway.

Peter opened it and poked his head in. "Morning ladies, may I join you?"

"Yes, come in," Lydia said, rising to get a cup. "Coffee?"

"Need you ask?" quipped Peter. He gave Patty a quick hug and sat down. "How are you doing?"

Patty's eyes filled. "Okay, I guess. It's so hard."

"Yes, it is. This is one of those trials James talked about. He didn't say if trials come but when trials come. That's when God can let you know he's standing right beside you, waiting for you to grab onto him. Then he can wrap his arms of comfort and strength around you."

"You're right, Pastor. But it's still hard."

"Yes it is, but that's what makes it so precious."

They sat silently for a few minutes, each thinking and praying in their own way.

"Patty," Peter started, "several of the farmers came this morning and told me they were willing to plant the rest of your crop. They know Charlie won't be able to get to it. They need to know which crop goes in which field. They're planning on next Monday. I'll announce it in church, but I expect everyone will know by then." He paused. "Ella will take care of planning for the meals, but I do think you'll need to be there, at least part of the day."

"You're right. I'll hate to leave Charlie, but I'll be sure to come and thank everyone."

"One more thing. I know you want to be here, but would you like to go out home to get some things and bring them back? Ella and I will be glad to take you."

Patty's eyes filled with tears again. "Yes, thank you. Do you want to go now?"

"This afternoon would be better. How about one o'clock? We'll be here in the buggy."

"I'll be ready." Patty smiled at the pastor.

"I should warn you, Janie will be along. She'll probably talk your ear off."

They all laughed at that. Then after a prayer Peter took his leave.

That afternoon after Patty had gone with the Lendreys, Sterling began cleaning and re-bandaging Charlie's injuries. He was grateful that Patty wasn't there as this would be a very painful process for Charlie. He'd asked Lydia to help him. She agreed but wasn't looking forward to it.

"Charlie, this is going to hurt like the very devil," Peter told him while he cut the bandages off the injured leg.

"I know, Doc." Charlie had woken up and spoken with Patty before she left. She'd wanted to stay but Charlie, having been a soldier in the Civil War, knew what was in store for him. Not wanting her to suffer along with him, he encouraged her to go.

"I'll give you some more morphine after we're done, but I want to see if you can move the shoulder by yourself." Sterling had wrapped the casted arm tight to Charlie's chest to keep him from thrashing it around while he slept.

"Why not do it before you do the leg, Doc? Then I could sleep through you messing with it." Charlie gave a wry grin.

"Because I like to cause pain, Charlie. You know that." Sterling grinned back at his patient.

"Why are you doing the leg before you give him more morphine?" Lydia asked. She stood by the bed helping hold the leg up so Sterling could remove the bloody dressing.

"He doesn't want me to get addicted, that's why," Charlie said. "You can. Ouch, easy there. Lots of soldiers went home addicted to the stuff from the war. Doc's just trying to keep me from that."

"He's right, Lydia. By waiting until later, his body gets rid of some of the drug. That will make it easier for him to wean off it." Sterling handed her the used bandages. "Here, take these dirty dressings and dispose of them, please."

She did as he asked and brought in the boiled water he would need.

Cleaning the wounds left Charlie exhausted, with pain etched on his face. Sterling had carefully cleaned away any sign of infection. Lydia held Charlie's hand during the most painful times, tears of sympathy coursing down her cheeks. Now Charlie slept, a benefit from the shot of morphine Sterling had given him.

"What do you think? How did it look?" Lydia asked. They sat at the kitchen table, Sterling with a cup of coffee and piece of cake, Lydia with a cup of tea.

"I'm fairly optimistic. There wasn't much infection and it didn't seem real deep. He moved the arm fairly well. It'll take a long time for him to heal. If there's no festering he should do fairly well. At least we'll pray he does. If there is festering, especially in the leg, it will be bad. It may be necessary to ... no, I won't say it. I'm not superstitious, but I don't want to speculate."

Lydia knew what he'd been about to say. If the leg festered it might need to be amputated. She looked down at her cup, praying that God would have mercy on Charlie.

"We'll have to clean the wounds twice a day, morning and evening."

"Will it hurt as much each time?" Lydia's voice held compassion.

"It'll get better over time, but not for a while. It was good Patty was gone."

Over the next few days Charlie's wounds began to slowly heal. Sterling and Lydia cleaned them carefully twice a day. Sterling wouldn't let Patty in the room while they did it, but Charlie's moans reached her wherever she was in the house. After the first time, she didn't ask again.

Charlie began to look better as he was able to take more nourishment and less morphine.

The day the neighbors planted Charlie's crops brought most of them into the clinic with quick greetings and well-wishes for Charlie. Lydia sent several covered dishes with Patty to serve the workers. She stayed home to tend Charlie while Sterling made his rounds and saw patients.

One afternoon Lydia, leaving Charlie sleeping in his room, sat down at the kitchen table and began a letter to Aggie.

Dear Aggie,

We've had an eventful few days. We are both well but tired. I was home alone last week when a wagon pulled up with a very badly injured farmer, Charlie.

She described the events of the previous few days and told Aggie of her fear that she hadn't helped in doing what she had done while waiting for Sterling to get there, and the difficulty of having to hurt Charlie in order to heal him. How, she wondered, had Aggie coped with the many injuries she'd treated without the training Sterling had? She was just getting ready to mention that Sterling hoped that Charlie could go home that weekend when she remembered the Rawlings were coming for Decoration Day.

She panicked. Jumping up, she grabbed a bucket and rag and, beginning in the dining room, started washing the windows with fast, furious motions. Without stopping for so much as a breath, she went from window to window, cleaning every one on the main floor except the one in the room Charlie occupied. She also washed the glass inserts in the doors. She opened the back door and tossed the water out, just missing Sterling who was coming up the back steps.

"Whoa, girl. What has you in such a frenzy?"

He could see the agitation on her face. Her hair was falling out of the knot on the top of her head.

"Two weeks. I only have two weeks to get ready for your sister and family. I completely forgot about it. Charlie and Patty have been my main concern the last few days. Now I'm behind in getting the house ready for their visit. The windows need washing, the walls and woodwork too. The bedrooms need to be cleaned and the bedding washed. My things will need to be moved. The meals planned and groceries purchased. The front porch needs scrubbed. So does the back. There's weeding, more planting and the tomato plants need set out. Then there are the regular things like washing, baking, meals. I'm so far behind now I don't know how I'll get it all done. Not that I begrudge helping with

Charlie. Of course that's most important, but now that he's better ..."

She stopped talking, turned and rushed into the kitchen. She put the bucket into the sink and began pumping water with quick jerky motions. When the water was flowing into the pail she grabbed up the soap bar and began whittling shavings into the water.

Sterling came up behind her and took the knife out of her hand. "Lydia, stop. You'll cut yourself with that. Slow down. It'll do no good if you have to have stitches because you were careless with the knife."

"But--"

"No. It'll be okay. Whatever you get done, you get done. If Margaret complains about something that isn't, I'll send them packing or tell her to do it herself."

Sterling put the knife in the sink then pulled her back against his chest and wrapped his arms around her waist.

Chapter 26

Mew, mew.

The late afternoon sun colored the clouds with pink and Lydia sat in the porch swing taking it in. She had spent the day cleaning the now empty patient rooms. Charlie had improved enough to be able to return home. Daniel, after finishing his morning route, had come with his wagon and taken the O'Sullivans home.

Mew, mew.

This cry had a slightly different tone. It came from below her. She peered under the swing, almost falling out in the process. Nothing under there. The mewing continued. Lydia left the swing, descended the steps, and leaning down, peered through the blooming tulips and budding peonies along the front of the porch.

Two pairs of yellow circles peered back at her.

Lydia sat quietly.

Mew, mew.

Stepping slowly, clumsily, two kittens tumbled through the flowers.

Lydia smiled. "Kitty, kitty, kitty," she beckoned softly. The kittens answered with their plaintive mews. They approached hesitantly and, finally, bravely climbed onto the skirt spread out around her.

"Hello, little ones. Where did you come from? Did someone decide you needed a new home so they left you off around here? You must have been born to a house cat, or you'd be scratching and hissing at me."

She reached out a hand. The kittens sniffed her fingers and climbed into her lap. Now, instead of mewing, loud rumbling purrs shook the minute bodies as they climbed and tumbled around her skirts.

"I think you might be hungry, aren't you? Let's go get you something to fill those little stomachs."

Picking up the kittens, she held them close as she went into the house. In the kitchen she closed the doors, keeping the kittens inside. They wandered, exploring under the chairs, table and stove, investigating everything in their low line of vision. The sound of their purring filled the room with its calming hum. Lydia brought two leftover chicken legs from the pantry's icebox, cut the meat into small pieces and put it on two saucers.

"Here you go, little ones."

She placed the saucers on the floor. The kittens came stumbling over, and after sniffing with suspicion began eating. Lydia watched as they first ate from one saucer before sniffing what the other had and moving over to eat from the other saucer. The fluffy balls of energy had fur that stuck out in all directions. Lydia thought this might indicate longer hair when the kittens grew into cats. One was a grey-and-black tabby with a tail reminiscent of a raccoon. The other had tabby markings on the back but from the nose down its chest and front legs were bright white.

With stomachs bulging, the kittens sat and began washing themselves. The kitten with the white front soon moved to the other and began washing its head. They finished giving each other baths, then curled up in one ball and went to sleep under the stove.

Lydia started supper, thinking of a way to keep the kittens. She very much wanted them. After the cat that she had when her parents passed away died, Cyrus wouldn't let her keep one in the house. There were barn cats, but none especially hers. These kittens obviously loved each other and she wanted to keep both of them. She didn't, however, know what Sterling would think of having cats. They would not, of course, be allowed in the clinic but that could be handled by keeping the doors closed.

Maybe I can keep them with me at night in my room, she thought. Sterling wouldn't know about them then. Lydia completely forgot that she'd be moving in with him shortly. If she could make sure they were outside or in the kitchen when he was here that might work. Or maybe in the cellar. She could fix up a box for them to sleep in and have a sandbox for them. She could even make sure they had food and water down there. That could work until she was able to feel him out on the subject of pets.

Finding a crate in the cellar, Lydia put part of an old blanket in the box. She brought down the saucers refilled with meat and a bowl of water. Not having sand at the moment, she went to the garden and dug up some dry soil and put it into another box, placing it near the bed crate.

She took the blanket lined crate back to the kitchen and continued with supper preparations, listening for sounds of Sterling's return. Often he would go to his office for a short while before he came to find her, but sometimes he came straight into the kitchen. She wanted to move the kittens down to the cellar before he came and discovered them. When supper was ready and keeping warm on the stove, she decided that caution was a wise choice. Getting down on the floor, she carefully reached under the stove to retrieve the kittens. They were startled awake, hissing for a moment before settling in her arms with contented purrs.

Listening for a moment for the sounds of Sterling's return, Lydia took the kittens down to the spot she'd prepared in the cellar. When she put them into the crate they immediately climbed out, mewing and trying to climb her skirts.

"No, no, little ones, you mustn't climb my dress. Here, see, your food is right here."

She successfully distracted them with the saucers. Figuring they would find the water and box of dirt by themselves, she hastily made her exit. Closing the basement door behind her and washing her hands, she listened carefully for any sounds coming from below. Hearing nothing, she breathed a sigh of relief. They were safe and secure for now.

She was setting the table when Sterling opened the kitchen doorway from the hall.

"Hello, wife. Why is this closed? You've never done that before."

"Oh, uh, I just thought it would be good to try it out before winter when we'll probably keep it closed to keep the warmth in." As excuses went it was a poor one, and when she turned away from him she rolled her eyes at her weak excuse. "You can open it if you like." Forgive me, Lord, she added sans voice.

Sterling did so, giving her a quizzical look.

"I cleaned both the patient rooms. They're ready, although I'll wash the drapes on Monday with the rest of the wash. You may want to think about another set for each room. That way there could be a clean set ready when I clean the room when a patient leaves."

"Hadn't thought of that. Might be a good idea. Would you mind making them?"

Lydia chuckled a bit. "Would I have suggested it if I minded?"

"I guess not." Sterling smiled at her, washed his hands and sat down as she placed the last dish on the table.

"I might even go wild and buy green fabric."

At that Sterling did laugh, then bowed his head and led them in giving thanks.

"Who did your laundry and the cleaning before we were married?"

"I took my laundry to the boardinghouse and Olive, the hired girl, did it. She also came here to clean once a week. I think she might be glad you're doing it now. She greets me more warmly. All those bandages were getting to her, I think."

Lydia nodded. "They can be rather intimidating, with all the blood. The things I washed after you treated Charlie, all the bloody towels..." She gave a little shudder. "I'm just glad that doesn't happen often."

"I agree. I never thought about how the bloody towels and things might make her feel. Maybe I should think about giving her something as a thank-you." He said it with a questioning tone, looking to Lydia for advice.

"That would be nice. What do you have in mind?"

"That's one of the benefits of having a wife. I can leave the decision of the thank-you gift to you. You get whatever you think she might like and would be appropriate."

Sterling took a sip of coffee and Lydia tried to keep the stunned look off her face. Imagine, Sterling trusting her to choose a gift for someone. It was such a foreign thought that even after he left she was still practically speechless.

In the morning, Lydia made sure she was downstairs early. She brought the kittens up, fed them and took them out to the back garden. Leaving them tumbling about under the fruit trees, she went into the kitchen and began breakfast.

Sterling entered with a smile and a warm, "Good morning."

"Hi, hope you slept well." Lydia took a quick look out the window to see whether she could see the kittens. She saw one climbing a tree trunk and the other pouncing on something in the grass.

Picking up the platter of sausage, toast and fried eggs, she joined Sterling at the table.

After a quick prayer and dishing up of the food, she asked, "What's your day like?"

"The usual. I have house calls most of the morning. I'm going out to the O'Sullivans' today to check on Charlie's injuries and see whether the shoulder's healed enough to start him moving it a little. He won't be able to do much, but it would be good to get it moving a little."

Between mouthfuls, Sterling said, "Clint Shaifer asked that I come out and check on Helen. She's had terrible morning sickness. She can't keep anything down and is losing a lot of weight. Then I'll come back to town for a couple of calls. I hope to be home for lunch. I may be late, though. Will that be a problem?"

"No, I'll plan on sandwiches. That way, whenever you get here will be fine. I need to go to Johnson's and plan to do it this morning. I thought I'd get the fabric for the curtains and look for a gift for Olive. I might stop in to see Ella to do a little more planning for when your sister's here."

"Sounds like we both have busy mornings ahead."

After Sterling left, Lydia dashed out the back door and down the walk to the fruit trees. "Kitty, kitty, kitty," she called when she arrived.

One kitten ran up to her and started to climb her skirts, crying plaintively. The other sat howling from the crook of a cherry tree in full bloom. Fortunately, Lydia found the kitten was within reach and was soon rescued.

"You mustn't climb up if you can't get down. I don't feel like climbing trees today. I have too much to do. You know I'm not a tree." She disengaged the other kitten, which had climbed halfway up her skirt. Both kittens were soon issuing loud purring from the cradle of her arms.

Returning to the kitchen, Lydia put a saucer of leftover egg and bacon on the floor. The kittens, hungry after their morning's play, eagerly dove into the offering. After shutting the kitchen doors she ran downstairs to scoop out the soiled dirt, not wanting any odor to reveal the kittens to Sterling.

They'd never talked about pets. She already loved the kittens and wanted to keep them. She decided to sound Sterling out about his feelings about pets before she revealed their presence to him.

Bringing up the blanket, she arranged it by the stove. The kittens were investigating under and around everything in the kitchen. Lydia called them, opening the back door. Rolling down the steps, the kittens jumped, ran and tumbled after her as she went to the back of the necessary. Spreading out the soiled dirt, she set each kitten on it. They quickly realized that this place was for them and, scratching, did their business. She took them back into the house and left them corralled in the kitchen.

Gathering her list, basket and hat she hurried down the steps heading to the store. Her plan was to get her errands run quickly, see Ella and be back in plenty of time to get the kittens squirreled away so Sterling wouldn't see them when he came home for lunch. The afternoon would be more of a challenge, as she knew he'd be in the clinic. She hoped the kittens would sleep most of the afternoon. She wanted to begin the second set of drapes for the patient rooms. If the kittens slept she could get them cut out on the dining room table.

Exiting Johnson's All-purpose Store, Lydia crossed the street heading for the butcher shop. She'd need scraps and leavings for kitten food, which the butcher sold very inexpensively.

"Well, good morning, Mrs. Graham."

Lydia turned to face the speaker, groaning inwardly.

"You're out early today." Magdelina Taylor looked Lydia up and down with a look of disdain as she approached on the boardwalk.

"Yes, I have a number of things I hope to accomplish today, so an early start seemed like a good idea." Lydia turned toward the butcher shop, hoping Magdelina would get the hint. As usual, she didn't.

"I saw your husband early too, in his buggy. I often see him leaving in that buggy, and you aren't with him. I've wondered about that."

Suppressing a sigh, she turned to face the girl who was older but seemed younger. She's not very good at insults, was the thought that flitted through her mind.

"Yes, Sterling uses the buggy when he goes on house calls to the surrounding farms. I don't go with him, usually, as I have my own work to accomplish at home. I won't keep you. I'm sure you have many of your own things needing to get done."

Lydia turned away and hurried to the butcher shop, knowing she left Magdelina frustrated that her attempted insult had failed.

"Does Magdelina Taylor work at anything?" Lydia asked Ella as the two sat in Ella's kitchen sipping tea. They'd finalized the plans for the Rawlings' visit and were simply visiting.

"Not really. As you know, her father, Eustace, owns the bank. She's the youngest and spoiled. The other girls have all moved away. Her parents give her everything she wants. They have hired help so she doesn't even have to do anything at home."

"That's too bad. She's so young and seems lonely." Lydia swirled the tea in her cup.

"I never thought of it that way. Come to think about it, I don't think she has any friends. She isn't very warm to people. She ..." Ella hesitated, searching for words that would convey the thought but would not sound harsh. "She tries to outdo others, trying to make them think she's better than they are."

" 'Let nothing be done through strife or vainglory," Lydia quoted, " 'but in lowliness of mind let each esteem others better than themselves.' "

"Philippians 2:3. A good concept to remember."

"Do you think she might feel unsure of herself? She sees others her age with husbands, families, homes, going to college or working, and she has nothing to do, nothing to accomplish." Lydia was looking out the window, not really seeing anything as she thought about Magdelina.

"You might be right. It might be good for us to include her in some activities, invite her to join us."

"How about while Sterling's sister and family are here? Maybe to the Sunday picnic at our house. That way she'd be part of the group and wouldn't feel left out or targeted in some way."

"Good idea."

"What's a good idea?" Peter said as he and Janie entered through the back door.

"Inviting Magdelina Taylor to the picnic we're having while Sterling's family is here," Ella said.

"We're wondering if she feels unsure, and sort of left behind with no husband and family, and nothing really to do that's worthwhile," Lydia added.

Peter put the cookie jar on the table and Janie climbed on a chair to reach in for the treat.

"Only one. Lunch is soon," Ella said.

"Okay, Mama." With a cookie in her hand, Janie jumped off the chair and started running down the hall. Just as her mother took a breath to tell her not to run, Janie stopped, glanced back with a wry grin and walked to the stairs and up to the second floor.

Peter had a cookie in both hands. "You seem to be making progress, my love. She stopped running without you saying anything."

"With her. Rye, on the other hand, well, let's just say he's a work in progress."

They all chuckled.

"You might be right about Magdelina. Several of her classmates have married, gotten jobs or gone to college. She's just living at home with no purpose." Peter took a bite of his cookie.

"She used to be popular. She had several good friends, but she's sort of been left behind. She has nothing to occupy her time. It hasn't improved her character one bit," Ella said.

"She's so young to have no goals," Lydia said.

"She's older than you are, Lydia."

"I know. She just seems so young. Like she stopped growing up some years ago."

"I think your idea of including her in some activities is a good one. Maybe some of what you both do will give her ideas of what she can learn and do."

"I'll talk with Sterling about it. I don't want to do something he wouldn't approve of. Her past of chasing him might make him uneasy about having her around."

"We can discuss it after service on Sunday," Ella said.

"Peter, did Sterling have any pets while he grew up?" Lydia asked, with an abrupt change of topic.

"Not that I remember. None that were especially his. I think there was a small dog at one time. His sister claimed it as hers and he didn't fight with her about it. If she was playing with the dog he was free to do what he wanted. Did you have some reason for asking?"

"I just saw Oscar go by the window and wondered. We haven't talked about pets yet." Lydia was glad she could answer truthfully without revealing anything about the kittens. "Well, I must be going. Sterling will be getting home from his calls and I want to have lunch ready. Thank you for the tea, Ella. We'll see you Sunday."

"I'm glad you came. It was a pleasant visit."

"And," Peter paused for effect, "you were privileged to get to visit with me."

The ladies groaned.

"Say goodbye to Janie for me," Lydia said as she went out the back door.

Chapter 27

    Arriving home later than he had anticipated, Sterling hung his hat on the hook. He stood for a moment listening to see if he could discover the whereabouts of his wife. She'd surely eaten lunch by now. He went to the foot of the staircase, calling her name. No response. Since it wasn't Lydia's habit to nap, he didn't go up but went down the hall to the kitchen. A pitcher of lemonade sat on the table along with a glass, and a cloth covered a plate. Lifting the cover, he found a large sandwich made from Lydia's bread, ham, cheese and pickles; just the way he liked it. He poured himself a glass of lemonade, took a long drink and picked up the sandwich.
    Rather than sit down at the table, he moved to stand over the sink. He remembered Lydia laughing the first time she'd seen him do that. Sterling had told her he ate over the sink so as not to scatter crumbs on the table or floor. It was a lesson his mother had drilled into him as a youth. After several times of having to sweep up the crumbs with a hand broom, on his knees, he'd learned the lesson well.
    Looking out the window, Sterling smiled. Lydia sat on the ground, her maroon skirt fanned out around her, her shirtwaist bright white in the afternoon sunshine. She had her hair down and tied back with a ribbon at the base of her neck. On her knee was a small kitten. It perched there, looking at the ground as if it were a hundred miles away instead of six inches. The kitten wobbled a bit then jumped, landing clumsily and hitting its chin on the fabric-covered ground. Lydia laughed and picked the kitten up, hugging it to her. Another kitten's head poked up from the center of her lap. He could see her say something as she picked that one up in her other hand. He continued to watch while he finished his sandwich.
    "So, what have we here?" Sterling said as he stepped out onto the porch.
    Lydia looked up suddenly with doubt in her eyes. She looked very nervous, so Sterling smiled broadly to show he wasn't upset about the kittens. He approached her,

knelt down and reached out a hand to stroke one of the furry heads.

"Where did you get these? I hope someone hasn't taken it into their heads to pay me with kittens." He continued to smile and pet the kitten.

"N-no." Lydia's nervousness was easing some but the stammer betrayed her. "I found them under the front porch."

Sterling picked up the kitten he'd been stroking and held it to him, listening to the loud rumble coming from the small chest. The white of its front legs blended with his shirt as it kneaded his chest.

"So, who are you, and what are you?" Sterling looked from the kitten to Lydia for the answers. She looked back in confusion. He laughed. "What's its name and is it a boy or girl?"

Lydia still looked somewhat confused. "I don't know. I just call them Little Ones or Kitty. I didn't think about whether they were girls or boys."

Sterling turned the kitten over and looked. "I think this one is a girl, but with kittens it can be hard to tell. Here, you take her and give me the other one." After checking he said, "This grey tabby is a boy. Brother and sister maybe?" He sat down beside her, putting the kitten back in her lap. "So, what are you going to name them?"

"You mean I can keep them?" Lydia was shocked that he assumed it was all decided.

"I don't see why not. You obviously love them, and I've always liked cats. They won't be able to go into the clinic, but I don't see why they can't be in the rest of the house--except my bedroom at night."

Lydia jumped to her knees, throwing her arms around Sterling and knocking the kittens off her lap.

"Oh, thank you. I've been so worried. When I found them the other day, I hid them thinking you wouldn't let me keep them. I was trying to figure out a way to ask, but was too nervous. Thank you, thank you." She hugged him tightly.

Sterling wrapped his arms around her and hugged her back. "If this is all it takes to get you to hug me, I'd have gotten you kittens long ago. No, you don't. Stay here and let me enjoy this."

Sterling tightened his arms around her when she tried to pull away. She looked at him for a moment then relaxed in his arms.

"Seems I have to keep asking you the same question," Sterling said, his chin resting on her head. "What are you going to name them?"

"I'll name the girl and you name the boy. Will you?" Lydia asked, her head on his chest.

"Okay, you first."

"I knew you were going to say that. Okay, Winnie. Her name is Winnie. Now the boy, what's his name?"

Sterling released Lydia and picked the kitten off his leg. "Ouch, your claws are sharp. No climbing the leg."

Lydia laughed.

Struggling not to smile, Sterling gave her a stern look but his lips twitched. "Hum. I'll have to think on that. You've known them longer. When did you find them? You said you were hiding them from me."

"I discovered them a couple of days ago. I was sitting in the lawn swing and heard them crying. I fed them and made them a box in the basement to sleep in. It was the day you found the kitchen door closed. They'd been playing and sleeping in there before I took them down to the basement. I forgot to open the door."

"So, now the truth comes out." Sterling grabbed her around the waist and began tickling her, causing her to wiggle and laugh.

"Stop, stop! Watch out for the kittens."

He stopped and smiled at her. She smiled back.

As his expression became more intense, she said, "So, the name of the boy kitty?"

"First, let's get off this damp ground and go into the house."

He helped Lydia to her feet, picked the male tabby off his pant leg again, scooped up Winnie and followed his wife into the kitchen.

Lydia closed the door into the clinic, and the doors into the hall and dining room. Sterling set the kittens on the floor.

"I ate the sandwich, which was very good, by the way. Now what?"

Lydia laughed. "Now I know why you wanted to come in. It wasn't the damp ground at all, it was your stomach. I should've known."

She continued to chuckle as she entered the pantry. She brought out a can of peaches, a small wedge of cheese, some crackers and a small paper-wrapped bundle.

"Let me feed the kittens, then I'll fix this up for you."

Sterling was pouring lemonade into two glasses. "Now I play second fiddle to a couple of cats," he grumbled in a teasing, pouty voice.

"They are little, you are big. You can wait, they can't." Sassily, she stuck her tongue out at him then proceeded to feed the kittens.

"Sterling," she began as she set his food on the table. "While I was downtown this morning I saw Magdelina. She tried to insult me again. She's very poor at it, really. Anyway, I got to thinking, and talked to Ella and then Peter about it. I think, and they thought I might be right, and we want to help her if we can, but I wanted to talk with you about it before we asked."

"Slow down." Sterling held up a hand, looking puzzled. "Just what do you think, and how are we going to help?"

"Well, I think she might be lonely, insecure and, well, bored. She has no husband or job or even a home of her own. The Taylors have hired help, so Magdelina doesn't even have chores to do. The friends she had in school have either gone away to college, or married, or gotten jobs. She's still doing what she did as a schoolgirl. We thought it might be nice to include her in our picnic while your sister and family are here. Maybe if she's included in activities she'll feel better about herself. Then she won't need to be so cutting in her remarks. I wanted to ask you if it was all right to invite her."

Sterling was quiet, looking closely at Lydia. "You would invite her to your home after she's insulted you every time she's seen you. You want to try to help her make her life better. I just want to take her by the shoulders and shake her until she cries and promises to stop."

"You'd never do that."

"No, but I've wanted to. She's followed me around since I returned from med school. Now she insults you continually, yet you think about becoming her friend." He paused. "I think your idea shows real compassion and is a good example of how Christ wants us to be."

"That's what I want, to be more like Christ, but don't think I'm better than I am. My hand has itched to slap her face when she's insulted me. I've had to confess my nasty thoughts more than once. I've been praying for a way to change my thoughts and feelings about Magdelina. I think this might be the way God wants me do that."

"Far be it from me to stand in the way of God. I'll pray about it, though, and let you know tomorrow. If God wants us to befriend her, he'll let me know."

The kittens slept with Lydia that night. She brought up the dirt box, food, water dishes and the old blanket for them to sleep on. Thinking that they'd actually sleep on the blanket was optimistic, she realized. They curled up on it while she was changing into her nightgown. A couple of minutes after she settled in bed the mews began.

"Shh, shh." Lydia spoke softly, which did nothing to quiet the kittens' cries.

Hoping that if she were very quiet they might settle down, she lay very still. She was wrong; they kept mewing in complaint. She felt a tug on the quilt covering her. First, Winnie came over the edge of the bed, followed by the nameless male kitten. Sterling had been called out shortly after supper, so he'd evaded her asking whether he'd chosen a name.

Having scaled the side of the bed, they now scaled Lydia. They walked up her body and their mews changed to purrs when they reached her head. Winnie decided the pillow was her destination, while the tabby sat on Lydia's chest.

"I am not cat furniture."

Lydia moved him beside her, then picked up Winnie and placed her beside her brother. She had to remove them from on top of her a couple of more times before they got the idea that they needed to settle beside, instead of on, her. Soon they were curled up next to her, purring loudly, as they drifted into sleep.

Lydia was so very glad Sterling let her to keep the kittens. He'd even seemed happy about them. He'd said they wouldn't be allowed into his bedroom at night, which she understood after her experience this evening. She would enjoy these few days sleeping with the kittens before the Rawlings came. At least until she moved back into this room.

Will I be back in this room? she wondered. Maybe Sterling would want her to stay with him.

The thought made her both nervous and excited. She didn't know which was stronger. She did know that she wouldn't be the one to suggest she stay. She also didn't know whether she would stay, if he asked.

Lydia thought over how close she was becoming to Sterling. Every day she learned new things about him, none of which made her like him less or made her more nervous. Instead, she realized, he made her feel safe and cared for. Enjoying the sensation, she smiled into the darkness, closed her eyes and went to sleep.

When Sterling came home from his call, he peeked into Lydia's room. Holding the candle high, he saw the dark spots of the kittens' bodies snuggled up to Lydia's back.

"Enjoy it while you can," he whispered, "because you won't join us when we share a bed."

Watching her while she slept made Sterling realize how easily Lydia had become the center of his life, second only to his Lord. He hadn't known there was something missing until he thought back to the time before that morning in March. Saying a silent thank-you to the Lord, he smiled at the trio, closed the door softly and went off to bed.

Chapter 28

Lydia awoke to Sterling poking his head into her room and saying her name.

"What?"

"I'm going to the livery to hitch up the horse and buggy. Then I'm heading out to the Griffith farm that's aways out of town. I call there every couple of months to see Granny Griffith. She's very old and can't come to town easily, so I go check on her there. I'll be gone most of the day."

"I'll get you some breakfast." Lydia was dislodging the kittens and climbing out of bed.

"Stay in bed. It's only five-thirty. I just wanted to let you know I'd be gone when you got up."

"No, I'll fix you breakfast. How about you go hitch up then come back here. I'll have breakfast ready by then. You can eat it before heading out."

"I'd appreciate that. Going on an empty stomach, which I've done frequently, isn't much fun."

Lydia heard him taking the steps two at a time. She smiled at the evidence of the boy still in the man.

When Sterling returned, Lydia, dressed in her nightgown covered by a light-blue robe, was placing hash topped with fried eggs, coffee and toast on the table. While he ate she made a parcel of sandwiches, and cookies.

"You take really good care of me, do you know that? Thank you," Sterling said, watching her bustle around the kitchen while he ate.

"You're welcome. I try," she said with a smile, then added in a long-suffering voice, "The Lord knows I try."

Sterling gave her a sharp look and laughed.

"You take good care of me, too." Lydia had her back to him as she tied up the parcel. The thought of them sleeping together flitted through her mind, making her blush. She turned to him, knowing her face was red.

Taking the last swallow of coffee, Sterling took the package and looked at her for a moment with puzzlement in his eyes. It seemed to her as if time stood still as he searched her face. She swallowed, forcing some unidentifiable yearning away. He leaned forward, kissed her quickly on the lips, winked and left.

Lydia stood watching him leave, her face maintaining its red glow. She lifted her hand, touching her lips, which still tingled from his kiss.

Lydia sat sewing in the sitting room and heard the screen door slam. Looking up, she saw her husband setting his bag down and hanging his Stetson on the hall tree. She set the sewing into her basket, rising to greet him.

"Hello, how'd your day go? Supper's still a while off. Would you like a snack?"

"No thank you, I just had coffee with Drew. He says hello, by the way. My day was fine. Mrs. Griffith is doing as well as can be expected for someone her age."

They walked together into the sitting room.

"That's good." Lydia sat back down, picking up her sewing. "I've started on the extra curtains. Mrs. Johnson had this green stripe she had mentioned before."

"You do know there's no real hurry for those, don't you?" Sterling was sitting in the matching upholstered chair that was separated from hers by a small table.

"Yes, but I want them ready when your sister comes. They're prettier than the plain navy ones."

"Are you still nervous about Margaret coming? She won't bite, you know."

"I know that, but yes, I am nervous about her coming. She grew up here, and she's never met me. I don't know whether she'll approve of or even like me."

"She has no right to approve or disapprove of you, you know."

"I suppose, but still ... I do want her to like me, at least for your sake."

Sterling reached over and took her hand. "I know she'll like you. You are a very likable person, especially to me."

Lydia turned her attention to her husband, wishing she could press the hand he held to her stomach. Lydia's stomach felt as if it had a million butterflies fluttering around in it.

The gloaming cast a peaceful end to the day as the couple sat next to each other on the lawn swing. Sterling used his long leg reaching the ground beside the swing to put it in motion. They chatted with those who walked by, content, enjoying the warm evening stillness. The kittens romped through the grass, stalking and pouncing on each other. Sterling laid his arm on the back of the seat, his fingers fiddling with her sleeve.

Lydia turned her head to look at him. "So, what have you decided to call him? You said you'd pick a name today."

Sterling glanced at her, a touch of panic in his eye. "Um ... ah ... um ... Max. His name is Max."

"You had last night and all day today to come up with a name, and you choose Max?"

"Uh, yes. It's a good, strong manly name that's fit for a tough tomcat."

Just then the kittens began to truly fight, growling, hissing and clawing at each other. Winnie managed to jump on top of Max, biting him on the ear. Max screeched, bucked Winnie off and ran to the swing, climbing Lydia's skirts. She picked him up and held him close.

"Did the little, weak, girly Winnie hurt the big, tough, manly Max?" Lydia's voice was thick with amused sarcasm.

"Okay, okay. Remember he's still a little kitten, not that tough, strong tomcat yet."

"Well, he is a sweetie."

Sterling looked down at his wife holding the kitten. Lydia had changed in the time they'd been together. When they'd married she was shy, unsure of herself and fearful. More relaxed now, she could tease him. He liked that. Thinking about the change in his life, Sterling realized he wouldn't want to be single again. He liked having Lydia in his life.

As for you, you meant evil against me, but God meant it for good. The passage from Genesis slipped into his thoughts. God could make this marriage of strangers work out. It seemed to him to have begun well. Silently he asked for the Lord to continue blessing them as he had so far.

Lydia glanced up, and their eyes met and held for a long moment before she dropped them back to Max.

Chapter 29

Done, Cyrus thought to himself as he put the planter away. Now I'm gonna find that girl and bring her back. He led the draft horses into the barn, planning how he'd begin his search. First off he would go to Aggie and make her tell him where Lydia was.

When he was finished tending the horses, Cyrus saddled his brown gelding for the trip to the neighboring farm. He was dirty and sweaty from his work, but saw no reason to clean up. He wasn't going to town. Going to intimidate an old woman didn't call for sprucing up. None of his other clothes were clean anyway. He didn't know much about washing clothes. The first time he'd tried, his efforts left him with two shirts and a pair of pants shrunk so much they wouldn't fit a boy of ten. He hated doing it and didn't much like cooking either. It seemed that everything was burnt or undercooked. He ate it because he had to eat, but nothing was very good. And the cleanup--he left that for as long as he could.

Cyrus really wanted Lydia back. After Gus and Lydia were married, he would talk Gus into letting Lydia come and do his laundry, housekeeping and maybe even some cooking for him. She'd have to come from town, but it was only a few miles for her to walk. A couple times a week wasn't much.

The memory of when he'd realized she was gone burned angry in his mind. Entering the barn after working all day he had seen that the cow hadn't been milked. Irritation took him to the house to find Lydia. Instead, on the kitchen table was cloth-covered food and a note. He'd sworn under his breath. The lazy girl had gone to that witch Aggie's to make soap and wouldn't be back until tomorrow. Not only would he have to milk the cow that night but the next morning as well. He'd have a couple of things to tell her that was for sure. At least she'd left him a loaf of bread, two-thirds of a peach pie and stew ready for warming.

The next evening when she still wasn't back he was angrier. He'd go get her in the morning, after he again did her chores. That evening he'd eaten the stew directly from the pot, leaving it and the now empty pie tin on the table.

Riding into Aggie's yard, Cyrus started yelling. "Hey, you old biddy, get out here right now, I want to talk to you."

The dogs danced around the horse, barking.

The door to the cabin opened and Aggie stepped out onto the small porch, her hands in her skirt pockets. The dogs stopped barking, coming to stand by the porch.

"I told you not to come snooping around here again, Cyrus Walcott."

"I don't care what you told me. I want to know where that stupid Lydia is, and I want to know now." He rode a little closer to the woman.

"I haven't seen her since the last time you were here, so I don't know. Now get outta here."

Cyrus dismounted. "You're gonna tell me if I have to beat it outta you."

With menacing steps he came at Aggie. Out of her pocket she pulled a Colt pistol and carefully cocked it.

Cyrus stopped.

"You just get off my land, Cyrus, and don't come back. Lydia's not here and won't be ever again, and you just have to get used to that. If you trespass on my land one more time, I'm gonna shoot first and get the sheriff after."

"You'll be sorry you didn't tell me where she is," Cyrus growled, then leapt onto his horse, whipped its side and took off at a gallop.

Chapter 30

Sterling placed his hand on Lydia's back, guiding her down the steps of the church following the worship service. Flickers of sunlight edged through the leaves waving in the gentle breeze. Seeing the Taylor family, with Magdelina standing a little off and behind her parents, Sterling leaned down to speak softly into Lydia's ear.

"Do you want to speak with her now or wait until Peter and Ella can join us?"

"Let's wait. I do want to invite her, but I'm nervous enough to want the support." She looked up at him with uncertainty in her gaze.

They slowly wandered in the general direction of the Taylor family, greeting and chatting with other parishioners while they waited for the pastor and his wife.

Lydia kept Magdelina in her line of vision as they moved. The young woman stood alone, behind her parents, next to the trunk of an oak tree. Lydia saw her eyes scan the crowd, a wistful longing on her face. Lydia's heart broke for the loneliness and longing in the beautiful eyes. *Please, Lord, help me to become a good friend to her. She needs one so desperately. Let me be a living witness for you.*

The Lendreys approached and Lydia and Ella exchanged glances. The two couples approached the Taylors.

"Good morning, Mrs. Lendrey, Mrs. Graham," Mrs. Taylor uncharacteristically gushed at the ladies. "How do you like my new dress? Believe it or not, I found it at Johnson's. I usually have all my clothing made at Hopkins' dress shop, but when I found this I just had to have it." She did a pirouette, showing off her pink and puce ruffled dress.

Lydia saw Magdelina looking down at the ground, her face flushed with embarrassment. Again, her heart went out to the young woman. She seemed so uncomfortable, not speaking with anyone, just standing in the shadow of the tree.

"It's very ... unique," Ella said after a moment, echoing Lydia's own words to Sterling in Johnson's store. "No one could wear it with as much aplomb as you."

Lydia let out a breath of relief when Mrs. Taylor smiled with pleasure. She nodded her agreement, not daring to utter a word, afraid she'd stick her foot in her mouth and spoil the older woman's pleasure.

Mrs. Taylor moved off to another group, eager to continue showing off her new dress.

Lydia squeezed Ella's hand then touched her husband on the arm. Sterling glanced at her, excused himself and took her arm. As a couple, they approached Magdelina.

"Magdelina," Lydia said when they stopped in front of her.

Magdelina had been looking off into the distance, and brought her focus onto them.

"We're having a picnic after church on Decoration Day. Sterling's sister and family will be here. We're having the Lendreys, the Stantons, the Phelps, Sheriff Drew and Mrs. H. We were wondering if you'd like to join us. It'll be simple and quiet, at least as quiet as three young boys will let it be." Lydia smiled at Magdelina, hoping the thought of the children would ease the nervousness she saw in the young woman.

"Yes, Magdelina, I hope you'll join us," Sterling said.

Magdelina looked from one to the other. "You're inviting me to your house for a picnic?"

"Yes, we'd love to have you," Lydia said. "Please say you'll come."

Magdelina hesitated for a moment. "You really want me to come?"

"We both do," said Sterling.

"Okay, thank you, I'll come." Magdelina looked at them, a small, genuine smile lighting up her face.

"Wonderful," Lydia said, wanting to squeeze Magdelina's hand but refraining. The girl was nervous enough as it was.

Then a new idea flew into Lydia's head, one that seemed so insistent she had to act on it. "Magdelina, may I ask a favor?"

Magdelina's expression became slightly guarded. "Yes."

"Would you be willing to come and help me decorate for the holiday? I've heard several other ladies talking about how they love to decorate for Decoration Day. I never have before and don't know how to do it." She leaned in a little closer to Magdelina, lowering her voice a touch. "I'm nervous enough about Sterling's sister and family visiting, and I don't want to do this part wrong. I could use your help."

A smile lit Magdelina's face, making her beauty shine. "I'd like to help you with that. I do like decorating of any kind."

Lydia let out a soft breath she hadn't even known she was holding. For some reason she didn't quite understand, it was very important that she and Magdelina, together, decorate the house.

"I'm busy with laundry tomorrow, so how about coming Tuesday morning and staying for lunch. We can make the plans then. We really only have this week to plan, and next week, until Saturday, to decorate. That's when the Rawlings arrive."

Magdelina was truly smiling now, "That's sounds fine to me. Is nine o'clock okay? That way you'll have time to get breakfast and the doc out of way." Her eyes twinkled a little.

Sterling laughed out loud. "I can tell when I'm not wanted."

Lydia laughed too, then, taking Magdelina's hand, gave it a gentle squeeze. "Thank you for agreeing to help. It really takes away a worry. I'll see you on Tuesday."

"Why don't you go to the clinic or out on a house call or something?" Lydia said as she wiped the kitchen table.

"You certainly are chasing me out quickly this morning."

"Well, Magdelina's coming shortly, and I want all my chores done so we can start planning."

"Why did you ask her to help you anyway? I thought we were just going to invite her to the picnic."

"So did I, but the thought of having her help me plan came into my head with such force that I just had to. Maybe it was the Holy Spirit, but it was so important I ask her. You saw how her face lit up. It was so right to ask her; it had to be the Holy Spirit. I'd never have thought to ask for her help. Now you just scoot, as Janie says."

Sterling went to the clinic. He didn't have anything pressing and thought he'd stay close for a while. If Magdelina was going to be nasty to Lydia he wanted to be near. If everything went well, he'd enjoy teasing and interfering, just to annoy Lydia. She was getting used to his teasing, but it always took her a minute to realize he was doing it. Her reaction when she did was great fun.

He was doing paperwork when he heard Lydia greet Magdelina. He decided to give them some time then go see how they were getting along.

"Good morning, Magdelina, come in." Lydia smiled as she opened the front door.

"Hello, I hope I'm not too early. The day is fine and looks to be warm. My walk over was very pleasant."

"I'm so glad. I was afraid after yesterday that the rain might continue today, making it difficult for you to come. I had to hang the laundry up in the basement. Actually, it's still there. It won't dry well down there."

They entered the kitchen. Paper and pencils were set out on the table ready for sketching and list making.

"I thought it would be too formal in the dining room," Lydia said. "It's a pleasant room, but I thought we'd be more comfortable and relaxed in here. Is that all right with you?"

"Of course."

Both women had a slight nervousness about them. They stood silently for a moment, taking each other's measure. Lydia broke the silence.

"Please, sit down. Would you like some coffee, tea or maybe lemonade? I also have some cookies." She placed the plate on the table as Magdelina sat down.

"Lemonade sounds wonderful, thank you."

Lydia poured glasses for both of them, then sat down at the end of the table. She picked up a pencil and fiddled with it. This is silly, she thought. We need to get past the ... past.

"Magdelina," she started, "I know you were disappointed at my marrying Sterling. If there'd been another answer I'd have gladly taken it. I'm so sorry."

Magdelina's mouth dropped open. She closed it quickly, blushed deep red, then smiled. "I like your directness. It's ... refreshing, not something I'm used to." She paused then went on. "Can I tell you a secret?" Lydia nodded, wide-eyed. "I never wanted to marry Sterling. Mother wanted it. I'm sort of, well, afraid of him."

This time Lydia's mouth dropped open. "Afraid? Of Sterling? He's the sweetest, gentlest man I've ever met. He doesn't get mad at me for the stupid little things I do. He's considerate, kind, generous. How can you be afraid of him?"

"I'm really not sure. He's so much older than I am. He was one of the big boys when we were in school. He and Drew Richards and Peter Lendrey were always together. They played lots of pranks on the littler kids. Nothing really bad--banging on the outhouse walls when you were in there, pretending to steal your lunch pail, picking you up and holding you so your feet wouldn't touch the ground ... Typical boy teasing."

Magdelina paused, her expression looking back into the past. "Now that I think about it, they were also the first to put a stop to real bullying. Several of the boys would try to lift up your skirts, throw dirt or mud on you or trip you. Sterling and the others stopped them. Looking back at it, I guess I just combined my thoughts of Sterling with the mean boys. He was the youngest of the three, and closer in age to the bullies. When Peter and then Drew graduated, Sterling hung around with the other boys. I guess that's when I lumped him with them. They'd stopped being mean by then. They were more interested in teasing to get the girls' attention. I never really thought about it before. I just remember thinking he was a bully."

"That's understandable. A child's experience and thinking."

"Then, Mother decided that I should marry Dr. Graham. As soon as he came back from medical school, she started in. I was still in school, but she'd talk nonstop about how wonderful it would be for me to marry a doctor. Especially Dr. Graham, since he was already here. She never let up. When I tried to protest that I didn't want to marry him, she threw such a fit I never said it again. I never did anything to promote the idea. I just let Mother think I was. Truth be told, I was relieved when you and Sterling married. It ended, finally, Mother's insistence that I marry him."

Lydia was stunned at the revelation. "She told us, the day after the wedding, that you'd spent all Sunday afternoon and Monday crying in your room."

"I knew I couldn't let her see my relief that I wouldn't have to listen to her harp about pushing myself at Doc. I stayed in my room until Tuesday morning. She was pretty much over her tirade by then and has never spoken about it since. She still doesn't know my real feelings." Magdelina's expression was a mixture of joy and chagrin.

"Why were you so insulting to me then whenever we met?"

"I thought I had to so Mother wouldn't suspect I was happy about your marriage. I'm so sorry about it. I do so want to be your friend. Please forgive me. Your invitation Sunday was so welcome. I almost cried and hugged you right then. You showed such grace to me after how I'd been to you." Magdelina stopped, her eyes brimming with tears of repentance.

Lydia took her hand and squeezed it. "Of course I forgive you. I'm so glad you told me. It really makes things easier. We can start here and now with a good solid friendship." She smiled, her eyes twinkling. "How about we seal the friendship with a cookie?"

"A marvelous idea," Magdelina replied, taking a cookie off the plate Lydia held out to her.

Sterling walked down the clinic hall to the kitchen a couple of hours later. He'd been busy with several patients, and this was the first time he could get away to check on Lydia and Magdelina. Concern for Lydia, and how Magdelina might be treating her, had been on his mind all morning. As he approached the door to the kitchen, he heard shrieks of pain and peals of laughter.

Rushing into the kitchen, he saw Lydia jumping around with Max on her back. She was trying to reach one hand over her shoulder and the other up from below to reach the kitten, which was clinging on with all his might. Laughter mixed with sounds of pain came from his wife.

Magdelina, laughing also, was trying to get Lydia to stop jumping and turn her back toward her so she could get the kitten off Lydia's back. Max, scared by the movements and noise, gripped Lydia's blouse and skin tighter.

Lydia stopped abruptly when she saw Sterling.

Magdelina snatched the kitten, holding him to her chest, soothing him with soft words.

"Sterling!" Lydia blushed red at the thought of him seeing her prancing around and squealing.

He grinned. "Dancing with my cat, I see. He doesn't seem to approve of the steps."

"No, he doesn't," Magdelina said, taking her seat with the kitten.

Lydia, her cheeks still crimson, deciding that a change of topic was in order, "Is it lunchtime already?"

"Not quite. I've had a busy morning. and thought a cookie might keep my strength up until lunch." He snatched a cookie from the plate. They heard the bell to the clinic ring, so Sterling, with a parting word, left to see who needed him.

"See, he's not so scary," Lydia said, sitting down to catch her breath.

"I know he isn't. I just never really wanted to marry him. Mother still sighs heavily when we're together and she sees either you or Sterling."

"Well, he can get scary when he's hungry," Lydia said with a twinkling eye. "I have sliced ham for sandwiches and the makings for potato salad ready for mixing, some canned pears, and of course the cookies. How about we get lunch ready for when the hungry man comes back?"

"Why don't we take your laundry from the basement outside and hang it up on the lines?" Magdelina said as they were finishing up the dishes from lunch. "That way they'll dry."

"I'd thought about that, but didn't have time before you came."

"Let's do it now, then we can go to Johnson's and see what they have that we might use for the decorating."

"You don't have to help me, you know. The laundry's my work, and I don't want you, as a guest, to do it."

Magdelina looked sorrowful and serious for a moment. "Lydia, I really want to help. Actually, I need to learn how to do all the things a woman knows about keeping a house. My mother thinks it's beneath her and never lets me help, or even watch Rosie, our housekeeper and cook. I don't know anything about laundry, cleaning, canning, and very little about cooking. I can sew a little, but not clothes, only fancywork. I've never dug in the dirt let alone planted and tended anything."

"You're kidding." Lydia was incredulous at the thought. "I've done those things ever since I can remember. How are you supposed to live when you marry and have to keep a house?"

"I was supposed to marry Sterling, remember. Since he's a doctor, we were supposed to hire all that done. As the banker's daughter" --Magdelina stuck her nose in the air and spoke in a perfect imitation of her mother-- "and doctor's wife, who needs to live up to the profession, having hired help is a must. Social status and all that, you know." She giggled.

"Oh, I see." Lydia joined in the giggling. "Heaven forbid getting our pretty little hands dirty with the filthy business of living. Okay, let's go get that laundry and hang it out."

That night at supper Sterling looked at Lydia with a quizzical eye.

"What?" asked Lydia.

"What's going on with Magdelina and you? You two were laughing and getting along like long-time best friends. Was that the same Magdelina who we invited after church or an impostor?"

"It was Magdelina. She never wanted to marry you. You scared her from her childhood days." Lydia took a bite of chicken casserole.

"Me? I scared her?" Sterling set down his fork, looking confused. "What did I ever do to her?"

"Actually, she realized today, as she spoke about it, that you'd always been nice to her. She said that you, Drew and Peter protected the younger children from being bullied. After they grew up and graduated, you were still there, about the same age as the boys who did the bullying. In her mind she not only connected you with Drew and Peter but also lumped you in with the bullies. Aside from that, it was always her mother who wanted the two of you to marry."

Sterling began eating again as Lydia went on recounting what Magdelina had told her.

"I understand her not wanting to marry someone she was afraid of, but I'm glad she figured out that you aren't a big scary man she needs to avoid. Did you know she was never taught any of the skills that a woman needs?"

"What, batting her eyes at the men?"

"No, silly, the important skills like cooking, cleaning, gardening, that kind of thing. What she'll need to know so she can manage a house when she marries."

"So who's supposed to do those things?"

"The maid and cook. Her family has hired help who do the cooking, cleaning, yard work and such. I just can't imagine it."

"Some women have mother's helpers or hire someone to help during busy times. Usually it isn't permanent help though. Like us hiring the Jorgensen boys. I know Peter hired Natalie Winston to help Ella when Janie was born. Natalie was younger than we were. She's since married and moved away."

"I can understand that, especially with Rye bouncing around as a toddler."

"My mother would hire help occasionally."

"I helped my mother do those things. That's how I learned. After she died I had to do them. What I didn't know I went to Aggie to find out how. Magdelina wants to learn how to do all of it. You know, Sterling, she's bored. She has nothing to do at home, and nothing outside of home either. She wants me to teach her all about keeping a home."

"So you two got along well?"

"Oh, yes, we had a great time. I'm really looking forward to getting to know her better. She has very good ideas for the decorating. We got a lot of the plans for the decorations worked out." Lydia's forehead furrowed a bit. "It'll cost some to buy the bunting and other items, but we'll save them and use them again."

"Well, since I'm not a big scary man I'll just say, get whatever you need. No, scratch that. Get whatever you want. Now, since I'm done with my meal ... what's for dessert?"

Lydia laughed. "Not a big scary man. Instead one with a big--no, scratch that--enormous sweet tooth."

Chapter 31

Hoooo, hoooo.

The sound of the incoming train startled Lydia from her reverie. She and Sterling were sitting on a bench outside of the station, waiting for the train bringing Sterling's sister Margaret and her family. Lydia's hands were sweating from her anxiety. Sterling didn't know this, even though he held her hand, because of the new white kid gloves he had given Lydia the day before.

Lydia and Magdelina had worked hard getting the house cleaned and the outside decorating done. Before decorating, they had scrubbed the porch floor and arranged the furniture into pleasing groups. The porch railing had red-and-blue bunting, which set off the masses of white peonies in full bloom in front of the porch. The columns supporting the roof were festive, with large white satin bows trailing long streamers that swayed in the breeze. The furniture also had bows of red, white or blue. Bunting looped across the frame of the lawn swing, with white bows on the corners. There would be white cushions on the seat come the day of the party. In the yard beside the house they had set up a crochet field.

During a break in the work Lydia had noticed Magdelina sitting in obvious serious concentration. "Magdelina, is everything all right?" she asked.

Magdelina was silent for several moments before saying, "Well, nothing is really wrong, it's just ... would you ... I mean ... I'd really rather ..." She looked straight at Lydia and with quiet intensity said, "I'd really rather be called Maggie."

"Oh, I'm sorry, I didn't know. I've never heard you called that."

"Mother hasn't let anyone call me Maggie since I was a small child. She said it wasn't dignified for a leader in the community to be called by such a common nickname." She paused. "I don't want to be distinguished or a social leader. I just want to be Maggie. It has a friendly feel to it. Magdelina is stuffy and snobbish. Maggie is just, I don't know, approachable and nice."

"Of course I will. It may take me a few days to adjust so remind me when I slip up."

That evening Lydia had told Sterling about Maggie's request.

He shook his head. "Her parents have always set store in being better than everyone else. 'Do nothing out of rivalry or conceit, but in humility.' 'Consider others as more important than yourselves.' In their desire for social superiority they've made their daughter's life miserable. How sad, and how wonderful that you listened to the Holy Spirit in befriending her."

"She's so much fun for me to have around. I've never really had a girlfriend before. I've giggled more than I have in years."

"She's really come out of her shell. I've noticed that she doesn't stand in that slouch as if she's trying to be invisible anymore. I never noticed it until she started coming here. Now she stands much more relaxed. You, Lydia, are a very good friend."

The train whistle blew again, much closer this time drawing Lydia's thoughts back to the present. The day was warm and sunny. A light rain had fallen yesterday morning, settling the dust and washing everything clean.

"Come, let's stand over here so we can see them come off the train." Sterling led her to the corner of the building so they'd be out of the way but be able to see the passengers debark.

With the roar and clatter of the great machine and the whoosh of steam, the train came to a stop. There was a flurry of activity as baggage was unloaded and passengers stepped down onto the platform. A man in a grey suit stepped down then turned, giving a hand to a small boy. Another boy jumped off the step and continued jumping, getting out of the way.

Sterling let go of Lydia's hand and moved forward. The man was helping a woman dressed in maroon carry a little girl down the steps.

"Margaret, Reese," Sterling called as he approached.

Margaret looked up, handing the girl to Reese and quickly reaching for her brother. Sterling swept her up in a big hug.

"Sterling, Sterling, it's so good to see you. It's been so long. And now you're married. How bad of you not to let me know beforehand." Margaret hugged him back then pulled back to look at him. "Well, well, you have turned into a reflection of Papa. I never thought of it before but you do have the look of him. Connor, Stafford, stay off of the baggage cart. The men need to be able to get our baggage onto it. Reese, say hello to Sterling."

"Yes, my dear." Reese winked at Sterling. "Good to see you. As you can see, Margaret is the same as always." He took Sterling's outstretched hand, balancing his daughter with the other.

"Welcome back to Cottonwood. It's good to see you too. Let me introduce you to my wife."

Sterling looked around for Lydia. She was still standing by the building. He could see apprehension on her face though she tried to hide it. He realized he could read her feelings by the tension in her face.

"Come, let's get out of the way." He led the group to where Lydia stood.

She smiled, but Sterling could tell that the smile was only on the surface. Underneath she was extremely nervous. Sterling took her hand and pulled her to him. With his arm around her waist, hoping it was a comfort, he began the introductions.

"Margaret, Reese, this is Lydia. Lydia, my sister Margaret and her husband Reese."

"Pleased to meet you. Welcome. We look forward to having you with us for the holiday."

"Introduce me, introduce me," piped the voices of two young boys.

The girl in Reese's arms stuck her thumb in her mouth.

"If you'll stand still long enough I will," Margaret said.

The boys, who had been jumping around the group, stopped, coming to stand beside their mother.

"Lydia, these two jumping beans are Connor," she touched the older boy's head, "and Stafford." She ruffled Stafford's hair in obvious affection.

Leaning down toward them, Lydia said, "I'm very pleased to meet you also."

Connor spoke first. "Are you Uncle Doc's wife? Mama said--"

"This one is Abby," Reese interrupted.

Margaret latched onto Connor's arm, halting his comment before it was voiced.

"Mama, I'm hungry." Stafford turned toward his mother, grabbing her skirt and looking up at her.

"We can solve that, my man," Sterling said. "We're lunching at Langston's Cafe. These young men will take your baggage to the house. Matias, Niles," Sterling called to the teens standing by the baggage cart. "Reese, how about you showing them which bags are yours."

Reese handed Abby to her mother, saying, "Why don't you and the boys start off to Langston's. We'll catch up with you."

Lydia nearly panicked. How was she going to make conversation with Sterling's sister, who had obviously said something against her that her son had heard? How long would it take for the men to catch up with them? Looking up the street, the cafe seemed a thousand miles away.

"Boys, come with me," Margaret said. "We're going to eat at a place I ate at when I was a child."

Lydia fell into step with them. Her mouth felt like cotton was stuffed in it. She desperately wanted to say something engaging, but absolutely nothing came to mind. A small hand reached out, touching her shoulder.

"Hi, Abby. I'm Lydia. Well, I guess it would be Aunt Lydia."

She smiled at the little girl. She was a fair child with curls of dark brown hair bouncing all over her head.

"Aun Ydia." Abby said and then smiled.

"You've made a friend, Lydia." Margaret looked a little surprised. "Seldom will she talk to someone she doesn't know."

Lydia smiled. She tried to figure out if Margaret was pleased or not as she had made the comment in a neutral tone. She decided to think the best and said, "I'm pleased. She's a charming, pretty girl. Your boys are bundles of energy, aren't they?" She smiled in delight at the boys jumping down the boardwalk.

"You're certainly correct in that. They'll go at lightning speed then collapse with fatigue. We have to get them to bed when that happens or they'll get a second wind and be off again. They were very good on the train. They aren't used to being still for so long. We left very early this morning." Margaret lowered her voice. "I hope they get their energy worked off now and during the walk home so they'll take naps this afternoon. I know I could handle them taking a nap."

Lydia stifled a laugh. Then she looked at Margaret's face and laughed along with her, the tension easing slightly.

"Would you like me to carry Abby? She must be heavy."

"She can walk if we go slow. When we get to the house she can run in the yard, but I don't want her getting away from me and into the street."

"Of course, that way the men can catch up with us sooner."

"Hold up, boys. Abby's going to be slower than you," Margaret called.

Connor and Stafford jumped back to the ladies as Margaret set Abby down and, holding her hand, began walking at the pace of the toddler. Abby tried to jump with her brothers. Margaret told her she could jump later but needed to walk now. Lydia was impressed with the obedience of all the children and told Margaret, who beamed with a mother's pride.

Arriving at Langston's, the two women and the children sat at a large table. Suddenly a shriek split the air. They all started, and turned to look at the doorway to the kitchen. Sally stood there with a huge smile on her face.

"Margaret Graham, as I live and breathe. I haven't seen you in years."

Sally rushed over as Margaret stood. The two women hugged long and hard.

"Sally, it's so good to see you. What are you doing here?"

"I'm married to Reg. We got married six years ago. We run the cafe now that his folks have retired. Not that they really have. They keep the girls. We have two."

"I didn't know. You know my brother. His letters leave something to be desired. These are my three, Connor, Stafford and Abby. We've come for a visit and to get acquainted with Lydia."

"Mama," Abby said as she squirmed in her seat. The adults recognized the movements.

"Children, we will all go out the back for a few minutes. Please excuse us, Lydia." Gathering the children, Margaret followed Sally out of the dining room, the chattering of the ladies drifting back to Lydia.

"Where are Margaret and the children?"

Sterling's voice caught Lydia by surprise.

"They'll be back in a moment. They just stepped out for a few minutes," Lydia replied. She was very glad the men had arrived. Although she and Margaret were getting along well enough, Lydia didn't know if she could have kept up a conversation if Sally hadn't come along.

Sterling took his place beside Lydia, Reese across the table. Sterling looked surreptitiously at Lydia. He knew how nervous she was about meeting his relatives, especially Margaret. He hadn't wanted to have the ladies and children walk without the men, but hadn't seen a way of changing that. Lydia's face showed nervousness, but not so much as to cause him concern.

"Lydia," Reese began, "it is a real pleasure to meet you. Margaret was pretty surprised when Sterling's letter came. She just about jumped on the next train and came down here. She didn't even finish the letter before she started packing. Fortunately I'd brought the mail home with me so I was home. I managed to stop her. She hadn't even read the entire letter and wasn't planning to."

Sterling pinched his lips together to stop himself from commenting, with ill grace, that the letter had said he would write again when he felt it was time for them to come.

He noticed Lydia's hands gripped in her lap and her eyes looking at them. It was a sure sign that she wanted to just disappear. He hadn't seen her in that position in many weeks. He didn't want her spending the entire week of their visit trying to be invisible. He hoped Margaret would be a considerate guest, but was afraid she might run roughshod over Lydia since she'd grown up there. Under the table he reached for and took her hand, holding it after giving it a gentle squeeze.

"Papa, Papa," the boys called as they all but ran over to the table, weaving around the chairs and tables.

Margaret was coming at a more dignified pace with Sally. The two were chatting as fast as their mouths could move.

"Well, my dear, I can see you're already having a good time." Reese stood to hold his wife's chair.

"You probably don't remember Sally. She was a good friend when we were children. Reese, this is Sally Langston. Sally, this is my husband Reese Rawlings."

Sally and Reese shook hands during the formal introductions, both saying, "Nice to meet you."

Sally reviewed the specials for the day and they placed their orders. As Sally left, Margaret turned her attention back to her brother and his wife.

"So, how do you like Cottonwood, Lydia? It's such a nice friendly town, don't you think?"

Lydia blushed and glanced at Sterling. "I have made some good friends here."

"I've been away so long. I plan to visit with some of my old friends and acquaintances while we're here. The Johnsons, Mrs. H., Francie, I don't remember what her married name is. I think of her as Francie Cottom."

"She's married to Daniel Windsor. He runs a dairy farm not far from town," Sterling interjected. "He came and bought the Burrows place. They decided to move on west. Daniel married Francie about a year later. He's a very good man. He delivers milk and eggs to us."

Then Sterling told them the story of Charlie O'Sullivan's accident. "Daniel brought Charlie in when the bull gored him. I was out on a house call at the time. Lydia really did a good job tending him before I returned, and while he stayed in the clinic. I was and am so proud of her."

"Charlie's wife was there too, Sterling," Lydia said. "She did as much as I did."

"I'm not married to Patty. I'm married to you and so you have to let me brag on you a little bit." Sterling smiled at her.

"Just a little. I don't want to have to live up to some fantasy you make up." Lydia smiled back at him.

As Margaret watched the couple, her worries about her brother's marriage eased somewhat.

"Don't touch me. Mama, Stafford's touching me."

"I am not. You're touching me."

The plaintive voices of the boys told of their fatigue from the journey.

"That's enough, no touching from either of you," Margaret said. "Your dinner will be ... here it comes now. We'll all eat a good meal then go on the house. It's the house I grew up in. I played in the yard, climbed the tree. All sorts of fun things."

"You climbed a tree, Mama?" Connor's eyes were wide with wonder.

Stafford's face had a puzzled look on it as he tried to visualize his mother climbing a tree.

The dishes were set on the table, and grace was said. Margaret and Reese began dividing the children's portions between them. The children settled in to eating quietly, not touching each other. The adults enjoyed their meal as Margaret asked questions about other friends and families she had known as a child.

Chapter 32

The walk to the house was only marred by two quarrels between the boys. Reese carried a sleeping Abby, and Margaret finally held the boys hands, which effectively ended the bickering.

Margaret apologized. "They don't usually act like this. The train ride first excited them, then made them restless. They had to wake up early so we could catch the train, too."

"We understand. The ride on the train tired me out also," Lydia offered, to ease Margaret's embarrassment at the boys' behavior.

Sterling glanced at Lydia. It was the first time since early in their marriage that she'd spoken of the train or that time. He hoped she was getting over the upheaval and trauma of that time. Please, Lord, he prayed silently.

"Oh, Sterling, the house looks beautiful. Mother used to do this for Decoration Day." It was obvious Margaret wanted to hurry to the porch, but she kept to the slow pace her tired boys could manage.

"Well, at least I managed to keep her peonies growing."

Sterling and Margaret smiled at each other.

"The peonies were our mother's joy," Margaret told Lydia and Reese, "and she impressed upon us that they were not to be played amongst. Both of us were the recipients of several spankings learning that lesson." Margaret's expression was wistful. "The yard swing is still here. And it's so prettily decorated." She looked closer and exclaimed, with a slight edge to her voice, "Oh, it's not white. It's yellow and green."

Sterling felt the hand in the crook of his elbow tighten. "It's a new one. The old one was broken. I think Lydia's choice of yellow and green is a good one. Matches the house, and all the porch furniture is white."

"Well, you know, now that I think about it and see it, I think it's a good choice, too," Margaret said.

Sterling felt the hand loosen slightly.

"Well, let's get the children in and settled for a nap, shall we?" Reese indicated a sleeping Abby in his arms. "She's getting heavy."

"I'm so sorry." Lydia released Sterling's arm and hurried to the porch and up the steps. "Come, I'll take you all up to your rooms."

The group followed her up the steps and through the door she held open. Sterling picked up a couple of pieces of the luggage that was waiting for them beside the door.

That evening while the Rawlings were settling the children for the night Lydia prepared a tray with a pitcher of iced tea and glasses. Sterling filled a plate with a variety of cookies Lydia had baked the day before, piling the plate high, higher than Lydia would have. She smiled to herself as he put more and more cookies on the plate.

The two couples met up on the porch.

"Come, Margaret, sit with me on the swing. It'll be nice to sit with you without the children squirming between us," Reese said as he held the swing still for her to seat herself.

The two couples sat enjoying the warm evening without speaking for a while, the stillness broken only by the rustle of leaves touched by a gentle breeze. As the sky slowly darkened with the setting of the sun, they shared items of news, catching up on lives that were lived apart.

At least three of them did. Lydia sat quietly listening. She really hadn't anything to share. Besides, all she could think about was when the evening ended she would head up the stairs and go down the hall to Sterling's room. She'd moved her things in over the past few days, setting the last of the items on the washstand just this morning.

Her stomach tightened with each minute that passed. Would he be in there while she changed into her nightgown? Would he change in front of her? She grew warm at the thought. She wasn't sure if it was because she was embarrassed about being there or because she was excited at the thought. All she knew was that, either way, she was about ready to jump out of her skin.

"You've been real quiet this evening, Lydia," Margaret said.

"Just listening to you all."

"Well, I'm tired and think I'll head in now. Would you like to join me?" Margaret's question was directed at Lydia.

"Yes, I will. Thank you."

The women rose. Margaret leaned down to give her husband a quick peck on the cheek. Seeing that, Sterling took hold of Lydia's hand and pulled her down toward his face. She leaned down. He looked in her eyes and saw her nervousness.

"Reese and I will stay here for a while. Don't worry about the dishes. I'll take care of them." He saw her tight nerves ease a bit.

"Ha. You just want to eat more of those cookies, little brother. I know you. The biggest sweet tooth there ever was. Come, Lydia, let's leave them to their cookies."

Margaret twined her arm around Lydia's, holding her head overly high in over-exaggerated haughtiness. "We at least will exit with our dignity intact. We will not make pigs of ourselves over some cookies."

Everyone laughed at her melodramatic demeanor.

Lydia flew through her evening ablutions, wanting to be changed and in bed before Sterling came. She wanted to be asleep but knew there was no chance of that. Giving her hair only half the number of brushstrokes she normally did, she braided it loosely and tied it with a piece of ribbon.

She hesitated, trying to decide which side of the bed to sleep on. Her mind was simply blank. She'd slept with him once. She changed the sheets every week. Why couldn't she remember which side of the bed he slept on?

A soft knock on the door startled her so badly that she nearly tripped as she spun around to face the door.

"Lydia," Sterling whispered loudly, "may I come in?"

"Of course." Lydia went toward the door just as he opened it to come in. "Oh." She jumped back, allowing him access to the room.

He carried his shoes and vest. "Reese and I didn't want to wake the children stomping up the stairs with our shoes on," he said, lifting the shoes.

Lydia simply stood looking at him. Her eyes were wide with the haunted look of a frightened doe.

Sterling closed the door, set his shoes on the floor and approached her. Lydia, he was pleased to note, didn't back away from him. Still, he knew he had to be gentle with her.

"It's all right, Lydia. All we're doing is sharing a bed. Nothing else, simply sleeping." Sterling took her hand and stroked the back gently with his thumb.

Lydia let out the breath she'd been holding since she heard the knock on the door. "I'm so sorry. I shouldn't be so--"

"Shhh." Sterling put his finger to her lips. "You just get in the bed. I'll change and then join you. We'll both just go to sleep." She seemed so scared. He'd hoped she'd be more comfortable after the night of the storm. She seemed more nervous than ever.

Lydia turned toward the bed. "I ... I don't know which side."

"Well, I sleep on the left but I'll move to the right if you want it."

"No, no, I'll take the right." Lydia scurried to the right side, lifted the blankets and slipped in. She pulled the covers up to her chin and curled up on her left side, squeezing her eyes tightly shut.

Sterling grinned at the image she presented: that of a little girl hiding beneath the blankets believing no harm can come to her when shielded by them.

He leisurely changed clothes, tidying the clothes he'd removed, then blew out the lamp. He watched Lydia in the moonlight as he climbed into the bed. She was trying so hard not to jump at his every movement. When he was settled he whispered, "I don't bite, you know. Well, not very hard anyway. Besides, I can stitch up any bite I make, so you don't have to be concerned."

A nervous giggle snuck out of the mound of blankets on the other side of the bed. Then a huge sigh. Lydia uncurled herself and turned onto her back.

"I don't know what I'm so concerned about. It's so stupid, really. I know you don't bite." Another nervous giggle. "I guess I've been so nervous about your sister coming that I let it overflow into other areas."

Sterling had turned toward her, supporting his head with his bent arm and hand.

Lydia turned her head and looked at him. "How can you be so good to me? Over and over you are so patient. My fears and insecurities overwhelm me and you never get mad or impatient."

"How would that help?"

"It wouldn't, I guess, but that doesn't stop others from reacting that way."

Sterling knew she was thinking of her brother. He reached over and stroked the hair by her face. "I'm not trying to control you by making you afraid. I'm not trying to control you at all. I want you to feel safe, protected. My getting mad and impatient wouldn't lead to that goal."

"I never thought of that--that you had a goal in how you treat me. I'll have to think about that."

"Well, think fast or I might just have to resort to biting." He leaned over quickly and gave her a quick peck on the cheek. "Go to sleep now. You'll need all your strength to keep Margaret from taking over tomorrow at the party."

"Okay. Goodnight, and thank you."

"Sweet dreams."

Chapter 33

Cyrus sat at the table in the kitchen, just having finished his not very tasty meal of burned stew. He looked around the kitchen and swore. The room was a mess: every surface was covered with dirty plates, bowls, pots, pans and tableware. Stray bits of dried food stuck to the dishes.

Hearing hoof beats, he got up and walked out into the yard. Gus was getting down off his horse.

"You found Lydia yet?"

"No."

"Well, you better find her soon or I'm finding me some other girl to marry." Gus turned back to mount his horse.

"Wait, Gus, I got a idea. That old Aggie says she doesn't know where Lydia is. She won't let me back on her place." Cyrus walked over to Gus standing by his horse. "I think she does. Lydia always went over there. Liked the old biddy. If Lydia told anyone where she was going it'd be Aggie."

"So, what's your idea?"

"You go over there and tell her you're concerned about Lydia. Worried that she might be in danger or something. Play it up big so she believes you enough to tell you where Lydia is. Whaddya think?"

Gus rubbed his chin. "Might work. I'll go there now and come back here to let you know."

"Good. I have a bottle we can share when you get back." Cyrus slapped Gus on the arm then held the horse's head while his friend mounted.

Aggie looked up from weeding the garden at the sound of hoof beats. "That better not be that low down Cyrus Walcott again," she muttered as she stood up, leaning back with her hands on her hips, stretching out the stiffness.

Gus Botwright turned his horse into the short lane leading to Aggie's house.

"Mizz Cuttler, good day to you, ma'am. I was hoping I could have a word with you." Gus got off his horse and took off his hat.

Aggie, suspicious, stood looking at him with a raised eyebrow.

"I come by to find out if you'd heard anything from Lydia Walcott. I'm supposed to marry her, and I ain't heard nothin' from her in a long time. I'm worried about her being safe and all."

"You think I know?"

"I knowed you're a special friend, like, to her. I thought she might'a let you know how she is and let you know her whereabouts. I'm mighty concerned." Gus furrowed his eyebrows into what Aggie thought was his idea of concern.

"I ain't seen the girl since she run off from that brother of hers."

"I know that, ma'am. I was a hopin' you might've heard from her. I'd like to know she's safe and maybe be able to find her so we could go and get married like we planned."

Gus's attempt at humility didn't fool Aggie one bit. She looked at him and didn't like what she was seeing. He had the strong arms of a blacksmith, and if he struck a woman he would most likely injure or maybe even kill her. Lydia had been scared to death of marrying him.

Aggie guessed that he was here because Cyrus had told him to try and sweet-talk her into revealing Lydia's location. They figure I'm pretty stupid if they think I'd tell Gus Botwright, any more than Cyrus Walcott, where Lydia is, she thought.

She put her hands on her hips. "You go on back to Cyrus and tell him I'm not stupid," she said angrily. "If I wouldn't tell him I sure wouldn't be tellin' you. Now get off my land."

Aggie turned her back to Gus and strode into the house, where she went straight to the gun rack. Picking up her shotgun in case Gus was stupid enough to try something, she looked out the window, checking on him. Gus had mounted and was riding out of her yard.

That's not gonna be the end of this, most likely, Aggie thought. She would need to take care. Who knew what those two might do.

"Damn it anyway. Who does she think she is? Lydia's my sister and I gotta right to know where she is." Cyrus paced around the barnyard.

Gus sat on a bench with a bottle in his hand. "She ain't gonna tell you or me that. You'll have to think of some other way to find out." He took another drink from the bottle.

"Gimme that." Cyrus grabbed the bottle and put it to his lips for a long guzzle. This was the third bottle they'd shared since Gus had returned. "We're just gonna have to figure out something. Don't know what yet, but I'll figure it out. Then I'm gonna find Lydia and get back at that old bitch, too."

"Yeah. Figure it out. Uh-huh." Gus lay down on the bench, burped loudly and fell asleep.

Cyrus walked over to the barn, taking another long pull from the bottle. He sat down against the wall and began to think of a plan. His eyes fluttered, then shut as a grin spread across his face.

Chapter 34

The sun shone brightly into Sterling and Lydia's bedroom, announcing that the day would be warm and pleasant. Lydia had woken up when the first rays peaked over the windowsill. She lay next to Sterling, trying not to squirm too much with her mixture of nerves and excitement. Today was Decoration Day, and on Sunday, too. The parade, then church service, then the picnic. Lydia knew all the plans and preparations were done but was still nervous at hosting her first large social occasion.

Looking at the clock, she saw that it was just before six. Careful not to disturb Sterling, she eased out of bed. Pulling on her robe and stepping into slippers, she took one last glance at the sleeping man, then left to go start water heating so everyone would have warm water to wash with.

Sterling reached across the bed. Nothing. No body next to his. He wondered if she'd left in the night, too nervous to stay and sleep with him. He turned his head and looked at the vacant space. There was a dent in the pillow but no indication as to whether she'd stayed all night.

There was a rattle at the door. It swung open to reveal Lydia carrying the pitcher, which matched the basin on the washstand.

"Oh, you're awake. I hope my clumsiness with the door latch didn't wake you. I got up a while ago to make sure there was hot water for everyone. Margaret helped with getting all the pitchers brought up. She's getting the children ready now."

Sterling realized that his fear was unjustified. Lydia had just gotten up quietly so as not to disturb his sleep. "Thank you. Have you washed yet? I can wait for you."

"Already done. I did mine down in the kitchen. I didn't see the need to bring water up for me to wash my face and then have to carry it back down."

She'd placed the pitcher beside the bowl and was setting his shaving equipment out on a towel. Sterling came up behind her and wrapped his arms around her waist, drawing her back against his chest. Her hair smelled like lilacs.

"Did you sleep well?" he said, looking at her in the mirror.

She looked back at him. "Yes, I did. You didn't kick or snore or steal the covers." Her timid smile indicated she was just a little uncomfortable with their position.

"Well, who knows, maybe I will tonight. What would you do if I did any of those things?"

"Ella says to kick you back, push you over or steal the covers back."

He grinned back at her. "Sleeping with Peter, I'm sure she knows all about all those things."

Their eyes held for a long moment.

"Let me go. I need to get dressed so I can finish breakfast. Those children will be hungry and we have church to get to. We need to be on time, too." She squirmed in his arms.

"All right." Reluctantly, Sterling released her.

She scooted out from between him and the washstand, grabbing her hairbrush. Undoing the braid, she began to style her hair in the chiffon she wore to church. Sterling went to shaving but kept peaking at her in the mirror as she did her grooming.

When she was satisfied with her hair she hesitated. Now she needed to change her clothing and Sterling could tell she was uncomfortable doing so with him in the room.

"Hold on." He wiped the last of the shaving cream from his face, threw the towel onto the washstand and left the room. A few moments later he reentered with a folding screen and set it up across a corner of the room.

"Here, dress behind this. I don't know why I didn't think of this sooner. It was in the sewing room. This will give you privacy. Me, too, for that matter."

"Thank you." Lydia's relief was palpable. She quickly gathered up the clothing she needed and vanished behind the screen.

Sterling dressed and was tying his shoes when she emerged from behind the screen. "You look beautiful," he said.

She was wearing the sapphire dress she'd purchased the day of the shopping expedition.

Lydia smiled. "Thank you again. You don't look too bad yourself."

He had on his charcoal-grey wool slacks, white shirt with black studs, crossover tie, and maroon-and-gold brocade vest. He would add the grey frock coat and black derby when they left the house. Both had worn their outfits before but the intimacy of dressing in the same room brought more awareness of the other.

Breakfast was a noisy affair with three children at the table. Lydia and Margaret worked together, getting the plates filled, keeping milk glasses from being overturned, and eating their own breakfasts. The men took the children into the drawing room when the meal was done, allowing the women to do the dishes.

"I'll wash so you can get started on the food. We can leave the dishes to dry by themselves," Margaret said, taking a pitcher to the hot water tank and filling it.

"Okay, thank you. I have a ham to go into the oven. I boiled potatoes and eggs for salad yesterday. I thought to make German potato salad. Is that okay with you and your family?" Lydia knew Sterling liked it but didn't want to serve something none of the Rawlings liked.

"Reese and I do. The children, well, today maybe, tomorrow who knows. Don't set your menu by us. What else are you serving? I don't know why we didn't talk about this yesterday."

Lydia chuckled. "You and Sterling spent the afternoon catching up on your lives and reliving childhood memories."

"You're right." Margaret smiled. "Then the children woke up. No wonder we never got around to discussing it."

Lydia brought the potatoes and eggs from the icebox. "I'll cut these up. Let's see. Then there's the potato salad, there's fresh bread in the breadbox we'll slice when we get home. There are pies in the pie safe and--"

"Hey, ladies," Sterling interrupted, sticking his head into the kitchen, "it's time we left. The parade will be starting soon."

"Be right there. Tell Reese to gather up the children and make sure they're clean enough to go," Margaret instructed. "We're all ready here. The dinner will be easy to finish up when we get home."

The parade ended in the cemetery honoring those who had fought in the War of the Rebellion on both sides. Several Confederate veterans and their families had moved into Cottonwood after the war. Some in the town hadn't welcomed them to begin with, but as the years passed friendships were made, families joined in marriages and the sentiments of the war were left behind.

Many of those who watched the parade followed on to the cemetery then went into the church across the street. The service also centered on those who had given their all for a cause they believed in.

Lydia and Sterling, standing in the churchyard following service, watched as Margaret was greeted by childhood friends.

Maggie approached them, bubbling with happiness. "I'm so excited about the party. I brought the cookies we baked Friday. I was afraid Mother would say something to spoil my day."

"Isn't she pleased that you're coming?" Lydia asked.

"Well, yes and no. She's not pleased that I'm being called Maggie instead of Magdelina, pleased that I have a social engagement but definitely not pleased that it's with you. You're the reason I'm not married to the doc here." She gave Sterling a quick wink.

"Maggie, you're welcome at our home any time. You've become a great friend to Lydia and I truly appreciate it."

"She's become a great friend to me, too. She has the patience of a saint. My cooking skills have sorely tested her attitude toward me many times."

"Now, you two stop it. You'll make me have a big head with all this sort of talk. Your cooking is getting much better, Maggie. You only burned one pan of cookies this time instead of three," Lydia said with a teasing grin.

They had reached the street when Mrs. H called to them from a few steps away.

"Doc, Mrs. Doc, Magdelina, I'd like you to meet my great-niece, Rachel Meyers. Rachel's staying with me for the summer."

Rachel was a tall young woman with black hair and brown eyes. Tall and willowy, she towered over Mrs. H and Lydia. She looked shy but smiled as she held her great-aunt's arm.

Greetings were exchanged then Mrs. H asked, "Is it all right if Rachel comes with me to your party? I know it's impolite to invite someone to another's event, but she only arrived yesterday and I didn't have an opportunity to contact you."

Sterling smiled broadly at Mrs. H., including Rachel within the scope of his gaze. "Of course you're welcome, Rachel. Mrs. H., don't think a thing about it. Besides, we want to tell Rachel all about the things she doesn't know about you. And we want her to tell us what we don't know."

"Thank you," Rachel said.

"We'll slip home and get the basket with my dishes and be along as soon as we can," Mrs. H. said.

"Just don't hurry yourself too much," Sterling warned Mrs. H with a serious look. "I don't want to be a doctor this afternoon, especially not with you as the patient."

"Don't worry, Dr. Graham, I'll carry the basket and keep her in line at the same time." Rachel's voice was teasing.

"Now, you two, stop fussing over me." Mrs. H fluttered her hands, waving off their concern. "Come then, Rachel, we'll be late since I have to crawl along at a snail's pace if we don't leave now." She took Rachel's arm and they turned away toward Mrs. H's house.

"We need to get going too," Lydia said, taking Sterling's arm. "I have things to get done before people start arriving. Come, Maggie, you can help me with that. You're the one experienced in entertaining so I'm enlisting your help. It looks like Margaret and her family may be a while."

They looked back at the Rawlings, where Margaret was busily engaged visiting with old acquaintances. Reese saw them looking and shrugged his shoulders as if to say, 'Who knows how long she'll talk?'

The children were running around with Rye and Janie. Sterling waved back. Holding his other arm out to Maggie, he escorted the ladies down the street.

"Sterling, Drew, set that table right here. Lydia, let's have the salads before the meats, then the breads and then the desserts. Reese, darling, that chair goes with this table, not that one."

Margaret bustled around arranging dishes, platters and bowls on the serving table as the men set tables and chairs under the shade of the big maple tree in the front yard.

Lydia and Maggie set their bowls on the table where Margaret pointed and turned back to the house to get more from the kitchen.

"Does she always boss people around like that?" Maggie asked.

"I don't know. I only met her yesterday." Lydia refrained from saying that Sterling had told her that his sister bossed him a lot when they were children.

"Hello!"

Ella's call caused them to turn around. Rye and Janie had already run over to the Rawlings children and started playing.

"Here, let me take that, Peter." Lydia took the large basket he was carrying.

"Yeah, Peter, come and do some man's work," Drew called.

"So what would that be?"

"Why, carrying chairs and tables of course. Can't let you off by just carrying a picnic basket, can we?"

Ella, Lydia and Maggie were heading into to the house when they heard the clatter of hooves and rattle of a buckboard.

Maggie took the basket from Lydia. "You're the hostess. Let us deal with the food. You go greet your guests."

Lydia shot a nervous look at her two friends.

"Go get Sterling and tell him to play host," Ella suggested. "Drew and Peter can finish up with the chairs and tables."

The thought of greeting people, even people she knew, as a hostess of a large social event caused a moment of panic in Lydia. Ella's reminder that she didn't have to greet the arriving guests alone relieved much of her agitation. She turned toward Sterling as he came toward her.

"Come," he said, "We have guests arriving. Let's go welcome them."

"Hey," Drew called, "aren't I a guest? When I got here you put me to work."

"Me too," Peter echoed.

Ben Phelps was helping Betsy down while Vince Stanton tied up the horses. The two families had come to town together for church and the party.

"Pa, come let down the back," Billy called, "I want out. The kids are playing without me."

"Hold on a minute, pipsqueak, ladies first," Ben said, giving his son a look that Billy knew meant he should be quiet and wait.

Betsy, on the ground now, reached up to take newborn Johnny from Millie Stanton so she could be helped down.

"Welcome, we're so glad you all could join us." Sterling shook the men's hands and nodded to the ladies.

"Thank you for inviting us," Millie said.

Lydia could tell that Millie was nervous. She wondered if Millie felt out of place with so many people so much older than she. If so, she understood how Millie felt. Lydia herself was closer in age to the young mother than to Sterling and his friends.

"We're just glad you came," she said to Millie. "Apart from anything else, we women all want to hold the baby." Lydia's smile was warm, and in helping to ease Millie's nervousness her own nervousness vanished. Lydia would always remember the baby's birthday since it was the night she slept in the livery.

"Hey, sheriff, where were you during church today?" Ben called to Drew, smiling. "Not a good example to set for the rest of the population."

"Had part of the rest of the population in jail last night for drunkenness. His wife came to get him and I ended up protecting him from her. She came with her frying pan ready to hit him over the head with it. Took most of the morning to get her calmed down."

Reese joined in. "You're excused, then," he said to Drew. "Marital peace is a worthy objective."

"Drew, Mrs. H and her niece just turned onto the street. Would you go and help them the rest of the way please?" Sterling asked.

"Sure." Drew's long legs took him out of the yard in short order.

"Sterling, are you playing matchmaker?" Lydia asked quietly, not wanting the others to hear.

"What? No, I just want to make sure Mrs. H gets here without being winded. She'll rush herself and Drew knows how to keep her at a safe pace without her knowing it."

"Okay. For a moment I thought you wanted to push Drew at Rachel."

"Not a chance. He'll have to find his own lady. I found mine without his help, he can find his own too."

The day was sunny with a gentle breeze tickling the leaves. After lunch Sterling helped Lydia with the cleanup. They wouldn't allow any of their guests to help.

Margaret and Reese's baby Abby was sleeping in the parlor, as was baby Johnny. Sterling watched as several adults and children knocked croquet balls around in some semblance of an actual game. Those not playing croquet were scattered around the lawn and the porch, chatting. He saw the swing in the yard and the one on the porch in motion; Mrs. H. was on the porch, and Peter and Ella were in the yard.

He saw Drew talking with Rachel, Mrs. H.'s niece, who was leaning against the trunk of the maple tree.

They were both watching the croquet game as they chatted.

"They're going to get married," Lydia said as she and Sterling stood at the top of the porch steps.

"Who?"

"Drew and Rachel."

Sterling looked over at the couple. "Why do you think that?"

"I don't know. The thought just came to me when I looked at them. They're going to get married."

"Now who's playing matchmaker?"

"Not me. I'm just an observer. They'll have to do it all themselves. Just remember I told you so when Drew asks you to be his best man. I'm going to sit and chat with Mrs. H. We haven't had a good chat in a while."

"Going to find out about her niece, are you?"

"No, of course not. But if she wants to talk about Rachel I'll listen." Smiling broadly, Lydia walked over and joined Mrs. H on the swing.

"And she accused me of matchmaking," Sterling mumbled to himself as he went down the steps.

Chapter 35

"I hope this doesn't spoil your Decoration Day," Sterling said to Ida Hopkins, the young daughter of Samantha Hopkins, who ran the dress shop. "Keep it out of water and come back in a couple of weeks so I can check it."

Egged on by her older brother Keith, Ida had climbed up to walk along a fence, fallen off and broken her arm.

"And you, young lady, don't let your brother bait you into doing something dangerous again. Remember, boys don't always use their heads and can get themselves or others into trouble." Sterling tweaked the nose of the girl sitting on the exam table.

"Yes, sir. Now my summer's ruined because of him." Ida's dejection was very noticeable.

"Not totally," her mother said, stroking the dejected girl's hair. "Keith has to do all your chores until the cast comes off."

"Even the laundry?"

"Yes. Even the laundry, with you supervising."

"Good. He deserves it. Making me walk that fence."

"Wait a minute. You chose to do it, so you need to take responsibility for your poor choice," her mother scolded gently.

"I know. I'm sorry."

"Well, I think the cast is dry enough now, so you ladies can go."

Ida jumped down from the table, stumbling a little as the weight of the cast threw her off balance.

"Thank you, Doc," said Samantha. "I appreciate you taking the time from your entertaining to fix her arm."

"You're welcome. It comes with the job. I know there are still deserts out. If you'd stay and have some I know the others would enjoy it. Ida, you could tell them all about how your mean old brother made you walk on top of that fence."

"Oh, Doc, don't encourage her."

Samantha's teasing frustration made Sterling smile.

"Can we, Mama?"

"I guess." With a laugh Samantha added, "One more thing you can hold over your brother."

"Margaret," Sterling called to his sister, who was standing by the table that was covered in cookies, pies and cakes. "This young lady is needing a treat to help with her broken arm. Can you fix her and her mother up with a selection of the delicacies you're guarding?"

"Of course. Come on, ladies. There's plenty here."

Sterling stood on the porch, looking over the yard at the adults and children enjoying the afternoon. Turning toward the porch swing, he saw Lydia sitting there holding Vince and Millie's baby boy. He watched as she chatted with the ladies. Wrapped in a pale-blue shawl, Johnny was nestled in her arms. Suddenly a longing for her to be holding a baby of their own flooded over him.

Sterling thought his heart would burst. The realization nearly overwhelmed him: he loved her. When had his feelings for her changed from duty and liking her to this consuming love?

He had liked her from the start, even when they had first been married. Granted he hadn't known her very well but he had sensed from the first that she was kind, considerate and giving, and was not one to ask anything for herself. He knew they had both been sure that they would do the best they could to make their marriage work. They had, he thought, gotten to know each other well during the past few months. He knew she was still fearful of making him angry, and that she didn't totally trust that he would support and protect her no matter what, but they seemed to be settling into a friendly relationship.

So when had his feelings grown from respect and friendly affection to this burning, almost aching love for her? Sterling wanted to rush over to her, grab her up in his arms and tell her how much she meant to him, how much he loved her. He knew now was not the time. Nor would it be right any time this week while his sister and family was there. Also, should he tell her? he wondered. Would she trust that his words were true? Or would she think he was only saying them because he wanted to consummate their marriage?

A burst of laughter broke through his reflecting. The ladies gathered around Lydia and the baby smiled and laughed. Lydia handed the infant to his mother, who held him away from her body as she moved to where she had things for the baby.

"Oh, Sterling," Lydia said, rising from the swing, "I didn't notice you there. We ladies have decided that the order of the evening is leftovers from lunch. None of us want to cook again today, and since there's plenty of food left over we'll serve it again before everyone heads home. Is that all right with you?"

"As long as there are still desserts left over I'll be fine with that. Otherwise, someone better start cooking now." He took Lydia's hand as they walked down the steps to let the others in on the plan.

Lying in bed that evening, Lydia reflected on the way she had felt holding Johnny. Oh, how she loved the feel of the precious little life in her arms. When she'd relinquished him to his mother she had felt an aching void. But she knew that she wouldn't know how it felt to hold her own child until she released her fear of intimacy with her husband. The desire for a child of their own grew greater every moment, but her fear held her prisoner.

A small voice in her head said, Let go. Fear is not of me. I am with you, always.

Lydia silently let go, releasing her fear to the One who was able to carry it.

Margaret carried the laundry baskets out onto the back porch while Lydia brought out pails of hot water. Abby's job was to bring the big bar of soap, which they would shave into the laundry tub.

"Thank you, Abby," Lydia said, taking the bar from Abby. "Do you want to put some of the things into the tub?"

"Yeth, pwease."

"Start with these, sweetie," Margaret said. "Lydia, I know you don't realize it but many of the items of furniture in the house are still the ones that we had as children. Also, a number of them are in need of repair or at the very least new upholstery. The paint and wallpaper hasn't been changed in longer than I can remember, and I'm not sure that if you washed the drapes they would come out as anything more than strings. I think we should redecorate the house, don't you?" She didn't wait for a reply. "We could start with the kitchen. Don't you think it would be lovely in a bright blue with new white curtains? You could make napkins and tablecloths in gingham check. Wait, maybe curtains in the gingham too. So very cheery."

"I'm not so--"

"No, maybe not. Maybe red. The sitting room is so very drab with that faded rose-covered wallpaper. The morning sun can make that room so warm and cozy, but that wallpaper and the out-of-fashion chairs and tables, ugh. Besides, the furniture really needs to be either repaired or replaced. Reese sat in one of the chairs and the creak it made caused me to wonder if it was going to break and dump him on the floor."

"Oh my, I'll look into that."

"And my bedroom, did you know it was decorated for me like that when I was seven or eight? I won't tell you how long ago that was, but you get the idea anyway."

Margaret continued outlining the faults she saw in every room, even the master bedroom, which she had seen for only a couple of minutes that morning.

Lydia tried a few times to slow Margaret down but she failed miserably. Margaret was speaking rapidly and with great enthusiasm about redecorating the entire house. She planned out color schemes, furniture styles and placements. She chose and discarded fabric types at lightning speed. New knickknacks, drapery styles, rugs were all talked about and compared within Margaret's monologue. Lydia didn't know whether half of what Margaret said was in style, or the names of colors, or the companies where all of this would be purchased.

"Mama, can I go pway wiff the kitties?" Abby said, tugging on her mother's skirt.

"Yes, sweetie, so long as Aunt Lydia says it's okay."

"You may." Lydia leaned down and smiled at the bright eyes of the toddler. "Just remember they like to be played with gently, with no tail pulling. If that happens they'll scratch or bite."

"Okay, me memember."

The two women watched as Abby's dress-and-pinafore-covered form scampered down the steps and along the path.

"It must be close to lunch," Lydia said. "I'd better go look and get started on it. Sterling's always hungry when he comes back from house calls. I try to make sure it's ready when he gets home."

"You go ahead. I'll finish this load and hang them up. After lunch we can finish while Abby naps."

As Lydia prepared lunch she wondered how Margaret could be so considerate and helpful, and so pushy and bossy at the same time. Margaret knew so much about decorating and styles and colors. She used words Lydia had never heard before: Gothic, Rococo, baroque. When Margaret first said the word "baroque" Lydia thought she was talking about something that was broken. Then she realized it was a style of furniture or lamp or, well, something that was new and popular. It made her feel very inadequate and stupid. Just like Cyrus had always said. How could she be a good wife and helpmeet if she couldn't fix up a room so it looked nice?

Lydia's shoulders slumped in despair. She hadn't known that the house was so badly in need of repair. It was a million times better and nicer than the house she had grown up in. She thought it was simply wonderful. She knew she couldn't pick out the right and proper colors and styles to make the house what it should be. She didn't know any of this sort of thing. She would never get it right. On top of all that, how would she ever even bring the subject up with Sterling?

She heard the front screen door shut. Sterling was home for lunch.

"Margaret," she called out the window, "lunchtime. Sterling's home."

Margaret waved, indicating she had heard and went to pull Abby away from the kittens.

Ladling soup into bowls, Lydia looked up as Sterling entered the kitchen.

"So, is the laundry done?" he said.

"We're getting there. Margaret is a big help. We should be done in the early afternoon."

Margaret and Abby entered then, with the ensuing enthusiastic welcome from Abby to her Uncle Doc. Taking their places at the table, they settled to their meal.

"You know, Sterling," Margaret said, "you haven't done anything to this house since I left. The entire house needs to be redecorated and so Lydia and I are going to get started on it this week."

Sterling looked at his sister as she made her pronouncement and then at Lydia. She was looking down at her soup. She slowly raised her spoon to her lips, not looking up at all.

Margaret continued describing her plans for each room, not paying any attention to Lydia's slow movements or lack of participation in the conversation.

Sterling watched Lydia, noting her pallor and the slight tremble as she raised her spoon for each bite. She's nervous about this, he thought. I'll bet Margaret's just declared that the house would be redecorated and never even asked Lydia what she wanted.

"Margaret ..." Sterling started. Just then they heard a frantic knock on the clinic front door. "I've got to go. We'll talk about this later."

Taking a last bite of soup as he got up from the table, Sterling leaned down and gave Lydia a quick kiss on the cheek. He wanted her to know he wasn't upset with her.

Just what we need, he thought as he went to answer the door. Another session of pushy Margaret.

"That's the last of the whites," Lydia said, dropping the blueing bag into the tub. "Thank you for helping."

"Many hands make light work." Margaret looked at the lines full of clean clothing and linen, and the towels and bandaging from clinic. "I do think Sterling should get you one of the new machines with the wringer attached. I don't know how you wring all these things out by yourself. I helped my mother when I was a child but I have a wringer now. You should tell Sterling that you need a wringer."

Lydia didn't say anything. She simply looked down, picked up the basket full of wet laundry and went to hang it up. She was certainly not going to "tell" Sterling that he needed to get her anything. She wasn't sure enough of herself to ask him for anything.

Margaret had moved to the tub and was agitating the wash water with the dolly plunger.

"When we finish with this let's take a break for tea and cake, shall we?" Lydia said.

"Wonderful idea. Abby will probably be waking from her nap soon and will want a snack."

Finished and in the kitchen, Lydia set the kettle on the stove and set out plates of oatmeal cake while Margaret went up to see if Abby was awake.

"Here's the sleepy one, all awake and hungry," she said, entering the kitchen carrying Abby who had her head on Margaret's shoulder.

"How about some cake, Abby?"

"Yeth, pwease."

"Margaret, about the redecorating ..." Lydia started when they all were seated.

"It's a daunting task, I know, but Sterling will just have to deal with the upset to his home while the work's being done. Reese complained the entire time we redid the house but now he appreciates the sacrifice."

"I'm sure, but--"

"Don't worry. After we finish eating we can start in the dining room and make a list of what's needed in each room. After that we can discuss colors and styles and furniture. We can get very organized so it'll be easier for you after I'm gone."

Lydia looked down at her cake. Only about two bites left. She didn't want to upset Sterling's sister, especially after all the help with the laundry, but she just didn't want to plan for something she was unsure if Sterling would even allow and that she knew she didn't know how to get accomplished. She felt so stupid and scared. Would Sterling be angry with her? They'd been getting along so well. Would this make him angry with her--that she couldn't stop his sister from making these plans? Would he think she didn't like the house?

"I have some work I need to do in the garden. You may go ahead and make your lists. That way everything gets done." Lydia chose her words carefully, neither endorsing nor rejecting the idea.

"Okay, if that's what you want."

"Yes, I need to gather some vegetables for supper and do some weeding. Abby can play outside with me if it's all right with you."

Abby immediately ran to where the kittens were napping in the sun, effectively putting that to an end, and began playing. Lydia took her basket and hoe to the garden.

Okay, Lydia, she told herself, you decided not to be scared anymore. *Okay, Lord, I come to you praising you for making me aware that I don't have faith in you when I'm scared. So, help me now think this through because I know in my head that Sterling won't be angry with me.* Now I just need to move that down into my heart where the fear lives. She took a deep breath, feeling the fear go out of her. Thank you, Lord, she said softly. Your love helped me see that I haven't anything to fear. Protect Margaret from Sterling if he is angry with her.

Chapter 36

Sterling watched Lydia surreptitiously at supper that evening. He noticed that although Lydia conversed, she only did so when she was spoken to directly. He knew she was nervous and upset. He knew she was concerned about the redecorating plans Margaret had made. She's afraid I'll get angry with her, he thought. Margaret was so pushy.

He decided that he needed to speak with his sister or Lydia would be a nervous wreck by the time the family left Friday.

"Margaret," he said after supper, "how about you and I go for a walk? We haven't had any time together, just sister and brother."

"I was going to help Lydia with the dishes."

"You go on and walk with your brother," Reese said. "I'll help Lydia with the dishes. The boys can help, too."

Sterling rolled his eyes, wondering what kind of help two boys would be. Abby seemed content to play with the mess she had made on the tray of the high chair she sat in.

"Yes, Margaret, your men can help me."

"Okay, I'll just go and get my shawl."

Sterling walked over to Lydia, reached his hand into the dishpan and gave her hand a squeeze. She looked at him, her eyes a touch uncertain. "You be good now. No ordering the Rawlings men around while we're gone," he said with a grin and teasing eye. Then he leaned in and kissed her on the nose. "Be back in a while." Hearing Margaret descending the steps, he went to join her.

They walked in comfortable silence for a while, enjoying the evening, waving to a few people sitting on their front porches.

"We've enjoyed having you with us, Margaret. Has meeting Lydia and spending time with her eased your concern for me about the 'hussy' who made me marry her?"

"Oh yes, Sterling. She's so sweet and so conscientious. A very talented cook, too," Margaret said with a smile.

"You need to be careful. Her desserts are going to make you fat." She poked him in the side as she said it. Sterling grinned at her.

"Did you know that she's very unsure of herself and feels she's stupid and incapable?"

"No! Why would she think that?" He heard astonishment in her voice. "She's very good at anything she does and is great at conversation. She told me that she plans to use Mother's yarn and knit scarves, hats, mittens and such for this winter. Her sewing is excellent."

"I know she's very smart. When Charlie was injured I wasn't there. She got him prepared for me to be able to get right to work on his injuries. She'd even washed his shoulder wound some and picked some of the grass and dirt from the wound."

"So why does she think she's stupid?"

"Her brother abused her both physically and emotionally, telling her she was stupid and worthless and couldn't do anything right. So she believes it."

"Poor thing. She didn't deserve that. No one does."

"You're right." Sterling paused. "Anyway, I have a feeling that your plans for redecorating the entire house scared her silly. I can tell she's nervous and probably afraid. She doesn't think she can do it. She's also afraid I'll get mad at her for the expense."

"Oh, my. I've done it again, haven't I?" Margaret said. Sterling nodded. "I've barged ahead with what I thought would be best without even asking if she wanted to redecorate or what her tastes are."

"Also, without giving her time to talk with me about it," Sterling added. "I know Lydia would be very afraid I'd get angry. She tries hard to convince herself that I wouldn't hurt her but she isn't always successful. Especially in new situations, areas she isn't confident in."

"I need to ask her forgiveness. I'm so sorry I made her nervous today with the plans. I just saw that the house could use some fixing up and it went from there."

"I know you didn't mean to upset her. It's just ... she wouldn't even tell me she needed new clothing or even ask for some fabric. I figured it out when I saw that she'd made a chemise out of the muslin wrapping from her rib injuries. So imagine how she'd feel about asking to redecorate the entire house."

"She pieced bandaging strips together to make a chemise?" Margaret's mouth dropped open.

Sterling grinned. "You should've seen the clothing she had when she came. It wasn't even fit for the ragbag. Her brother wouldn't let her get new and made her use their mother's clothes. She had to adjust them as she grew up. When I finally noticed, a month into our marriage, it shamed me. We went that day to Johnson's, and even though I would've let her purchase everything she wanted, she bought the bare minimum and then fabric to make the rest. When we realized the old lawn swing needed replacing she was very unsure of herself. I had her speak with Johann without me there. I wanted her to decide what she wanted without looking to me for approval."

"That's why she never said anything when I said she should tell you she needs a wringer for the laundry. She wouldn't have asked you for one. She would just continue with wringing the water out by hand. Really, Sterling, you should get a wringer. It makes it so much easier to do the laundry."

"Okay. I'll tell her tonight to get one."

"No, brother mine, wait until we're gone. Then she won't think I complained to you."

"She'll be fine. I'll speak with her about the redecorating and let her know it's okay to do whatever she wants. Actually, I told her she could when we had the swing made and picked yellow and green paint for it, but she needs convincing still."

"Well, I plan to apologize to her for my pushiness."

The last light of the day lit the edges of the house as Sterling and Margaret came up the walk. Reese was the only one in view, sitting on the porch swing.

"Where are the children?" Margaret asked.

"Lydia's putting them to bed. I don't think she plans to come out again. I'm enjoying the quiet. Want to join me?" Reese grinned at Margaret, who smiled back.

Sterling thought they might like their privacy and said, "I've got a little paperwork to do. I'm going to finish that and then go on up. You stay out as long as you want. But be good," he added with a teasing grin.

But instead of doing the paperwork, he just sat at his desk in his office. Margaret isn't the only one who did it again, he thought. Why can't I see what Lydia needs? Why don't I notice? He knew she wouldn't ask, so why couldn't he keep watch and figure out when something should be bought or changed? He sat in the dark room, in his despair not bothering to light a lamp.

It was as if he didn't see her working everyday. He was gone a lot or busy but he knew he had the time to check in with her several times a day. He thought about the opportunities he had had on the days she did laundry to come to the back porch with a cup of coffee and a treat and chat with her while she worked. It wasn't as if he didn't know about wringers. He had seen them in the store and had even treated a child who had caught his fingers between the rollers on a dare from his brother. So why hadn't he noticed that Lydia wasn't using one?

"Put other's needs before your own," the Bible said. I know better and need to do better, Sterling thought, echoing the words Peter had told him the day he had confessed his neglect of Lydia's wardrobe. They had talked about a checklist, about how Sterling used a mental checklist when he examined a patient. He needed to develop some sort of checklist concerning Lydia.

Sterling lit the lamp and pulled a piece of scratch paper out of a cubby in the desk and a pencil from the drawer. Okay, Doc, he told himself, heal thyself.

He wrote down a list of aspects in life: emotional, physical, environment, work, entertainment, relationships. These were all areas that he felt he could check on every day, or at least periodically, to see if any adjustments were needed. He could run through the list in his head and act on what he noticed right then, not when something or someone else brought it to his attention.

Figuring he would need some kind of reminder until it became a habit, he wrote the list on several small cards. He stuck one in the place for a label on a cubby drawer of the desk. That way there would be one he'd see whenever he sat at his desk. The second he placed in his vest pocket. The third he would put in with his shaving equipment. Satisfied with this plan, Sterling blew out the lamp, hoping to have a talk with Lydia about the redecorating before she was asleep.

In the bedroom, he found Lydia in her nightgown, sitting cross-legged on the bed brushing her hair. Realizing this intimate action revealed that she was more comfortable being in the same bedroom, he smiled big on the inside but smaller on the outside so as not to make her nervous. He wasn't going to tell her about his checklist but he noticed that her brush was old and missing sections of the bristles. He thought he would surprise her with a new brush and comb set soon.

"Did the children go to bed easily?" he asked as he removed his vest, fingering the checklist in the pocket.

"Yes. I had to read three stories to the boys but Abby was very tired and went right to bed when we got her nightclothes on."

Going behind the screen, Sterling changed into his nightshirt. When he returned to the main part of the room he noticed that Lydia had finished with her hair, which now hung in a thick braid over her shoulder. She was under the covers now, sitting up against the headboard. He really wanted to loosen the braid and run his fingers through her hair. Stifling the urge to say or do something that would make her nervous, he put his dirty clothes in the basket in the corner.

Rounding the bed he climbed in beside her, pushing the pillows into a pile behind his back. "I spoke with Margaret about her bossiness about the redecorating. She's sorry and will tell you so tomorrow. She is right about there needing to be some work done, but not everything and not all at the same time. It also needs to be what you want, not her."

He tried to figure out what Lydia was thinking but couldn't. She was propped up on her pillows, fiddling with the end of her braid.

He leaned over and laid one hand on hers. "Talk to me. Let me know if you're really angry with my sister. Tell me that you want to kick Margaret and her family all the way back to Des Moines in the morning."

Lydia turned to look at him, her eyes wide with shock at what he was saying. "No, Sterling, I'm not mad at Margaret. She means well. It's just that I feel so stupid. I didn't understand half of what she was talking about. All those words I'd never heard before. I couldn't figure out why she would want to replace the things we had with something broke. I'm so stupid. It took me so long to figure out that 'baroque' was a style of decorating. I can't possibly redecorate. I'd make a mess of the whole thing."

Sterling just about laughed out loud about the baroque and broke mixup, but realized just in time that she really thought she wouldn't be able to do the redecorating successfully.

"Lydia," he said as he squeezed her hand, "can I make a suggestion?"

"Of course. Why would you ask?"

"I don't know really. It's just that I know you don't feel like you can do the redecorating, and I was thinking ... What about asking Margaret to help you with, say, one room. She could help you learn how to go about making the choices and knowing what needs to be thought about. I, certainly, don't know anything about it." He could tell she was thinking about it. He waited, patiently, allowing her time to process what he knew would be conflicting feelings and thoughts.

Lydia looked at him. "Okay, I think that's a good idea. Having someone who's done it before, and can teach me, will make me feel better doing it."

Sterling squeezed her hand. "Good, we can talk to her in the morning about it."

Thu-thump. Thu-thump. Lydia was wrapped in the warmth of her father's embrace, her head against his chest, hearing his heartbeat. It had been so long. So long since she had felt so secure. So loved. She started awake. The arms tightened around her.

"Don't move."

It wasn't her father's voice. The heartbeat was not her father's. She was wrapped in her husband's arms, her head lying on his chest. Opening her eyes, she saw dust motes floating lazily near the window in the early morning sun. She lay still, listening to the steady beat of Sterling's heart. He raised an arm to stoke her hair, which was coming free from the loose braid she customarily wove it into before retiring. She felt him gently pull more strands out, running his figures through its softness.

"Lydia, when my sister and family leave, stay with me. Don't go back to the other room." Though spoken as statements, they were really questions.

"All right," she said, so softly that he felt the response rather than heard it. Again the arms tightened the embrace. Lydia was swamped with the feeling of security she remembered from her dream. She sighed and relaxed in her husband's embrace.

With no knock beforehand, the bedroom door opened about an hour later. Margaret swooped in, still in her robe. Sterling sat up quickly. Lydia slid out of his arms, retreating further down in the bed, pulling the covers over her head and curling into a ball.

"Reese and the boys are going fishing with Peter and Rye today. Hopefully we'll have their catch for supper, but I'm sure there's something we can fix if they come home empty-handed. I'll help Lydia with the chores while you work, Sterling." Margaret stated as she crossed the room.

"Get out, Margaret." Sterling's voice was quiet but stern. He had placed his hand on Lydia's back and could feel her tremble. What had happened to cause such a reaction to an interruption like this?

"What?" Margaret was looking out the window.

"I said get out. This is my house and our room. You have no right to come bursting in here without even knocking, let alone waiting for permission. Now, close the door behind you as you leave." Sterling's voice was like steel.

Margaret looked at him almost in shock. Then she turned from the window, crossed the room and pulled the door shut quietly behind her.

Sterling turned his attention to his wife. Lydia had pulled her pillow over her head and had her arms crossed over it, clutching it tightly. He lay down next to her and wrapped his arms around her, pulling her against his chest.

"It was only Margaret being rude and bossy. You're safe here. I'm not going to let anyone hurt you." His words were whispered beneath the pillow near her ear as he held her.

Slowly her trembling stopped. She pulled the pillow off of her head and took a deep breath.

"I'm sorry. I shouldn't have reacted that way. It's just ... Cyrus ... when he was drunk sometimes or angry he'd come into my room and start hitting me. The door opening like that, so suddenly, I thought ..."

"Shhh, it's okay." He kissed the top of her head. "I'm sorry Margaret's actions made you remember those times."

Lydia turned over in his arms and snuggled closer. "I'm better now. You being here helps. Thank you."

They lay holding onto each other for a few minutes until the clock struck seven.

"And here I thought we'd slept late," Sterling said, rolling over and eyeing the clock. "She didn't even let us sleep until seven. Not that we normally do, but we were doing so nicely until she interrupted."

"Well, we need to get up now. You have to get ready for work and I need to fix breakfast." Lydia threw back the covers and got out. "Get up." She shook the blankets at Sterling, who was stretching and making no effort to get up.

"Convince me," Sterling said, with a teasing glint in his eyes. He tapped his cheek as if requesting a kiss. His reward was a pillow thrown into his face and a smile on Lydia's. "Okay, okay. You convinced me."

Chapter 37

"You what?" Reese only just stopped himself from shouting the words. "Margaret, that was extremely rude and intrusive of you."

"I realize that now. I just never gave it any thought. I always just went into his room when we were young." Abby had gotten up earlier and Margaret was dressing her while telling Reese of her gaff.

"That was rude of you, also. Even as a child he deserved his privacy. I know the boys don't have rooms to themselves but how about Abby? Would you want the boys just barging in on her any time they felt like it?"

"Well, no, I suppose not. Like I said, I never gave it any thought." Margaret was distressed not only with Sterling and Reese's reactions but also with herself for just assuming she could barge into another adult's bedroom.

"My dear," Reese said, and quoted Philippians 2:3–4. " 'Do nothing from selfish ambition or conceit, but in humility regard others as better than yourselves. Let each of you look not to your own interests, but to the interests of others.' "

"You're right. I need to apologize to both of them. For today, and also to Sterling for the past."

"Yes, you do."

They had been getting dressed, Margaret in a dark-blue and green plaid dress, Reese in a tan vest over a blue shirt and black pants. They left the room to see if the boys were awake. The boys were up dressed in clothes that were fit for small boys to go fishing in. They started talking excitedly when their parents, after knocking on the door, entered.

"I'm gonna catched the biggest fish and eat him for supper," Stafford said as he pulled on his shoe.

His mother smiled. "It's on the wrong foot, sweetheart. Shall I help so you can get to breakfast sooner?"

Stafford pulled off the shoe and handed it to his mother.

"Go fish?" Abby asked, looking up at her father.

"Not this time, sweeting."

"Boo. Want to go fish." Her lip stuck out in a pout.

"I need you to help Aunt Lydia and me with our chores. You're such a good helper." Margaret saw Reese roll his eyes. Then he mouthed the word liar. She just grinned back.

"Okay, Mama. Me hep."

"Okay troops, are we ready?" Reese saluted, turned and marched out of the room. The children marched along behind their father, trying to stay in step. Margaret followed behind, nervous about seeing her brother and Lydia, and chewing her lip as she thought about what to say in her apology.

Sausage was frying in the skillet and Lydia was stirring up pancakes when the Rawlings family marched into the kitchen. She smiled a little uneasily, noticing that Margaret wasn't smiling or marching, and her expression was pensive.

"Troops, halt! Parade formation." The children scurried into a line by Reese's side. "Greet!"

"Good morning, Aunt Lydia," the troops said, with Abby pronouncing her name 'Ydia.'

"Good morning. How about you all take your places? Pancakes coming up as soon as I get them cooked." Lydia turned back to the stove and began pouring batter onto the hot griddle.

"I'll pour milk and coffee," Margaret offered.

"Thank you." Lydia's reply was somewhat stilted.

"Sterling's not down yet?" Reese asked.

"He'll be down shortly. He's a little slow this morning."

"We're going fishing with Pastor Peter and Rye. We're gonna catched lots of fish and have them for supper," Stafford said excitedly. "We're gonna go as soon as we eat breakfast."

"That sounds like fun for you." Flipping the pancakes, Lydia glanced over her shoulder and smiled at the five year old. She heard footsteps descending the stairs and Sterling entered the kitchen.

"I'm not too late for breakfast, am I? You hungry bear cubs didn't eat all the pancakes, did you?"

"We still are hungry bears, Uncle Doc," Connor said before his brother could reply. "We haven't had any yet."

"Here you go." Lydia placed a plate piled high with steaming pancakes on the table. A plate of sausage joined it next to the butter crock and maple syrup pitcher.

After breakfast was finished Reese and the boys went off on their fishing trip, leaving a somewhat pouty Abby behind. Lydia started washing the dishes. Sterling was still seated at the table, enjoying another cup of coffee as Margaret folded the drying cloth and sat down next to him.

"I want to apologize to both of you," Margaret said. "I never should have come barging into your room this morning. Abby had gotten up and after I put her back to bed I just decided to make sure you knew what we were doing today. I acted just as I had as a girl when I went into your room, Sterling."

"Yes, you did." Lydia could hear the resentment in his voice.

"Sterling," Lydia said sharply from her spot by the sink. "Margaret is apologizing. Hear her out."

"Thank you." Margaret looked at Lydia then at Sterling. "I shouldn't have done it as a child and should definitely know better as an adult. I'm sorry, Lydia, for bursting in on you this morning. Sterling, I'm sorry for today, and also for not respecting your privacy as we grew up. Please forgive me." Margret's eyes were gleaming with tears as she looked at her brother.

Sterling looked at her for a moment, then reached out and took her hand. "I forgive you, both for today and for the past. But if you come into my bedroom unannounced again prepared to be pitched out the window." The last was said with a twinkling eye, which Lydia was glad to see.

Lydia came to stand beside her husband. "I forgive you, too."

"Thank you," Margaret said, squeezing her brother's hand and giving him a repentant smile.

While Margaret was making beds, Lydia and Sterling walked through the downstairs. They discussed the various rooms, trying to decide which one they would redo first. They still hadn't chosen when Margaret finished her chore and joined them in the parlor, along with Abby.

"Margaret," Sterling started, "Lydia and I have been talking, and, well, we'd like you to help Lydia redecorate one room. She's never done anything like this and really would like you to show her what's involved."

"Do you really, Lydia, or are you just trying to make me feel better?"

"I really would like your help. I've never done anything like this before. It's quite overwhelming." Lydia waved her hand, encompassing the room.

"Is this the room you want to do?"

"We haven't decided yet," Sterling said. "We were just discussing it." He walked toward the dining room, indicating that the ladies follow. "I have just enough time for a cup of coffee before I need to go make my house calls. Let's talk about it in the kitchen."

Sterling was watching Lydia pour the coffee when he leaned back in his chair. With a crack his chair leg broke off, landing him on the floor with a loud crash. He lay on the floor and started to laugh. Lydia had rushed to him and was kneeling beside him. His sister looked over the corner of the table at him with a big-sister smirk on her face.

"Oh, Sterling, are you all right?" Lydia said.

He looked into her worried face. "Yes, sweetheart, I'm fine. I think we've just figured out which room we should redo."

Still laughing, he allowed Lydia to help him rise from his ignominious position. Once he was standing, he picked up the chair, looking it over closely. Then he looked over the other three, making Margaret get up out of hers. Lydia fussed over Sterling, which he enjoyed immensely, brushing at his clothing as if it were dusty.

"I didn't realize these were in such bad shape. There are cracks in the legs, which are also coming loose from the seat." He pushed at the table, causing it to wobble. "This is coming apart too."

"Well, I don't remember any other table and chairs. We even had this set in the apartment above the office," Margaret said.

"Looks like we need a new table and chairs. What do you think, Lydia?"

She quit brushing at him. "Well, I suppose that's the best idea, but ... where would we get them? There's no place to buy furniture in town."

"I guess we could order a set from Johnson's."

"Who knows how long it would take to get here." Margaret sat down, carefully, on the chair Sterling positioned for her.

"Do you suppose Johann would be able to build them? He did a wonderful job building the lawn swing." Lydia placed a cup of coffee before Margaret and handed one to Sterling, who was leaning against the sink counter. He'd decided he didn't trust any of the remaining chairs.

"I don't see why not," he said. "I'll see if I can find him while I'm out today and ask him to stop by to see you. That way you can talk about what you want." He saw Lydia's eyes take on the panicked look she got when she was afraid she'd make or had made a mistake.

"Remember, I said that the way the house was decorated was up to you. I promised to like, or at least tolerate, whatever choices you made. Even if they're pink with purple polka-dots."

Lydia grinned. "It was purple with pink spots."

Sterling saw Margaret's puzzled look and chuckled. "Lydia will explain it to you, sis. I've got to get going." With a peck on Lydia's cheek, he exited by way of the clinic door.

Lydia and Margaret looked at each other and started laughing.

"Who knew," Lydia said, "that we'd decide so easily on the room to redecorate." Becoming more serious she continued, "I appreciate you helping me with this. I know nothing about how to go about it."

"I've redone rooms a number of times. Reese is really good to me that way. He lets me change things more often than most husbands do. Abby, no, no, you mustn't carry the kitten by its head."

"Are you finished with your coffee?" At Margaret's nod Lydia took the cup, placing it in the sink next to Sterling's. "Since it's not too safe to sit in here, why don't we go to the sitting room to talk about this?"

"Okay, but first let's look around in here and get a good idea of what needs to be done. The table and chairs of course. Do you want to change the wall color?"

"Yes, I think so. See here?" Lydia pointed to the wall behind the sink. "And here?" She indicated the area behind the stove. "The paint's been scrubbed so many times it's beginning to get pretty thin."

"You're right. What about the floor? Does it need another coat of varnish?"

They looked carefully at the kitchen, back hall and pantry. Taking paper and pencils, they continued their planning in the comfort, and safety, of the sitting room.

"I think I've seen wallpaper books at Johnson's," Lydia said. "I've never paid any attention."

Lydia and Margaret were walking to the business district. They'd left Abby napping in a patient room with Sterling nearby seeing his afternoon patients.

"You're probably right. It'd be something they'd most likely have. I think your notion of painting the walls and putting a border near the ceiling is good."

"You do?" Lydia was surprised that Margaret voiced approval of her idea. Then she reminded herself that no one but Cyrus thought she was stupid.

"Yes, painting the walls will make them easy to clean and the border will dress it up some."

They'd reached the corner where they would cross the street to the block dominated by Johnson's All-Purpose Store. As they crossed an excited voice called, "Lydia, Lydia." Looking toward the sound, Lydia saw Maggie, wearing a navy wool skirt, and navy-and-white striped shirtwaist, rushing up the street waving her arms. Climbing the steps to the boardwalk, they waited until she caught up with them.

"What has you so excited, Maggie?" Lydia smiled at her friend as they stood in the shadow of the building.

"You'll never guess. I got a job!" Maggie's face showed her delight and pride in her achievement.

"That's wonderful. I didn't know you were trying to find one."

"I decided I needed something to do, not just embroidery or reading or shopping. So, I thought about what I could do, and went to see Mr. Dalhrimple at the newspaper."

"Leon Dalhrimple?"

Lydia looked at Margaret, hearing her astonished query.

"Yes, he owns the newspaper and print shop," Maggie explained.

Margaret laughed. "It's hard to believe. Leon Dalhrimple was in my grade. He just never was one to read or write anything. To think he owns a newspaper..."

"I'd walked by yesterday and saw the help-wanted sign in the window. Today I went in and inquired about the job. It's part time to start with. Being a receptionist, mainly, but he also wants me to try writing an article on a social event. If he likes it then I'll get to write on others. He doesn't like to go to social things."

Lydia saw Maggie's excitement and gave her a big hug. "Congratulations! How exciting! What does your mother think?"

Maggie's happiness dimmed, and the smile left her face. "She doesn't know yet. I haven't told her."

"Won't your mother be pleased?" Margaret asked.

Maggie looked at Lydia then back at Margaret. "No, I'm supposed to be a 'lady of leisure'. A job ruins the image of high society." She said this emphasizing the 'lady of leisure' in a snooty way.

"Oh."

"Well, I for one, Maggie," said Lydia, "am very happy for you. I think you'll do marvelously."

"I hope so. I'm just sort of afraid to tell my parents."

Margaret took Maggie's hand, giving it a comforting squeeze. "Tell your mother that by having this job you'll be able to go to all the 'high society' functions that go on in Cottonwood." Margaret imitated Maggie's snootiness at the 'high society' and smiled.

"Do you have to go tell them now?" Lydia inquired. "We're going to pick out paint and a wallpaper border for the kitchen. Sterling and I decided to redo it. Margaret's helping me with the planning. Would you like to join us."

"I'd love to. Anything to put off telling my parents about my job." Maggie's voice went from delighted to grudging.

"I catched fish. I catched fish," came the call from the backyard as Reese, Peter and the boys came in through the gate.

It was late afternoon. Lydia and Margaret had chosen the paint and border and returned home by way of the Lendrey house, helping Ella carry her contribution to the evening meal. Janie danced around, telling what she and her mother had done that day.

As they worked in the kitchen, Lydia looked out the window, swallowed a laugh, and said, "Come look at this."

Taking the large pot from the shelf above the stove, she started pumping water into it. Ella and Margaret joined her at the sink while Janie ran to the open back door and looked out the screen.

"Mama, look," Janie exclaimed. "They're a muddy mess. Are you gonna get mad at Papa and Rye?"

The ladies all laughed.

"No, sweetie, it's fine. That's why they wore those old clothes," Ella said. "Fishing can be a very messy activity."

Lydia set the pot on the stove to heat water for the baths that were needed by three boys and two men. Then, with Margaret gathering up Abby, they went out to great the mighty fishermen who were standing in the yard.

"Pee-uw! You stink!" Janie scrunched up her nose and backed away from Peter, whom she'd run to.

"Yes, my sweet girl, I'm sure we do." Peter carried a creel along with fishing poles.

"It was great," Rye said. "We went down to that special secret spot by the river."

"Yeah, and we catched lots of fish." Stafford couldn't stop jumping around in his excitement.

"Staff fell in the river." Connor tattled on his brother.

To Lydia, it looked like Connor wanted Stafford to get into trouble. She glanced at Margaret.

"Well, he's not so sweet that he melted, I see." Margaret ruffled her younger son's hair. "So you were successful and we're having fish for supper?" she said to Reese.

"Yes, my dear, and I know... them what brings them home cleans them." Reese grinned at his wife, then acted as if he was going to grab onto her. "How about a big hug and kiss before I start?"

"No," shrieked Margaret, scurrying back to the porch quickly.

Lydia saw Ella look at Peter, who bounced his eyebrows up and down playfully. Ella, with little dignity, hurried up onto the porch too. With Sterling in the clinic she felt a little left out of the fun.

"I have water heating for baths, which, by the way," Lydia said with a grin, "you all are in desperate need of."

"But I got wet in the river, why do I have to take a bath?" came Stafford's stricken question.

"Because, my dear son," Margaret explained, "you, as Janie so apply put it, stink." Everyone laughed at the boy's dismayed expression.

"Peter, I brought you and Rye clean clothes, so you don't have to go home," Ella said from her safe place on the porch.

"Thank you. How about, Lydia, if you bring out a wash tub so we can clean up out here and not mess up your kitchen." Peter set the creel on the ground by the poles Reese had put there.

"Okay," Lydia said, "and we'll take ourselves into the parlor or sitting room until you're finished."

The ladies and Janie entered the house to finish preparing for the baths while the men set about cleaning the fish with three boys watching avidly.

Chapter 38

"I can't believe it's already Friday." Lydia placed the bowl of scrambled eggs on the dining room table beside the dish of fried potatoes, the platter with sausages, and the basket of fluffy biscuits then returned to the kitchen.

"I know, the week's gone so fast. We've had such a wonderful time." Margaret, coming from the pantry with a crock of butter and jar of jam, smiled broadly. "Even with my bossiness, which you so graciously forgave."

"Well, it led to Sterling putting off past resentment and my learning what baroque decorating style is; also, the plans for redecorating the kitchen."

"It certainly was funny when the chair broke, landing Sterling on the floor."

They both laughed. They heard the rest of the household gathering in the dining room and hurried in.

"The luggage is out on the porch waiting for Luke to come pick it up." Reese was settling Abby into the highchair.

When everyone was settled, grace said and the food served, Margaret asked, "So, when are you, brother dear, going to bring Lydia to Des Moines for a visit?"

Lydia looked at Sterling. He grinned at his sister. "Oh, I don't know, three or four years, I'd say. This visit should hold you for that long, don't you think, Reese?"

"Three or four years!" exclaimed Margaret, turning from helping Abby to look at her brother in dismay.

Sterling just laughed. "Gotcha."

As they walked to the train station, after helping Luke load the luggage into his wagon, the adults reminisced about the activities of the past week. The boys ran ahead then back, burning off some energy. Reese carried a squirming Abby, who wanted to get down and run with her brothers.

"Maybe," Lydia said, "we'll plan to come before Christmas, before winter has set in."

Sterling, with his wife's hand tucked in the crook of his arm, agreed. "That might work well. I could use a few days off by then."

At the train station Sterling looked at Reese, who simply shook his head. The women were hugging each other, fighting tears that threatened to spill over.

"Now, you promise to come in the fall whether Sterling comes or not." Margaret held Lydia at arm's length then hugged her close again.

In the distance the whistle of the train announced its pending arrival.

Margaret released her sister-in-law, becoming the attentive mother again. "Come, children, settle down. The train's arriving and we must be prepared to board." She rounded up the boys who were running around the pile of luggage waiting to be loaded. Abby jumped up and down, squealing as she watched the chase.

Sterling stepped up to his sister and put his arms around her in a heartfelt squeeze. "I'm glad you came. It's been a wonderful visit."

He saw Margaret's eyes tear up again. "I love you, brother mine."

"I love you, too."

All too soon the Rawlings family was peering at Sterling and Lydia from the window of the train. The couple waved as the conductor called, "All aboard."

"It's too bad they live so far away." Lydia's voice sounded so forlorn. "I've come to love your family in the short time we had."

"I know what you mean. This is the first time I've ever been with my sister that hasn't left me frustrated and angry. I'm glad."

Sterling tucked her hand into his elbow, drawing it close to his side. "Well, wife, what are we having for lunch?"

Lydia burst out laughing. "Are you always hungry? We just finished breakfast."

"Well, I ... um ..."

She laughed, looking up at him. "Don't. No need to try and explain. You are always hungry."

Lydia and Sterling walked home in near silence, each one content with their own thoughts. Sterling had two totally different thoughts competing within his head.

One caused an immediate anticipation for when they arrived home. The other, more intense feeling, he had longer to contemplate, but it held a much greater reward when evening came.

He looked down when Lydia reached over and picked a piece of lint from his lapel. She smiled and held it up before turning her face and blowing the bit of fluff away.

Sterling drew the hand tucked by his elbow down, entwining his fingers with hers. He gave the hand a small squeeze, hoping for and then receiving a soft press in response.

As they continued their slow stroll home, Sterling thought back, comparing how Lydia had reacted to him in the beginning of their marriage and how she was at the present time. She had been so very wounded, both in body and soul. Nervous and afraid of doing anything wrong, she'd jumped and shied away from him if he came upon her unaware. Several times she had shielded her face with her arms, as though thinking he might strike her. Now she was voluntarily touching him, with little thought about the intimacy of her picking some lint off his jacket. She was much less nervous about his responses to questions or suggestion. He thought of the witty ways she poked fun at him, and how she caught onto his teasing much more quickly now, not fearful that he was angry or upset.

Lydia had said she'd stay in his bed now that the Rawlings had gone and Sterling sincerely hoped she would keep to her word. He had plans for the night.

When they arrived home Sterling pulled Lydia toward the kitchen. "Come with me, I have something to show you."

"What?"

"It's out on the back porch."

Sterling opened the door for Lydia and followed her out. Taking her hand, he led her to the area she used for laundry. Drawing her to the washtub, he patted the brand-new wringer now attached to the side.

"Oh, Sterling, I asked Margaret not to mention a wringer."

He could see her distress. "You know my sister now. What makes you think that if she thought you, or she for that matter, needed something she'd keep silent about it?" He grinned at her. "I kept my word concerning it. I wanted to get one right away but she made me promise not to do so while they were here."

"They just left. How did you get it here and attached? We've been together all morning and it wasn't here when I was out here before."

"I had Luke bring it and hook it up after he delivered the luggage to the station."

"Thank you. I don't truly need it, but it will make laundry go so much faster."

"That way you'll have more time to make desserts."

Lydia laughed and slapped him gently on the chest, leaving her hand resting there for a moment. "Come, you hungry man. I'll fix lunch and then you can have your dessert."

That evening before supper Sterling gathered his shaving equipment and took it downstairs to his office. He planned on shaving after they had their devotions and Lydia went upstairs. He often did a little office work before going up. Tonight he wanted to be sure his face was smooth. Sterling planned on kissing Lydia a lot and didn't want a scratchy face deterring her response.

He knew she was nervous about marriage intimacy. Having no experience made him nervous too. He loved her, and wanted her with a mounting passion. He knew his love would allow him to gently, slowly, take them into the closeness God had intended for husband and wife.

"Sterling," he heard Lydia call from the entrance to the clinic hallway, "supper's ready."

"Coming." On his way out of the office he glanced at the clock. Only six-thirty. They didn't generally go to bed before nine, and now that the daylight lasted longer it was often later. Around three hours to wait. How would he fill those hours? It normally wasn't an issue, but tonight three hours seemed to stretch to eternity.

Entering the kitchen, he noticed a basket sitting on the bench with rolled white fabric items filling it. "What's this?" He pointed at the basket.

"I decided to try out the wringer, so I stripped the beds Margaret and family used and washed the linens."

Lydia stepped up to him, startling him a little when she slipped her arms under his, wrapping them around him in a big hug. "I want to thank you again for the wringer. It makes the work so much easier."

"You're welcome." This bodes well for the evening, he thought.

"As a special thank-you I made lemon meringue pie and sugar cookies." Her smile delighted him as she pulled away, allowing him to proceed to his chair.

"Let's have our devotions out on the porch tonight, shall we?"

Sterling looked around as Lydia came into his office. As usual he'd spent the time she was doing the dishes in his office working on paperwork. He'd long ago given up attempting to help her with cleaning up the kitchen after their meals. She just wouldn't let him.

"That sounds pleasant. I'll go get the Bible and meet you outside." He rose from his seat then grinned as Lydia raised her hand, already holding the Bible.

"I knew you'd agree, so I just brought it along."

He laughed. "You know me so well." Ushering her ahead of him, they paced to the porch swing.

They settled next to each other silent for a few minutes, simply enjoying the evening air. Sterling picked up the Bible that lay on the small table beside the swing.

"We're still in Ephesians." Opening it to the place marked by the ribbon bookmark, he began to read.

" 'Speaking to one another in psalms, hymns, and spiritual songs; singing, and singing praises in your heart to the Lord; giving thanks always concerning all things in the name of our Lord Jesus Christ, to God, even the Father; subjecting yourselves one to another in the fear of Christ.

Wives, be subject to your own husbands, as to the Lord. For the husband is the head of the wife, and Christ also is the head of the assembly, being himself the savior of the body. But as the assembly is subject to Christ, so let the wives also be to their own husbands in everything.

Husbands, love your wives, even as Christ also loved the assembly, and gave himself up for it; that he might sanctify it, having cleansed it by the washing of water with the word, that he might present the assembly to himself gloriously, not having spot or wrinkle or any such thing; but that it should be holy and without blemish. Even so ought husbands also to love their own wives as their own bodies.

He who loves his own wife loves himself. For no man ever hated his own flesh; but nourishes and cherishes it, even as the Lord also does the assembly; because we are members of his body, of his flesh and bones. For this cause a man will leave his father and mother, and will be joined to his wife. The two will become one flesh. This mystery is great, but I speak concerning Christ and of the assembly. Nevertheless each of you must also love his own wife even as himself and let the wife see that she respects her husband.' "

Sterling sat mulling over the words. "Most of the time when people quote this they stop at 'Wives, be subject to your own husbands.' When you read the entire passage the emphasis isn't on the wife submitting, but on the husband loving. 'Husbands, love your wives, even as Christ also loved the church, and gave himself up for it.' That really puts more responsibility on him."

"Why do you say that? Aren't wives supposed to submit to their husbands?"

"Yes, that's true, but just think about what the instruction to the husband is: Husbands, love your wives the way Christ loved his church. He gave all for us. Even dying for us. He served man, not demanding to be served or holding his position as God over us to make us do what he wanted. Here I'm directed to give all for you: to serve you in the manner of Christ. It seems to me that I have the greater responsibility. You're simply instructed to do as your husband thinks best. I'm to love you totally sacrificially."

He could tell Lydia was seriously considering his words. "I think that if the husband does that it would be very easy for the wife to submit to him. He wouldn't only be thinking about his wants but also what his wife wants and needs. He might even put hers before his own."

They each sat contemplating the verses and how they applied to themselves.

"Dr. Graham, Mrs. Graham." Eustace Taylor, Maggie's father and the man who had seen Sterling and Lydia in the livery, was coming up their front walk. "May I please have a word with you?"

Sterling glanced at Lydia. Her smile had faded and her expression was serious.

"Of course, would you like to speak here or go inside?" Sterling stood, extending his hand as the man approached.

"I think inside. That way we won't be interrupted."

"Yes." Sterling helped Lydia to her feet, allowing her to proceed him and Eustace into the house.

Once they were seated in the parlor the couple waited for Eustace to begin. Sterling could tell he was nervous and wondered why.

"Um ... I ..." Eustace hesitated, clearly ill at ease. "I needed to speak with you and ask for your forgiveness. My actions back in March were not compassionate or even considerate. I never meant for you to have to marry. I didn't think about how people would take it. I was wrong to go out of the livery without knowing what had really caused you both to be in the stable that night. Since the worship service that Sunday when you married I've been thinking about what Pastor Peter said in his sermon. Those verses he used have eaten at my soul ever since."

Eustace quoted: " 'I will silence whoever secretly slanders his neighbor. I won't tolerate one who is haughty and conceited. He that utters a slander is a fool. There are six things which Yahweh hates; yes, seven which are an abomination to him: haughty eyes, a lying tongue, hands that shed innocent blood, a heart that devises wicked schemes, feet that are swift in running to mischief, a false witness who utters lies, and he who sows discord among brothers.' "

"I'm guilty of these and most likely others. I ask you to forgive me. My sin had consequences that changed your lives in ways I never, ever thought about. I am sorry."

Sterling saw genuine anguish and remorse in the banker's eyes, which were swimming with tears. He looked at Lydia, who had turned her head to look at him. He reached for her hand, giving it a small squeeze and hoping she would agree with his intent. Her corresponding press of his hand answered as he had hoped.

"We forgive you, Eustace, and thank you for coming and confessing the sin. It takes a humble man with a willing spirit to listen to the Holy Spirit's prompting."

The strain left the older man's features and his body visibly relaxed. "Thank you so very much. This has been eating at me. I just had to let you know I regret what I did. I've been reading the Bible and in Leviticus it says to make restitution more than the value of the crime. I have no idea how to. I'll do whatever you think is best."

Thinking how to respond to Eustace's concern Sterling searched the Scriptures he could remember that dealt with restitution. All he could think of concentrated on injury, death or material examples. The verses dealing with gossip and lies seemed to focus on the perpetrator's relationship with God.

"Eustace, have you confessed this to God and asked for his forgiveness?"

"More times that I can count. I ask for it every day."

"Do you think you've been forgiven?" Sterling watched him consider the questions. It was evident when the revelation came.

"I finally do. I've been carrying this burden of guilt around since that day in March. Now, I feel it's finally been lifted away."

"I'm glad." Lydia entered the conversation. "I hope you can now leave it behind."

"I hope so, too. I know I've learned why God says gossip is evil. It spreads lies and half-truths, and causes innocent people harmful consequences."

Sterling looked at Lydia again then turned back to Eustace. "We're doing well. For my part, I think we will make a good marriage."

"You relieve me of a nagging worry. My actions caused this marriage, so the success of it is part of my responsibility. If ever I can help you with anything do not hesitate to ask. Whatever I can do, you can be sure I will."

Although he knew he would probably never take advantage of the offer, Sterling knew he had to accept it. "We will, Eustace. It's comforting to know there will be support if we are ever in need."

Eustace rose from his position on the edge of the chair. "Thank you. Now, I've taken enough of your time."

Both the Grahams stood also, allowing Eustace to lead the way to the front door.

"Thank you for coming, Eustace," Sterling said holding out his hand for Eustace to shake. "It took courage, and also the willingness to humble yourself before us. I respect you for that. I think I speak for by Lydia as well when I say, we'll pray for peace in you that passes all understanding."

"I'm grateful." Eustace placed his hat atop his head. "Good night." He pushed open the screen door, stepped onto the porch and headed down the steps before starting his walk home.

Chapter 39

Instead of going back out onto the porch, Sterling and Lydia went to the kitchen.

The desire for dessert was fluttering on the periphery of Sterling's mind, but Eustace's visit still captured his attention. "God certainly has been working on Eustace." He opened the cupboard and reached up to take two bowls down.

"Yes, I didn't think it would be bothering him after all this time. It's good to see the evidence of God convicting people of sin." Lydia stepped into the pantry emerging with a pan of peach cobbler and bottle of cream. She began dishing up the cobbler as Sterling got spoons.

"That he would come asking for forgiveness shows his commitment to Christ and wanting to be more like him," Sterling said. "Remember when Peter told us at the cafe after the wedding that some people had come to him confessing their participation in the gossip?"

They sat down at the table, each pouring cream over their bowls of cobbler. Sterling's bowl held considerably more than Lydia's.

"Yes, he said that not many would come and tell us about it and ask forgiveness. No one has come to me. Has anyone come to you?"

"Not until tonight. It shows Eustace's growing character than he would humble himself in this way." Sterling savored every bite of the biscuit topped fruit. He saw Lydia pause with the spoon midway to her mouth. He knew she was thinking about something and waited until she was ready to talk about it.

"I'm glad for Maggie as well as Eustace and us. I don't think her mother cares for more than what she wants. At least her father, though he made a terrible mistake, is trying to do right."

"Is it so terrible?" Suddenly Sterling's plans for the rest of the evening looked grim.

Lydia smiled, reached across the table and patted his hand. "No, it's been very good for me. I'm truly happy here with you."

Relief flooded him. "I'm happy also. You are a wonderful helpmeet. I like having you around."

Lydia's eyes twinkled with mischief. "I like having you around too." Standing and grabbing up his empty bowl and spoon, she spun from him. "Most of the time anyway."

"Hey." Sterling jumped up from his seat trying to catch her, but she set the bowls in the sink and ran out the back door.

"I need to ..."

He heard the tinkle of her laughter as she ran down the walk. Smiling, he moved to the sink, turned the dishpan over and began pumping water into it. By the time Lydia returned he had washed the bowls and spoons and was in the process of drying them.

"You didn't need to do that." He could tell she was distressed to find him doing the dishes.

"I know. I just wanted this to be one of those times you liked having me around." Sterling set down the last spoon and hung the towel neatly over the side of the sink. He thought about how to get her to go upstairs without him so he could have the time he needed to shave before he joined her.

"I have a little office work I should finish up tonight. You don't have to stay down here. I'm not sure how long it will take." This wasn't unusual so he knew she wouldn't suspect he would be shaving. It also wasn't a lie. There were a couple of notes he needed to make.

"Okay, I am rather tired. I did the sheets from the other bedrooms today. Thank you for the wringer. It made the job much easier and my hands aren't sore from the squeezing and twisting to get the water out." She walked up to him and gave him a hug. "Thank you. You do so much for me." She surprised him by lifting her head and giving him a quick peck on the cheek. "I'll head up now. Don't get absorbed in your paperwork and stay up too late."

Sterling stood watching her leave the kitchen. He definitely would not get lost in any paperwork tonight.

Once he knew Lydia was upstairs, Sterling pumped warm water into a pitcher, carrying it to his office and setting it on the desk. He jotted the patient notes on a paper then threw the pencil to the back of the desk. He took the pitcher to the exam room and poured some of the warm water into a bowl. With a little water, shaving soap and brush, he worked up lather. Just before he began dabbing the lather onto his face he noticed the shirt, ascot and vest he was still wearing reflected in the mirror hanging on the wall.

He set the brush down, quickly removing the garments. His hand shook a little while he spread the foam over the bristles. Calm down, he told himself. Don't slice yourself. Carefully moving the sharp blade across his skin, he cut the stubby hairs, leaving his face smooth with no blood oozing from cuts. Slipping back into his shirt, he carried the now dirty water to the kitchen and poured it down the drain. As he walked to the stairs, he prayed that God would bless them as they moved, this night, into a deeper relationship.

The room was in shadow, with one lamp burning on the small table by his side of the bed.

"Lydia?"

Softly saying her name, he walked to the bed. She didn't reply. He turned the lamp wick up so he could see her in the brighter light.

Lydia lay on her back in a white nightgown. The gathered neck ruffle was flipped up, hiding her neck, the lace edge dusting her cheek. Her russet braid, tied with a green ribbon, graced her shoulder and down onto her chest. She had her arm bent with her hand resting on his pillow. From her mouth came a soft gentle snore.

Disappointment nearly made Sterling groan out loud, but he stilled his urge. She must be exhausted from the week. Resigning himself to nothing but sleep tonight he changed into the nightshirt Lydia had laid out for him. Folding the clothes with a sigh of regret, he climbed in next to her.

On his side Sterling watched her sleep. Just before closing his eyes he slipped his hand onto hers, lacing their fingers. "Sleep well, my love."

Lydia awoke to soft tugs on her hair. It took her a moment to realize Sterling was behind her running his fingers through it, tenderly undoing the braid. Rolling onto her back she found him leaning on his elbow, her hair filtering and curling around his fingers. Looking into his hazel eyes, the pupils dilated in the first blush of morning, Lydia saw the question. Studying him for a moment she realized he would accept whatever answer she gave him.

With a timid smile and welcome in her eyes, without a word Lydia gave him the answer he so desired. Eyes joined, she watched as he lowered his mouth. Her lids fluttered shut as his lips met hers.

Chapter 40

"The cherries are ripe. I'm going to pick today and start canning. If you're really good I might just bake a pie for dessert."

Lydia and Sterling were finishing breakfast. The late June morning was bright and warm.

"If I'm not good, will you bake a cobbler?"

"No dessert for you if you're not good."

"The ultimate threat. I'll be good." Finishing his coffee, Sterling got up from the table. "I have a call out at the Hansen farm. I think I'll be back by lunch. If not, don't wait for me."

Leaning down, he gave Lydia a peck on the cheek. He made a point of showing affection whenever he could. "See, I'm being good. Now I'll get out of here so I don't have a chance to be bad."

Lydia laughed, watching as he left the room. She shook her head a little at the thought of his ever-present sweet tooth. She'd make sure there were enough cherries pitted so there would be a pie waiting for him when he returned.

When the dishes were done, she changed into one of the dresses she'd brought from home. She only wore them now when she worked in the garden or did other very messy chores.

Sterling had brought a stepladder up from the basement the other day, placing it near the fruit trees. Carrying a bucket in each hand filled with one kitten each, Lydia walked down the center path looking the trees over. They were both dotted with clusters of red ripe fruit. Her mouth watered at the thought of the tasty dark red Bing cherries they would eat fresh. She dearly loved sweet cherries, looking forward all year for the few weeks in late June. One year she'd almost made herself sick eating so many and she hadn't cared one bit.

First, though, she would pick the pie cherries. She would pit and can them for use the rest of the year, and bake others fresh into pies, cobblers, muffins and bread while they lasted on the trees. She wanted to pick as many as she could before the birds could get to them.

Setting the buckets on the ground, she laughed at the kittens struggling to get out. They were definitely growing, but they were still kittens with all the clumsiness that went along with it. As they chased each other around in the grass, she began picking the low branches rapidly, filling her first bucket. Delighted, she saw that not even half of the branches she could reach were clear of the tart ruby jewels. The second bucket filled just as quickly.

If she could pick enough today she would invite Ella over. They could share the work of pitting and canning, dividing the yield between them. Doing the boring job of pitting with someone else made the work go much faster and was tremendously more enjoyable. Aggie had been the one she'd done this with before; they had done joint canning of nearly everything from their gardens and fruit trees each year.

Lydia missed her grey-haired friend and longed to see her. She wished she could go for a visit but knew it wasn't possible. There was too much risk of running into Cyrus or Gus. Putting the desire aside with a decision to write a letter later in the day or tomorrow, she stood back from the tree and surveyed the crop still hanging within the branches. Birds flew in and out, harvesting their own pickings.

"Get out of here." Lydia yelled and waved her arms, startling the birds. They ignored her, aware she couldn't reach where they were enjoying the sweet juicy fruit.

Lydia carried two full buckets of pie cherries into the kitchen. She wanted to pick sweet cherries for eating but didn't have any more buckets. Setting her burden on the table, she thought about what to put her pickings in. Furrowing her brow, she figured how to create what she needed. She ran from the kitchen, up the stairs and into the sewing room. She pulled out a drawer in the bureau, extracting a square of muslin. Back downstairs, she entered the clinic exam room and pulled clean, used muslin strips from a shelf. She tied the strips to the corners of the fabric. Slipping the straps over her head and shoulders, the pouch formed by the muslin square hung in front of her waist. She smiled at her ingenuity as she went out the back door.

The kittens met her, crying pitifully.

"You're both just fine. I didn't leave you very long." She picked them up, giving each a hug before setting them back on the ground. "Come along. There are more cherries to pick, and these I'm going to eat as well as put in my pouch."

Winnie and Max darted in front of her as she walked back to the line of fruit trees. The branches with the sweet cherries began further up the trunk; she'd need the ladder to reach the fruit. For a while she climbed the ladder, picked what she could reach--eating her fair share also--and descended to the ground and moved the ladder, only to have to climb up again. Unhappy with the system, she took what she'd picked to the kitchen and poured them into a large bowl.

There has to be an easier way, she thought. All that up, down, move the ladder, up, down, move the ladder. She studied the tree. Although the branches started fairly high, they were evenly spaced around and up the trunk. The age of the tree gave its limbs sturdiness she thought would easily hold her slight weight.

Her steps were determined as she went to the ladder, moving it near the lowest branch. Climbing to the top she transferred her foot to the branch while grasping a branch above. Feeling pleased with her accomplishment she swiftly picked the cherries hanging within reach in front, above, behind and around her. Stepping from branch to branch, she gradually picked, moving further up and around the tree. The pouch as well as her stomach filled with the crimson nuggets, swollen with sweet juice.

"I think that's enough for now," she said to herself. There was enough for the two of them, the Lendreys and Mrs. H to share for a few days.

She began her descent, cautiously balancing her load of cherries as she moved her feet from bough to bough. She was making good progress when she felt a tug on her skirts. Straddling between two limbs, she looked back groaning in dismay. Her skirt was hooked on the stub of a pruned twig. Turning and planning to retrace her path, she found herself stuck. The strap of muslin crisscrossing her back caught on another stub. Twisting and turning in her attempt to free herself from the grip of the tree only succeeded in catching the other strap. She let go with one hand, hoping to be able to free even a single strap but this caused her balance to shift, nearly toppling her. She grabbed the limb again, saving herself, she was sure, from reaching the ground faster, and more painfully, than she desired.

Well, I am truly stuck, she thought.

She stood in the tree, her feet and hands divided among four branches, with a fifth holding tightly to her skirt that was stretched back and around the trunk. She couldn't tell whether the straps were held by a single branch or two.

"Oh, no!" She realized it must be close to lunchtime. Sterling should be home soon. She remembered that he'd said he might be late.

She looked down at the kittens, now curled up under the ladder sound asleep. "You two aren't much help. You're not even keeping me company in my distress."

Lydia took some time considering her options. There wasn't a way she could think of to free herself. She'd definitely needed help. Maybe if she yelled someone would hear and come to help her, but not wanting to again be the center of gossip in the town she rejected that idea. She would just have to stay there and wait until Sterling got home. She frowned. He'll never let me live this down, she thought. He'll tease me about it for years to come.

Lydia stood stock-still. Realization flooded her with joyous abandon. She wasn't afraid or nervous of his reaction when he found her. The knowledge that he would come help her get out of her predicament without censure or condemnation brought a huge smile to her face.

Thank you, Lord. Thank you. It was all she could think of to say. His peace had carried her and assured her of his love and protection while she learned that Sterling wasn't Cyrus but a caring man devoted to helping her heal from her fear and insecurity. She was no longer fearful that a mistake or mishap would bring critical words or physical harm. Now all she had to worry about was the teasing he was sure to heap on her for getting stuck in a tree. A wry grin accompanied her thoughts.

Lydia didn't know how long she had been in the tree before she heard Sterling's voice calling for her as he usually did when he came home. She did know of her pressing need that grew with each minute that passed.

"I'm out here." She raised her voice, hoping desperately he would hear her and breathed a grateful pray when he appeared on the porch. "Over here, in the cherry tree."

He searched with his eyes before he stepped off the porch and paced along the path toward her.

"What have we here?" He was smiling up at her. It was clear he'd assessed the situation, finding the humor she knew would frame his dealing with it.

"We have a wife stuck in this cherry tree."

"I see that. Are you in need of your husband's help?" His eyes fairly screamed the laughter he held back.

"Yes sir, I do believe I am."

"Ah ... so, my dear wife, what benefit for me shall I receive in helping you out of the predicament you are presently in?"

"A cherry pie?"

"You promised me one at breakfast."

"Some of the fresh sweet cherries I've picked?"

"You've eaten your fair share, I can see. Your lips betray you." Sterling walked around the tree, taking in her circumstances.

"I needed to see whether they were good enough for you to eat. I most certainly wouldn't want to serve you under-ripe cherries."

"That's your primary concern, I'm sure. Again, what benefit shall I receive for aiding you?"

"You will receive dessert each day, which you will not receive for a month if you don't help me down immediately." She smiled sweetly as she said it.

Sterling broke into laughter. "Oh Lydia, what a marvelous reply. I do love you so."

Lydia's mouth dropped open in shock at his words. Speechless, her mouth pumped open and closed like a fish in the air.

"Yes, my dear, I do love you. Please accept it without feeling the need to reciprocate. I don't expect you to, but do hope you might one day."

She simply stared at him. No thoughts formed in her mind, and nor were there words for her to speak.

"Now let's get you out of this tree." Moving the ladder behind her, he climbed up and released her skirt. "One trap freed, onto the next." When he'd released both the straps of the pouch he instructed her on how to place her hands and feet, allowing her better balance and a more secure stance.

"Can you remove the pouch? Very ingenious, by the way."

"I think so."

With his help Lydia was able to slip the straps off allowing him to take the pouch, which he set on the ground. She worked her way down through the branches until she stood on the lowest one.

"Will you put the ladder here so I can climb down?"

"No."

"What do you mean, no?"

"You're unfamiliar with the definition?"

"No."

"Then you understand?"

"No."

"Previously you stated you were in need of your husband's help, not that of a ladder."

"Well, I need a ladder now."

"As your husband, I say you have no need of a ladder."

"So, dear husband, just how is your wonderful wife supposed to complete her descent?" Lydia finally realized the game, smiling sweetly. "Shall I jump?"

"No need. Your husband is willing and able to help you come down from your perch." His corresponding smile told her he appreciated her participation.

"How is this going to be accomplished?"

"You, my love, will stand there and I shall wrap my arms around you, carrying you out of your predicament and set you safely on the ground."

Lydia sent him a dubious look. "You're positive of my safety? What if you drop me?"

"You forget I'm a doctor. If you're injured I can patch you up. Now shall we proceed with the rescue, my damsel in distress?"

She hesitated. "All right, but don't you drop me or no dessert for two months."

"The ultimate threat."

Sterling, having moved the ladder away, stood before her and wrapped his arms around her legs just above her knees. "Let go of the branch."

Lydia did as she was told. He lifted her slightly, carrying her along the branch as she pushed the higher ones out of her way. Just as they neared the end of the branches one caught in her hair, momentarily pulling her off balance. She shrieked as Sterling stumbled. She felt his arms loosen and squealed in fear. Her body slid down along his as he struggled to remain standing. The battle ended in his defeat. They landed with Sterling on his back and Lydia lying atop him, her face just above his. His arms held her tightly.

"Are you all right?" His voice held concern.

Lydia, feeling safe within the circle of his embrace, nodded. She searched his face, seeing a desire there which matched her own. Slowly she brought her mouth down, her lips aching to touch his.

Chapter 41

Crash, clatter, stomp, stomp, crash, clatter, clatter, stomp!

Sterling watched, extremely disappointed, as Lydia jumped away just before her lips touched his. Turning over and springing up from the ground, he saw the last few stumbling steps Drew took before catching his balance. He grabbed his wife, now crimson faced with embarrassment, around the waist before she could flee, holding her close to his side.

"Sorry." Drew called from among a pile of metal bins and bowls, now scattered, that Lydia kept beside the garden to use when she harvested. He'd been trying to back away from the couple lying on the ground so he wouldn't disturb them. "I ... um ... huh ... didn't mean to interrupt."

"Well, you did a fine job of it anyway." Sterling, though a little irritated at the sudden end of the moment, was very pleased that Lydia had accepted his declaration and had taken the initiative as they lay on the ground. Now though, he couldn't figure out why she was squirming so much, trying to get away. He knew she was embarrassed, but she had been in more uncomfortable situations before and handled them well.

"Let me go, Sterling. I need to go. Now."

"It's only Drew. You don't have to be that embarrassed. He won't say anything to anyone."

"No, it's not that. I need to go." Lydia dragged his arm from her waist, lifted her skirts high and ran down the path, turning at the intersection toward the outhouse.

Sterling grinned then followed more slowly, approaching a sheepish Drew. "You picked an awful time to visit, my friend."

"I know, I'm sorry. You two seemed to be getting along pretty well."

"The moment was sweet, until a certain friend of mine barged in." Sterling laughed as he punched at Drew, pretending to hit him in the chest.

"What are friends for but to cause problems?" Drew held up his hands, allowing Sterling to mock punch them.

"So, what was so important you had to interfere with a private moment with my wife?"

"Let's wait until Lydia returns. She'll want to hear this too."

"Okay, I'll go get the cherries she picked. You clean up the mess you made." Sterling thought of telling Drew about Lydia getting stuck up in the tree but decided against it. It was a sweet personal event between the two of them. Especially his revelation to her of his love. That had slipped out so naturally, coming as a surprise to her. At least she hadn't rejected him. Someday, he hoped, she would return his love, but she knew now and he'd be able to tell her as often as he wanted.

As he was returning with the pouch of fruit Sterling met Lydia coming from the necessary. He slipped his arm around her waist again, pulling her close. "I kept your little adventure to myself. It's a moment I'll treasure forever."

"Thank you, me too." Her reply was soft-spoken and gave him hope.

They went into the freshly painted kitchen, the men settling on the new chairs while Lydia rinsed the cherries. Setting the large bowl of fruit in the center of the table, along with saucers for the pits, she sat next to Sterling.

"So, my friend, what brought you here this afternoon?"

"Not much really, I just needed to ask one of my best friends if he would do something for me. The other of my best friends will be busy that day."

Puzzled, Sterling reached for a cherry. "What do you need me to do?"

"Would you stand as my best man at Rachel's and my wedding?"

"Ho, ho, I told you so!" Lydia jumped from her seat, running around the table to give Drew a big hug. "I'm so happy for you, and for me. I've come to love Rachel and wasn't looking forward to her leaving in the fall. You aren't moving away, are you?"

"No, we'll live here in Cottonwood." Drew looked at Sterling. "I have your wife's delight, now how about an answer to my request?"

"Of course I will. It will be an honor. When's the wedding?"

Drew told them that the mid-September wedding was to be held in Cottonwood, with Peter officiating, rather than the bride's home since her aunt, Mrs. H., was unable to travel. Then the couple would journey to her childhood home where a celebration was being planned.

"You see, Sterling, I was right, right, right." Lydia's voice held delighted humor as she sat down next to him. "I was so right and you didn't believe me." She snatched a cherry, popping it into her mouth with a big grin.

Drew looked confused. "What were you right about?"

"The first day when we all met Rachel at the Decoration Day picnic, we noticed you and Rachel standing under the tree talking. I told Sterling that you two were going to get married, but he didn't believe me." Lydia poked Sterling in the side, emphasizing her words and laughing.

Sterling grabbed her finger then shifted his grip to lace his fingers with hers, effectively stopping the teasing pokes as he held her hand. "You were right, I admit it. I'm also honored that you asked me to stand up with you."

"I stood up with you so I figured you could hold me up when my knees collapse from nervousness," Drew said with a silly grin.

"Where are you going to live? You only have a room in the boardinghouse."

Sterling wondered the same thing but Lydia had asked the question.

"I'm buying Mrs. H.'s house. She's going to be living with us and took that into consideration when she set the price. It will be good for both Rachel and me, and Mrs. H."

After extracting her hand from Sterling's, Lydia began pitting pie cherries while the men talked. Lost in her thoughts, she wasn't paying any attention when the bell to the clinic rang. Both men got up from the table, signaling an end to the conversation.

"Looks like I have an unexpected patient." Sterling reached out his hand to Drew, who grasped and firmly shook it. "Congratulations, my friend." Sterling headed through the back hall to the clinic.

"Thanks, Lydia." Drew turned to exit through the house hall. "The cherries were wonderful. I won't tell Rachel, she might be jealous." He gave a quick chuckle.

"Drew, why don't you, Rachel and Mrs. H. come for supper tonight? We can have a small celebration. I'm making a cherry pie and Rachel can have some of these sweet cherries so she won't have to be jealous."

"Sounds good. What time do you want us to come?"

"Six o'clock for the meal but come earlier if you want. Be sure to tell them not to worry about bringing anything. I'll cook it all."

"Will do." With a wave, Drew walked down the hall to exit through the front door.

The events of the past few hours swirled in Lydia's mind as she pitted cherries and planned her menu. The surprise of Rachel and Drew's engagement, the upcoming wedding, deciding what else to serve besides cherry pie. What held her most enthralled was Sterling's confession that he loved her. His declaration coming right on the heels of her realization that she felt total security in her relationship with Sterling nearly overwhelmed her. She hadn't had time to understand the change within herself; Sterling's feelings for her added another layer of confusion.

One thing she was certain of was her disappointment at Drew's interruption, no matter that the reason was joyous. While she lay atop Sterling beneath the fruit tree, her desire bloomed more intensely than ever before. She didn't know if it was because of her realization that she wasn't afraid or uncertain anymore, or the words he had spoken as he looked up at her trapped within the branches. It may even have been a combination. It spun in her mind as if in a whirlpool. She hoped the swirling would soon settle into a calm, clear pool so she could see clearly to the bottom of her emotional sea.

Chapter 42

Summer always meant gardening and canning for Lydia. This one was no different. There were differences, though. Aggie wasn't there, but Maggie and Ella were, and Janie with her run-on sentences and innocent interest also. They talked, laughed and joked as the two experienced women taught Maggie the process, with a four year-old giving advice.

Cherries, peas, beets, cabbage, broccoli, followed by beans, carrots and onions along with copious zucchini filled July. Early apples meant applesauce and fresh apple pie. The jars from the cellar changed from pale-blue dusty vessels to a myriad of colors promising nourishment throughout the winter. August brought potatoes, cucumbers for pickles, salads and sandwiches, and tomatoes: mounds and mounds of tomatoes. The women canned and dried the bounty daily, dividing the jars and bundles between the two families. Maggie wouldn't take any, knowing her mother didn't approve of her daughter's activities. Plans were made to give a goodly number to Drew and Rachel as wedding presents.

This morning was an unusual one since Lydia would be working alone. Maggie was attending a social function with her mother in a nearby town and Peter had stopped by saying that Janie had a stomach ache so Ella and she were staying home.

Sterling was in the clinic seeing patients when Lydia carried her large enamel bowl into the garden. Tomatoes needed to be picked as well as more cucumbers. She'd cook the tomatoes down into sauce and make bread-and-butter pickles with the cucumbers and onions.

Lydia spent much of the morning thinking about how living with Sterling had changed her from an insecure, frightened young woman into one who loved to laugh and tease, confident in herself, secure in her position as his wife. And he loved her. This was the hardest to fathom. When she tried asking him about how and when he'd realized it, Sterling pressed his finger to her lips and told her not to analyze it, just live within it.

Doing so was easy, so easy Lydia was afraid she'd start taking it for granted. He'd always been polite and courteous, patient, caring and protective. His distress over her clothing had endeared him as a generous provider. Now she saw a gentleness and affection that had crept in. She was mulling all this over as she picked the vegetables. Sterling wasn't perfect: he often left dirty socks on the floor when the hamper was close by, and occasionally he invited people over for supper and forget to tell her until lunch the day they were to come. He'd smacked her several times in his sleep when turning over, flinging his arm across her pillow. Lydia smiled at the memory of how she'd smacked him back a couple of times, waking him up. Then he would wrap his arm around her waist, pulling her close. She liked waking up nestled close to him without having woken when he reached for her.

Winnie bumped her head against Lydia's arm as she pulled a branch of the tomato plant up to get at the dark red globes.

"Do you need some loving?" She picked up the half-grown kitten, looking around for Max. He was sleeping, belly up, in the sun between rows of onion and garlic. Stroking Minnie, she thought about how secure these two furry waifs were in their new home. Just like she was, and it was all Sterling's doing.

She thought about the conversation they'd had about the passage in Ephesians instructing wives to submit to their husbands. Lydia found submitting to Sterling easy since he was loving her as Christ loves the church: sacrificing rather than demanding her submission. He had what was best for her as his goal. It wasn't that he always chose what she wanted but he did always consider her thoughts, needs and desires.

Her bowl now filled with tomatoes and cucumbers, Lydia set Minnie down and called to Max, waking him up. Carrying her produce, she went into the house followed by the kittens.

"My, I'm tired," she told the kittens.

She set the bowl on the table then turned to the sink to pump water into a glass for a drink. Facing the table again, she looked at the large bowl heaped with the green and red vegetables and grimaced. She was bone-tired and didn't really want to do them, but they were ripe and needed to be done. Setting a couple of large tomatoes aside and slicing a cucumber into sour cream for lunch, she began the work of preparing the tomatoes to cook into sauce.

While they cooked she sat at the table slicing cucumbers and onions for the pickles. Weary, her knife moved slower and slower. Soon it stopped and her head sagged until it finally lay on the table as she slipped into an exhausted sleep.

Sterling walked down the clinic hall at noon and sniffed. There was a slight scorched smell. Drawing his eyebrows together in concern, he hurried into the kitchen. On the stove was a kettle with steam rolling out the top. Taking long strides he pulled the pot from the heat. Turning toward the table, his heart skipped a beat as he took in Lydia, her head on her arm, which was stretched across the surface with a knife still in her hand.

"Lydia?" He pressed two fingers to the side of her neck. Her pulse was strong and steady. "Lydia?" Sliding the fingers up to her forehead, he found no fever. "Lydia, sweetheart, can you hear me?" He was getting alarmed and his voice was louder, with a touch of panic.

"Huh? What?"

Relief flooded him.

Lydia lifted her head and looked at him in confusion.

"Are you all right?" Sterling knelt by her chair.

"Yes, what happened?" She yawned so wide he could see the back of her throat.

"You must've fallen asleep. I think your tomatoes scorched. I could smell them in the clinic hall."

"Oh no!" The emerald eyes shimmered with tears. When they overflowed Sterling wrapped his arms around her.

"It's okay. There are more tomatoes."

"I know, it's just ..." She laid her head on his chest and cried.

Sterling held her, letting her cry, trying to think of what could be the cause of the tears.

Lydia dropped the knife on the table and wrapped her arms around his back. "It's just that I'm so very tired. There was all the work picking, and getting them into the kettle to cook, and now they're all ruined."

"It's all right, no real damage done." He felt new wetness on his shirt. "Let's get you upstairs. You're done working for today." Helping her rise, he put his arm around her waist and began guiding her from the kitchen to the stairs.

"But the cucumbers, I need to make the pickles." When she tried to pull away he bent and scooped her up into his arms and continued toward his goal of the bedroom.

"Not today, doctor's orders. I'm going to put you to bed where you will spend the rest of the day. I'll do the cooking tonight."

"You can't cook."

"I can do well enough for one meal."

"Two."

"Two what?"

"Two meals, we haven't had lunch yet."

"I can make that too."

They'd reached the bedroom so Sterling set her down and began unbuttoning her dress.

"What are you doing?" Lydia looked down at his fingers then yawned again.

"Putting you to bed where you will stay the rest of the day."

"I am tired."

He'd gotten her dress unbuttoned and was pulling her arms out of the sleeves. Once her dress was pooled at her feet, Lydia stepped away then climbed into bed on top of the blankets. "Will you please get me a cover?"

"Certainly." By the time he'd gotten a blanket and covered her, Lydia was sound asleep. Sterling removed her shoes and stockings then stood looking at her. He thought he knew what was the cause of her extreme fatigue but needed to speak with her to confirm his suspicions.

Something smelled wonderful. Lydia came slowly awake, inhaling the luscious aroma. Opening her eyes she saw Sterling placing a tray on the washstand.

"That smells good." Her words brought him to the bed and a big yawn from her.

"So you finally decided to wake up, sleepyhead." Sterling sat on the bed smiling at her.

"What time is it?" His body blocked her view of the clock.

"Almost seven o'clock. You slept the afternoon away. Every time I looked in you were sound asleep." She saw a teasing twinkle light up his eyes. "You even snored some."

"I did not."

"How would you know? You were asleep." Teasing now sounded in his voice.

"I just do. I do not snore." Lydia realized how pouty she sounded and laughed. "So, what did you fix for supper? It smells wonderful, and I'm hungry." As if on cue, her stomach started rumbling, causing both of them to laugh.

Sterling stood. "I have a confession to make. I didn't fix anything. I was busy with patients all afternoon so I got this at Langston's."

"Well, at least I know I'll be able to eat it. I wasn't sure about your cooking," Lydia teased.

"I can take this back to the cafe and cook up something for you instead if you'd rather."

"No, no, I wouldn't want to put you to all that trouble." Her grin widened.

"Minx." He turned and picked up the tray.

Lydia sat up and arranged the pillows behind her. "I've never had supper in bed before. Never breakfast either. I feel very special."

Sterling, holding the tray, carefully sat beside her. "To me, you are very special. I love you."

"Thank you." Lydia knew he wanted her to say that she reciprocated his love but simply couldn't. She was still unsure of her feelings. Lifting her hand, she caressed his cheek. "You are very special to me too."

His smile conveyed his disappointment, but he turned into her hand and kissed her palm. They spent a moment looking at each other then she pulled her hand away. Lydia's stomach growled again.

"Okay, you're hungry." Sterling laughed and turned his attention back to the tray. He removed the cloth covering and revealed fried chicken, green beans, coleslaw, fluffy biscuits and two big pieces of chocolate cake.

"Oh, it looks so heavenly." Her stomach growled again.

"I'd better say grace fast so you can feed that beast within you."

They held hands and Sterling thanked God for the meal, asking that the Lord bless the people who had prepared it.

Lydia concentrated on her food for a while then looked at Sterling, who seemed to be studying her. "What?"

"I'm just wondering about your fatigue today."

She waved the piece of chicken held in her hand dismissively. "I've just been working so hard the last couple of weeks. Obviously I planted too much garden. I think I'll see if the Jorgensens would like some. I don't think they have a garden."

"I think that's a good idea. See if the boys will come to pick and weed for you, too. I don't want you working so hard. Especially now."

"Why now?"

"Well, I think there may be an additional reason for you to be tired."

Lydia thought about all the work she'd done for the past few weeks. This time of summer was always very busy. She had the garden to maintain as well as harvest and preserve. The fruit, in addition to the vegetables, needed to be canned and made into jellies, jams and preserves.

"It's always like this during the summer. It's been hot, too, and I haven't slept that well, so I suppose that makes me extra tired."

"I'm putting on my doctor hat now, Lydia, and want to ask you a few questions." They'd finished with the meal so Sterling took the tray, still holding the desserts for later. He set it on the washstand, and climbed back on the bed, settling close to her.

Now she was becoming nervous. Did he think something was wrong with her?

"Have you been feeling well, or has there been any nausea you haven't mentioned?"

"No, I've felt fine."

"Good. When was your last menses?"

"My what? Oh." She blushed and stammered. "Well ... um ... let me think. Just before your sister came." Her eyes widened as she began to understand what his questions might mean. "Oh."

"Is it regular?"

"Yes." Lydia looked at his now grinning face. "Oh, Sterling, do you think ..."

"Very possibly. I want to check you out but I think you're expecting."

Suddenly Sterling's arms were wrapped around his wife, who'd flung herself at him. He could feel the rapid beat of her heart as she held him tightly.

"So you might be just a little happy about this?"

She pulled back from him. The delight on her face matched his. "Oh, yes. Ever since we ... I've thought how wonderful it would be to have a child. I had no idea how long it would take."

"Not long, it would seem." They laughed. "Let me check you out so we can be sure." His joy increased as she leapt off the bed and began undressing, obviously wanting the confirmation. He rose and pulled the blankets back.

The exam proved their suspicions were correct. "I'd say you're due in early to mid March." He leaned down and kissed her. "So, do you want a boy or girl?"

Her arms came around his neck and held, forcing him to sit beside her. "I don't care at this point." She kissed him.

He didn't either.

Chapter 43

Aggie twitched her shoulders. Standing on her porch in the late afternoon, she watched the buzzards circling off to the north. She'd lived on this farm for more than thirty-five years and been content. Now something called her to leave. The sensation had begun in June and gotten stronger each week. Now she realized God was calling her to a new place. Her shoulders moved involuntarily again.

Stepping off the porch, she walked to the barn and saddled up her mare. Climbing into the saddle she whistled to the dogs. "Come on, you two old hounds. We're gonna visit Gerald Newman."

The ride wasn't long to the neighboring farm. The dogs greeted Aggie with familiarity. At the noise Gerald and his son Randal came out of the barn.

"Well, howdy Aggie. What brings you here? Not that you aren't always welcome."

While Gerald spoke the young man held her bridle and Aggie climbed down from the horse.

"I want to have a parley with you and the boy here."

"How about we go into the kitchen for some coffee and a sit-down? I'm sure Marcy has something sweet to go along with it."

"Sounds good. My bones don't like standin' around doin' nothin'."

Once they were settled at the table Aggie began.

"Gerald, you've been farmin' my place since my man died and the children went west. You done a good job of it too. Randal, I hear you're lookin' to marry up with Ginger Townsend and you're needin' a place to set up housekeepin'." Aggie paused, looking at the two men. "I'm offerin' to sell my farm and house to you. I'm not lookin' forward to another winter of tendin' stock and shoveling snow. Now's the time to move. What do ya say?"

The huge smile on Randal's face told her that only the price was left to be negotiated. This was accomplished in good time, with both sides satisfied.

"Oh, one more thing, and it's a deal breaker. You don't agree to this and I'll be lookin' for someone else to buy the place." Aggie watched with silent mirth as the men's expressions turned suspicious. "Buster and Angus become your dogs the day we sign the papers."

Randal laughed, jumped up, ran to Aggie and hugged her. "It's a deal. They're here or our dogs are there most of the time anyway." He stood, grabbing his hat from the hook. "I'm going to go tell Ginger. Tell Ma not to expect me for supper. We've got plans to make."

Aggie and Gerald laughed as the screen door slammed behind the young man. He ran to the barn and a whoop of delight echoed in the room.

"You sure made his day, Aggie. We'd just about given up on finding a farm around here. Randal and Ginger didn't want to move away but we couldn't find anything. This offer is God's answer to prayer."

The older woman sipped the now tepid coffee. "For me too, Gerald. For me too." She paused, prayed silently then spoke. "I'm gonna tell you something and I need your solemn promise not to tell anyone. I've prayed about whether to tell you but I'm a needin' your help. It ain't somethin' wrong, just needs to be kept to yourself. Don't even tell Randal or Marcy, okay?"

"I promise." Gerald's voice was serious and sincere, giving Aggie confidence in revealing her secret.

"I'm a gonna be moving to where Lydia is. God's given me a powerful callin' to be with her."

"So you know where she is?"

"Yes, I helped her leave and know where she's livin' and doin'. Cyrus and Gus have both been to my place wantin' me to tell them. I'm afeared that if they know, Cyrus'll go after her. You know what he'll do if'n he finds her."

"Yes, I know. I'll keep it secret. What kind of help do you need from me?"

"I'm gonna pack up my things in crates and leave them till I'm ready to have them sent. I'm hopin' you'll send them to me. On the day we sign the papers on the farm I'll be givin' you an envelope with the address. You keep that sealed until I write for my things to be shipped. Once they're shipped off I want you to burn that paper."

"That's an easy promise for me to make, Aggie."

The following day Randal and Ginger came to visit and see the house. Aggie was delighted at the excitement of the couple. Their joy was infectious, bringing back memories of her youth.

"I'm not gonna be needin' all this stuff. How about I decide what I'm not gonna be wantin' to take and see if you wanna buy it? Small things I'll just be givin' you for a wedding present."

"Oh that's too generous, Mrs. Cutler." Ginger looked distressed at the offer.

"That's why I said I'd be sellin' most of it to you. We can settle on the furniture and such. Then I'll go through the smaller things as I pack 'em up and if I don't plan on takin' somethin' you can have it or get rid of it. Some of this stuff's just plain junk." Aggie winked at Randal, who laughed.

"It's generous of you and I'll be giving you a fair price."

"I'll help you with your packing. It's the least I can do." Ginger squeezed the older woman's hand in gratitude.

"Deal. Now let's go see what I wanna take with me."

Chapter 44

"You can still back out, you know." Sterling was straightening Drew's tie just before the ceremony began. "It's not too late until the preach says the vows."

"I'm not backing out. It's taken me this long to find her and I'm not going to let her go."

Sterling laughed. "All right. Hold out your hands."

"Why?" His voice suspicious, Drew moved his hands behind his back.

The two men were in a small room next to the altar area.

"I just want to see if your hands are shaking. Mine were when I got married."

"This is very different from your wedding. We want to get married." Drew paused then continued. "You seem pretty contented these days. From what I saw in the garden in June I think the two of you are making your marriage work." Drew had a big grin on his face from the memory.

Sterling simply smiled. He didn't need to tell his friend that he loved Lydia, figuring it was fairly obvious to someone who knew him so well. He also didn't say anything about Lydia's condition. They wanted to keep it between themselves for a while. They enjoyed this private time of joy, talking about names and colors for the nursery. The news would travel quickly through the town when they decided to share it. Both were just a touch afraid that Margaret would descend, taking over all the planning.

Piano music coming from the sanctuary signaled the start of the service.

Sterling looked at Drew, seeing his face pale. "Don't faint now. You'll be married before you know it. Just respond when Peter tells you to say something." Punching Drew in the arm, he opened the door and led the way into the sanctuary.

Sitting next to Ella with Janie tucked against her other side Lydia watched the joyous expressions on the faces of the couple getting married. This was the first wedding in Cottonwood since she and Sterling were wed. She remembered her confusion, nervousness and fear as she had stood exchanging vows with a stranger. Seven months later she was carrying his child and, more importantly, she knew he loved her. Rather than doubts and worries she was filled with security, trust, and something else.

Lydia focused her gaze on Sterling, standing beside his friend. Standing in his black suit, his dark brown hair carefully combed, the profile he presented kept her eyes locked on him as Peter spoke the vows. He was so handsome, but she knew that was only on the outside. He was beautiful on the inside too. His passion for his patients, his devotion to God, his desire to do what was right, his determination to make their marriage work. Those were the important things. Sterling's name describes his character, she thought.

The thoughts flowed through her mind unclouded and sparkling. Then realization struck.

I love him. How could I not have seen it before?

Lydia sat perfectly still as the ceremony went on without hearing one word. She thought back, trying to figure out when her liking for Sterling had moved past the threshold into a zealous love. Her heart beat rapidly, excited with the discovery. Then she realized when it had started. The love for him had crept in slowly. The day he'd taken her shopping for clothes began a continual shower of caring, thoughtful, purposeful acts intended to help her feel safe, secure and treasured.

He had loved her until she was able to love her back. He had never pressured her. At times he'd chastised her, but only for her own good. She smiled at the memory of his scolding when she did too much gardening before her back healed. He'd been gentle but firm. Lydia continued thinking of the last seven months, and all the ways he'd loved her even before he realized it.

Now she'd discovered that she loved him back. Smiling to herself, she began thinking of how she would tell him. He had just let it slip out, but she wanted to make her own declaration somewhat special. Something unique to him. A way that would be remembered by them just as his confession would always be.

"I now pronounce you man and wife. You may kiss the bride."

The declaration brought her back to the present. Shifting her gaze to the newlyweds, Lydia left her rumination for another time. Along with the rest of the congregation she applauded as Mr. and Mrs. Andrew Richards walked down the aisle followed by the bridesmaids and groomsmen.

Sterling was waiting for her on the church lawn. Lydia smiled brightly as she approached. "It seems to me that you look especially handsome today."

"Why, thank you, madam. You look beautiful as well. There seems to be a special glow to your face." Sterling leaned close, whispering in her ear.

Lydia wondered if her newly discovered love was evident on her face, then realized he was referring to her expectant condition. Smiling, she took the arm he extended to her.

The day was warm and sunny, with just a hint of fall coloring the leaves. A cake and punch reception was set up on the lawn. Sterling kept a close eye on Lydia, watching for signs of weariness. Fatigue still dogged her and he didn't want her to become overtired. He was watching her chat with several women when Peter approached.

"You sure are watching your wife closely. Any reason for it?"

"She's become a beautiful woman compared to the bruised and broken soul you married me to in March." Sterling glanced at his friend then returned his gaze to Lydia.

"You're right." Peter also centered his attention on Lydia. "She's healed not only physically but emotionally as well. I'm proud of how you two have made a strong marriage."

"I think we have. I try to be a good husband." He grinned. "I know she gets aggravated with my dirty laundry left on the floor. One time she scolded me, telling me I should bring my neatness of the clinic into our room."

"I'm glad to hear you've progressed to sharing a room." Amused, Peter watched Sterling's face turn bright red. "I'm also glad she can scold you. She must be safe and secure with you to do that."

"She is. Lydia knows how important she is. It took a while for her to relax and stop being afraid." He paused then smiled at his friend. "Now I have to be afraid. She threatens to stop making desserts if I'm naughty."

Peter laughed out loud, drawing attention from several groups scattered around the churchyard. "The ultimate punishment. Your wife is a smart woman and knows you well."

Watching his friend turn his gaze back to his wife, Peter noticed the soft smiles they gave each other. *Thank you, Lord. You've let them fall in love with each other.*

Lydia spent the next few days trying to figure out a meaningful way to let Sterling know that she returned his love. She really wanted it to be memorable. Walking to the All-Purpose Store one morning she heard her name being called and turned to see Peter hurrying up the street.

"Good morning. How are you this fine day?" Peter slowed as he approached her.

"I'm well. And you?"

"I'm happy to say that my family and I are all well. Janie has been a bride all week with a dishtowel veil and bunches of black-eyed Susans for her bouquet."

"Who's the groom?"

"His name changes several times a day. Such a fickle thing, she is. The place beside her during the ceremony is usually occupied by Oscar. Sometimes the cat escapes to nap where she can't find him."

Lydia laughed with delight. "She's such a delightful girl. You are very blessed."

"I am."

They walked in silence for a few moments then Peter spoke again. "I wonder how Sterling has been lately?"

"He's fine. Why do you ask? You saw him at the wedding the other day and also at church service."

She saw the teasing light in the pastor's eyes and wondered what he might be up to.

"I was just wondering if you've had to take away any of his desserts. He told me of the consequences if he isn't good."

"Now I know what you two were talking about at the wedding reception. I had wondered about that. The expressions on your faces told me Sterling had revealed something that embarrassed him." Lydia was relieved that Sterling hadn't told him about the baby.

"Just that you're secure enough in your relationship that you scold him for leaving dirty laundry around. I'm glad of that. I've prayed for you both, and for you especially. God has answered my prayers. You have a good marriage, and you've blossomed from a terrified waif into a beautiful woman, both in looks and character."

"You're making me blush." Lydia covered her burning cheeks with her hands.

"I'm sorry, but it's the truth. I'm very glad for you both. Now I must be heading in a different direction. I told Mrs. H. I'd stop by this morning. Have a wonderful day. I hope you won't have to take any of Sterling's desserts away from him any time soon."

After they parted Lydia walked slowly considering his words. She stopped. An idea had come to her as to how she could let Sterling know of her love. Picking up her pace, she swiftly completed her shopping wanting to get home with time to execute her plan that afternoon.

"Sterling?" Lydia stood in the doorway to his office.

Seated at his desk, he turned to look over his shoulder at her. "Yes?"

"Will you please come to the kitchen?"

Puzzled, he stood. "Of course. Is anything wrong?"

"No."

He drew his eyebrows together with concern. Lydia usually explained whatever she wanted and why. Now she was silent. He followed her down the hall. Entering the kitchen, he glanced around the room quickly trying to discern what the issue was. Everything looked fine.

No, something was odd. On every surface were pies, cakes and cookies. The counters, the table and even the chairs had some kind of sweet on them.

"What's all this? Is there a social event I don't remember that you're taking desserts to?"

"No." Lydia was smiling now.

"Why did you bake so much then?" He knew expecting a baby could make women crave foods but he'd never heard of them baking so much just to fulfill it.

Lydia took his hands and faced him, her back to the bounty. Looking up into his eyes she said, "This is to show you how much I love you."

Sterling looked at her face then lifted his eyes to the items arrayed before him. He looked back at her. Drawing Lydia close, he wrapped her in his arms. They stood savoring the moment. Putting a finger under her chin, Sterling lifted Lydia's face. Lowering his, their mouths met in a long, sweet kiss.

"I love you," Lydia said when the kiss ended. "I've been trying to think of a way I could tell you how much. This is how much." She swept her arm around the room, indicating all the various desserts.

"I love you too. You certainly chose a wonderful way to let me know." He kissed her again. Drawing back, he kissed her again laughed. "How am I supposed to eat all this? There's enough for an army."

Lydia laughed too. "You're not going to. I love you enough not to let you."

"You wound me. It's not all for me?" Sterling put a wounded expression onto his face but couldn't hold it. "Then what are you going to do with it all?"

"I thought we'd give some to the Jorgensens'. I don't think they have desserts very often. Drew and Rachel will be home tomorrow so I'll take a pie over there. Maggie's in her new apartment now. A housewarming gift of cookies might be nice. I thought Ella and family could take some off our hands."

"Wait a minute. I get to eat some. It sounds like you're giving it all away."

Lydia reached up giving him a peck on the cheek. "You get to choose your favorites and have them for breakfast, lunch, supper and evening snack."

Sterling took her in his arms again. "God certainly had a plan when he placed us in the livery stable that night."

Lydia, her head resting on his chest, nodded and hugged him tighter.

Chapter 45

Sterling closed the clinic for the day and walked to the exam room to gather the used instruments for cleaning. He heard a knock on the front door and Lydia's footsteps as she went to answer it. He'd just picked up the full pan when Lydia screamed. Scattering the instruments as he dropped the pan, Sterling ran, praying that her brother hadn't found her and arrived at their home. Throwing open the door to the clinic, he flew out ready to do battle. He stopped short, seeing his wife and a tiny grey-haired woman in a tight embrace.

"Aggie, Aggie, Aggie." Tears clouded his wife's voice as they rocked back and forth.

"I know, I know."

Sterling watched the older woman stroke Lydia's hair. He could see the love between them. He relaxed, walked to them and stood waiting for the initial greeting to end.

"Sterling, look, it's Aggie." Lydia reached over, took his hand and drew him close. "Aggie Cuttler, this is my husband Dr. Sterling Graham."

He smiled down at the petite woman who was looking up at him with an assessing expression.

"I've heard so many good things about you, Mrs. Cuttler. I owe you a great debt." He watched as her countenance changed to questioning. "You enabled Lydia to escape and travel here to become my wife."

Aggie smiled then. "Call me Aggie. Mrs. Cuttler stopped being me when my husband died. You're very welcome. God had it all planned out. His ways aren't ours and if we'll just get out of the way he can do great things in our lives."

"Come," Lydia said to Aggie, "supper's nearly ready. I need to get back to fixing it. We can talk in the kitchen. Sterling, Aggie's bag must be on the porch. Would you mind bringing it in?"

Lydia wrapped her arm around Aggie, holding her close to her side as they walked to the kitchen.

Sterling found himself standing alone in the foyer. Why do I suddenly feel superfluous? he thought. But he smiled at his wife's excitement and did as she'd asked, bringing in the worn leather bag that sat outside the door.

"Sterling, Aggie's moving to Cottonwood." Lydia was so happy she couldn't contain her joy, rushing to him as he entered the kitchen carrying the pan of dirty instruments. She nearly bumped it out of his hands as she grabbed him to hug.

"Careful there, I've already dropped this once. You'll be the one to pick up everything this time." He was holding the pan high with one hand, wrapping the other arm around her. "You'll have to excuse her, Aggie. Sometimes she can be a little clumsy."

"Hey, you." Lydia poked his side with her finger. Her delight would not be contained. "Let's put these in to soak. Supper's ready."

When grace had been said and plates filled, Lydia began asking questions.

"Why did you decide to move to Cottonwood, Aggie? I never dreamed you'd leave your farm."

"A couple of reasons. I'm gettin' old and I didn't want to spend another winter doing outdoor chores, tending stock, chopping wood and the like. Decided to sell the place to Gerald and Randal Newman. Randal's gettin' hitched to Ginger Townsend soon and needed a place. It was the final confirmation that God was telling me to come."

Lydia looked at her friend in confusion. "God was telling you to come?"

"Since June I've been knowin' God was tellin' me he wanted me somewhere else. I didn't know where he wanted me but I knew he'd let me know when and where when it was time. A few weeks ago he finally told me. I thought it might be to one of my children. It was, but not one I birthed. He told me to go to the child of my heart. So here I am."

Lydia reached across the table, taking Aggie's hand. "I love you like a mother, too. You'll stay with us, won't you?"

"I plan to look for a house here in town, but not for a while. Not until that baby you're carryin' is born at any rate."

Lydia looked from Aggie to Sterling. "I didn't tell, I promise."

Turning back to Aggie, she said, "We haven't told anyone yet. How did you know?"

"I've been a midwife for over forty years. I can spot a woman with one in the womb sometimes before she even knows." Aggie chuckled. "Why else would God send me here, now, with such insistence other than you bein' with child?"

Sterling chuckled, drawing her attention to him. "When the Lord started telling you to leave your farm is around the time Lydia conceived. He has the plan all worked out in advance. We simply need to obey."

Lydia could feel herself blush. It seemed discussing conception was just a little more embarrassing to her than to Aggie or Sterling.

"We'll need to start telling very soon," Sterling said. "You're increasing earlier than some women. It'll become evident and several of your friends will be disappointed if they hear it from someone else."

"You're right. I'll invite Ella, Maggie and Rachel over to meet Aggie. Oh, and Mrs. H. also. We can tell them then. Is that all right?" Lydia looked at Sterling for affirmation.

"Just be sure I'm out on a house call. I don't want to be around when the squealing and giggling start."

"Oh, you don't want to be there?" Lydia was slightly disappointed for a moment then rallied. "No, we'll be talking babies and all that goes along with that. You'd just be in the way." She stuck her tongue out at him then grinned an overly sweet grin. "You might try to let Drew and Peter know at the same time."

Aggie chimed in. "Definitely in the way. Besides, he'll want to swagger through town as if becomin' a father's somethin' new and original."

"I guess I'll have to practice my swagger then."

They all laughed and continued eating.

Over dessert Lydia noticed the concerned look on Sterling's face. "Is something wrong, Sterling? You look worried."

He looked from Lydia to Aggie. "From your letters we know that both Lydia's brother and Gus came to you trying to find out where Lydia was. How did you move here without them finding out?"

Now Aggie and Lydia both became serious.

"I did as much as I could to keep where I was goin' a secret without seemin' to," Aggie said. "Those at church I told I was gonna live with one of my kin. Lydia's as much my kin as any child I birthed. Maybe not in a legal way but in my heart."

Reaching out, she touched Lydia's shoulder and then Sterling's. "That makes you kin, too. The only one who knows what town I went to is Gerald Newman. He's a good man and won't tell a soul. Not even his wife or son. I only brought my bag and one trunk with me. The rest will be shipped later."

"Did you leave your trunk at the station?"

"Yes, didn't want to take the time to find someone to bring it. Stationmaster said he'd arrange for it to be delivered, most likely tomorrow. I can get by tonight. I just wanted to get here and see my girl."

Lydia smiled but thoughts of Cyrus or Gus finding her left her sober. "What if they do find out where I am? What if they come?"

"Sweeting, I did what I could and prayed about it. All we can do is trust that the good Lord knows and has it all planned out if they do."

Lydia and Sterling exchanged glances and then he took her hand in his. "No matter what, Lydia, I'll do whatever it takes to protect you. You have my solemn word."

Several days later the gathering of women chatted, drank tea and ate cookies in the parlor. Janie, who'd come with her mother, sat studying Aggie. When she couldn't stand not knowing any longer she climbed down from the settee and walked over. Looking up at the stranger, Janie waited until Aggie noticed her.

"Yes, Janie, do you want to talk with me?"

Shuffling her feet and biting her lip, Janie nodded.

"Are you wondering about me?"

She nodded again. Just as Aggie was preparing to encourage her Janie began. "Did you hit Aunt Lydia and make her all broken and bruised when she got here?"

The entire group of women went silent. Lydia started to speak but Aggie held up a hand.

"Oh no, child. That wasn't me. That was a mean man. I bound up her broken arm and helped her get away on the train. I came here because I love Lydia like my one of my own girls. I missed her too much so I decided to move to where she lives."

"I'm glad it wasn't you. I wouldn't want that mean man to come and find her. He might hit her again." Big tears swam in the blue eyes.

Aggie picked Janie up and held her close. "Me too. I know one thing. The Lord will protect her just as he did when she moved here. He has it all planned out."

"How?"

"God has given Lydia a good husband who will protect her, and lots of friends who will too."

"You mean me and Uncle Doc?"

"Yes, along with your mama and papa, and all these ladies here and their husbands and all the other people here in Cottonwood who love her."

"Okay. I just don't want her to be hurt again even if it was fun to help smear on the cast and get it off. But not the cushion Rye got that day."

Lydia told Aggie the tale of Rye's accident and Lydia's cast removal. Then she decided to let everyone in on her secret.

"You all are such special friends of mine and I wanted you to meet Aggie. She's moved here because God told her I needed her. As always, he's right. I am going to need her. In about mid March there will be a new person coming to live with us."

She paused, wanting to see if anyone would figure it out. It wasn't long before Ella jumped up and with a squeal of delight rushed over to give Lydia a huge hug.

"A baby ... you're going to have a baby. I'm so happy for you. What a blessing."

Shrieks, giggles and hugs dominated the room. Talk now turned to diapers, names, offers of baby clothes, help with sewing. The three women who had been through childbearing shared their reminiscences.

Sterling, peeking in from the sitting room, beat a hasty retreat. He'd told Drew and Peter that morning but wasn't ready to face a room full of women filled with the excitement about a new baby. Besides, he had an errand to run he didn't want Lydia to know about. He'd put his coat and hat in his office when he'd returned for lunch. Now he donned them for his walk to Johnson's store.

The day was sunny but the chill of early October bit. Several people waved or smiled as he progressed, causing him to remember the day Lydia had been discovered with him in the livery stable. They'd both changed since then. The waif, beaten and scared, had blossomed into a secure, confident young woman. And now she was expecting his child. The thought made him smile and his heart pulsed with love for the little one growing in her womb.

"Hello, Doc." Hal was stacking canned goods on a shelf when Sterling entered the store. "What can I do for you today?"

"Afternoon, Hal, I'm wanting to order a sewing machine for Lydia's Christmas gift. She's going to be doing a lot of sewing over the winter." Sterling struggled to keep his face passive; he so dearly wanted to smile.

"You don't say. I thought she'd done quite a lot getting her dresses and things made."

"Oh, this sewing isn't for her." The smile won the war, breaking out large on his face. "We're expecting a baby so she'll be making things for it."

"Well, congratulations! You seem pretty happy about it." Hal placed the last can, vigorously shook Sterling's hand and turned toward the back counter leading the way.

"We both are. I thought a sewing machine would help in making all the things she feels are important for a baby to have. I'm sure she'll be in purchasing flannel and muslin and who knows what else."

"I'll go get the brochure so you can pick the one you want." As Hal rounded the end of the counter he picked up a shotgun leaning against the wall and placed it on a shelf under the surface.

"That's a nice shotgun. Do you keep it there?"

"Yes, you never know when you might need it. I never have but several times I was glad it was there. I was showing it to Mitchell Constant. He's looking for one. I forgot to put it back."

Hal pulled the brochure from a shelf and opened it, displaying images of the sewing machines. At the top of the page was the word "Singer."

Sterling looked the machines over, asked Hal a few questions then pointed to one. "I don't know much about these machines. Is this a good one?"

"Must be. It's what most people order and I haven't had any complaints about them."

"Can it get here by Christmas?"

"It should make it with you ordering it this early."

The door opened causing the bell over it to giggle. Sterling turned to see who it was. His welcoming smile turned a little sour when he spied Mrs. Taylor.

"You just get that ordered for me, will you, Hal?" he said.

He moved down an outer aisle hoping to avoid the nosy gossip. He calculated the wrong aisle.

Mrs. Taylor stepped in front of him through a break in the shelving. "Good afternoon, Dr. Graham. A pleasure to see you. My Magdelina is visiting your wife today."

Sterling thought he heard a bit of derision in her voice. "Yes, Maggie was there when I left. The ladies seem to be having a good chat. My wife is introducing them to her friend Aggie, who has moved to town."

"Well, there aren't many unwed men left in Cottonwood, what with you and Sheriff Richards both having married."

"I suppose not. I rather doubt Aggie will be looking for a husband, but I could be wrong."

"I don't suppose you've met another newcomer. I hear he's an English lord. He's living with the Ralstons at the moment but I'm sure he'll be finding a house to buy soon. I hear all the English aristocracy is very wealthy."

Sterling wanted to glance back at Hal, who hadn't come out from behind the counter to greet Mrs. Taylor. Traitor, he thought. "Well, Mrs. Taylor, I must be going. I have ... uh ... some other errands to do for my wife. I'll tell her you said hello."

Adeptly sidestepping her, he made it to the door just as she said, "I'm sure my Magdelina will catch the eye of the lord before your Aggie does."

Stifling a laugh, Sterling replied, "I'm sure you're right," and closed the door behind him.

Chapter 46

The late November day was miserable: snowy, cold and getting colder. Gus didn't want to go to the train station to pick up his expected delivery but he needed the iron to make the hooks, horseshoes and wrought iron fencing he had orders for. He pulled his collar up so the snow wouldn't go down his neck. Spitting tobacco juice onto the street, he strode to the station.

Under the eve were boxes and trunks ready to be loaded onto the train. He slouched next to them, trying to stay dry and hoping the train would be on time. Surveying the piles, he read the names of the owners and destinations of the various crates printed in large letters on the sides. Then he straightened, eyeing three trunks with the words Agnes Cuttler, Cottonwood, Iowa.

He knew Aggie had left the area. He and Cyrus had found that out when they'd sneaked onto the Cuttler property planning to grab the old lady and use a little 'friendly' persuasion to get her to tell them where Lydia was. They had watched as Randal had come out of the barn whistling and walked into the house. They had gone back to Cyrus's farm trying to figure out why the man had been there.

Later Cyrus went back on the pretext of a runaway hog and Randal told him that Aggie had moved away. He said he had bought her place because he was getting married next month. The only thing the man could tell Cyrus was that Aggie had gone to live with some kin.

The train whistle sounding in the distance announced train's pending arrival. Gus thought fast. He'd help with the unloading and loading so he could chat with the men working there. Maybe they'd know more about the kin Aggie had gone to. He strode to the baggage car when the train stopped.

The baggage handlers began wrestling with luggage, and then began unloading trunks, boxes and crates.

"I'll help you with that," Gus said.

"Much obliged."

Gus nodded to the speaker. He knew him to be a talkative, gossipy man often poking his nose where it didn't belong. He waited until they began loading the waiting containers.

"I see this one says Agnes Cuttler. Is that old Aggie who lives out on that farm off to the east of town?"

"Yeap, but not anymore. Hear she sold the place and moved west."

"You don't say. I always thought you'd have to pry her outta there with a crowbar. Now she up and moves."

The man laughed. "I did too. I heard that she's moving in with one of her children. I always thought they all went farther west, but what do I know?"

Gus finished helping with the loading then put his shipment of iron on a dolly. "I'll be bringing this back when I get the iron unloaded at the smithy."

"You always do. Glad we have it here for people to use."

Pushing the load along the boardwalk, Gus thought he and Cyrus needed a confab. He also thought Aggie's children had all moved farther west. What if she'd gone to Lydia instead of one of her own? The orders could wait. He'd get the dolly back to the station and ride out to talk with Cyrus about this.

Cyrus looked at the nearly bare shelves. They should be filled with jars of garden produce. He'd raised a small garden this year but didn't know anything about canning and preserving. The jars that were left were ones Lydia had canned last year. This winter he'd have to buy tinned food in town.

Maybe he'd spend the winter finding some woman to marry. That way he'd have someone to do the gardening, canning, cooking, cleaning and laundry. That was all women's work and he was a man. Besides, if they found Lydia and brought her back she'd be living in town with Gus. Even if she came out to do cleaning and laundry for him there was still the cooking and gardening to do. Gus wouldn't want her doing all that for him.

Yes, he'd look to finding him a woman who'd do what he told her to do. Not a stupid one like Lydia.

Hearing hoofbeats, Cyrus looked out the window and saw Gus ride into the yard. He threw a log into the stove and pulled the coffee pot forward. "Come on in and out of the snow," he said when Gus came to the door. "What brings you here?"

Gus shrugged out of his coat and tossed it with his Stetson onto a chair. "I think I might know where your sister is."

"What makes you think that? With Aggie gone how'd you find out?"

The two sat at the kitchen table drinking coffee and making plans based on what Gus had found out at the station. Cyrus, mad at Lydia for leaving and irritated from his survey of the lack of canned food for the winter, became angrier. His contributions to the planning were littered with swearing and diatribes on how his sister had been selfish when she'd run away.

"Gus, I'm gonna go to this Cottonwood and get her back for you. She owes me the work she'd a done this summer and you for not being there to marry you."

"You got that right. When are you going?"

"I think next week. Let's let Aggie's junk arrive and let them think we don't know anything about where they are. Then I can go and stay in town near the general store until Lydia shows up. I can grab her and make her come home."

"Sounds like a good plan. I'll tend your stock while you're gone. How about coming to town with me now and we'll celebrate?"

"You help me with the evening chores and I'll just do that."

Chapter 47

"Lydia, you do have that glow women who are expecting have."

Mabel Johnson stepped from behind the counter of the All-Purpose Store as Lydia, Sterling and Aggie walked up the aisle.

"Thank you." Sterling smiled back, taking the compliment.

"Oh stop, you," Lydia said. "Pay no attention to him. He thinks he has something to do with my condition."

"I do."

"Not that much or I'd make you be as big and round as I am. Who'd think I could be this big with three months left?"

"You're simply beautiful to me."

"You'd better say that or she might make you sleep on the sofa. Or maybe, as my wife did, burst into tears at odd moments." Hal came through the curtained doorway leading to the back room carrying a shotgun.

"What's that for?" Aggie walked up to the counter. Sterling saw her assessing the gun's quality.

"I keep it under the counter just in case. I've had to bring it out a few times but never had to shoot it."

"Smart thinking. Nice gun. I have one too. Don't think I'll be needing it much here in Cottonwood, though."

The trio separated then to gather the items they'd come to purchase, each having a list prepared by Lydia. She stayed close to the house more now at Sterling's instruction. She had grown larger than normal as her pregnancy had progressed and he wanted to be close in case something went awry. She'd protested at first but Aggie had smoothed her ruffled feathers, commenting that not many husbands would think to consider her health and safety. Today was the first in over a week that she'd been anywhere other than home and church.

Sterling quickly got the things on his list and put them on the counter. He leaned close to Hal while glancing back to see where Lydia and Aggie were. "Is it here yet?"

"Not yet, but I received the bill of lading so it's on its way. Should be here next week."

Sterling saw the conspiratorial smile on Hal's face. "Good. I'll need to figure out how to get it home without her knowing about it."

"It'll be in a crate but I can't guarantee it won't have the company name on it."

"I think the word Singer might just give away what her present is."

Hal laughed. "It most likely would. I'll see what I can do. Maybe have Luke paint over it if the name's on the crate." Hal cleared his throat, indicating the approach of the ladies.

"Sterling, I'm going to go over to the butcher shop. Is there something special you'd like me to fix?" Lydia touched his arm, letting her fingers rest there for a moment.

He covered her hand with his. "Everything you fix is special. Especially the desserts, but nothing at the butcher will help with that."

"Mincemeat. I can get the meat parts at the butcher."

"Remember my fondness for turnips?"

"You don't like them."

"The same goes for mincemeat." He was delighted with her smile.

"Aggie, would you like to go with me to the butcher?" Lydia said.

Sterling followed Lydia with his eyes as she walked to Aggie, who had wandered over to the shoe aisle.

"Do you want me to go?" Aggie said.

"Not if you have something you want to look at."

"I'll stay here then and try on these shoes. I ain't had nice shoes in so long. Only work boots."

Sterling nodded as Lydia waved at him as she went out the door.

"You've got it bad, my friend." Hal's comment pulled him back.

"Yes I do, Hal, I certainly do." Sterling smiled at the storekeeper, not at all ashamed of his love for his wife.

Cyrus smiled. She'd gone in with a man and Aggie but now was coming out of the store alone. He couldn't believe his luck. Only in Cottonwood two days and

Lydia was all alone, ready for him to take her. He knew she'd put up a fight so he had his story all planned. Lydia was not totally right, he would explain. She would seem normal for a while, maybe months at a time, but then all of a sudden she would change into a maniac, breaking things, biting and tearing her hair out. He'd been looking for his dear younger sister for almost a year. Praise the Lord now that he'd found her. He'd take her home where she'd be safe.

Cyrus had gone over it many times on the train so he knew the story well. He'd control his frustration and anger, not wanting to let it show. He didn't want to raise any suspicion among the townspeople.

A cold wind gusted and what Cyrus saw turned his controlled calm into a raging anger. Lydia's cloak blew open before she could grab and hold it together, and the fact that she was carrying a child slammed into Cyrus.

"You bitch, whore, slut!" He charged out from beside the corner of the feed store where he'd been watching. Running into the street, he grabbed Lydia by the arm. "You slut! First you run away, and now look at you. How long was it before you jumped into some bastard's bed? Not long from the look of you!"

Held tightly by the arm, Lydia watched in horror as Cyrus swung back his arm and brought it down, slapping her hard across the face. She couldn't believe it. He was here in Cottonwood. What would he do to her now that he'd found her? She crouched down, curling into as much of a ball as she could to protect her belly. Nothing could happen to her baby.

He wrenched her back up and she looked at the livid face of her brother. "No, Cyrus!"

He backhanded her. "Don't you talk back to me, you slut. I don't know if Gus will have you now. Well, then, you can just stay with me. That bastard in your belly can go to an orphanage."

"Sterling!" Aggie's scream made his blood go cold. "He's here. Cyrus is here and has Lydia."

Sterling looked at Hal, who had already pulled the shotgun out from under the counter. He tossed it to Sterling, who caught it and ran down the aisle. Aggie held the door open and he flew through it. Seeing his wife being slapped nearly caused him to point and shoot without thought. Capturing the fury, he cocked the gun and stopped a few yards away.

"Let go of my wife and back away. I'm ready to fill you so full of buckshot it'd take me a week to dig it all out."

The steel of Sterling's voice stopped Cyrus's fist as it began its downward path to Lydia's face. "Just who the hell are you to tell me to let her go?"

Sterling's voice became colder. "Let her go." He took a step forward. He could see nothing but Lydia and her brother. Everything else was blurred, bringing them into sharp focus.

"Let. Her. Go." He took another step closer. "At this distance I can shoot you easily, making sure that no harm comes to my wife. Believe me, I dearly want to shoot you."

This time Cyrus heard the word 'wife' and the intent in Sterling's voice. He released his hold on Lydia's arm.

Sterling's anger didn't abate. Although Lydia scurried from his vision, the only thing he saw was Cyrus standing there, his arms held away from his body. He took a step closer, the shotgun aimed, his finger pressing firmly on the trigger.

"I had hoped you were smart enough to leave Lydia alone. I should've known you weren't. Anyone who beats a woman deserves to be shot. I tended the injuries you beat into your sister. Maybe I'll be gentle when I treat yours, but then again, you weren't gentle with her."

"I just needed to get her attention. She's pretty dense when it comes to what I want."

"I've been able to get her attention without beating her. She's pretty able to figure out what I want."

"I can see that," Cyrus sneered. He made motions indicating a rounded belly.

Sterling's grip on the shotgun tightened. He lifted it to his shoulder and looked down the barrel.

"Sterling." Drew's voice, calm but grave, penetrated. "I know you want to shoot him. I do, too, but you can't. Aggie has Lydia. She's safe. Let me handle this now."

Sterling's finger on the trigger itched to wreak vengeance. He stood stock-still, torn between the desire to inflict pain on Cyrus as he had on Lydia, and allowing the sheriff to take over. His mind flashed images of Lydia standing in Ella's kitchen with a bruised back and face, a broken arm and broken spirit. Her face terrified when he startled her. Not meeting his eyes but face turned to the floor. His finger tightened on the trigger.

Into his consciousness slipped the sound of Lydia sobbing. Turning to the sound, he shoved the shotgun towards Drew, held out his arms and strode to Lydia, who met him halfway. Nothing was said as they held each other in a tight embrace. Neither noticed the crowd that had gathered. Neither cared.

Sterling held Lydia close during the ride home. Theo Ralston, the livery owner, had provided a brougham, allowing the trio privacy. She was still trembling uncontrollably as he helped her up the stairs to the bedroom. He nodded to Aggie, who told him she'd make a calming tea. He helped Lydia into her nightgown and tucked her into bed.

When he pulled away she grabbed and held on tight. "No, don't leave me. Please don't leave me." Her hands were frantically pulling him closer.

"I'm not. I'm staying right here. I just want to take off my coat and shoes." He sat on the edge of the bed next to her. Lydia kept her hand on him the entire time. "I'm going around to my side of the bed. I won't leave you."

When she was settled against his chest with blankets tucked under her chin she gave a shuddery sigh. "I was so scared. He just grabbed me from the side and started yelling, calling me terrible names."

Sterling stroked her hair and made indistinct comforting sounds, hoping to encourage her to talk out her fears.

"Then he slapped me. It was like I'd never run away. I was so afraid of him. I was so scared for our baby." Her tears soaked his shirt. His arms held her more firmly. "I thought he might try to hit me in the stomach. He was so angry, telling me I'd have to put the baby in an orphanage and I'd have to stay with him."

"He couldn't do that. I'd never let him. You're my wife and I love you."

"I was so relieved when I heard your voice. Even though I was still scared, I knew you wouldn't let him hurt me again."

"I wanted to shoot him so much. All I could see was him holding you, wanting to hurt you. Even after he let you go ... I wanted to pull that trigger. I wanted to hurt him far worse than he'd ever hurt you. It was hard letting Drew take over. Then I heard you crying and all I wanted was you in my arms."

Lydia's body had finally stopped its tremors. They lay quietly, allowing their emotions to settle. A soft knock on the door sounded.

"Come." Sterling helped Lydia into a sitting position.

Aggie entered carrying a tray with a teapot and cups. She set the tray on the washstand and stood looking at the mirror. Her reflection showed Sterling puffy eyes and a nose red from crying, understandable given the events of the day. Aggie turned around, tears streaming and her distress vivid.

"Oh Lydia, I'm so sorry. If I hadn't come he never would have found you. Please, please forgive me."

Never having thought Aggie was responsible, Sterling began to say so but was stilled when Lydia sobbed.

"Aggie, no ... no. I don't feel that way. I love you."

Lydia raised her arms to the older woman and suddenly there were three people on the bed holding each other.

Sterling realized how much he, too, cared for Aggie. "The Lord told you to come," he said to her. "We'd still be living under the cloud of wondering whether Cyrus would find her if you hadn't moved here." He kissed Aggie on the cheek and then pulled back to let Lydia and Aggie have one more hug. "Besides, who will be the baby's grandmother if not you?"

The loving look Lydia gave him for that affirmation and the slightly stunned pleasure on Aggie's face settled the matter in Sterling's mind.

"How about some tea?" Aggie climbed off the bed.

"Sounds wonderful." Lydia snuggled closer to Sterling.

Sliding his arm around her shoulders, he said to Aggie, "You didn't happen to bring some cookies along with the tea, did you?"

Epilogue

"Aurgh! You lied to me!" Lydia screamed at Sterling, her eyes blazing fire.

"What? When? How?" Sterling replied, stunned at the accusation.

"You promised you'd never hurt me! You lied. I'm in terrible, awful pain and it's your fault."

Sterling and Aggie exchanged somewhat amused glances on the sly. It wouldn't be good if Lydia saw their amusement.

"I know, sweetheart. It's all my fault. Push now."

Lydia bore down, holding her breath, and Aggie's hand, with all her might.

"I can see the top of the head. Relax, then on the next contraction push again."

Lydia didn't have time to relax. The contractions were coming hard on the heels of each other.

"Auggh!" She screamed again. This time the baby slipped from her body.

"It's a boy," Sterling said with more satisfaction than he really wanted to show.

The baby's cries filled the room. Aggie hadn't heard such a beautiful sound in a long time. She worked her hand out of Lydia's and grabbed the towel warming by the stove. Sterling cut the cord and lifted the squalling baby up so his mother could see him before quickly giving him to Aggie.

"Let me know when the contractions start again." Sterling slipped back into physician mode.

"You mean I have to do this again," Lydia complained, then, as another contraction came upon her, "Auggh!"

"Sorry, sweetheart, you're not finished yet."

While Aggie washed and swaddled the baby, Lydia continued to complain of the pain Sterling had inflicted upon her.

"Almost here, my darling," Sterling said with sympathy. "Give me another push."

Taking a deep breath as another contraction rolled down her body, Lydia pushed and felt the next little body slide from hers.

"You got your girl this time," Sterling said as he cut the cord, his daughter competing with her brother in a howling contest.

Aggie had placed the boy in the cradle by the stove, and took the new arrival from Sterling.

"They're both beautiful, my girl," Aggie said. "Look at all that hair."

The baby girl indeed had masses of dark, wet hair all over her head. Aggie held the baby so Lydia could see her for a moment before taking her aside to wash and swaddle.

"They're beautiful, aren't they, Sterling?"

"Yes, my love. Another push now."

"Another one?" Lydia's voice held fear that there would be another baby.

"Just the afterbirth," Sterling said, hiding a grin at her distressed plea. "Push."

Lydia pushed.

"There now, all cleaned up, but you're very tired, aren't you?" Aggie tied the braid with a ribbon after brushing out the tangled mess. "I'll get the babies for you, if I can pry them away from their papa."

Lydia now lay in her own bed after giving birth in one of the clinic patient rooms. Sterling sat with a baby in each arm, rocking them in the rocking chair Johann Jorgensen had made for Lydia when he'd heard she was expecting.

"Oh, I guess I can give them up to their mother for a second." He stood up, somewhat awkwardly, with no arms to help him rise.

Aggie took one baby, carrying it to the bed and laying it in Lydia's outstretched arms.

"Oh, my. My little Nathan." Tears rolled down Lydia's face unnoticed as she looked at his face.

"How can you tell?" Sterling asked.

"He only has a little baby fuzz on his head. Hannah has a head full of hair." She hadn't taken her eyes off her son at all.

"Oh, you're right. I really hadn't noticed. I guess I was just looking at their faces as well as checking to see that all the parts were there. Would you like to hold your daughter?"

Aggie stayed just long enough to see Lydia holding both babies, then slipped from the room leaving the new family to themselves. *Oh my Lord, she prayed, you told her to go with no knowledge of where you were taking her. Thank you. You provided for her in her need, healed her broken soul and have given her a new life, a loving husband, and now two wonderful new lives. Bless her, and them, with your mercy and grace.*